THE NAHAN SERIES

OURSELVES

For Diana—

Let's buckle up
for a whole new world.

Enjoy!

ALSO BY S.G. REDLING

Flowertown
Damocles
Braid: Three Twisted Stories
The Widow File (A Dani Britton Thriller)
Redemption Key (A Dani Britton Thriller)

THE NAHAN SERIES

OURSELVES

S.G. REDLING

47N●RTH

Text copyright © 2015 S.G. Redling
All rights reserved.

Published by 47North, Seattle

www.apub.com

Amazon, the Amazon logo, and 47North are trademarks of Amazon.com, Inc., or its affiliates.

ISBN-13: 9781477820391
ISBN-10: 1477820396

Cover design by Stewart A. Williams

Library of Congress Control Number: 2014912636

Printed in the United States of America

This book is for my agent, friend,
and separated-at-birth sister, Christine Witthohn.
Thanks for never giving up on this story.

TABLE *of* CONTENTS

．．．．．．．．．．．．．．．．．．．．．．

We have always been among you.

Since humanity first huddled together on the windswept plains of Asia Minor, cobbled shelters on the steppes of Russia, and carved viable land in the cliffs of Liguria, we've been in your midst. Were we ever as you are? When did our paths diverge? We are blue-eyed people with the dark hair of the east and the pale skin of the north. Nowhere in our line are there tales of tenderness or frailty. Our heroes, our legends are full of cunning and lust and appetite.

You've passed down names for us for a thousand years. "Still Ones" in the ancient language of the mountains; "Terrible Night" among the desert dwellers; the indigenous people of a rainy area charmed us with the title "Those Who Hold the Sky in their Eyes."

Who are we?

In our tongue, we are Nahan, "Ourselves."

You are simply the common.

Our children are in your schools. We live in your neighborhoods and work side by side with you in every profession. Our world within your world touches you in a thousand ways you can never imagine. You have your massive population, your gods, your technology, and your fears. We have only Ourselves.

We are the Nahan and we have always been among you.

．．．．．．．．．．．．．．．．．．．．．．

Chapter One

NAHAN DA LI

....

Nahan da li: literally, *Are you Nahan?* A traditional welcome,
a friendly greeting, affectionate

Stell knew there was something wrong with her. Something dark
lived inside of her. She didn't know what it was or how the others
could see it. She might not even have known about it herself if she
didn't see it in the eyes of the congregation and feel it in the fists
of her uncle. When she was little, she used to look for it in the rib-
bons of blood that poured from her body when the ritual knives
cut into her.

Now she knew better.

Whatever was wrong with her couldn't be cut out like a splin-
ter underneath her skin. Whatever was wrong with her was wrong
to the bone.

Since she couldn't cut it out or pray it out, Stell took herself and her darkness out of the compound at every opportunity. She'd climb through the hole in the wall behind her bed, crawl through the forsythia, and run hard and fast up the steep western side of Calstow Mountain. She'd run like someone chased her although she knew the congregation wouldn't miss her. Her classmates wouldn't. Stell drew the wrath of Uncle Rom like a magnet to a lodestone and everyone gave Stell a wide berth.

She thought maybe her mother missed her when she took off into the woods of Calstow Mountain. She thought maybe Malbette might worry about her daughter alone in the darkness of the mountain forests, might wonder if her child was safe and unharmed running through streams and climbing trees, sleeping under the stars and waking in beds of pine needles day after day. She thought her mother might miss her but Malbette's eyes had a distance in them that was impossible to read so Stell didn't think about her mother much.

After all, Stell wasn't a kid anymore. She had to be at least twenty by now. Maybe closer to twenty-five.

Nobody had ever told Stell how old she was. Nobody ever told Stell anything except to shut up and to repent and to pray. Nobody cared whether or not she could read. (She could but she hated to.) The teachers didn't care that Stell never looked at the maps or listened to the Traditions or that she learned her numbers quickly. Stell never asked questions and nobody noticed or cared.

When she was little, before she knew better, she'd asked questions.

She'd asked why she had to pray so hard, why she had to bleed into the bowls in the filthy church room. She'd stomped her foot and cried and clung to her silent mother as the two of them were led to Uncle Rom's waiting ritual chamber to be cut and bled before the pale faces of the congregation.

Uncle Rom had answered those questions with snarls and threats and long recitations of Tradition but those weren't the questions that silenced Stell. Malbette had done that.

Stell had asked about her father.

She didn't know how old she was when she'd asked but since she hadn't been tall enough to look out the window, Stell figured she'd been pretty young. Young enough to press her luck. Stell had demanded her mother tell her why she didn't have a father like the other kids in the compound. Stell had shouted and pled, whined and wept, badgering Malbette to tell her who her father was and why he wasn't with them and why nobody would tell her anything about him.

Malbette hadn't answered her. Instead, she ignored her daughter's dirty, grasping hands and settled into the only chair in the small shack they called a home. She folded her hands in her lap, stared into the grimy wood of the near wall, and fell silent. At first Stell had raged as small children do. She cried and pulled but Malbette wouldn't move. She climbed into her mother's lap but the larger hands made no move to comfort her. And finally Stell got quiet too. She curled up on the floor beside her mother's chair, thumb tucked securely in her mouth, her cheeks pressed into the scratchy wool of her mother's skirts.

They sat that way for three days.

When Malbette rose from the chair on the third day, smoothing her skirts, and walking off as if nothing unusual had happened, Stell wiped at the tears and spit and snot that had dried on her face. She headed into her room, pulled the cot away from the wall, and kicked at the loose board behind it. She crawled through that hole and ran up to the mountain.

On Calstow Mountain it didn't matter what was wrong with Stell. Whatever darkness she had inside her didn't bother the raccoons or opossum or hawks. The wild turkeys kept their distance but the streams and poplars didn't mind her. The only ones that screamed at her were the blue jays and they screamed at everything. They even screamed at the common.

Stell loved those moments when she heard something crashing through the brush louder than any forest creature would. Birds would fly and Stell would climb as fast as she could up into the nearest tree, folding into herself and being as silent as an owl so she could watch and listen to the strangely dressed, heavily burdened common making their way along the forest trails. She listened to their voices; their English sounded so different from hers, no trace of a Nahan accent at all. And sometimes if she really stared at one of them, if she really focused on one particular part of one particular common, that common would freeze. Stell would bite her lip, trying not to giggle as they scanned the forest around them, some ancient instinct alerting them to a danger they couldn't see.

Stell didn't know why they would fear her but she loved it when that happened.

Maybe that had something to do with the darkness within her.

She didn't care. The common would go and Stell would climb down and the mountain would be hers again. It was hers today and Stell lay in her favorite spot, a thick blanket of moss between the creek bed and a thicket of blackberry bushes. Summer had only just started warming up the mountain and it would be weeks until the blackberries appeared but Stell had peeled off her gray, woolen dress as she always did once the snow melted. She'd tossed the hated garment up into the poplar branches and sprawled out along the chilly moss.

The canopy overhead hadn't thickened fully yet and the sun warmed her pale skin. Bits of mud flaked off her body as she stretched long. She must have fallen asleep because she didn't hear the rattling of the blackberry branches or the swearing until it was too late to hide. Stell leapt to her feet, blinking away the sleep, as the branches closed together, catching the skin of a young man who pulled at the thorns.

They stared at each other. Stell knew her eyes and mouth were as wide open as his.

He was Nahan. She could see it and smell it and feel it.

And he was beautiful.

"Nahan da li?" she asked, smiling at this wondrous sight before her.

He looked nothing like the congregation. His clothes weren't drab and rough. His skin shone with a health she had never seen. And most wondrous of all? His surprised gape turned into a smile.

"What? Oh yeah, yeah." He nodded but Stell didn't think he blinked. "I'm Nahan. I'm . . . I'm . . . I'm Thomas. Tomas. Tomas is my real, you know, my real name, um, that we, you know, use here because my grandparents . . . that's my name when I'm here. I mean it's my name but I use Thomas when I'm home but here I use, you know, my name. Tomas."

Stell watched the words pour out of his beautiful mouth. She wanted to touch the shadows of pink that rose on his pale cheeks as he talked and talked. He said more to her in that minute than anyone had said to Stell in months.

"I'm Stell," she said but he seemed to want more. "All the time. I'm only ever Stell."

The pink on his cheeks settled into a glorious rose shade that matched the lower lip he licked. His teeth shone white as he bit into it and Stell couldn't think of a single reason to ever look at anything else again. She watched his mouth move and waited for more words.

"Why are you naked?"

"My dress is in the tree."

"Do you want me to get it down?"

"No."

"Oh."

Everyone thought there was something wrong with Tomas. He knew it. And they were probably right. His cousin Louis had spent a lifetime taking care of him—defending him in school-yard fights and smoothing things over for him socially. Aricelli and the other girls in their group hid their eye rolls, ruffling his hair and treating him more like a puppy than a guy. It wasn't just because he was the youngest in the group either, although that didn't help. Especially since it took him longer to graduate from high school than anyone else.

Even among the Nahan, twenty-four was a little old to be taking high school chemistry.

The Nahan aged differently than the common, much more slowly, so it wasn't unheard of to take that long to graduate but it was more than just being a late bloomer. Tomas could never get the hang of social interaction. Louis assured him that even with his awkwardness, his looks more than made up for his shortcomings with the girls. Or would if he ever got up the courage to try.

The problem was, his problem wasn't just with girls. It was people in general—Nahan and common. Crowds unnerved Tomas and four voices speaking in a room at a time sounded like thousands to him. The Nahan community in Deerfield assumed he was just shy, sheltered as he was by his socially cunning cousin, and so let Tomas slide under the radar. But now he had graduated, a moment the group had been waiting for so everyone could take their *avalentu*, the Nahan word for *flight*.

That was the plan for the summer, to map out their routes, to solidify their arrangements, and pick their travel mates. Tomas would travel with Louis. Aricelli and Kitty would no doubt travel together. They'd crisscross the country, away from their families and the watchful eye of the Council for the first times in their lives. There would be no Heritage School, no parents, no rules. They could explore and party and feed from the common with a freedom they never knew at home. *Avalentu* served as a rite of passage into adulthood for the Nahan and the thought of it scared the crap out of Tomas.

But he'd come to his grandparents' farm here in upstate New York as he did every summer. Louis and Aricelli and the others would be showing up soon too as they always did. They'd have a few weeks to get the last pieces of advice and to make their last-minute arrangements and then they'd be off.

Tomas would be in a pick-up truck for weeks with Louis. His cousin wanted to head west. There would be bars and parties and festivals. There would be girls both Nahan and common. There would be guys too for Louis, who made no effort to hide his preference. And for Tomas there would be an unrelenting pressure to interact and open up and drown himself in the hammering wall of noise that came with people people people.

So he'd run up onto the mountain.

The higher he ran up the eastern side of the slope, the calmer he felt. Noises from the town below him fell away and the feel of voices ringing in his ears grew fainter with each step. He didn't worry about getting lost; he'd been running on this hill every summer of his life although today he'd climbed higher than ever before. The mountain leveled out here and there and the forest stretched out in every direction. He heard a creek running behind a thicket of blackberry bushes and Tomas didn't let himself question the wisdom of charging through the thorny bushes in just his shorts and t-shirt.

And there in the clearing stood a completely naked girl.

Tomas felt his cheeks redden and could feel his usual stammer coming on but something about the way she just stood there, smiling at him, made his nerves melt away. She looked nothing like the girls in his group and not just because she was naked. Her long, black hair hung matted and clumped with leaves and dirt and he'd never seen eyes so pale. She didn't move to hide herself. Mud streaked across her small breasts and green and brown stains on her kneecaps broke up the line of her long, slim legs.

She looked like a wild creature.

"I'm Stell," she said and he heard Nahan in her voice. "All the time. I'm only ever Stell."

Something inside his chest loosened. He couldn't think of anywhere he would rather be at that or any moment. He thought that Louis would be proud of him for stepping forward and taking the girl's hand. They sat together on the moss and started to talk.

. . . .

Tomas played a precarious game of avoiding his grandparents and assuaging the curiosity of his cousin.

"Just tell me who she is," Louis demanded.

Tomas sighed. "I don't know."

It was a lie and it was the truth. Nothing had prepared him for what was happening on Calstow Mountain. Heritage classes at the Council, brutal social coaching from his cousin, everything he thought he had learned slid from his mind with Stell. Just saying her name made him light-headed. He wanted to talk to Louis about what was happening but it seemed too enormous an experience to pull from his mouth with words.

He knew it would seem ordinary to his far more experienced cousin, and that more than anything kept him silent. Really, what had he and Stell done that thousands of other Nahan kids weren't doing any given hour of any given day? If anything, their slow, sweet encounters on the forest floor would probably seem tame. They talked forever.

Or really, Tomas admitted with a stab of anxiety, he did most of the talking, didn't he? Did he talk too much?

He could see Stell sprawled out beside him, her pale body draped over dark green moss, as she listened to his stories, her mouth slightly open, her eyes almost closed. He told her stories of Nahan legends. He told her plots of science fiction movies. He made up stories from the shadows in the farthest corners of his mind. She would laugh and she would shudder and occasionally interrupt in that strange combined Nahan and English of hers to voice a concern or applaud a heroic action. He couldn't tell if she understood that the stories were fantasy. She would listen and listen and then reach for him, running her hands over his face and neck and chest as if she could divine the source of this wellspring of adventure.

Their kisses were slow and long, sometimes lingering to the point that Tomas would snap out of their trance with a jolt, wondering if he were taking too long doing what they should have been doing. He would open his eyes and see her pale blue eyes hooded under heavy lids, that small smile lingering in the corners of her mouth.

In many ways, she frightened him. She could be so still, so utterly and perfectly still. When she moved, she moved into his hands like water, warm and filling every crease.

Naked with her on the fallen leaves and stones and mosses, his body felt like an explorer on an alien planet. Stell was not only the alien lifeform; she was the entire climate, the blue sun, the salty wind, the whisper of strange red stones.

While his mind wandered, his body moved to its own natural desire, tasting her skin, arching to feel her teeth on his shoulder, his chest, his stomach. She would straddle him, sliding him inside of her, rocking gently at first then increasing in speed and need, finally wrapping herself around him to roll on the earth until the sweetness of her would make him cry out in release. They would lie there, tangled together, feeling as if his heart was her heart and, just when he was sure he would never know a moment sweeter, he could feel his body tell him "More."

. . . .

A breeze moved the branches enough to let a sliver of moonlight fall on Tomas's face. His mouth was open, one arm flung over his head, the other lying behind Stell, who sat cross-legged above him. She watched him sleep, watched the forest come alive at night around them, opossum and raccoons and foxes padding past, curious and unafraid. Stell was afraid. She was afraid to touch this boy, afraid to awaken him. She was afraid of the hot, red scars she could see marring his smooth skin.

Bloodlust. How many times had she heard the word hissed from the pulpit? How many endless hours had she been forced to pray for deliverance from the curse of her people? Uncle Rom stalked her mind, gnarled and angry, the words *backslider* and *abomination* rolling out of his mouth like a foul smoke. She had never understood what those words meant. Now, however, in the damp privacy of Calstow Mountain, when visions of Tomas turned to visions of blood, Stell understood.

She had taken his blood.

Not just a drop, not just the surface of a scrape. She had drunk deep. And he had drunk from her. They had dug at each other's skin like crows on a kill. She had dug and clawed and bitten and torn and he had gone along, following her, unable to resist the power of the evil that had come over her. She saw his eyes as he'd fallen asleep. They were different, faraway. He would never want her again. Turning away from him, Stell spread her arms wide, gathering the forest debris. She pulled it over her head, burying herself in misery and fallen leaves.

. . . .

"I'm sorry, Tomas."

Tomas tried to focus on the pale face before him. His lips felt soft and swollen as he smiled. "For what?" He raised himself on his elbows, feeling dampness from the moss on his back. "Have you been sitting up all night? Can't you sleep?"

"I'm sorry for what I've done to you. For what I am."

"What have you done?" He added with a laugh, "Besides blow my mind?"

"I've given in. I've turned my back on my higher self." Her Nahan accent thickened as she spoke words that sounded like Tradition, but no Tradition Tomas had ever heard. He sat up, hearing something serious in her voice. "'And the fever of the blood will boil within you and your flesh will fall away. Touch and you will spread this pestilence among those of your kind and all will know you are forsaken.' I have done this to us. I have done this to you." She held her arms out before her, staring at the scratches and bruises. "Forgive me."

Tomas stared at her. None of this made sense. "Stell, these marks, they're not a pestilence." She shook her head, wrapping her arms around her body. "They're not. This isn't a fever or a curse." He trailed his hand down her arm and felt her shiver. "This is natural." The word sounded ridiculous under the circumstances. It felt like those awful heritage classes when the mentor would talk in excruciating detail about their bodies and everyone would laugh and pretend not to devour every word. He sounded just like Mentor Davenheim discussing saliva and blood clotting.

"You're afraid," he said and she looked at him as if he had just noticed the sky was blue. "Are you afraid of me?"

"You should be afraid of me." She closed her eyes. "Look what I did to you."

"What you did to me?" He leaned in and whispered in her ear. "Stell, we did this to each other. We wanted this." She shook her head, her eyes still closed, but she didn't pull away.

"Do you love me?" he whispered. "Because I love you. Stell, this is what people in love do. This is Nahan." He drew her into his arms. "This is life. We belong to each other."

They rolled over the moss, tangled in each other. Whatever doubts Stell might have had burned away in the heat between them. Tomas kissed the protests off her lips and shouted down her worries with murmured reassurances and whispered delights. They more than doubled their scars.

. . . .

"Are you going to get in trouble for staying out all night?"

Stell shrugged and watched him tie his sneaker laces.

"I don't think my grandparents will care. Do you think your family will notice? Most of the scratches are healed. Maybe they won't know about . . . this."

Tomas felt Stell drifting away from him. It was like she had a window into herself that she could open and close at will, letting him in or keeping him out. The window was sliding shut and he didn't know what to do to stop it.

"Will I see you tomorrow?"

"Maybe."

Tomas couldn't catch her eye, so he rose to his feet and began dusting himself off. "Yeah, I should hang out with Louis for a while. He's probably freaking, wondering what's happened to me. I think I'm pushing his lying skills."

Stell looked up. "You've been lying to him?"

"He's been lying for me. About where I've been. I'm supposed to be, you know, hanging out with him and everyone else who's in for the summer."

"Not with me."

He stepped in close to her. "They don't know you. Yet. You should come down and meet my grandparents at least." She turned from him and jumped over the log onto the trail, yanking her dress down from a branch. "Or not." He spoke to her back. "You know, whatever. See you in a few days." He watched her disappear into the forest. Even when she was moving, she looked like she was standing still.

. . . .

"Are you sure you don't just want to start a crabgrass ranch, Grandma?" Tomas hacked at a thick clump of wiry grass. "It might turn out to be valuable or something."

"Well normally crabgrass isn't such a problem in my tomato patch. Of course, I used to have a grandson that would stay on top of the weeding."

"Really? I wonder what ever happened to him."

"From what I gather, he's staying on top of something altogether different these days." Tatiana shot Tomas a look through the tomato plants and caught his blush.

"Is that what you heard?"

"That's what I've heard." She strolled by Tomas, playfully swatting him with a bundle of clipped parsley. "So are you going to spill the beans, young man?"

Tomas kept his head down, grinning as he pulled a long dandelion root from the earth. "Sounds to me like you're pretty informed."

"Mm-hmm. No names, though. Tell me, is it one girl? Or have you found an easy patch of hay to roll in?"

"Grandma!"

"What?" Tatiana asked, her mock indignation bringing out traces of her Russian accent. "You don't think I know what you're doing? How do you think you got here? Your father? Your mother? Do you think we sprung up from the ground like those weeds?"

"I know the birds and the bees, thanks. But a 'patch of hay to roll in'? Really?"

"There are many beautiful Nahan girls in town this summer. Including Aricelli, if I'm not mistaken." Tomas nodded, turning back to the weeds. "Have you seen much of her this summer?"

"A little. She and Louis ran by the other day when I was out fixing the gate with Grandpa. They want me to go to the movies with them tomorrow."

"And are you going?" Tomas shrugged. "Aricelli is very beautiful, no?" He nodded, still not looking up. "You don't think she's beautiful?"

He pulled a patch of grass apart, nodding. "She's really . . . tall."

"Tall is nice. You are tall." She watched her grandson, trying to divine what was going on behind his eyes. "Of course, there are many girls out there."

Tomas sat back on his heels. "Her name is Stell, Grandma. She's a local."

"Nahan, of course?" Tatiana asked.

"Of course Nahan. I don't want a common. I mean, I want them to, you know, but not, like, for a girlfriend." Tatiana thought his blush made her grandson even more handsome and he rolled his eyes at her smile. "Don't pair me off just yet. I mean, I like her. A lot. She's really pretty. But not like Aricelli. She's not glamorous, you know?"

"She's not tall?"

Tomas knew she was teasing him. "No. She's nice and short. About two feet high, big potbelly, bare butt. You'll like her." He pointed to the plaster garden troll nestled in the flower garden against the house.

"Oh, I'm sure you two will be very happy." Tatiana kissed the top of her grandson's head. "Smart aleck. Do we get to meet this mysterious troll or does she only live under the mushrooms?"

. . . .

How long had she been sitting here on Calstow's western slope? Stell couldn't be sure. She knew there had been at least one long night, maybe two. Her body, fortified by the new sustenance it had received, felt stronger, strong enough to go another week without moving, without eating or drinking. The only difficult part had been overcoming the sense of bounding in her muscles, the feeling that she wanted to run and run. Whenever she had thought she had to move, she would open her eyes, see the fences and the tin roofs of the compound below her and, seeing nowhere to run, would settle back down silently.

Stell watched a group of her schoolmates pulling a wagon of heavy stones across the pitted dirt road. They were laughing and pushing at each other, none of them in a hurry to complete their chores. Some were younger than Stell, some were nearly adults but they each had homes to go to, real houses within the fenced-in compound. Stell waited until the laughing group moved behind the community barn before she slipped down the hill, through the forsythia and into her bedroom.

"I'm home, Mother." Stell brushed her knees off after climbing through the hole behind her bed. The house was small, more of a lean-to shooting off the rear wall of the church than an actual house. Her room furnishings consisted of a sagging camp cot under a canted window; a wooden chair with several dog-eared books stacked upon it, and a wall cupboard covered by a flimsy curtain. It took no more than three steps to cross the length of the room and still it made up almost a third of their living space.

Malbette stood in the doorway that led to their windowless living room and, when she saw her daughter's face, sucked in a sharp breath. Stell couldn't read her mother's reaction, couldn't gauge if there was disapproval, but as always erred on the side of caution. She remained silent, meeting her mother's stare without flinching.

Malbette broke the gaze first. "Well." Her voice trailed off as she turned to step back into the dark room behind her. "Well."

Stell felt her natural reserve evaporate under the heat of this new force that pumped within her. She choked back her words as long as possible, then stomped to the door of her bedroom and challenged Malbette.

"Well what?"

"Who is he?" Malbette sat in the only chair in the room, her hands folded, as she had all those years before when Stell had asked about her father.

"He's not from here."

A snort of derision escaped Malbette. "I wouldn't think he was."

Stell clenched her teeth. She wanted to say something cutting, something permanent to make Malbette rise from her chair shrieking and weeping. Before any words came, her mother leaned her head back against the chair and sighed.

"There's no one here fierce enough for you."

And just like that, Stell unfolded, her shoulders dropped, the roaring in her head subsided. Malbette opened her eyes again and smiled at her daughter. She held out her arms and in two strides Stell was on her knees, her head buried in her mother's skirts.

. . . .

She couldn't wait at their clearing. Holding her shoes in her hand, Stell ran down the path Tomas took over the mountain, jumping over rocks and fallen trees, giggling to herself as she saw him working his way up the path toward her. She didn't want to sit down on any of the rocks around her but found standing in one place almost impossible. She bounced from bare foot to bare foot before she remembered she held shoes in her hand. Fumbling to get them on, she winced at the straps of the inexpensive white sandals against her roughened feet. Tomas hadn't seen her yet and she wanted to look perfect. She was glad she'd let her mother brush out her hair and wash it in the old tub in the washroom. Her mother had surprised her with both the sandals and the new summer dress, a simple sundress made from lightweight flowered cotton.

"I was saving this for a special day," Malbette had said, pulling on the hem of the dress to straighten it. "I don't suppose there is any day more special than meeting his family, is there?"

"If I do get to meet them," Stell had said, trying to catch her reflection in the small mirror on the wall. "He's coming up the mountain tomorrow. I can feel it."

. . . .

Tomas stopped short, realizing Stell was less than ten feet before him. "You came. You knew. You look . . . you look . . . you look so beautiful."

She grinned and spun around. "You said you wanted me to meet your grandparents. Today? Can we do it today?"

Tomas laughed, three days' worth of tension dropping out his feet. He had been sick thinking something had gone wrong. Stell hadn't returned to the mountain. His grandparents and his friends had wanted his attention. For three days he had weeded and worked and even gone to the movies. Last night, however, he had sent up a cry, his body broadcasting farther than his mind could ever dream and now, here she was, looking like a country schoolgirl. He would have preferred no dress at all, but figured once they'd had lunch with his grandma and grandpa, they could take care of that. He took her hand and led her down the mountain to the farm below.

. . . .

"Grandma Tat?" Tomas called as they stepped onto the porch. "We're here." He could hear his grandma in the kitchen setting out plates, but Stell dug in her heels and refused to move past the screen door. "What are you doing?" he whispered as Tatiana stepped up to the screen door, wiping her hands on a dishtowel.

"Tomas! You're back sooner than I thought." She smiled at Stell. "Is this your friend?"

Stell squeezed Tomas's hand and cleared her throat. *"u fealte, sed 'im sete."*

Tomas blushed. Who asked formal permission to enter a home anymore? He started to speak, when Tatiana answered, smiling. *"Set fealte, 'u di."* She opened the door to let them in. As they stepped past her, she smacked her grandson on the back of the head. "You could learn a thing or two about manners, young man."

Stell tried not to gawk at the rooms before her. Everything was so clean, so full of light and space. There were bookshelves full of large, hardcover books. Photographs peeked out on end tables and on walls. The pine floor shone underneath a sunny hooked rug. She clutched Tomas's hand as he led her to the kitchen.

"I hope you don't mind eating in the kitchen, Stell. May I call you Stell?" Stell could only nod at the energetic woman before her, at the energy all around her. Plates were set; bowls, silverware, glasses clinking and catching the light. A tall, white-haired man entered, introduced himself as Charles, Tomas's grandfather, kicking off a new flurry of activity as they settled around the table.

And then the food started—enormous bowls of green salad, pasta salad, warm bread, soft butter. On and on it came. She had never seen so much food on one table in her life.

"Is this all right?" Tatiana asked. "Do you like olives? I can make you a sandwich if you don't like pasta salad."

Stell didn't know where to look. "I like everything."

"Good," Tomas said, "because the hamburgers are coming right up."

"Tomas!" Tatiana smacked his head again, then rolled her eyes at Stell. "So vulgar. Forgive my grandson. He has the manners of a goat. He and his very cool friends find it amusing to bring up nauseating topics like carrion at the table."

When she could think of nothing to say to that, Tomas kicked her softly under the table. "I'm kidding about the hamburgers. We don't eat meat. We're all Nahan. Nothing dead here."

"That's right, Stell." Charles said, taking a seat at the table. "The only dead thing at this table is Tomas's chance of borrowing the truck this summer." Tomas began to protest when Tatiana cut them off.

"Could we please stop talking of dead things? Please? We're eating."

. . . .

Tatiana wondered if Stell was a farmer. Tomas had said she was local and none of the Nahan children that came in from the city would be seen in such a simple dress. There were Nahan far out along the county roads, farmers and orchard keepers, but it was unlikely Tomas had strayed out that far from the farm. Her table manners were odd; she ate quickly, her head bowed, as if embarrassed and unaccustomed to being seen eating. Something about the simplicity of the dress kept pulling her attention until it came to her with a jolt.

It was the light colored floral fabric that had distracted her, that had put out of her mind the dark and drab clothes of the dour religious compound on the other side of Calstow. *En Na 'u 'an* they called themselves. "The True Family." It had to be. They were close enough to the farm that an ambitious hiker could reach them, and Tomas was certainly ambitious when it came to this young lady. The foreignness, the formality, it all made sense now. This could prove to be a long summer.

. . . .

"Knock-knock. Anybody home?"

Stell looked up from the last bite of her strawberry shortcake to see the most beautiful Nahan girl she had ever imagined come strolling into the kitchen.

"Do I smell strawberries?"

"Aricelli!" Tatiana rose to embrace the young woman. "This is a surprise. Are you by yourself?"

"No!" A male voice called from the living room. "I'm here too, but I'm stealing your chocolate kisses. You're going to have to find a better hiding place, Grandma Tat."

"I've long given up hiding any sweets from you, Louis. Don't be a dog. Come in and say hello to Tomas's friend, Stell."

Stell felt glued to her chair. Aricelli was like a goddess of myth standing before her. Where Stell's hair hung straight (thankfully clean and brushed), Aricelli's fell in lustrous tumbling waves of black with copper glints. Her eyes, a more vivid blue than Stell's naturally, shone all the brighter for the carefully applied eyeliner and her tall, athletic body held few secrets within the clinging pink camisole and brief plaid shorts. She even smelled lovely. Stell had never seen herself in a full-length mirror, but instinct told her she looked nothing like the young woman before her.

"Why don't we step out onto the porch for some lemonade?" Tatiana said. "It's crowded in here."

As chairs scraped back from the table and the crowd made their move toward the porch, Stell tried and failed to catch Tomas's eye for reassurance. The shorter, stockier young man who was obviously his cousin Louis watched her from the corner of his eye; Stell could see the smirk on his face. It was the only part of the afternoon that reminded Stell of home.

. . . .

Tomas followed Tatiana, reaching over her into the upper cabinets for lemonade glasses.

"Go on out on the porch, everybody." Tatiana called out. "We'll just be minute." Aricelli and Louis surrounded Stell, leading her out the door with warm smiles and, Tomas would probably guess, hell in their eyes.

"You haven't introduced Stell to your friends yet, Tomas?" He said nothing but made a great effort of putting napkins into a basket. "Are you keeping her a secret?"

"No, Grandma. There just hasn't been time. Or an opportunity."

Tatiana put her hand on his arm. "Have you told them what she is?" Tomas turned away, brushing her hand off his shoulder. "Tomas, I am speaking to you. Do you know what she is?"

"She's just a girl." He wouldn't meet her eyes.

"No, Tomas. She's part of the True Family."

"You don't know that."

"Tomas." She lifted his chin to look him in the eyes. "You know it."

He did. More than anything in the world he wished he didn't but for weeks now the message had been coming to him, no matter how hard he tried to ignore it. Her odd manner, her strange scriptures, they were all signs of the True Family, a fundamentalist cult of Nahan that preached the inherent sinfulness of the Nahan nature. They hated themselves. They hated other Nahan. Their lives were lives of repentance and prayer.

"I don't think she's like them."

Tatiana stroked his cheek. "Maybe, maybe not, but this will not be an easy relationship to maintain. I can only assume her family does not know about you?"

"I don't think so."

She sighed. "Well, she is here now and so are your friends. You cannot leave her alone with the likes of Louis. It may be, sometime soon, you will have to make a choice between your friends and your girl."

"Why?" His eyes told her he had been worrying over that very thought.

"Because, my dear boy, your life will be bigger than Calstow Mountain. And for Stell? The world may be too big."

....

On the porch, Charles and Louis sprawled out in wicker chairs, Louis insisting that Stell join Aricelli on the porch swing. Aricelli leaned back easily, one shapely leg tucked under her, the other pushing the swing with her white canvas sneaker. Stell knew nothing of the fashions of the outside world, but she had a pretty good idea that her simple cotton dress and white sandals, the very clothes she had nearly burst with pride putting on only hours ago, were grossly out of place. Every way she sat seemed wrong, every sound she made sounded slow and out of place. Despite all the smiles and the attempts to include her in the conversation, Stell felt every bit as miserable as she did at any church service. When Tomas finally pushed through the screen door, lemonade in hand, it was all she could do to not cry out.

"There they are!" Charles applauded. "Thought you'd flown to California to pick the lemons yourself." Tatiana bustled around setting up a table, which led to a general commotion on the porch, everyone but Stell rising and making gestures of helping out, however useless.

"Here, Tomas." Aricelli stepped away from the swing, brushing close past him. "You sit on the swing with Stell. I'll sit here on the floor next to Louis."

Without an actual protest, Tomas settled next to Stell, close but not touching.

"So we were talking about our *avalentu.*" Aricelli clapped her hands. "Kitty and I are going to head to New York City and do a few weeks there."

"You can keep it." Louis said. "We're heading west, aren't we, Tomas? You and me and the big red machine. I've got a good feeling

Vegas will be on our itinerary. Next Thursday, dude, we are outta here."

The words fell out of Stell's mouth before she could stop them. "You're leaving?"

"I meant to tell you about it," Tomas said, his cheeks burning. "It's this thing we do when we're old enough. We get some money and go out on the road. Technically we're supposed to be looking for jobs but no one does. We just hang and hunt and find out what we're good at and stuff like that."

"It's our *avalentu*." Aricelli said as if the word explained itself. "Have you had yours? Do you get to go anywhere?"

Stell looked from Aricelli to Louis, who both watched her with veiled amusement. Charles and Tatiana met her eyes with gentleness but she could see the shade of embarrassment behind their smiles. It was when she looked at Tomas, wondrous Tomas, that she saw the true gap yawning between them. The six inches that separated them might as well have been the gorge off northern Calstow. She didn't belong here.

"I am only going home."

Tomas jumped up and reached for her hand. "Don't go. Or at least let me walk you."

Stell freed her hand from his, clasping them behind her back, and gave Charles and Tatiana a small bow. "Thank you for your hospitality." She looked up at Tomas. "Stay with your friends. It is a long way to my home."

Before he could protest, she was off the porch and well across the yard. Not caring if they watched, she ripped the uncomfortable sandals off her feet and ran up the hill into the forest.

Chapter Two:
AVALENTU

....

Avalentu: Literally *flight*; a road trip or excursion taken by
Nahan youths as a rite of passage into adulthood

AUGUST

Tomas drove with his elbow out the window, hot wind drying the
sweat on his face as the Kansas landscape sped by. Beside him in
the pick-up truck, Louis laid his head back on the seat and sighed.

"Wow."

Tomas nodded. "Wow."

"Maybe we should rethink college."

"Think they'd let us in a sorority?"

Louis grinned. "They let us in that one."

One look from Tomas and the two cousins burst out laughing.
They'd just spent one astonishing night in the Kappa Delta house
at Kansas University. They'd followed a trail of rush parties and
ended up groin deep in a sea of drunken college girls.

Tomas blushed at the memory. "I thought it would be tougher getting common girls to do that. I didn't think it would be so easy, that they'd be so . . . so . . ."

"Persuadable?" Louis arched his brow. "For a late bloomer, you certainly got the hang of it quickly. How many did you have in that bed? And weren't they all cheerleaders?"

"No, two of them were. The other was on a gymnastics scholarship." Tomas grinned and Louis swore in disbelief. "You didn't do too bad yourself, from what I saw. It sounded like you had that one girl meowing."

"Well yeah but there's nothing surprising about that. I've been tapping commons since grade school. You on the other hand"—he patted Tomas on the shoulder, ignoring his cousin's eye roll. "All I'm saying is that I'm glad you're coming out of your shell. If it took getting your cherry popped by a True Family member then so be it."

"Don't say that."

"I mean nothing bad by it. Seriously. As long as you've got her out of your system and are now ready to act like a grown-up, I'm cool with it." Louis cupped his hand around a cigarette to block the wind while he lit it. He blew a stream of smoke out the window. "You're still writing to her, aren't you?"

"Sometimes. I send them to Grandma Tat. I don't know if she's getting them."

Louis sighed. "Yeah, I guess you can't address them to Cult Road One, Back Ass Nowhereville, huh?" Tomas just stared out at the flat land ahead and Louis shifted in his seat. "I know you liked her and I'm glad you got that out of the way."

"Can we drop it, please?"

"Sure. I'm just saying that I'm not going to be around forever to smooth things over."

"Is this what you call dropping it?"

Louis slouched down in the seat and closed his eyes. After three weeks on the road together, Tomas knew that was his sign of surrender. They'd been having versions of the same almost-argument since they'd rolled off of Calstow Mountain. Louis wanted Tomas to admit that Stell was just a passing thing and Tomas refused. The problem was he couldn't wholly deny it.

Stell didn't feel like a passing thing. What he'd experienced with her on the mountain moved him; it changed him. He didn't know why he hadn't told her about their upcoming trip. He tried to fool himself by saying he assumed she'd understand the *avalentu* but he didn't get far with that. Stell had never heard of Star Wars or gas stations. Something told him her education lacked some pretty big chunks of information.

If he was honest with himself—and unbroken hours on Midwestern highways made that almost unavoidable—he hadn't wanted his worlds to collide. He didn't want Stell to know Louis and Aricelli. He didn't want her to know the Tomas that Louis called *cousin*. Alone with Stell, Tomas wasn't the awkward weird kid hiding behind Louis. But that train of thought led down an ugly track. Tomas didn't seem weird with Stell because Stell was weird. Tomas was downright normal by comparison.

It was hardly the stuff of eternal romances.

But he knew what he felt and, as usual, was unable to express it in any sort of rational method. So he and Louis had fallen into their same old patterns—Louis taking the lead, Tomas following along. He couldn't complain. The trip had been educational, to say the least. Tomas had discovered that he had a knack for creating back stories and aliases to ease them into whatever scene drew their attention. While Louis would have been content to just introduce himself with a fake name and seduce a common or two for a tumble and some quick feeding, Tomas found he liked to engage them in conversation. He liked to tell them lies, to seduce them, to lure them in with more than just Nahan pheromones and charm.

Tomas discovered that he liked the common.

Funny that after all those years surrounded by commons in school and in the neighborhood, it had taken a trip across country to learn that.

. . . .

The bus was old, its white paint rusted through. Both sides were painted in a shaky print "Fellowship of God's Word." Beside her, Stell could feel Malbette tremble with—what? Anxiety? Excitement? The high-pitched hum of her energy made Stell's heart beat even harder than it had when she had received word that she would be going out into the world.

"Is this our *avalentu*?"

Malbette turned at that and Stell felt an ugly pleasure in surprising her mother. Again. Things had changed since her luncheon with Tomas. Malbette had been waiting for her when she returned to the house. Stell had fought back tears the entire run. They'd clouded her vision and one or two had slipped down her cheeks as she thought about Tomas hiding the truth from her, hiding her from his family.

But when she saw the look of pity on her mother's face—expectant pity, anticipating pity, pity wrapped up in the certainty that it would be needed—the tears dried up.

Stell hadn't explained. She hadn't said a word about it. She didn't slip out to go back up the mountain but danced in tense silence with her mother in the cramped shack for days until Malbette had sprung the news of the trip.

"I doubt Uncle Rom would use that word." Malbette folded a woolen skirt and slid it into a satchel. "He would call it our pilgrimage. You probably don't remember the last outing several years ago. Maybe if you would attend school once in a while, you would have heard people talking about this." The criticism was lost in her carefully controlled enthusiasm.

"Where do we go?"

"We pack up all the jellies and jams we've produced, all the quilts, any carvings or crafts any of us have made since the last pilgrimage. Arrangements have been made for us to visit churches that are having revivals. We have permission to sell our wares and sing the good news and hopefully make enough money to last for another three or four years." She smiled into the bag, smoothing the cloth beneath her fingers.

"Nahan churches?"

Malbette laughed. "No, Stell. Not Nahan churches. We're going to be Christians for the week." Stell stared at her, not understanding. "You know, Jesus."

"Jesus." Stell nodded, trying to remember what she had learned of this god. "He was born in a basket of reeds, right? And ran from the king with the locusts?"

Malbette put her hands on either side of Stell's face. "My sweet button, on this trip, try not to speak."

Stell shook off her touch. "How is it we are allowed to go? We haven't made anything."

Malbette chuckled again, a strange sound to her daughter and not altogether unpleasant. "Well, at first I was going to beg but I knew how far that would get me. Then I used the one tactic that I knew could not fail. I let someone overhear me saying how happy you would be to finally be free of your classmates for a whole month. They couldn't get us on the bus fast enough. Don't forget to take a book. It's a long drive."

By the time they made it to the highway, the handle of Stell's satchel was damp from her tight grip. She could feel the anticipation, could hear the giggles and whispers of the girls around her, and watched the roughhousing of the boys. Like many of her companions, this was the first time she had ever been in a motorized vehicle. The sound and vibrations moved through her, distracting her. Beside her, Malbette hummed under her breath, occasionally catching her eye and winking. For the first time since running up Calstow Mountain, thoughts of Tomas didn't twist in her stomach like stones.

As farmland turned to suburbs then turned to strip malls and cineplexes, Stell felt something opening up inside of her. She watched commons in their cars, wearing fashionable clothes like those worn by Aricelli and Louis. She saw Starbucks and Walmarts, exotic names that had dropped from Tomas's lips like the names of gods. Those places were real. She was out among them. Even in the heavy woolen clothes, the clumsy shoes, the uncomfortable black cotton head scarf, she was out. This was the world.

. . . .

It was a long ride, long and bewildering, broken up with stops at 4-H camps and state parks and ugly tents in muddy fields. Every stop had lumpy women with piles of hair introducing themselves as Sister This or Sister That, and pawning them off to sweaty men called Brother Something Else.

Everyone smiled and everyone shouted, "Praise the Lord!" while they stared at the congregation, checking out the dark clothes and head scarves. Once Malbette had caught Stell staring back at a woman gawking at her heavy shoes. Her mother had elbowed Stell hard and the gawker, realizing she'd been caught, clasped her hands between her enormous breasts and cried, "Praise Jesus!" Malbette had dragged Stell away.

In and out of tents and Quonset huts and cinderblock buildings they filed. The first time the Nahan congregation stood up and sang in harmony, Stell could only gape.

When did they learn that?

Was this what she'd been missing by skipping school? All Stell knew of Nahan church and Uncle Rom were beratings and threats, punches, hair pulling, and ritual knives.

When did Jesus-singing come into the picture?

Stell had so many questions and only her mother to answer them but there never seemed to be any time to talk. They were forever being herded into and out of revivals, each one hotter and more crowded than the last. Stell thought she might be bruised from all the hugging and grabbing. One preacher had even smacked her on the forehead, forcing Malbette to once more hold her back.

The bus offered no chance to pummel her mother with questions either. Chatter on the bus stayed low since Uncle Rom walked the aisle at every chance. He'd stalk up and down, staring into faces as he passed. Stell made a point of keeping her eyes down.

Rom walked the aisle as they crossed into Ohio. "You did very well last night, my children. I am proud of you." He smiled that yellow smile of his. "For many of you, this is your first interaction with the common and I am sure many of you were sorely tested." His eyes roamed over the faces before him as if he knew exactly of whom he spoke.

"This pilgrimage of ours is not about raising funds for our way of life. That is simply a side benefit of our good work. No, children. It is far more than that." He made his way down the aisle, the lurching of the bus only adding to the hypnotic rise and fall of his voice. Stell noticed he was paler than usual and his skin wore a sickly waxen sheen. "It is on this pilgrimage that we move among those we are compelled to slaughter. It is on this pilgrimage that we are forced to rely on the kindness of the very people our abomination compels us to devour." He grabbed a young man by the hair and shook him violently. "Did you feel that bloodlust, brother?"

"Yes, Uncle Rom." Tobias could barely choke the words out past the shaking.

"And did you lower yourself into that debauchery, brother?"

"No, Uncle Rom. I swear!"

"You swear." The old man dropped Tobias's head like a handful of trash. He addressed everyone on the bus, his voice dropping to a menacing whisper. "He swears when what he needs to do is pray. Prayer. Atonement. Vigilance. That is what keeps the curse of our people at bay. Prayer. Atonement. Vigilance. Prayer. Atonement. Vigilance. Say it with me."

"Prayer. Atonement. Vigilance." The crowd spoke in one muffled murmur, repeating the chant, rising in volume, until the words ran together, joining with the rattles and groans of the old bus as it made its way to the next revival.

. . . .

During the last revival in Ohio, Stell caught her classmates Davina and Luanna sneaking away from the group, followed by Thor and Lucas. She tracked their escape at two more stops and at the third, Thor caught her watching them and flicked her ear hard with his finger.

"You keep your mouth shut, tree frog." His whisper was a low growl.

"I won't say anything. I don't know anything."

Davina pushed past her, mocking her in a singsong voice. "I don't know anything. I just roll around in dirt and talk to birds all day."

Luanna choked back a scream of laughter, grabbing at Stell's long hair. "Take a bath, tree frog. Then maybe you'll know what you're missing!"

To Stell, they looked different than the rest of the congregation. Their movements were faster, brighter somehow, as if all the other Nahan were on newsprint, and they were leaping out of the pages of the glossy magazine Stell had seen Luanna sneak from her bag.

Then Stell realized what was different about them. She could smell it. She smelled it on their skin, on their breath, in their hair. They smelled like blood. But not the way she had smelled of Tomas; this was not Nahan blood.

The revival took forever to finish. Stell wanted so badly to be alone with Malbette to ask her about what she had learned but there was always someone grabbing her hands, hugging her or commenting on her simple clothes. She wasn't used to spending this much time around anyone, much less this many anyones, and she needed the solitude of the forest that ringed the campground.

Stalking off into a copse of beech trees, Stell settled on a soft patch of moss to relax. The cool green under her fingers made her ache for Calstow Mountain, for Tomas, for the nights of freedom. She saw her mother making her way through the clearing, heading right for her.

"Always sneaking off into the trees, aren't you, my sweet?" Malbette wrapped one arm around a slender beech tree, pressing her cheek against its white peeling bark.

"That's why they call me tree frog, isn't it?" All day she had longed to be alone with her mother and now that the moment was here, her mood soured.

"Tree frog. I think it's sort of cute."

"They don't mean it to be cute."

Malbette released the tree and came to sit beside Stell on the forest floor. "That's because they're stupid, Teherestelle." Stell jumped at the sound of her full name, the name her mother rarely used for her, but Malbette's eyes were focused on the crowd before her. "They're small and mean and stupid. They're liars and hypocrites, just like me."

"What do you mean? You're not like them."

"Aren't I? I'm worse than them. I'm a coward."

"Malbette, no . . ."

"Don't be upset, my sweet. Like you, all this Family time is getting to me. Tonight, after supper, let's you and I take a long walk."

. . . .

Dinner was set out under a tent next to the picnic shelter. Stell was heading back for seconds when Malbette gestured for her to hold back. People milled about the buffet table and even Uncle Rom seemed to be in what passed for good spirits on him. She felt her mother tug at her sleeve and followed her lead as she stepped to the side of the stone picnic shelter.

"Let's take a walk along the creek, Daughter." She spoke in English, not Nahan. They had been instructed to use their own tongue as little as possible while out in the world. She spoke loudly enough to be overheard but not enough to seem obvious. There was a coy tilt to her head as her eyes flickered past her daughter's face to a point beyond. Stell followed her gaze and saw a common man in workman's clothes hauling tubs of ice into the shelter. The man had noticed Malbette and was trying not to smile too broadly. Her mother linked her arm in hers and led her across the campground to the stream that wandered into the forest.

"Are you flirting with that man, Mother?" They were alone along the creek bed, but she could feel her mother's attention drawn behind her.

"Yes, my sweet. I am."

"Why? He's a common."

"Oh, Stell," she turned to face her daughter, smoothing her hair and stroking her cheek. "Will you ever forgive me?"

"For what?"

"For living here among these people. Keeping you from the Nahan. The real Nahan, not the Family. When you came home after you met your young man, I realized what a coward I'd been, how selfish I've been, hiding with you in the mountains, thinking

33

I could keep you a child forever. But look at you. You're a young woman. You have the whole world before you and now I have so little time to teach you what you should have known all along."

"Mother, you're scaring me."

"Don't be afraid, my button. This is"—A cracking tree branch behind them cut her off. It was the workman from the campsite hurrying to catch up to them. When they turned to him, he seemed embarrassed for having been caught.

"Brother Daniel." Malbette's voice was smooth. "How nice of you to join us."

The big man blushed. "I just wanted to make sure you knew that there are copperheads along this creek. You might want to be extra careful jumping up on any rocks. That's where they like to sun."

"Copperheads. Oh my goodness." Malbette glided closer to Daniel. "I must say I have no fondness for snakes. Do you think we're in danger?"

"Well, if it would make you feel better, I'd be happy to walk along with you."

She took his arm. "I can't tell you how much better that would make me feel. Shall we?"

Stell fell in step behind them, unsure she should follow until she caught a slight hand gesture from Malbette. Her mother was a woman transformed. The inward focus had vanished, replaced by a demure creature, by turns flirtatious and coy. Their shoulders touched often and more than once Malbette leaned on Daniel for help she didn't need. Always when she spoke to the much taller man, she looked up under her lashes but mostly, Stell noticed, when she spoke or laughed, she breathed on him softly. Brother Daniel didn't seem to think or care if there was anything calculating in her performance. His eyes rarely left her face.

They reached a narrow clearing, where the creek slipped under a sun-warmed expanse of slate. Malbette curled her feet under her and invited Daniel to join her. With a subtle flick of her hand, she motioned for Stell to hang back. Over the laughter of the creek Stell could just hear the soft sounds of her mother's voice as she spoke very closely to her companion. Not wanting to disturb them, yet unable to overcome her curiosity, Stell stepped behind them. When she was very near, she realized Malbette was whispering in Nahan, running her fingers over Daniel's eyes and lips, her breath softly rustling his hair.

She put her hand behind his head and lowered him onto the rock. He seemed to be sleeping, a dreamy smile smeared on his face, his eyes just slightly open. Malbette continued to stroke his face softly as she smiled up at Stell. "Come see a common man up close." Stell settled down on the other side of Daniel, curious to be so close to a common and feel no danger.

"His skin is so rough." Stell marveled at the small lines and ruddy complexion. "He looks older than he should."

"Their skin doesn't heal as quickly as ours, so it shows their lives easily. It's a bit like a patina on a bronze statue or the yellowing of an old book. It's fragile."

"What are we doing, Malbette?"

Her eyes were light. "Whatever we want. Did you see how I took him, Stell? Did you notice the attention, the thoughts I brought to the front of my mind?" Stell nodded. "Collect your thoughts, whatever you want to be before you, and breathe them out. Never panic, sometimes it takes longer than other times. Sometimes if your mind drifts, you can find yourself with some surprising results. Whatever you do, don't let your mind drift to your young man unless you are ready to take the common into your bed."

"A common? You mean, be together like me and Tomas? Together naked?"

Malbette laughed again, her fingers brushing Daniel's chest. "Don't sound so shocked, Daughter. Sex is sex. Pleasure is pleasure. And their bodies can be a lovely diversion."

"But I love Tomas."

"Of course you do. This has nothing to do with that. Tomas may be love but this is life." Malbette pulled at the simple silver band she had put on before they'd boarded the bus. She twisted the ring and revealed a slender hooked point. It was little more than a flattened needle, but even in the fading light of dusk Stell could see how sharp the outer blade was.

"A memento of happier times." She stared at the blade for a moment and then returned her attention to Daniel. "The silver keeps the bruising down. Your tongue will make the wound clot. If you do it properly, there will be no scar. Still, it's best to find a suitable location to feed, just in case. The crook of the elbow is a good choice, especially for a laborer. They are used to bruises and scratches."

Stell was speechless as she watched her mother push up the sleeve of his work shirt. A ring with a blade? Her mother feeding? On a common? In one short walk in the woods, Stell's entire life had been thrown up in the air and was now bouncing through the tree limbs crazily. She stared as her mother sucked on the muscular arm of the man sleeping before her. Her sighs were deep but she fed only a minute. Her fingers pressed against the wound as she rose to face Stell.

"Come here, child. Taste your life."

. . . .

Tomas hadn't spoken for over an hour.

"No hard feelings?"

Tomas glared at him. "You've got to be kidding me."

"It was a nice motel at least."

"Don't." Tomas's voice was a warning.

"I think you made a good call pretending to be Hungarian."

"Dude, you left me in a gay bar."

"You did great."

"You. Left. Me. In. A. Gay. Bar. Left me! Took the truck and left me."

Louis shrugged. "We needed to be alone."

"I was stuck there all night. Until closing. Supposedly not able to speak English. Can't exactly call a cab when you don't speak English especially in the middle of nowhere. Plus I didn't know the name of the fucking motel. Four hours, Louis, four hours in a gay cowboy bar in Arizona not speaking English."

"Hey, you're the plan maker. Besides, Kevin seemed to like the exotic side of you."

Tomas glared at Louis once more until, despite himself, he began to laugh. "Fuck off, Louis. I could kill you."

Louis threw his head back laughing. "Hey man, I've had nothing but poontang for three thousand miles. This trip is supposed to be for our personal development. Have you forgotten what you learned in Heritage School about not letting orientation and biases interfere with—"

"I know, I know, with necessary feeding. You've brought that up a thousand times. That's for when there's no other source in sight, not 'How to Spend a Night in Arizona.'"

"C'mon." Louis punched his arm. "It wasn't that bad, was it?"

"Dude, you left me in that bar. I felt like the last gumdrop surrounded by fat kids."

"No, but Kevin turned out to be cool, didn't he? I mean, you woke up with him." Louis winked luridly. "Did you get some?"

"Don't even go there."

"I'm going there."

"I got what I came for."

"You didn't even try it? Dude!"

"Dude! I don't like dudes! How much clearer does that have to get?" Tomas turned his head away quickly.

"You did try it, didn't you?" No answer. "C'mon, admit it. You got a little something."

Tomas rolled his eyes. "I kissed him." Louis waited, nodding his head expectantly. A long moment passed before Tomas gave in. "Actually he was very nice." They stared at each other then both exploded in laughter.

"Look who's got a boyfriend!"

"I will kill you if you ever do that to me again, I swear. You're lucky he was a decent guy and wouldn't leave me when the bar closed. We drove up and down that stupid highway trying to find that fucking motel. What was I supposed to do? Leap out of the car and run away?"

"Of course not. You did the right thing."

"I'm going to punch that smirk right off your face."

"So you brought him in and . . . what? A little dancing, a back-rub?"

"Yeah right. If he'd grabbed me he'd be in the back of the truck right now wrapped in plastic. No, he just talked. I wasn't supposed to be able to understand him so I just nodded. Apparently nobody in his life knows he's gay. He's in some kind of trouble at work. He's from out of town and was just passing through."

"Sure he was."

Tomas lit a cigarette. "I think he was telling the truth. Why would he lie? He thought I couldn't understand him. I leaned in to kiss him, which was no fun by the way, and he was under in like two minutes. Took my drink from his arm and called it a night."

"And spooned him the rest of the night."

"I really hate you, Louis. I do."

"I know. But for what it's worth, thank you."

"You owe me big time."

"I bet I can make it up to you. How does a suite at the Bellagio in Vegas sound?"

Tomas raised an eyebrow. "Sounds like a nice place to start. How are you going to pull that off? We're almost out of money. We should be heading up to Budrowe soon." Budrowe, Utah, was the location of the nearest Nahan-friendly bank, where there would be cash and extra sets of identification for the many Nahan youth crisscrossing the country this time of year.

"This is on the way."

"Las Vegas is on the way from Phoenix to Utah? I like your map."

. . . .

Louis led them through the crowded lobby of the Bellagio to the elevators.

"Where are we going?" Tomas asked. "Do we have a room?"

"No but someone we know does."

Tomas held the elevator door open. "Uh-uh. No more surprises. I swear to god, if you've gotten us tickets to 'Thunder from Down Under all male revue' I'll kill you."

Louis laughed and slapped his hand away from the door. "Relax, tough guy. We're going to a party in the Grand Lakeview Suite with one Mina Harker."

"Mina Harker?" Tomas leaned back against the wall as the elevator rose. "Who does that make you? Dracula?"

"Naturally."

They could hear the music bumping from the suite before they reached the door. Inside, a small but energetic crowd of beautiful commons danced and drank, champagne glasses and beer bottles raised high. Louis and Tomas, grimy from the drive, cut through the crowd looking for their hostess. Despite their road-weary appearance, or perhaps because of it, several young women and a few young men eyed them appreciatively.

"Where's Mina?" Louis shouted to one glassy-eyed brunette in a shiny halter.

"Who?" She stumbled against him.

"The person who's throwing this party."

"Yeah it's a great party, isn't it? *Whooooo!*" She spun off in search of more champagne.

They pitched their bags into the space behind the couch and, turning back to the party, came face to face with two ice-cold bottles of beer.

"Looking for these?" Aricelli stood before them, beers in hand, looking cool and unperturbed by the chaos around her. "I thought you'd never get here."

Louis took his beer and kissed her on the cheek. "We almost didn't."

She held the other beer close to her throat so Tomas had to reach out for it.

"So you're Mina Harker tonight?"

"It's Daddy's idea. His big surprise for me. Sort of my debutante celebration." She seemed charmingly embarrassed by the excess around her. "Let me show you guys where you can clean up." Tomas grabbed his bag and followed her; Louis hung back, sneaking Aricelli a knowing wink.

In the relative quiet of the luxurious bedroom, Tomas took a deep drink of his beer and sighed. He hadn't fed well or slept well the night before, thanks to Louis's stunt, and his shoulders were stiff.

"Don't you get tired of it?" Aricelli sat on the edge of the bed, her long, ivory legs stretched out before her.

"Of what?" He couldn't help but stare at the swell of her breasts in her skimpy camisole.

"The smell of them. The noise of them. The common, I mean. Don't get me wrong, I have totally loved this trip. We've had an amazing time." She flipped a wavy lock of hair over one perfect shoulder. "But we were the only Nahan for days. Just me and Kitty. I've eaten enough to live for a year but sometimes that isn't enough, is it?" She rose and stepped in close to Tomas. "Or am I just being selfish?"

He breathed in her scent, part honeysuckle soap, part Nahan woman. He had forgotten how smooth skin could be. Her breathing deepened as his eyes roamed over her face and shoulders. The sight of her pink tongue flicking over her lower lip made him lean in to her and he felt a spark of heat everywhere their bodies made contact.

"Why do I get the feeling that this is a set-up?" Tomas asked.

Aricelli smiled. "Whatever do you mean?"

"I mean, Louis is worried I'm not over Stell and suddenly I find myself alone in a bedroom with the most beautiful girl in the world."

"Oh, flattery. I like that."

"So I'm right, right?" He could see the shine on her lips where she licked them.

"You make it sound far more nefarious than it should. Is it so wrong that we should meet up on our trips?"

"How much orchestrating did this take?"

She laughed. "No offense, Tomas, but we could have rebuilt the *Titanic* in your underwear and you probably wouldn't have noticed." She bumped her nose against his. "You're very good-looking but not especially cunning."

He laughed. "That makes one of us."

"Do you want me to apologize?" She sighed. "This is our *avalentu*, Tomas, our time to fly. This is our time to do things and try things that we've only thought about."

He spread his legs to give her room to press in closer. "Have you thought about this?"

"Haven't you?"

Tomas laughed, having a hard time thinking with the nearness of her. "Yeah, but I'm me and you're you. You're . . ." His eyes roamed over her body. "You're you."

"And you're sweet. Are you through with that beer?" Aricelli's fingers slid down his wrist, across the back of his hand, and wrapped around the neck of the bottle. She brought the beer to her lips and drank deep, her eyes never leaving Tomas's. Her throat working to swallow, her lips wrapped firmly around the brown glass, the small sounds of satisfaction she made as she drank, were all Tomas needed. He leaned in, burying his face in the base of her neck. She smelled like everything he hadn't realized he had been missing.

"I'm not sure you're going to like the way I smell after two days in the truck with Louis."

She pulled his t-shirt over his head and began to kiss his chest, her tongue tracing arcs on his smooth skin. "I love the way you smell. You smell like a man." She put her forehead to his, tangling her fingers in his hair. "You look like a man. This trip agrees with you."

"I don't want to talk about this trip." He picked her up and placed her on the bed. "I don't want to talk about anything."

. . . .

Gary Hunter III of Glenn Creek Freewill Baptist Church looked forward to the autumn revivals at the county fairgrounds every year. Each summer and fall, busload after busload of young, impassioned country girls rolled through his little town on the highway that was known among churchgoers as the northern loop of the Bible Belt. Pentecostals, Seventh-day Adventists, snake handlers, Southern Baptists, even a Methodist or two made it to his little acre with their families to find another piece of the Lord. Gary felt he was doing his part as he made a point to get at least one young woman per revival onto her knees, although he joked, it was usually him that wound up saying, "Oh god!"

When the Fellowship of God's Word bus pulled up and what looked like a truckload of nuns piled off, he was at first dismayed.

Upon closer inspection, however, he realized that under those incredibly ugly clothes, even by revival standards, were some lovely young women. Putting on his best "come to Jesus" smile, Gary Hunter III greeted his northern guests and helped them settle in the Conestoga Lodge, the mildewy cinderblock barracks they would call home for the night.

It was difficult to put an age on the women. In their frumpy clothes they could have been fifteen or forty and from the looks he was getting from some of them, he suspected this was not their first rodeo. While he appreciated an experienced woman as much as the next man, this weekend he was looking for something a little fresher, a little more challenging.

That's when he saw her.

How to pick her out? She was simply another dark-haired girl in ugly clothes. And was it just him or were all their eyes blue? Either a huge coincidence (unlikely) or some serious inbreeding (far more likely, he figured). But this young woman didn't meet his eyes boldly. She didn't giggle with the other girls on the bus, or push and play with the boys around her. No, this girl clung to her mother and, when she caught him staring at her, ducked behind her mother to hide. *Yes,* Gary thought to himself, *sometimes a man wanted a challenge.*

"May I get you a lemonade, Sister?"

. . . .

Stell could feel his intention as clearly as if he were humping her leg. Pretending to be struck with shyness, she kept her eyes downward, knowing Malbette would play her part.

"That would be very kind of you, Brother." Her mother's voice was strident, like that of a wary guardian. She too had noticed the leering smile of this young man. "My daughter and I would appreciate a nice cold drink."

"It would be my pleasure, ma'am." Gary tried to catch Stell's eye and she rewarded him with the briefest glance. As he stepped away, Malbette chuckled.

"Not exactly a prince but I suspect his experience on his back could make up for any shortcomings while upright. I would suggest however"—she pulled Stell close, her voice low—"that you keep your encounters with him in absolute privacy. All of it, including whatever passes for flirting in this county."

Stell didn't question her mother's advice. She had been dazzled by her mother's proficiency at luring men away from the crowd and not only lowering their defenses but leaving them grateful for the encounter.

As always the revival seemed to last forever. Singing and praying and waving arms, people dropping to the floor and speaking in tongues, it had all become a prelude to what she and many of her congregation members considered the main event of the evening. During the supper break, Stell pretended to be engrossed in the endless selection of green bean casseroles but was instead following Gary's course to get her alone.

"Is it all right if I sit with you?" he asked.

Stell looked around worriedly. "It might seem improper. We haven't been introduced. My mother . . . my preacher . . ." Gary stared hard at the ground and Stell could feel his concern that she was simply too hard to get. She let him sweat for a moment then blurted out in her best mousy-but-bold voice, "We finish our singing at eight." She bit her lip as if she had revealed her deepest secret and Gary took the bait.

"Well then, Sister, I'd best let you eat. Why don't I get your mother and let her have my seat and maybe, just maybe, we shall see each other after your performance?" Stell allowed a pensive smile to escape as Gary turned to go. Malbette joined her a moment later.

"For heaven's sake," she said, "did he just bow to you?"

44

Gary Hunter III was nowhere to be found during their singing performance. He found the revivals easier to endure with a large mug of Mountain Dew and vodka. Sipping his cocktail through a straw, he leaned against the back wall of the picnic shelter, waiting until the unbearable singing was over. There was the usual applause, the shouts of his father, Preacher Gary Hunter Junior, and general commotion as yet another choir took the platform. He waited until he saw the dark-clad group filing out of the tent, seeking fresh air and cold drinks. In the failing light he had trouble picking out his little songbird, but knew he didn't need to worry. He had seen the look in her eye. She would find him.

And there she was. While the other girls gathered together to giggle, he saw one skinny one looking around the crowd. That was his girl. Her mother hovered nearby. Ditching her would have to be the girl's problem. He'd been caught once with his pants around his ankles by an angry father and vowed, as the bruises healed, never to be so careless again.

Staying on the edge of the grassy field, he walked slowly, keeping his eye on his little target. He knew the moment she spotted him, for she ducked quickly behind her mother. This time, however, it wasn't to hide modestly, but to signal to him without her mother's knowledge. She waved, her eyes wide, and he pointed to the picnic shelter. She nodded and waved him away, just as her mother turned back to her. Gary laughed as the girl smiled innocently, certain of the lies that slipped out of her mouth as easily as he planned to slip into hers. Making his way back to the picnic shelter, Gary Hunter said the only prayer he ever prayed.

"Thank you, Lord, for dumb country girls."

It was nine thirty before he heard footsteps coming around the corner. He was half-drunk from his latest cocktail and had nearly given up on getting any action tonight. Seeing her smiling at him, he wondered for a moment if he had had too much to drink to perform adequately, but then reassured himself that a little chicken like this one would never know the difference.

"Good evening, Brother." Her voice was breathless.

"And good evening to you too, Sister." Gary struggled to his feet.

The girl looked around nervously. "I'm sorry I took so long to get here. I didn't think my mother would ever settle down with her scriptures. I was afraid you wouldn't wait for me."

Gary stepped close to her and slid the cotton kerchief off her hair. "Now why on earth would I not wait for such a pretty girl as you?"

She ducked her head and he knew she was blushing. "I . . . I am only plain. I'm not really allowed to be alone with boys. If anyone should come back here . . ."

He took her hand and led her along the path to the barn. "Then let's take a walk, Sister. I grew up in these fields. Why don't we find a quiet place to look at the stars?"

. . . .

Gary settled them down on some soft grass that Stell noticed was well out of earshot from the revival. She could smell the vodka on his breath and see the glassiness in his eyes. Malbette had never told her how to handle a drunk common, but she wasn't worried. It was clear from the bulge in Gary's trousers, he was planning on making the first move. Filling her mind with thoughts of desire, she parted her lips and let her thought-breath drift toward his grinning mouth.

Lulled by vodka, Gary dispensed with the niceties. He lunged toward Stell, his lips clumsily bruising hers as his tongue forced its way into her mouth. She wanted to laugh at the juvenile gesture but instead pretended shock.

"Wait!" She cried, letting visions of helplessness mix with desire, wordlessly urging Gary on to his ill-laid plan. "What are you doing?"

He pushed her down onto the grass, his hand pushing up the heavy, woolen skirt. When he realized the stockings she wore only went as high as her thighs and that everything from there up was bare, he forgot the little decorum he had held and climbed on top of her. Stell made as if to fight him off, her own strength more than enough to flip him, yet enjoying his false sense of superiority. She was going to enjoy bleeding him.

"Relax," he growled in her ear, fumbling to open his pants.

"Please wait!" She allowed a whimper to escape. "I don't understand."

He buried his face in her shoulder, the vodka keeping him from being fully erect. He banged at her, trying to force his way inside of her and beneath him, Stell rolled her eyes, trying to feign fear at this ridiculous situation. Finally he was able to enter her and pumped furiously within her.

"That's right. That's right. Oh, it feels so good, baby. It feels so good."

Maybe it was hunger, maybe it was trip fatigue or maybe Gary Hunter was just that sort of person, but all at once Stell found it impossible to maintain the facade of fearful desire any longer. Ignoring his pitiful thrusting, Stell felt around until she found the small folding knife her mother had slipped into her pocket. Wrapping her thighs around him in a forceful grip, Stell slipped the blade up to his neck. Thinking he had finally awakened her desire, Gary began to urge her on.

"You want it, don't you, baby? I know you do."

"I do. Oh, I do." She slid the knife on the tender part of his neck below the ear and attached herself to the wound.

Still not understanding his situation, Gary Hunter continued to thrust and grunt until weakness overtook his muscles. He tried to pull back from Stell, but found himself locked in her grip. The vodka and blood loss combined with his natural stupidity kept him from understanding the true nature of the encounter until Stell flipped him onto his back, never breaking contact with his jugular vein. He began to panic, screaming, wrestling in vain to free himself.

But the forest ignored his cries as it had ignored all the cries of all the girls he had brought to this very spot.

The blood flowed more powerfully than she had ever known possible. She saw stars and heard symphonies as his heart pounded bravely, struggling to meet the demands of his rapidly depleted body. Stell sucked and swallowed, her body covered in sweat as his heartbeat became a whisper. And still she drank. The moment his body fell still, Stell released her grip, the echo of his death shocking her brain, making her body recoil. In the haze of her blood high, she marveled how quickly a living thing became a dead thing and, rolling onto her back, she stared at the stars, puzzled. Her body floated through the night, her nerves and muscles alive. When she heard her mother speak, she thought she must be dreaming.

"Wake up, Stell. We don't have much time." Malbette stood over her, a satchel in her hand and a faraway look in her eyes.

Chapter Three:

R 'ACUL

....

R 'acul: to kill common by feeding from them, draining
them of blood; can involve violence.

Malbette stood beside her, looking down at the dead body in the
forest. She who had always been so difficult to read was as clear as
a picture window to her blood-high daughter. Her eyes were filled
with sadness and resignation but there was something else, something Stell could smell, almost taste. She had never known it before
but she would have sworn it was a touch of pride. Stell searched
her mother's face for more information but Malbette turned away.

"We don't have time for this now. We have to hide him."

Stell looked at the body at her feet. "He was a pig."

The sting of her mother's hand on her cheek spun her around.
"He was not a pig. He was a human being, a common. I assure you,
they are far more dangerous."

Stell tried to concentrate on her mother's directions as they picked up the body and began carrying it through the woods. Her mother was teaching her as they worked, trying to give her necessary information even as they both knew Stell was in poor shape to learn. The echo of the end of life pounded within her, making the dark forest twinkle with light. The body in her hands was so uninteresting compared with the flares going off in her mind and body.

"Burning is usually a good option for bodies. It hides the cause of death and destroys evidence." Malbette hefted the corpse by its armpits. "But the forest is too dry now. We'll put him in the lake. Put some stones in his pockets. And we'll have to widen the wound."

"Why?"

"To make it look like somebody cut his throat to kill him. Stell, you have to think. You have to concentrate. I won't be with you to tell you what to do."

Stell dropped Gary's feet. "Where will you be?"

"Pick him up. We have to keep moving." Stell obeyed, her eyes fastened on her mother. "I'll stay with the Family. You have to go. Don't drop him again!"

"Where am I supposed to go?"

Malbette put her end of the body down. "Take off your clothes. We're getting in the water." They searched the edge of the lake for stones to fill his pockets. Malbette used Stell's knife to lengthen the wound under his ear to reach the other side of his neck.

"It wouldn't fool a thorough autopsy, but hopefully the water will do our work for us. Get him in the lake."

Despite the weight of the stones and the depth of the cold water, Stell felt stronger than she ever had. Beside her, her mother struggled under the burden, so Stell took the body from her and towed it out toward the middle of the lake. The shore was still brilliantly clear to Stell's hyperalert eyes when Malbette told her to stop.

"This is probably as deep as it's going to get. Push the body as far down as you can."

Stell used her legs to push Gary beneath her, plunging them both down into the murky depths of the small lake. In no time, her feet pushed off of the sandy muck below, rushing her back to the surface.

"I bet it isn't even twenty feet here."

Malbette treaded water, looking around for anything that might help them. "He won't stay down long here. But this is all we have. Go back down and step down hard on his stomach and chest. Try to get as much air out of him as possible. Drive his body into the mud." Stell dove back down into the blackness. The cold water on her naked skin felt marvelous and she was hardly aware of what her feet pressed into as she pushed off the bottom and broke the surface with a joyful breath.

"Do it again." Her mother's voice was cold.

Again and again Stell dove and rose, dove and rose, loving the feeling of strength that pulsed through her muscles, the explosion of the sky as she broke the surface over and over. By the fourth dive, she had forgotten why she was diving, lost in the physical sensation of it.

"That's enough, Stell. Let's head back to shore."

She floated on her back, watching the stars peeking through the trees all around them. It was beautiful here. It was almost as beautiful as Calstow Mountain. On shore, Malbette rummaged through the satchel she had brought with her.

"Teherestelle, I need you to listen to me." Stell tried, but the night air on her wet body was so distracting. Her mother grabbed her by the shoulders. "Stell, you have to listen to me. I know this is a lot. This is my fault that it's happening so quickly but it is happening and you have to pay attention."

Stell nodded, trying to focus on her mother's face.

"Put this on." It was the cotton dress from her luncheon at Tomas's grandparents. "I'll leave the shoes in the bag. I know you hate them but you have to wear shoes in town. There's money in here too. It isn't much but it was all I could grab from the till. You're going to head south from here. The highway is less than five miles. Do you remember the road we came in on, Stell?" The quiet urgency in her mother's voice began to pierce the high she was on. She nodded again, trying to absorb everything her mother said.

"Take that highway west. You'll sense the sun rising before you see it. Turn your back on it and walk as quickly as you can. Do not catch a ride with anyone. Stay out of sight until you get to town. There is a bus station next to the post office. I saw it when we came in. Stay out of sight until the ticket window opens. Buy a ticket to Iowa City. Can you remember that, Stell? Iowa City." Stell felt tears burning her eyes and saw those same tears in her mother's.

"There is a bank in Iowa City. It used to be called First Fidelity Trust on South Clinton Street. Ask for directions. They should still be there."

"Where are you going to be?" Stell could only whisper.

"There isn't time. If you can't find the bank, look for signs. Look for the blue signs. Look for Nahan. I don't think there's any Family there but be careful. Don't tell anybody where you're from or who you are. Just ask them for help. They'll help you, Stell."

"Malbette . . ."

Her mother hugged her tightly. "Maybe you can find Tomas. There are sunglasses. You'll need them. And a bag of candy. Orange slices. Your favorite, remember? I brought them back from town when you were only five and you ate the whole bag and you cried because your stomach hurt." They clung to each other, rocking each other for comfort until Malbette pulled away and grabbed her face.

"Listen to me, Stell. Don't let Rom's words into your mind. Don't believe the poison he's poured over you. You are not evil. You are Nahan and you are fierce. This feeling you have right now, this giddiness, it will pass. Maybe badly. And when the blood high fades, you may feel a flood of emotion—guilt, shame, pain. You may see his face over and over but don't dwell on it. That will pass too. It will. Don't let it in, Stell. We all kill at least once in our lives and we survive. You will survive it.

Malbette smoothed her daughter's hair, her tears glistening in the starlight. "Never come back. You are so fierce. You are Nahan." She kissed Stell, pressed the bag of clothes into her hands, and ran off back toward the campsite. Stell watched until she couldn't see her mother anymore then slipped the dress over her head. Picking up the small bag, she ran away from her mother as fast as she could.

. . . .

She didn't have enough money to get all the way to Iowa City. The woman behind the ticket window told her she had enough to get just to the edge of the Illinois border about thirty-five miles east of her target. The route was a rural one and the trip would take a whole day to complete. Stell handed over her money, getting a few small bills in change and paced the depot to wait.

She was surrounded by common. She had remembered to put on shoes and in the motley crowd that made up the bus goers, she didn't seem to stand out. She was thankful for the sunglasses. When the sun had come up, Stell winced at the brightness of the dawn off the windows around her. The fluorescent lights of the depot flickered and made her flinch. The smell of frying meat from a café across the street made her stomach lurch.

Near the restrooms, Stell spied a row of pay phones. She had seen those at the rest stops on the pilgrimage. Malbette had shown her how they worked. She put her bag at her feet and read the print on the front of the phone. Taking a deep breath, Stell picked up the receiver and punched in a number.

"Directory Assistance. City and state, please."

"Calstow Bend, New York."

"What listing?"

"Desara, Charles and Tatiana."

"Hold for the number."

. . . .

Tomas fell out of a dream, his heart pounding. He had dreamed of doors, of whispering doors. It meant something. He knew it. He felt it. He opened his eyes and knew—

"Shit, Louis!" Aricelli grumbled as Louis flopped into the bed, elbowing Tomas in the stomach. Sheets billowed and flopped, pinning him to the bed between them.

"You kids sleep okay?"

Tomas felt his face get hot when Louis grinned down at him. Aricelli fluffed the pillow behind her, sitting up in the bed. Even rumpled with last night's makeup smeared under her eyes, she looked spectacular.

"We slept fine. Give me a cigarette." She reached over Tomas to take the pack from Louis, who also propped himself up against the headboard. With both of them pulling at the sheet, Tomas nearly disappeared. They talked over him as if he were a pillow. "I must say, Louis, I had no idea your daffy little cousin would turn into such a delightful playmate."

"Why are you surprised? I've been grooming him for years."

Tomas felt his face get even hotter. He really wanted to change the subject. Plus his dream wouldn't leave him. "Hey, you guys—"

"Did Kitty make it back last night?" Aricelli asked.

"Nah," Louis grabbed the lighter. "She left with that guy in the ugly shirt. You know the one. He said he was a record producer. He kept telling her she could be huge. Then he made the mistake of telling her she looked good enough to eat. I suspect she is answering in kind."

Aricelli flicked an ash off the covers, ignoring that it fell into Tomas's hair. "Let's hope she doesn't wind up on YouTube doing it."

Tomas tried and failed again to get their attention as they launched into a gripe session over the perils of digital surveillance.

"It was so much easier for the other generations," Louis said. "Grandma Tat used to tell me stories about being at court in Paris. If things got dicey, you just had to slip out and get into the country. No photographs, no IDs. She said all you needed was gold and guts."

Aricelli laughed. "And hope nobody screamed 'Vampire!' and tried to cut your head off."

"Well there was that."

"You guys," Tomas tried again. The meaning of the dream pressed on him.

"Daddy told me to really watch it here in Las Vegas," Aricelli said. "There are cameras everywhere. You're photographed a million times a day."

"It's getting like that everywhere." Louis dropped his cigarette into an empty beer bottle. "They say London is one of the worst. Every move you make is recorded. The good part about that is maybe it'll be easier to see my parents. They're flipping."

"Really?" She laughed. "You get to move to England? Are you going to fake an accent or play the ugly American?"

"I'm not going to need an accent because I'm not going." His voice took on a tone of false brightness. "It looks like I'm the first kid on my block to be *osviat*. How cool is that?"

That got Tomas's attention. *Osviat* was the Nahan term that meant both *to disappear* and *liberated*. It signified the inevitable split between generations of Nahan when, due to the slower aging process, parents had to change their common identity separately from their children.

Aricelli reached over Tomas and grabbed Louis's hand. "But you're still so young!"

"I know, but it's my dad's job. He's going to London to be part of their immigration security crackdown. It's a major flip. Working for the government, he's going to be thoroughly vetted. I guess it's been in the works for a long time, creating this identity for him and Mom. And because there's so much technology involved, the Council decided he had to be kind of young, like thirty-two or something, and even the Council can't justify a thirty-two-year-old man with a twenty-five-year-old son. So . . ."—he smoothed the sheets—"I will very soon be completely independent."

Tomas didn't know what to say, even if they had been listening to him. This would happen to each of them but like most major changes in life, each thought they would have more time to be ready.

"When are they going?"

"As we speak." Tomas heard the tamped-down emotion in his voice. "Dad thought it would be easier to do while I'm out, you know, in case there's any surveillance at home."

"My god, what are they joining? Al-Qaeda?"

"Hey, look at the bright side." He lit another cigarette. "At least I don't have to hurry home. And speaking of hurrying home, you guys aren't in any hurry to get back, are you? I mean you haven't been taken by any great flashes of inspiration to work in a coal mine or anything?"

Tomas started to speak, glad he'd brought up the topic, but Aricelli cut him off. "No, but speaking of great flashes, do you guys remember Tabby Adair?" Tomas remembered the short, intense Nahan girl who had hung briefly at the edge of their social circle. "Mother told me she's been on the road just over a year. She was in Nashville. Had to leave. Let's just say she took a real liking to *r'acul*. Big time."

Louis's eyes widened. "She's already killing? How many?"

"Like five, I think, before her grandfather came down and made her leave. Made her go see the Storytellers."

"Oh god, poor girl. Like it's not enough to go blood crazy, then you have to go see those weirdos. Tabby Adair, who would have thought?" Louis eyed Aricelli. "So I take it you and Kitty haven't done it yet either?"

Aricelli shook her head. "No. We came really close in New York. We were at this club and these girls were all over us. But then we both got spooked."

Tomas burrowed down into the pillow. "I can't imagine what it's going to be like."

"I know," Aricelli said, her voice hushed. "They say it's really intense. I know we're all going to do it but how do you know if you're going to love it? Like Tabby?"

"Or even worse," Louis said, "what if I hate it? What if I'm a total puss and can't stop crying about it? What if I freak out and join the True Family?" He cringed and looked down at Tomas as he realized what had just come out of his mouth.

"Awkward." Aricelli whispered.

Tomas laughed. "No, it's okay. But there was something—"

"See?" Aricelli smiled. "One night in my bed and the True Family is no longer an issue."

Louis grinned. "I never doubted you."

"You guys know I can hear you, right? You know I'm lying right here."

Louis patted Tomas's head. "Right where you belong, buddy."

.G. REDLING

"In bed with your cousin?" Aricelli coughed on her smoke. "That's a little weird."

"You guys—"

"You know what I mean."

"You guys!"

"What?" Louis laughed.

"You're not even listening to me."

Aricelli brushed his hair out of his eyes. "You're not saying anything, darling."

"I'm trying."

"We're all ears, Cousin."

With their undivided attention, Tomas felt the words freeze in his throat but the pressure from the dream wouldn't leave him.

"I think I need to call the Storytellers."

Aricelli's eyes widened and then Louis barked out a laugh.

"Thanks a lot, Tomas!" She folded her arms in mock hurt. "Was I that bad in bed?"

"It's not you." Louis shouted over Tomas's protest. "It's because we're starting to wrap it up out here. We've got to head back home and you know how Tomas's parents are."

"No, it's not—"

"Oh god, Tomas, you don't need the Storytellers." Aricelli winked at him. "Nobody expects you to have a plan yet. Do you really think Louis and I are ready to start a career?" When Tomas tried to interrupt, she reached over him and smacked Louis. "You shouldn't have brought up being *osviat*. Tomas has got years before that."

"No, you guys, I think—"

Louis smiled. "Dude, seriously, relax. We're family. We've got nothing to worry about. My parents head up Security. Aricelli's dad is the number-one money man for the Central Council. Your mom is the queen of real estate for everyone from Chicago to

Denver. We're going to be fine. You don't need to go running to the Storytellers for guidance."

"But I think—"

He coughed when Aricelli blew smoke down into his face. She fanned it away, shaking her head. "Don't call in the Storytellers and don't let Daddy hear you talking about them. I mean, with all due respect to the Storytellers"—she and Louis shared an eye roll—"they're not exactly reality based."

"Feel better, Cuz? Tomas?" Louis ruffled his hair again. "Are you okay?"

Tomas opened his eyes and sighed. "I want to call the Storytellers because I think . . . I just . . . I think I might be one."

. . . .

The bus stop at North Fork, Illinois, was part depot, part convenience store, part farmers' market. Clutching her satchel, Stell centered herself mentally, silencing her pounding heart and racing mind. The high of killing Gary Hunter had long worn off. She wasn't feeling any of the terrible emotions her mother had warned her of. She just felt tired and hungry. She had never been so far from home and, except for the solitude of Calstow Mountain, had never been truly alone.

She had called Tatiana to tell Tomas where she would be but Tatiana seemed to think Tomas wouldn't come. The older woman had told her it would be better for everyone involved if Stell found shelter with local Nahan and maybe tried to contact Tomas at a later time. In her addled state, Stell couldn't seem to explain to her that she wasn't looking for Nahan. Her dreams of the outside world didn't include socializing with Nahan farmers that she didn't know.

Tomas was the only person who knew her, who cared about her. All she had managed to do was elicit a promise that Tatiana would tell Tomas where she would be. That was all it would take, Stell was certain. Until he arrived, she would simply make the best of it.

That had been almost two days ago. The bus had broken down just over the Illinois border and they had waited hours by the side of the road for a replacement bus. She only had a handful of dollar bills left and used them sparingly to buy the sugary sodas that kept her head from pounding. By North Fork, she had exactly two dollars and seventy-eight cents to her name and, after a quick glance into the convenience mart, knew she couldn't afford to stay there long. Instead, she settled on one of the orange molded chairs bolted to the floor of the bus-depot end of the building and tried to relax.

Around her, commons came and went, yelling and laughing, eating foods that tantalized her like popcorn and candy bars, as well as foods that nauseated her, like hamburgers and corn dogs.

She distracted herself watching a group of people setting up long tables and a grill. Some people hung signs, others laid out paper plates and napkins. Two young men were in charge of loading the grill and getting the charcoals lit, which involved a great deal of lighter fluid, eyebrow scorching, and laughter. So engrossed was she in the varying levels of flame that she didn't notice the two Nahan women until they were within twenty feet of her. Stell quickly closed her eyes, leveled off her breathing, and focused on being still.

Tomas was coming for her. In the chaos that had become her life since she had taken the life of one simple common, she had one certainty to hold on to and that was Tomas. He was different. He had looked at her, really seen her. It didn't matter that he hadn't told his friends about her. He said he loved her. He had to mean it. Once he knew where she was, he would come for her. He had to.

Stell had watched the Nahan women ask at the ticket window, probably about arrival times and departures. It didn't matter; they hadn't seen her. When they had left, Stell let her head fall backward, breathing deeply and relaxing her neck. She felt a quick jolt of fear as she noticed a woman staring at her. Had she missed one? But no, the woman was common. She smiled at Stell and went back to her business.

· ·

Erma Reynolds had been the youth group leader of Crossroads Methodist Church of North Fork for more than fifteen years. In that time she had worked with bad kids from good families, good kids from bad families, and every combination in between. Just this year she had counseled kids through two unwanted pregnancies, a quickly developing drinking problem, and several episodes of declining faith. Sometimes she succeeded; sometimes she failed but she never gave up. Erma believed the Holy Spirit had given her a gift for helping troubled kids and it was not a gift she was going to waste.

When she saw the young woman in the homemade dress sitting by herself at the end of the bus depot, Erma knew this was a girl with a story. There was no one there to meet her. She had no luggage and for nearly two hours she had not moved from her chair. That she had arrived in North Fork the same day the youth group was there to sell hot dogs for their mission trip to Belize could have been seen as a coincidence, but Erma Reynolds did not believe in coincidences. If nobody came for the girl in the next hour, Erma planned on stepping in.

People started lining up for hotdogs around eleven thirty and by twelve thirty the serving crew had their act together sufficiently for her to leave them to it. Casually, and with years of experience with runaways, Erma strolled toward the young woman sitting so still. There was a book open on her lap, but Erma could tell she was sleeping. As soon as Erma got within five feet, however, the girl bolted upright, staring up with eyes that were a shocking shade of pale blue.

"Sorry!" Erma laughed, raising her hands in mock surrender. She knew how important it was to keep the encounter casual. "Didn't mean to sneak up on you!" The girl clutched the book to her chest and she could make out the title on the yellowed dust jacket. "*Wuthering Heights*, huh? Isn't that the one with Heathcliff and Cathy on the moors? Very romantic." The girl didn't move or speak, only held her gaze with those chilling eyes. It was not the first time Erma had been stonewalled by a teenager and she was not intimidated. Instead she smiled and gestured toward the busy group outside.

"I noticed you've been sitting here a while. My name is Erma Reynolds. That's my youth group out there. We're having a fundraiser today, selling hotdogs and the like. I know how hungry you get traveling and I just wanted to make sure you knew that if you get hungry or would just like a little company, you're welcome to join us. We'll be washing cars soon. I know that doesn't sound like much fun but when you watch some of these kids try to handle a garden hose, believe me, you'll laugh." The girl glanced out to the parking lot where, indeed, hoses were beginning to create quite a mess. Erma took this small interest as a good sign. "So, that said, I'll leave you to your book. Again, I'm Erma and I'd love to have you over there."

With a jaunty wave, Erma turned and headed back outside. It never worked to press too hard. Either the girl would follow or she wouldn't. If she hadn't moved in another hour, however, she would try again.

. . . .

Stell watched the woman walk away and heard the crowd laughing and calling to her as she stepped outside. This woman seemed different than the types she had encountered in tents the past weeks. For one thing, she didn't call herself Sister anything. There were no awkward hugs or blurted out praises to her Lord. It wasn't enough to make Stell trust her, but it did make her curious about the common around her. It was strange out here. She wished Tomas would hurry.

Forty-five minutes later Stell's stomach demanded action. Knowing a cold drink in the convenience mart would finish off her funds, she screwed up her courage and headed toward the smoky, soaked, and laughing crowd that was the Crossroads Methodist Youth Group Fundraiser. She studied the price list on the table.

"Not a big menu, but it'll get you full!"

Stell looked up into Erma's smiling face. "May I buy a Coke and a bag of potato chips?" This would leave her with just over a dollar.

"Don't you want a hotdog? They're good. We've got all the fixings."

Stell averted her eyes from the blackening meat and tried not to inhale the smell. She shook her head and held out two crumpled dollar bills. Erma filled a large paper cup with cold soda and grabbed a bag of chips.

"Traveler's discount, honey. This one's on me." Stell shook her head, suspecting a trick. "I'll tell you what," Erma bargained, "I'll treat you to lunch if you sit with me on my break. I've been on my feet all morning. One condition, though, and I'm serious. I don't want to hear a word about Belize!"

Uncertain who or what Belize was, Stell accepted the offer. Grabbing her chips and drink, she followed Erma to a bench beneath the awning of the building several yards away from the madness.

"I tend to do all the talking, honey. What's your name?"

"Stell." The word popped out before she could stop it.

"Oh that's a pretty name. So much better than Erma. Erma. Who names their kid Erma?" Stell had no idea what the proper answer to that was and so busied herself opening her barbecue potato chips.

"Where are you from? You're not from around here. I know everyone around here."

"New York." Her mother had told her not to tell anyone where she was from, but this was a common. Plus she was so lonely, it felt nice to be with someone, anyone.

. . . .

Erma stirred her ice with her straw. It was all she could do to not reach out and hug the child beside her but she knew she was gaining ground by keeping it casual. "What brings you out here?" The girl tensed up. "Don't mind me. I'm as nosy as the day is long. Can't help myself. It's just that you've been waiting a while and, well, I don't want to seem like a mother hen, although heaven knows I am one, I'm just wondering if anyone is coming to pick you up."

"Oh, yes." Stell said. "Tomas is coming for me."

"Tomas? Is that your boyfriend?"

"Yes. He knows I'm here. He's on his way."

Erma nodded, smiling on the outside, hiding her doubt. How many girls had she seen waiting for boyfriends that never appeared? She wondered if Stell was pregnant.

"When's he's supposed to get here?"

"I'm not sure. I'm not sure where he's coming from but his grandmother told him when I would get here so I'm sure he's on his way."

"We're pretty far from everything out here, you know. It's easy to get lost on these farm roads. If something should happen that he doesn't show up—"

"He's going to show!" Stell's voice was louder than she intended but Erma just smiled.

"Well, honey, you know him better than I do. But if something should happen that delays him, maybe car trouble or something, you come find me. I've got plenty of room at the house and I just love company. We can leave word with Billy at the ticket window to call me if anyone shows looking for you."

Erma caught the momentary look of panic on Stell's face. This girl was clearly in trouble and almost definitely a runaway. She reached out and touched the young woman's hand. "You're going to be okay. You're among friends now."

"He's on his way."

"Good. I can't wait to meet him. Maybe we can all be friends." She rose to her aching feet. "You get hungry, you come on over and see me, okay, Stell?"

Stell nodded, trying to build up a strong enough anger at Erma's meddling to eclipse the fear that was chipping away at her resolve.

. . . .

They had gone through two cases of hotdogs and three cartons of paper cups by the time they decided to call it a day. Bagging up the garbage and wrapping up leftovers, the youth group members laughed and called to each other, congratulating themselves on a job well done. The sun was just beginning to sink behind the depot when Erma decided she would not take no for an answer. Stell had headed back to her orange chair after their conversation and Erma would swear she hadn't moved a muscle in the next five hours. *You didn't have to be psychic,* she thought, *to know there was no boyfriend coming, and she for one was not leaving a teenage girl alone in a bus depot overnight.* Bracing herself for the inevitable argument, Erma wiped her hands on a wet rag and headed into the depot.

"Erma! Are we still washing cars?" Teddy Lass called out to her as a red pick-up truck braked sharply at the curb in the midst of the crowd. Erma turned, fully prepared to give the driver a piece of her mind for driving so recklessly but didn't get a chance. The driver, a slim boy with longish hair, jumped from the cab, the engine running, and ran into the depot leaving another young man within the truck smoking a cigarette. The boy stopped inside the doorway, scanned the room, and began to run. What happened next brought tears to Erma Reynold's eyes and a rare curse word to her lips.

"Well I'll be damned."

Inside the depot, the young woman in the flowered dress exploded in a smile of such joy and light you could see it from the parking lot and threw herself into the arms of the young man running toward her. He lifted her off her feet and swung her around, burying his face in her neck. She clung to him and began kissing his hair, his shoulders, and his forehead. Finally he set her down and, wrapped around each other, they headed for the door. As she climbed into the passenger door of the red truck, Stell leaned out.

"Thank you, Erma. You've been very kind."

Erma could only shake her head as the boy with the cigarette slid behind the wheel. Stell and her boyfriend began to kiss as the driver flicked his cigarette into the bucket of wash water on the curb.

"I guess I'm driving."

. . . .

Tatiana and Charles had not told their son or daughter-in-law about the girlfriend Tomas had taken during his stay on Calstow Mountain. Tatiana figured it was better to avoid a fight over something that might simply fade away but when she saw the letters piling up from Tomas and then received the frantic bus-stop call from Stell, she realized she might have underestimated the relationship. She called around, knowing someone would be tracking the kids on their *avalentu* and found Tomas in Las Vegas. Then she bit the bullet and filled Richard and Beth in as best she could.

· ·

After receiving his grandmother's phone call, Tomas had struggled for all of twelve minutes before announcing he was heading east to pick up Stell. Louis tried to put his foot down, explaining to his cousin the folly of his plan but for once Tomas would not cave. Aricelli handed over the bulk of her remaining cash and Tomas saw the loaded look she and Louis shared.

Louis refused to allow Tomas to drive across the country by himself, partly to help with the driving, mostly to try to talk him out of the choice he was making.

"One minute you're talking about trying to, what, break in? Convert? I don't even know what you've got to do to be a Storyteller. And the next you're driving all the way across the country—and wrecking our *avalentu*, by the way—for a girl you've known for, like, two weeks. I get it. She was your first. We all think our first is some big deal but—"

Tomas gripped the wheel. "Don't talk about her like that. You don't know Stell."

"Neither do you."

"It was different with Stell. I was different with Stell."

Louis snorted. "Apparently. One summer with her and you're ready to be a Storyteller. And what happens when that doesn't work out? Going to apply to be an astronaut? At least that you can train for."

"Louis." Tomas hated the way his voice broke. "Please." He heard Louis sigh and knew his cousin was helpless against an upset Tomas.

· ·

There had been a flurry of activity upon their arrival at Tomas's house. Hugs and kisses and exclamations of worry flew around the room, easily dodging Stell, who hung back. Since Louis's parents were already gone, the fuss was shared equally between the two of them.

Tomas waited until dinner to drop his bombshell, telling his parents his desire to become a Storyteller.

Richard met Beth's eyes for a moment before speaking. "You know that's a tough path you've chosen." Tomas nodded and gripped Stell's hand under the table.

"When did you decide this?" Beth glared at Stell. "Or did someone decide this for you?"

"No, Mom. It's my idea."

"It seems to me to be an odd time to come up with such an enormous decision. You and Louis have only been out for a few weeks and you've already chosen your life path?"

Stell continued to eat, keeping her head down.

"And what do you think, Stell?" Beth asked. "Did you have some part in this?"

"I think Tomas tells beautiful stories," Stell said. "Why is the decision so difficult?"

"Well, there's more to being a Storyteller than just telling good stories."

Stell looked at Richard. "Oh, I didn't know that. What does a Storyteller do? We didn't have them on the mountain."

"They're not exactly on every street corner." Beth shot Stell a look that both Tomas and Louis knew well. It was a look that in the past had usually ended with both boys being grounded. Tomas was surprised when Louis spoke up.

"Maybe he can do it," Louis said. "While I'm loath to lump my cousin in with people like the Storytellers, we just spent a lifetime traveling through every wide spot in the road in America. He's really got a gift."

"And what do you know about Storytellers, Louis?" Beth snapped.

"I'm going to do it." Tomas said. "It's my decision."

"Well, it certainly doesn't seem as if you need my advice then, does it? Six weeks out and you know all you need to know. By all means, maybe your father and I should just move out and let you play house here with your new playmate and your personal adviser—"

Tomas began to talk over his mother, both of their voices rising until Richard banged his hand down on the table to silence them.

"That's enough! Both of you." His tone softened to a peace-making level. "Now, Beth, the entire purpose of their trip was to find out what they want to do with their lives."

"I think a reality check is in order here—"

"Please don't interrupt me." He turned to Tomas. "Son, you have to understand what you are proposing. You're not talking about becoming a banker or a police officer. Do you even know what's involved in becoming a Storyteller? What the lifestyle is like? It's not the glamorous calling you think it is."

"I don't think it's glamorous, Dad. I can't even . . . I just . . . I think I have to do it."

Beth could not hold her tongue. "You could do a lot of things, Thomas. But you have to think first; you have to make good decisions."

"Beth."

"It's true, Richard, and you know it. What about school? If you had applied yourself more in school you would have had the grades to get into any college you chose but instead you and Louis had to party and play and fool around. And now neither of you will be able to get into college on your own. Do you think Aricelli is going to need her transcripts doctored? No, she managed to get the grades—"

"Mom! We're not talking about Aricelli. Or college. This has nothing to do with—"

"It has everything to do with college! It's called having options, Thomas."

"And stop calling me Thomas! My name is Tomas!"

Beth threw her napkin onto the table. "That ridiculous affectation of your grandmother's."

"It's my name! You gave it to me!"

"I never should have let your father talk me into agreeing on it. Tomas. What's wrong with Thomas? Thomas Wilkinson. It's a fine name."

"Wilkinson? That's my common name. Common, Mom! You do remember that these really aren't our names, right? Or has it come to this? Have you actually become Beth Wilkinson? Going to become a Methodist and have barbecues on Sunday?"

Beth leaned over the table. "You watch your tone with me, young man. You may think you have the world all figured out but I assure you, there are plenty of surprises ahead for you."

"Yeah, well here's a surprise for you. I'm calling the Council tomorrow and finding out what I need to do to apply." He rose and held out his hand for Stell. "And then I'm leaving."

. . . .

There is a word, *saht,* in Nahan that literally means *flood.* Colloquially it is used to describe the feeling that permeates the air when young lovers are around. The passion, the self-absorbed hunger and overflowing pleasure are said to spread like a smell throughout the house, thereby flooding the other occupants with desire of their own. Under normal circumstances, the lovemaking of Stell and Tomas would have flooded the house with pleasure, leading Beth and Richard to a few passionate evenings of their own. Instead, the pleasure they were creating was like grit between Beth's teeth and smelled like the smoke of spent bullets.

In bed that night, Richard lay beside his wife feeling the frustration pulsing off of her. He had heard the sounds of pleasure coming from his son's room and knew the effect it would have on Beth. She let out a deep sigh.

"He thinks I hate him."

"He doesn't think that, Beth. He's just angry."

"He's angry? What does he have to be angry about? He has never lived up to his potential. Another dream world, another comic book, and now he wants to be a Storyteller. A Storyteller! We have built our lives to position him to have any job in the Council he wants and he picks the one position nobody can give him. Nobody wants to be a Storyteller. Why would they?" She kicked her feet out from beneath the covers. "And what the hell is he doing with that creepy piece of ass he picked up in the mountains? And why didn't your parents tell us about her, Richard?"

"Mom said she didn't think it would amount to anything."

"Her grandson is running around with the True Family and she doesn't think that's important? Honest to god, I don't know how that woman raised you."

Richard put his arm behind his head and let out a sigh. "Maybe Dad will have some luck with him. I always listened to my grandfather."

"You always listened to your parents too for all the good that did you."

Richard didn't argue with her. He knew it was pointless until her anger cleared.

She was wrong about him listening to his parents. Sometimes when he looked at Tomas, he wondered how it was possible that this strange boy could be his son. Then he would remember his own turbulent relationship with his father and how so often the only voice of reason he could find was from his grandfather. He could see the pattern repeated with Tomas. While Tomas and Richard rarely actually butted heads, a conscious choice on Richard's part to avoid creating the same battleground he and his own father had shared, he could see the natural bond between Tomas and Charles. They seemed to understand each other, to be natural with each other in a way neither father-and-son pair could manage. Grandpa used to say that your grandchild was your reward for not killing your own child.

Richard hoped Tomas had a child of his own soon.

....

Charles and Tatiana arrived early the next morning. Tomas and Stell were still in bed, giving Richard and Beth the chance to speak openly about the situation.

"He thinks he might be a Storyteller."

Tatiana raised her eyebrows in surprise but said nothing.

"He says he's going to call the Council today and ask what's involved. Then he says he's going to leave."

"Where is he planning to go?"

Beth poured her father-in-law more coffee. "We thought he might have told you. You both seem to be far more knowledgeable of our son's life than we are."

Tatiana refused to rise to the challenge, long accustomed to Beth's biting tongue. "He has said nothing to us. How is the girl?"

"Strange." Richard looked into his coffee as he spoke. "Hard. Not the sort of girl I ever would have pictured Tomas with."

"Especially if he has even a chance with Aricelli Capp."

"Aricelli is a lovely girl," Tatiana said, "but perhaps she is a bit too lovely for Tomas?" At the questioning glances, she continued. "Aricelli is perfect in every way. She is lovely, she is gracious, and she is very polished. She would be a feather in any young man's cap but maybe our Tomas does not want a feather in his cap or a cap at all. I don't think I am saying anything new when I say that our Tomas, while a lovely young man himself, is a touch . . . odd."

"Odd? Our son is not odd."

Tatiana gave a conciliatory nod. "Maybe odd is the wrong word. He is unique. I think he may be full of surprises, our Tomas. Perhaps he is Storyteller material. They are an unusual lot."

"I thought my ears were burning." All heads turned to see Tomas and Stell in the doorway. He smiled and moved across the room into the outstretched arms of his grandmother. Stell followed close behind.

Tatiana held Stell out at arm's length. "Look at you in your city clothes!"

"Do you like them?" Stell tugged on the hem of the formfitting t-shirt, pulling it down against the faded jeans. "Tomas bought them. He said my dress was . . . it didn't . . ." She let the words die off, hiding behind Tomas as he stepped in front of her to pour coffee. But Tatiana caught her shy smile when Tomas whispered in her ear.

"So I understand you are planning on calling the Council today."

"I already have, Grandpa." Across the room Beth faltered for a moment then continued to butter her toast. "I talked to Mentor Davenheim about how to apply. He said someone would call me back so I could set up a meeting with a Storyteller."

"You actually meet with one?" Charles sounded impressed.

"Davenheim said that was the only way to apply. He said there were all kinds of requirements to go through with the first meeting."

"Such as?"

"Such as he has to meet my family first. And my closest friends. Otherwise he won't meet with me." His eyes drifted up to his mother.

"That shouldn't be a problem," Beth said without looking up. Instead she took crisp swipes at crumbs on the table. "You do live here. Your grandparents are here, one set at least. Louis is welcome to stay until the meeting and, of course, your . . . Stell, you are welcome to stay as long as you like."

Stell nodded and the whole room seemed to exhale as one. Forty-five minutes later, after Louis had joined them for breakfast, the phone rang. Tomas raced to pick it up and went into the next room to talk. When he returned, his cheeks glowed with spots of high color.

"I've got the appointment. Thirty-three days from today."

"Thirty-three days?" Richard asked. "Why so long?"

"The Storyteller who does the interviews is in San Francisco right now and that's the soonest he'll be out this way. His name is Albion."

Louis reached into the fruit bowl for an apple. "So what are you going to do for thirty-three days?"

Chapter Four:

OSVIAT

....

Osviat: literally, *to disappear;* also *liberated;* figuratively, the
point at which, due to slowed aging, parents and children
must assume identities separate from each other; also used
to describe the general separation of generations by lifestyle

"I'm hungry."

"There's a Denny's down the street."

"That's not what I'm hungry for."

Tomas rolled over and looked at Stell, sprawled naked on top
of the sheets beside him. He ran his hand along the tender skin of
her inner thigh. "Then let's get you something to eat."

They had spent two days holed up in a roadside motel just
over the Virginia border, unable to keep their hands off of each
other. It had been obvious to all involved that they couldn't stay
with Tomas's parents and so they had decided to take a road trip
of their own. Free at last to be together, they shut out the world.
Only blood could break the spell. They left the room littered with

damp sheets, soda cans, and candy bar wrappers and headed back onto the road.

Wilson's Kool Stop had the same jukebox selection Tomas had heard in every bar across the country. Bon Jovi, Alan Jackson, and The Allman Brothers were never more than two songs away. He and Louis had entered countless bars like this as rednecks, foreigners, and drunken college students looking for a fight. Entering a dive bar in Virginia with a woman changed the dynamic. He caught the admiring looks Stell received as she sidled up to the bar and Stell let the bartender lean in closer than necessary to take her order.

Tomas slid his hand against the small of her back. "Better rein that in a little before we have a gangbang on our hands."

Stell leaned in to Tomas, looking out over the small crowd, and whispered in his ear. "I don't know what a gangbang is, but I think I'll like it. When do we start?"

"Drink your beer, hot stuff. Let's just see how the night goes."

It was the first bar Stell had ever been in. Still early in the evening, the men were sober enough to be friendly, the women's clothes and makeup were still fresh. Fascinated by the activity around her, Stell peppered Tomas with questions. How did they get their hair so fluffy? Should she also wear that kind of short skirt and the boots with the pointy toes? Would Tomas rather she wore the tiny t-shirt that showed her belly? Would he teach her to dance?

Tomas laughed and answered her questions as best he could. He told her he would buy her a belly shirt at the next opportunity and begged her not to wear makeup. He watched her profile as she watched the bar. The faint throbbing of her pulse below her jawline beckoned to him. Unable to resist, he placed his lips on her throat, feeling her heartbeat.

Her pulse quickened at his touch. "When do we eat?"

"Anyone here strike your fancy?" Tomas had several choices picked out.

"Who's the man at the end of the bar?"

Tomas didn't need to look to see who she meant. "People avoid him. Good choice."

Stell bit her lip. "He's really big."

Tomas leaned close and bit her lip as well. "Big enough for two?" He whispered his plan into her ear.

"Do you understand?" She nodded. Tomas rose, sliding his hands out from beneath her shirt, where he'd been rubbing her back. "Then I'm going to go play some pool. All that sugar you've been holding in? This would be a good time to let a little out." He winked at her then turned to join the men playing pool across the room.

Stell let her body sway to the southern rock pulsing from the speakers. Nerves gave way to anticipation. She and Tomas were together now; this was her life, her future. She let the smells and sounds wash over her, move through her.

The room had gotten considerably drunker as the night wore on and several women were dancing together suggestively. Stell watched them, studying their hip swings and hair tosses as she made her way down the bar. When she reached the man sitting alone, she leaned against the bar.

He turned to look at her, his dark eyes cool. His nose was large and slightly hooked, caramel colored skin smooth over high cheekbones. Stell admired the planes of his face.

"Are you an Indian?"

"You figure that out by yourself, sugar britches?"

"I've never met an Indian before."

"You still haven't." He turned back to his beer and Stell giggled. She took a deep drink from her beer and leaned in closer.

"Do you want to dance?"

"That depends."

"On what?"

He looked over his shoulder at the pool game across the room. "On how big a piece your pretty boyfriend over there is carrying." Stell laughed out loud, her breath sweet on his face.

. . . .

At six foot five, John Running Deer knew he was big enough to handle most drunken bar fighters. At forty-two years of age, he had seen more than his share of drunken bar whores getting horny as the night grew old. Plus he was not especially attracted to white women, their pasty skin reminding him of something cold and dead. Still, there was something about this particular white girl that kept him from leaving.

Her eyes were the palest blue he had ever seen, almost diamond-like in the darkened bar and her skin was so white and unmarked as to seem flawless. But it was the way she moved that held his attention. She didn't dance, didn't sway drunkenly. She seemed to undulate within herself, moving ever closer to him. Hell, he figured, maybe he was just horny, but John Running Deer decided to let this little girl give it her best shot.

She placed her hand on his shoulder, running her fingers along the seam of his denim shirt. "My boyfriend's not carrying a gun."

"I've heard that before."

She giggled again and the sound sent a bolt of electricity down his spine.

"I don't think he'd mind if we danced."

"Dance with your boyfriend."

"I want to dance with you."

Running Deer glanced past her and saw Tomas staring directly at them.

"I don't think your boyfriend would like that."

"You'd be surprised what my boyfriend likes." She put her lips to his ear, her tongue flicking his earlobe. "He likes to watch."

John Running Deer waged a brief internal war then quickly resolved the issue. Grabbing her ass roughly with one hand, he pulled her to him as he rose to his feet. She pressed the length of her body against him, her head at his chest.

"Then let's get out of here and give him something to see."

. . . .

They slammed into the side of the pick-up truck, her legs wrapped around his waist, her hands pulling his shirt free of his jeans. He had one arm underneath her holding her up as the other arm was braced to keep them upright.

"Right here. This is our truck."

"Where are we going?"

Stell reached over and flipped open the tailgate. He tossed her into the truck bed and watched as she slid out of her jeans. "You are one crazy bitch." He grinned as he unbuttoned his jeans and climbed in beside her.

. . . .

Even knowing what was coming, knowing it was only a common, it was still difficult to watch another man's hands clutching Stell's body. The light of the distant streetlamps was enough for him to see the muscles in the large man's back working as he moved on top of Stell. Tomas stepped closer to the truck and rested his arms on the side of the bed. Stell sank her teeth into her lover's shoulder and stared directly into Tomas's eyes. The look he saw there dispelled every trace of jealousy and he felt his body stir. Sensing a presence, the large man threw his head up and saw Tomas.

"Shit." His voice was hoarse but level. He held himself still above Stell and stared at Tomas. "We have a problem?"

Tomas shook his head. "I just like to watch."

He had to see the way Tomas's eyes moved over his body. Beneath him, Stell smiled, arching her back, her hips moving against him. He held Tomas's gaze for a moment then resumed his rhythmic dance inside the girl. He spoke aloud to no one. "This is fucking weird."

Tomas chuckled. "It's going to get a lot weirder."

. . . .

They shared a wound on his right arm. As Tomas drank, Stell moved to the other side of the truck bed and ran her hands over the sleeping man's body.

"He's very smooth. Are all Indians this smooth?"

Tomas lifted his mouth from the wound. "Gee, Stell, I don't know. This is the first time I've shared an Indian in a parking lot."

She ignored his sarcasm. "I don't like it when they're really hairy. Sometimes they feel like bears. I like smooth skin like this."

Tomas closed the wound and looked up at Stell. "Then maybe next time we'll get a woman. I think I'd like that better. A lot better."

She ran her fingers down the brown skin of his stomach, over his pelvis and traced the part of him that was now soft. "He's really big." At Tomas's cry of protest, Stell laughed and leaned across to kiss him on the mouth. "Don't worry. I still like yours better."

Tomas bit her lower lip. "I should say so."

She leaned back against the side of the truck, grinning. "But he was really big."

Tomas threw her jeans at her, laughing. "Next time we're definitely sharing a woman."

. . . .

They slept all the next day and as the sun went down, followed the highway a few towns down and stopped at another bar on a small side road.

"It's just like that place last night," Stell marveled.

"They're all like that place last night."

As promised, Stell let Tomas pick out their target, and as promised, he picked out a shapely young woman named Caroline in a tight t-shirt that read "I <3 <TS set as icon?> VMI boys." Stell bristled but played along when Tomas introduced her to Caroline as his sister. After luring the girl back to their motel room, however, she balked at Tomas's preferred feeding location.

"I am not putting my mouth there." Caroline's legs were spread wide and Tomas was preparing to make a small cut in her upper thigh.

Tomas laughed. "This is what you get for picking that big Indian last night."

"I didn't make you touch his thing!"

"No, you just waved it around saying how big it was!"

Stell shoved Tomas playfully and he wrestled her down next to the unconscious Caroline. "I'm not doing it," she said.

He kissed her deeply, his tongue teasing hers. When he pulled back she could smell the desire on his breath. "Do it for me." She rolled her eyes as beside them Caroline stirred slightly.

"Just this one time. And I'm giving her a bruise."

Tomas grinned and settled back to watch the show.

. . . .

By the time they crossed the North Carolina border they had come to an agreement. They would feed on couples or not at all. Tomas taught Stell to drive the truck as they made their way through the rolling mountains. She thrived on his company. She learned the songs on the radio and laughed at all of his jokes. The air was getting cold in the mountains and the trees were exploding with color. One night they slept under blankets in the back of the truck, deep in the forest. Stell's skin was as hot as a charcoal as she curled up beside him.

"In all my life, I never thought I could feel like this. I never thought I would be off Calstow Mountain."

Stell hadn't told him about the circumstances that led to her fleeing the congregation. Although she didn't doubt his feelings for her, she wasn't ready to risk his reaction to her killing urge. She leaned up on one elbow and looked down into his face.

"Why were your parents so upset? What does a Storyteller do?"

He caught a piece of her hair in his hand and twined it around his finger. "Didn't you have any Nahan contact up on Calstow Mountain?" Stell shook her head. "No Council? No heritage classes? I can't imagine what that would be like."

"It was like living with a bag over your head." She bent down to kiss Tomas. "Don't change the subject. What does a Storyteller do?"

"I'm not exactly sure."

"Then how do you know you want to be one?"

"It's just a feeling, you know? And once I let it into my head, it wouldn't let me go. The Storytellers are the ones who see the big picture. They're the ones who oversee where the Nahan are in the world. They oversee identity flips. Not the little stuff, not like us going from Parkers to Wilkinsons, but big moves. Big situations."

"Charles made it sound as if Storytellers are strange, different from everyone else."

Tomas nodded. "That's what they say. They say that they hold the whole Nahan world inside of them, that they know all the stories that'll ever be told." He watched the leaves move in the night breeze. "Everyone's scared of the Storytellers because they're supposed to be so weird but I've always felt weird. Sometimes it's like what I see isn't the same as what everyone else does. When people talk, I hear them speak but it's like I hear something underneath their voice, some echo or something and I can tell things about them that they haven't told me. And the longer I'm out, the more I feed, the stronger the feeling gets." He looked into her eyes. "Do you think I'm nuts?"

She shook her head. "So tell me, Storyteller, what do you see when you look at me?"

Tomas laughed. "Here's where it gets really crazy and probably blows a hole right in my ambition. From the first minute I met you, I never heard a thing from you. When I look at you, it's like all the world goes dark and you stand out clear and bright. I can't come up with a single story for you. I hope this doesn't mean you are my undoing."

. . . .

They spent a week in Greensboro then circled around to Asheville. Stell loved North Carolina. She loved the green mountains that were transforming into red, orange, and yellow jewels. The air was cold and, although it made her miss Calstow Mountain, it also made her feel at home. Tomas shared with her his insight into the people around her, his ability to divine hidden secrets growing every time they fed.

Feeding was easy in the small college town; there were plenty of people coming and going. They moved from hotels to motels to bed-and-breakfasts, never staying more than a night or two, always paying cash. Sometimes they drove out to the edge of town and slept under the stars, in the truck.

Stell felt strong and alive. There were moments, however, when she felt a tug deep down in her gut, a hunger she tried to ignore. She knew she couldn't do so indefinitely any more than she could hide it from Tomas much longer. Night after night, as they fed and laughed and made love, she could feel this dark part of her rising ever closer to the surface.

. . . .

"You're thinking about going back to Deerfield, aren't you?" Tomas watched Stell as she dried off after a shower. She had been quieter than usual all day. "It won't always be that tense. After I meet with the Storyteller, I'll have some idea about what plans we can make but I promise we won't stay at my parents' house."

Stell nodded as she tossed the towel onto the bed. She slipped into a pair of jeans and rummaged around in her bag for a shirt. She wanted to talk to Tomas about what she was feeling, what she was hungering for, but couldn't find the words. So much of what she had learned of the Nahan culture she had learned from him. Everything she had learned about the common she had learned from him. If the hunger within her was something she alone felt, if it was maybe some sort of aberration from her years in the True Family, she wanted to wait as long as possible to reveal it to Tomas. She pulled the t-shirt over her head and saw him watching her.

"Promise me something, Tomas."

"Anything."

"Promise me you'll never send me away."

Tomas laughed. "Send you away? I'd die first."

"Promise me anyway."

"I promise." He kissed her.

. . . .

For their last night on the road, Stell wanted to go to a highway bar, somewhere away from the small town's center. Tomas obliged and within a half an hour they pulled up to Shirley's Chatterbox Bar and Grill. Tomas hesitated at the word *grill* but a few sniffs in the air assured them both that Shirley's grilling days were long behind her. The bar was mostly for bikers and the sort of people who were not particularly stimulated by the college bar scene.

Tomas took a quick mental sweep of the room but was distracted by Stell, who clung to his side more tightly than usual. He nearly tripped over her feet as she walked in step beside him, her breath in his ear confessing her hunger and edginess.

"What's the matter, Stell? Is something in here frightening you?"

She shook her head against his neck and allowed herself to be settled at the bar. Tomas made small talk with the bartender, watching the scene behind him in the mirror. Occasionally he would whisper some ideas for the night in Stell's ear, rubbing her leg reassuringly. Shortly after they arrived, a young couple came in and settled down beside them.

"I didn't think I'd ever get out of the freaking car." The man stretched his arms over his head, swaying his back. Already over six feet, the move made him seem enormous.

"Pull your shirt down, Virgil. These people don't want to see your hairy belly poking out at them." The woman smiled past Virgil at Stell. She was in her mid-twenties with blond hair that fell down her back in tattered dreadlocks. "Don't mind us. We're from Ontario; been driving forever. We've been in the car for eight hours today, which is like four days when you're Virgil's size and you're in a Honda. You gonna make it, old man?" Virgil groaned and excused himself to the bathroom. The woman ordered two beers and held out her hand.

"I'm Stacy. That's Virgil."

Tomas smiled when he felt Stell squeeze his leg, signaling her approval.

"I'm Dylan. This is my girlfriend, Abby."

Virgil and Stacy did most of the talking and most of the drinking while Tomas let his thought-breath wash over them. Beside him, Stell fidgeted and sighed, letting him know her hunger. Within an hour, Tomas noticed Stacy found reasons to brush against him and Virgil openly eyed Stell's small breasts under the t-shirt fabric.

Tomas whispered in Stacy's ear, "I think we're ready to go."

He told Stacy and Virgil to pull out onto the highway and they would follow a few moments later. After the couple left the bar, he wrapped his arms around Stell and kissed her.

"You ready?" She pulled him even closer. Her hunger and desire burned through her clothes. He bent his head and bit down hard on her neck. She let loose a low growl, her fingers digging hard enough into his waist to draw blood. "Let's go party."

. . . .

They were waiting by the side of the highway. Tomas flashed the truck's headlights at them as he drove by and they pulled out behind them on the dark country road.

"We'll take them out where we parked the other night when we slept outside."

Stell looked over her shoulder at the car following them. "We don't have a campfire or anything. No tent. Won't they notice that?"

Tomas slid his hand between Stell's thighs. "Do you really think they're going to notice? Stacy's just aching to show me her tattoos and Virgil doesn't seem that hard to sway."

Stell bit into his shoulder, shifting herself against his caressing hand. "Why do they want anyone else? They said they had lived together for three years. Why are they sleeping with other people? Doesn't that bother them?"

"Well, we're sort of helping them along in that decision." He breathed softly in her face and her own hunger became nearly unbearable. "Besides, you love me and we both know what you're going to do tonight."

"It's totally different and you know it." Stell plunged her hands between his legs, climbing partially onto his lap, her mouth at his throat. The truck veered off the road as he tried to concentrate.

"Save it for Virgil. We're here."

He climbed out of the truck, Stell's crotch grabbing making his walk awkward. Stacy and Virgil unfolded themselves from the small Honda, Stacy holding her hands up triumphantly. "First bowl's on us!" She held up a pipe and a small baggie.

"Excellent." Tomas took the pipe from her and handed it to Virgil. "Let's get busy." As predicted, neither noticed the lack of a campsite and settled on the blankets Stell pulled from the truck bed. Tomas wasted no time getting Stacy onto her back, his hands and mouth moving over her welcoming body. If Virgil noticed his girlfriend's infidelity, it didn't bother him. Instead he thudded to the ground beside Stell and began to pack the bowl of the pipe.

"Judging from the look in your eyes, young lady, I'd say you've had enough." He took a deep hit from the pipe and held the smoke in. With a cough and a laugh he passed the pipe to Stell. "But then who the hell am I to say what's enough?"

Stell refused the offer and rose onto her knees before Virgil. He was large, his sandy hair and beard making him seem older than he was, and she could feel the raw strength of his body. He watched her watch him, then glanced at the passionate encounter on the neighboring blanket.

"Well now, I guess we're swinging tonight. Come here, Blue Eyes." His touch was gentle and his kiss was soft on her lips. Stell let his hands roam under her t-shirt and didn't resist as he pulled it over her head. His large hands cupped her small breasts and he admired her in the faint starlight.

"Don't they have sunshine in New Mexico?" His hands slid down her waist. "You're like a china doll. Like a hot, stoned china doll." Stell continued to stare down at him. "Don't talk much, do ya. That's okay. What's this?" His fingers reached into the front pocket of her jeans.

"A knife, huh? You gonna kill me in my sleep? Why, this blade's got to be . . . two inches long." He laughed and tossed the pocketknife over his shoulder. "I guess you're going to have to take me by force."

He kissed her stomach, his windblown hair and scraggly beard tickling her skin. His mouth was at the fly of her jeans when she grabbed him roughly by the hair, pressing him into her. She ground her hips against him, her head lolling back on her shoulders as he began to work at her clothes in earnest. As he pulled at her jeans, she pushed him onto his back, kicking the pants away. Just beyond Virgil's shoulder, she could see her pocketknife in the grass, beyond her reach. Beside her she could feel Tomas whipping Stacy up into a frenzy. Beneath her, Virgil smiled, watching her look around.

"Are you okay, Abby?" She tried to focus on his face. "Because we can wait if you want. It's no big deal." If she had been able to focus, she would have seen the gentle smile on Virgil Demillo's face, the same smile that had made Stacy Varnier fall in love with him three short years earlier. Unfortunately, all she could see was the pulse beating under his jaw. All she could smell was the blood within him and all she could think of was her hunger.

She ran her hands over his eyes, but her heart was beating too hard to relax him. He closed his eyes and sighed as she began to kiss the side of his neck. He ran his hands over her bare back, encouraging her to settle in on top of him and, at the first bite, he pinched her playfully.

"Hey watch it! That hurts." He was attempting to adjust her body to give him more leverage when the second and final bite came. Stell attached herself to his neck. He pulled at her hair, swearing, but she wouldn't be moved. He jerked, stiffening, and took a panicked breath to cry out when Stell's hand clamped down over his mouth. She was impossibly strong and even though he had six inches and a hundred pounds on her he was unable to dislodge her or get Stacy's attention.

The blood exploded from his carotid artery and it splashed on Stell's face, soaking the ground beneath her. The wound was jagged, a tear, and her mouth struggled to cover it. She drank and drank, the blood alive with Virgil's adrenaline and Stell could feel an ecstasy overwhelming her. He was like a child in her hands, his enormous body helpless beneath her hunger and despite his youth and strength all too soon the life spark went out of Virgil Demillo. A choking gasp escaped her lips as pleasure rocked her body and the shock of death tossed her from the corpse beneath her.

Not six feet away, Tomas had just put Stacy down and was opening his knife when Stell rolled beside him, smeared in blood and ecstasy.

"Holy shit, Stell! Holy shit!" He climbed off Stacy and grabbed Stell by the shoulders. "What have you done?" She sat up, oblivious to the gore on her face, the blood high setting fire to the night around her. She reached for Tomas but he grabbed her hands roughly.

"Did he try to hurt you? Did he grab the knife? Where's your knife?"

Stell swung her arm to the left. "He threw it away." She leaned in close, the blood on her chin black in the night. "I don't need a knife."

Tomas collapsed back on his heels and Stell swayed under the stars.

She giggled. "Uh-oh. Somebody's awake."

Stacy pulled herself up onto an elbow and rubbed her eyes. Her voice was thick with sleep. "Dylan? What are you doing?" She noticed Stell kneeling naked beside her. "Abby? Are you okay? What's on your face? Where's Virgil?" When she noticed what was left of Virgil, her breath came in short harsh gasps and her eyes flew from the blood-soaked blanket to the two naked strangers kneeling beside her. Understanding only her own fear, she began to crawl backward, pulling the blanket to her as she went. Tomas watched her, frozen on the spot, as Stell continued to sway and giggle.

"You'd better get her."

Those same words pounded through Tomas's mind as he saw Stacy putting space between herself and the killing field. A thousand options whipped through his mind but all ended the same way. Faster than she could follow, he sprang upon her, getting her neck in an iron elbow lock. She tried to scream, her breath partially blocked, and she punched and kicked to free herself to no avail. Tomas held her in place as easily as he would hold a pile of laundry, her cries for help unheard as his mind raced for a solution. He locked eyes with Stell.

"I'm sorry, Tomas. I wanted to tell you. This is who I am." She nodded to the struggling girl beneath his arm. "I'll do it if you want."

Tomas held Stacy down and stared at Stell. *This is who I am.* He could see the words floating around her. Blood dripped from her chin onto her slender white body, the body he had longed for, the body he would throw his whole life away for. He shook his head.

"There's a shovel in the back of the truck. Dig a hole. A deep one."

Stell rose on unsteady feet and walked to the truck. As she passed, she ran her fingers over his face. He caught her index finger between his teeth and held her for a moment. She smiled down at him, her eyes black in the night, and pulled her finger free.

Tomas looked down at the girl's tear-soaked face and expected to feel a jolt of pity, a weakening of his resolve. Instead he felt only a distance, a curiosity that he should ever have found this creature attractive. He felt no anger, no vengeance, simply purpose and hunger as he slid his fingers over her eyes. She wouldn't be calmed and Tomas was glad. He could smell her fear and it excited him. He lowered her to the ground where she lay with no fight.

"Why?"

He pushed the braids away from her neck, exposing her skin. He considered his knife but, glancing at the body across the way, decided against it. He breathed in the scent of her skin and fear and sweat as she asked once more.

"Why?"

"For Nahan." He bit down hard.

The night exploded. On his back, the stars burst into flame, lighting up the night sky, and the rustle of the leaves amplified into the sound of thunderous applause. He could hear Stell digging several yards away, could feel the earth scream each time her shovel pierced its skin and Tomas could see the diamonds of light that burst from her skin with her exertions. He whispered her name and the sound flew into the night like a rocket.

She came and stood over him naked, dirt and gore streaking her pale skin. The riot of stars behind her made her seem to Tomas a fierce goddess of legend.

"You can't lie there all night."

"Yes I can." His fingers traced circles in the blood-soaked mud around him. "Who's gonna stop me?"

Stell straddled him and lowered her face to his, her hair falling like a curtain around them. Tomas opened his mouth, breathing in the smell of her as she leaned in until they were nose to nose and he could see his reflection in the black pools of her eyes.

"Your pupils are huge."

Stell laughed and ran her tongue along his bloodstained mouth. "Look who's talking. And look who's not helping. Get up and help me do something with these bodies."

She pulled him into a sitting position, where he surveyed the area.

"Fuck 'em. Let's get out of here."

Stell laughed again, wrapping herself around his neck. He had voiced her thoughts exactly but she knew they had to do otherwise. "Think, Tomas. You had a plan."

He didn't let her extricate herself from his arms as he tried to make sense of what she said. He could remember no plan, no big picture. His body had plans of its own and from what he could tell, they were wonderful. Stell shook him, pushing herself onto her feet, and pulling him up with her. He sighed and examined the scene.

"My mother told me burning works well."

Tomas shook his head, focus returning, the plan falling into place.

"That should work."

"What should work?"

"My plan, Stell. Weren't you listening?"

"You never said anything."

"I did. I just told you"—Tomas closed his eyes, trying to remember what he had said. His thoughts were coming so quickly it was like he was backtracking and spinning in circles trying to start from the top. He couldn't remember if he had actually spoken but still his mind clicked ahead with plans for their getaway. Stell broke his reverie with a kiss.

"You don't have to tell me the whole plan. Just tell me what to do."

He took the shovel from her and told her to get both bodies on one blanket. "Don't drag them. We'll lift them and carry them here."

The hole dug as deeply as they could manage, they each grabbed a corner of the blanket and lifted the two Canadians. Even with their increased strength from the kill, the burden was cumbersome. Stell giggled and nearly dropped her end when Tomas huffed. "Shit, Stell. You've got to start picking smaller guys." They finally dropped the bodies into the hole. Tomas stared down at them.

"Let's make sure they don't have cell phones on them. Or those key fobs. We don't need some twenty-first-century "Tell-Tale Heart" scene." Stell didn't understand the reference but jumped into the hole. From Virgil's blood-soaked jeans, she pulled a phone and tossed it to Tomas. There was nothing else in either of their pockets, so she climbed back to the surface, kicking the blankets over the dead as she came out.

"I'll fill in the hole. You go back over there and build a small campfire where the majority of the blood is."

"Why didn't we just burn them?"

He shook his head. "It would have to be too big a fire to really burn them up. We'll just burn the ground to hide the blood. Try to kick the worst of it into the fire." He threw a shovelful of dirt into the hole then stopped. "Hang on a minute. You might as well burn the other blanket and our clothes. There's blood on them too. There's lighter fluid in the truck."

Stell watched him gather up the clothes, smiling at his naked skin glowing in the exaggerated starlight. "You sure have a lot of things in your truck."

"Grandpa Charles loaded it up. I guess maybe he knew what was coming." He tossed his sticky clothes to Stell and resumed his chore.

The dawn was still hours away when they finished cleaning the scene. The campfire had burned down, the charred ends of logs and blackened ash disguising the stains in the soil. Tomas scattered the dirt left over from the impromptu grave and pulled vines and branches over the bare earth. Stell collected the shovel and lighter fluid, put them back into the truck's toolbox and joined Tomas as he overviewed the finished product.

"This will have to do. As long as nobody has a reason to look for them here."

"What about their car?"

"That's next. But first we've got to get cleaned up. We look like grave robbers."

"Do you have a shower in your truck too?"

Tomas saw her laughing look and grabbed her around the waist. "Maybe I just do, funny girl." He bit softly into her neck. Her sweat tasted like salty wine and, mingled with the coppery taste of blood and the earthy smells of dirt and smoke, the effect was heroin. He couldn't let her go and together they tumbled onto the freshly dug grave of Virgil Demillo and Stacy Varnier.

Dawn was closer when they finally pulled apart.

"Seriously, Stell, we have got to get moving."

She groaned as she rose to her feet. A bottle of water and a washcloth got the worst of the gore and dirt from their faces and hands and Tomas assured her a fresh change of clothes would hide the rest until they had a chance for a proper shower. Grabbing an extra t-shirt from his bag, Tomas used it to keep his fingerprints off the inside of the Canadians' car as he searched it.

"The keys are in the ignition. Her purse is in the back and his wallet's in the glove compartment. Just one more thing to check." He popped the trunk and looked inside. "This is good. It looks like all their bags are here so they probably didn't check into any motel yet. I think we've gotten lucky. Can you drive the truck?" Stell nodded uncertainly. "Just follow me down the highway. Don't speed. If I get pulled over, keep going and I'll catch up with you. If you get pulled over . . . well, don't get pulled over." Covering the keys and steering wheel with the t-shirt, Tomas started the Honda and pulled slowly from their campsite, Stell following close behind.

They drove south for over an hour. The sun was streaking the sky with pink when Tomas pulled the small car onto an almost invisible rutted road. He left the Honda running as he climbed out and waited for her. Stell wasn't certain the big truck would make it, especially with her driving, and pulled off onto the shoulder.

"Drive up the highway at least ten miles, then find a turn-around and come back for me," Tomas said and Stell nodded, her hands sore from gripping the wheel so tightly. He winked at her. "You're doing great. I can't wait to get you into a motel."

When she returned from her brief trip down the highway, Tomas was standing by the side of the road waiting. He climbed into the driver's side, much to her relief.

"I made it look like they had camped there. You know, a blanket on the ground; they had some empty beer bottles in a garbage bag in the back. We're far enough away that even if they do find the car, there's no reason they would look back at our campsite. And speaking of which, I want to stop by there when we go past it."

"Why, Tomas? Isn't that dangerous?"

He put his arm around her and pulled her close. "I want to get some dirt. That was definitely sacred ground."

. . . .

Sunglasses were an imperative by the time they made it back to the campsite. Tomas scooped two handfuls of dirt into an empty Doritos bag, promising Stell they would find some beautiful boxes crafted by North Carolina artists to store it in. Stell laughed and stuck her nose inside the bag for a sniff. If it had been up to her, the nacho cheese–scented bag would have been sufficient, but Tomas wouldn't hear of it.

He told her of the various small boxes that were displayed throughout his house, most of them from sites important to his parents and a few antique boxes of his ancestor's with sacred soil. Her favorite description was that of the highly varnished pine box that bore the words *Calstow Mountain, NY,* that Tomas had picked up at a souvenir shop. Inside, it held a handful of dirt and moss he had grabbed from their spot near the blackberry bushes beside the creek. She clutched the smelly chip bag to her chest and rested her head on Tomas's shoulder.

They drove north for another hour and a half, taking winding roads, enjoying their shared blood high. Tomas felt he could drive forever, that he could do anything forever, but around him he was increasingly aware of the common and his curiosity demanded to know what it would feel like to be among them in his altered state. They pulled into a truck stop diner on Route 23. Tomas took Stell's hand as they crossed the parking lot.

"Do I look okay? My clothes, I mean?"

Stell laughed. "You're asking me?"

"I mean, can you see any blood?" He pulled her close and kissed her.

"No, but I smell it." Her hand slid under his shirt along his still-sticky skin. "And I know where I can find some."

"Behave!" He pulled open the door of the diner and pushed her in front of him. When the door closed behind him, he staggered against the glass, unprepared for what awaited him.

"Tomas? Are you all right?"

His mouth hung open, his breath shallow and harsh. They were attracting attention and Stell pulled him into a booth. Tomas spun his gaze around the room. He couldn't speak, could only stare, until he finally had to close his eyes and cover his face with his hands.

"What is it? What are you seeing?"

He shook his head as an older, heavyset waitress whose nametag read Dee approached their table. "Everything okay here?" Tomas let his eyes move up to her face and let out a small sigh. He nodded and looked back down. "You gotta order."

"Pancakes," Stell said, squeezing Tomas's hand. "And Coke. Cokes."

Dee shot them a withering look and turned to the kitchen to put in the order.

"Please tell me what's happening, Tomas."

Alone with her on the highway, he could feel the presence of the common all around him, hear them like the whir of crickets at night. But here, within the greasy confines of the crowded diner, his mind staggered under what lay before him.

"You know how I told you I can sense connections between people, what they want, what they think?" His speech was slurred. "I can just sense it. I didn't know how. But now, now there are these . . ." He gestured widely with his hands over the crowd around them, "these . . . tubes?"

It wasn't the right word but his mind couldn't grasp the vocabulary to describe the columns of solid-looking smoke that snaked out of each common around him, some thick and dark like the shells of armadillos, some wispy and transparent like cigarette smoke. They whipped and undulated, appearing and disappearing as their sources ate and spoke and rose to use the restroom. Dee dropped off their drinks and tears filled Tomas's eyes.

"She hates us." He whispered to her retreating back. "Drugs. She thinks we're on drugs and she hates that. Her brother—her little brother—is doing time, that's what she calls it, 'hard time' for drugs. He killed someone." The words tumbled out. "She hates our drugs. She would save us. If we asked her she would give us anything to get us off the street. Why won't we save ourselves? No one can do it for us she wants to tell us but she won't because we're just another set of junkies coming in, hippies, useless. Oh, Stell." He put his head down on his hands. "We've got to get out of here."

Stell dragged Tomas onto his feet and out the door. Outside the bacon-stench of the truck stop, he began to breathe more easily, his mind clearing. He looked through the windows at the curious stares of the people within. The smoke snakes had disappeared. There was nothing connecting the common within except their curiosity about the dark-haired hippies in the parking lot. They climbed into the truck and headed back onto the highway.

. . . .

They were over the Kentucky border before Tomas would speak. Twice Stell offered to drive and twice he shook his head. He needed something to focus on, somewhere to direct his concentration to anchor himself while he sorted through his mind.

How could he describe to her what had happened? It was as if his mind had touched a live wire in the universe and the power of the jolt had thrown him deep within himself. He could feel the blood coursing through his body, could feel his muscles and nerves rejoicing and rejuvenating even while his mind scrambled for equilibrium.

"Did you hate it, Tomas?"

"Hate what?"

"*R 'acul.*"

"No. I didn't hate it. That wasn't your first, was it?" She shook her head, and he reached over to stroke her cheek. "Why didn't you tell me?"

"I was afraid you would think I was . . ."

"You were what?"

"I was dangerous."

Tomas pulled her close to him. "My beautiful Stell," he spoke in a whisper. "You are very dangerous. You are *oascaru.*" The word meant *deadly* and among the Nahan it was high praise indeed. Stell pushed her face into his neck, breathing him in as he stroked her hair.

"Did you feel this too, Stell? Is this what they talk about after killing, this sick pain? These visions?" He felt her stiffen in his arms. She kept her face turned away.

"I didn't feel anything like that," she whispered. "I didn't feel anything bad."

"Figures it would tear me up." He sighed and kissed her hair. "Another Tomas Desara success story. I can't even feel bad things right. And now I've got to get back for my interview with the Storyteller. What if I've screwed this up?"

By the time they reached Deerfield, their blood high was wearing off and the sun was setting. The Desara house was lit up when they pulled into the driveway. Beth opened the front door and stood with her hands on her hips.

"Could you have cut that a little closer, Tomas? He's going to be here tomorrow afternoon."

Tomas set his bag down. "I know, Mom. That's why we hurried."

"No, hurrying would have been to get home yesterday so you had time to eat and rest and gather your thoughts. Instead, you're flying by the seat of your pants, as usual."

"Mom—"

"You're the one who said how important this is to you—"

"Mom!"

"But it's obviously not important enough for you to actually plan for—"

"*Mom*!" Tomas grabbed his mother's shoulders. "I'm home! I made it!"

Beth clenched her lips, looking at her son through a puddle of tears.

"Why are you crying?"

She smoothed his hair and tried to keep her voice steady. "You may find this hard to believe, young man, but your happiness is important to me. I'm your mother. I worry about you. If being a Storyteller makes you happy, I want that for you. And if this so-called expert coming in tomorrow can't see what a wonderful man you are . . ." Her voice broke and she pulled Tomas close to her. They rocked each other for a moment before Beth pulled away, her brusque self recovered.

"And of course you make this no easier for me. Showing up at the last minute. You have no idea what we've been going through."

Tomas turned from her to embrace his father. "Has she been like this the whole time?"

"The whole time."

"Fine! Fine! Make fun of me!" Beth threw up her hands and marched to the kitchen. "When you get disqualified for not following the directions, don't come crying to me."

"What directions?"

Richard pulled a letter from the bookcase. "This arrived earlier this week from Mr. Albion. It's a set of very specific instructions for your interview. If this is any indication of what it's like being a Storyteller, I can't imagine what you're in for."

Tomas read over the directions. "Kind of particular, aren't they?"

"It doesn't sound like any of it is negotiable either." Richard read the letter over his shoulder. "Your mom and I fed earlier today. You're grandparents are out now. Louis and Aricelli said they'd be ready too."

Tomas let out a worried breath, glad for his father's calm help. "What do you think he's going to ask? Why does he need everybody here? Why all these superspecific instructions?"

Richard shook his head. "I have no idea. I've never worked directly with a Storyteller before but I've seen them around the Council complex. They're an odd lot but, then again, they've got a big job. Without them, we never would have made it among the common. Do you understand what you're getting into, Son? This is more than a job. If you get accepted, if you become a Storyteller, you're responsible for the survival of our people."

"Thanks, Dad. I didn't think it was possible for me to get any more nervous."

Richard laughed and pulled Tomas into a hug. "My pleasure, Son. How about a beer?"

. . . .

"It should be on the next block, Mr. Albion."

"Thank you." He centered himself as the car pulled up to the curb of a modest ranch house. His driver held the door as he took three deep breaths before stepping out.

As instructed, the front door had been left ajar. That was one small victory. He always forwarded very specific instructions.

They weren't arbitrary. His job was difficult enough without having to slog through family chaos and local traditions. The family was seated as he had requested and no one raised their eyes as he entered. Most of his colleagues made the same requests of interviewees, particularly the request for no unsolicited eye contact. Each Storyteller had his or her strengths but as a group they found eye contact to be especially exhausting.

He stood for a moment in the living room, taking in the surroundings. It was a nice house, comfortable and welcoming. There were family photographs in frames and he could spy at least two boxes of sacred soil. That was a good sign. Everyone seated wore shades of blue, showing their respect for tradition.

He stood before the parents and touched them on their cheeks, their sign to meet his gaze. They looked up together. The father was calm, the mother slightly defiant. Albion could feel a protective energy around her, which was to be expected from a parent, but he could feel nothing unbalanced. These were all good signs but not enough to make him optimistic.

He nodded to them and stepped to the couch to the elder couple seated there. He studied their bowed heads until he could discern their identity. They were the paternal grandparents. He could feel their son in them. Touching them on the cheeks, he looked into their eyes. His fingers lingered on the grandfather's face and learned of the bond between grandfather and grandson. This was not a picture-perfect family. There was no real dysfunction, simply the usual generational friction.

Albion bowed slightly to the elder couple and crossed the room to the three young Nahan sitting uncomfortably in wooden dining-room chairs. He made a point as he moved to not see the young man in the doorway at the end of the room. The first one he came to hid her face behind a wave of lustrous black hair. He touched her head and as she turned her face to him he couldn't help but smile.

She was a beauty and, despite her early years, she was already adept at using it to her advantage. Albion liked working with beauty. Not for any lascivious reasons of his own, but because beauty was the easiest tool to wield and brought the sweetest results with the least effort. He enjoyed her face for a moment and could feel her understanding of his enjoyment. There was a potential for hardness within this one and, if he had been called to do so, he would have some warnings for her parents. He touched her head again and she looked back to the floor.

The young man beside her raised his head at his touch. It was an interesting combination, this young man and the beauty beside him. The young man had an edge, not exactly cynicism but a keen eye for reality. Albion felt the affection and nervousness of the young man before him, could feel how badly he wanted to help his cousin. A touch on the head and the Storyteller stepped before the last young woman.

There was suspicion in her eyes as she looked into his face and that set him off his pace for a moment. Who was she to look at him with insolence? He gathered his thoughts and breathed deeply. Then he saw it. She was True Family. Or had been. For the second time in the visit he felt a smile play on his lips. One thing this candidate had in abundance was fierce women. Did it mean he would qualify? Probably not, but at least it gave Albion a break from the endless grind of the interviewing process. He put his hand on the girl's head and nearly laughed as he was forced to actually press to get her to lower her eyes. What a family.

Albion stepped into the center of the circle to collect his thoughts one last time before approaching the boy. Part of him wanted to hurry it up, part of him wanted to delay. Despite all the disappointments, despite the fact that it had been nearly four years since a new Storyteller had been admitted to the training, each failed interview was a bitter disappointment. He, like all Storytellers, was hesitant to face another failure.

Albion stood before the boy but he didn't see him. He closed his eyes, preparing to ask the same question he had asked eighteen times so far on this journey, that he and his colleagues had asked hundreds of times over the centuries. He wondered which of the variations on the theme he would hear:

"What do you mean?"

"Could you be more specific?"

"I'm not sure."

Different words that meant the same thing—he had wasted yet another day of his life. He put his fingers under the chin of the young man before him and, when he felt his face rise, looked him in the eye and asked his question.

"What does it look like?"

. . . .

It took a heartbeat for the words to register to Tomas. They banged around his head before he understood the question. When he went to speak, however, his voice failed him.

Tomas burst into tears.

His eyes didn't well up, his voice didn't break with emotion. Rather, his body convulsed with ugly, wracking sobs that bent him in two. The question tore through him like a knife thrown with force. Around him the room dissolved into chaos, Stell leaping to his side and pushing the Storyteller away. Beth and Richard fought to comfort him and beyond the raw sounds that issued from his throat he could hear his mother screaming at Stell, blaming her. He wanted to stop, to correct her, to assure everyone he was all right, but the sobs tore at his abdomen, bending him double as if he had been punched.

When he heard the front door close, Tomas felt a small dose of composure return. His throat was raw and his eyes burned as he fought to be heard in the din.

"Stop! I'm all right." The room quieted as he raised his tear-stained face. "I don't know what happened. I just, oh god. He's gone, isn't he? I blew it, didn't I?"

Nobody spoke. He could see their concern changing to embarrassment.

Tomas rose to his feet. "This is nobody's fault but mine. I don't . . . this is . . . I'm sorry I wasted everybody's time." He wiped his fists across his face, noticing for the first time a wadded up note in his hand. "What is this?" He unfolded the crumpled sheet and fell back into the chair.

"It's the address of a hotel in Chicago. It says 'Conference Room B, 11 a.m.' Am I in?"

. . . .

Conference Room B was bedlam. Long tables packed the center of the room, set up at right angles in no discernible pattern, creating a maze teeming with Nahan men and women waving their arms, shouting out messages, and flinging papers and files. Tomas stood on the periphery. No one had greeted him. No one had acknowledged him until one sharp-nosed woman in a Chanel suit stood too close to him, glaring up at him over the edge of her reading glasses.

"Who are you?"

"Tomas Desara."

"Who?"

"Desara. Tomas Desara. Mr. Albion sent me."

"Albion?" She said the name like it tasted bad. "You're the candidate for Storyteller? You look like a cabana boy." She held his sleeve in an iron pinch and yelled to a man digging through a cardboard box beneath the nearest table. "Wilson. It's Albion's boy. Our future."

From somewhere to his left, a voice yelled out, "In those shoes? We're doomed!" Laughter scattered through the room and Tomas glanced around helplessly. Whatever he had expected of his training, this pandemonium was not it.

"I got him." The man she called Wilson took his arm and led him deeper into the fray. Nahan both young and old moved and talked and passed files around him as if he were no more than a pitcher of water. "I'm Wilson. You gotta listen, kid. Don't say anything. Don't try to talk to anyone. Just listen."

"To what? It's chaos in here."

"Exactly."

Tomas saw stacks of bank records, computer code printouts, contracts, divorce decrees, even a document that claimed to be an annulment with what looked like official stamps from a Catholic church. He kept his hands behind his back to fight the temptation to rifle through the documents. Doors on both sides of the room opened and closed as messengers came and went. People shouted into cell phones and screamed at laptops. When Wilson took a break from the file folder he had been studying Tomas ventured a question.

"Are these all Storytellers?"

"Are you kidding me?" Wilson asked. "A room full of Storytellers? I'd put a gun in my mouth. No, kid, this is just a quick info confab. We've got three days here for Region Six *I-M-F* to get as much damage done as they can, then we're off." Tomas nodded as if he understood what any of that meant and continued to follow Wilson.

A voice from the doorway shouted, "Who left the spook in the lobby?" Nobody answered so the young woman who had asked the question fought her way deeper into the fray, two laptops filling her arms. She dropped one computer off with a worried-looking man chewing a pencil and searched the room for the recipient of the second laptop. "There's a girl in the lobby with suitcases. We calling in hookers?"

"That's my girlfriend." Tomas spoke and immediately regretted it.

"You brought your girlfriend to a confab?" It was the hook-nosed Chanel woman. "And left her in the lobby?"

Tomas shrugged, uncomfortable with the attention he was getting. "I didn't know what to do. If we would be staying. How long it would be. Mr. Albion didn't say—"

"Albion." The woman snorted again, then snapped her fingers over her head. The sound carried to a young Nahan man waiting by the door who rushed to attention. "Derek, go out to the lobby and check in our lost little girl. They've got a room. Destry or something."

"Desara."

"Whatever. Get her out of the lobby." She dismissed her assistant and spoke to herself in a voice meant for the room. "Doesn't say much for our Storytellers if they can't even check themselves into their own hotel."

"Lay off it, Lana." Wilson pulled Tomas to another table. He was shorter than Tomas, and his hair was thinning on top, giving him a fragile look. "She's like that with everyone. She's good though. That woman could pull money out of a pig's ass." A heavy plastic binder slid down the table past them, caught by a girl not much older than Tomas. The noise was giving him a headache and there seemed no order or purpose to the madness.

Then, as if a blanket had been thrown over the crowd, the sound muffled down. The people in the room grew still, papers were held in place, voices lowered to silence. Laptops were closed quietly, groups congealed and whispered among themselves as they pulled apart, leaving a clear aisle from the front door to a grouping of tables near the back wall. Wilson placed an unnecessary hand on Tomas's arm to silence him. Tomas peered over the heads around him, needing to see what could bring quiet to this room.

It was three Nahan, two men and one woman, who had entered the room as a group and settled themselves at the only clear table. They didn't speak to anyone around them, murmuring only to each other as they lined up at the table facing the wall, their backs to the room. The room held its collective breath as the three adjusted their seats, poured a few glasses of water, and after passing nods among themselves, leaned back as one and placed their folded hands on the table.

Noise returned to the room. People began to whisper, shuffle papers, then resumed business as usual. Tomas noticed people heading to the table of the newcomers and placing papers on their desk. Nobody spoke to the newcomers. Nobody looked directly at them. They simply placed their documents before them and stepped away. Wilson guided him toward their table. As they got closer, Tomas could see most of the documents on the table were photographs, close-ups of faces or tight shots of groups, many with sticky notes bearing the name of a city or company. He was trying to read some of the headings when he realized Wilson had left his side and he stood before the table alone.

He clasped his wrists behind his back, a nervous gesture he'd picked up from Stell.

"Hello." His voice sounded high and childish.

The tall man on the right answered him. "Is that your girlfriend in the lobby?"

"Yes, sir."

"True Family. Interesting choice."

The woman in the middle spoke next. "Why did you bring her?"

"I didn't want to leave her. With my parents, I mean."

"Then why didn't you check her in?"

"I didn't know I had a room."

The man on the left spoke, his voice gravelly despite his youthful face. "You didn't know you had a room? What did you think? This is a day school?"

"What did Albion tell you?" the man on the right said. Tomas could not help but feel he was being interrogated by three sides of the same person. For his own sanity, he labeled them Tall, Woman, and Growler.

"He didn't tell me anything."

"What do you mean, he didn't tell you anything?" Woman said.

Tall said, "He must have told you something. You're here."

Tomas shook his head, feeling his cheeks burning. "He handed me a note with the address and left."

Growler: "He didn't say a single word?"

"Well, he asked me a question."

Woman: "What was your answer?"

Tomas felt a trickle of sweat slip down his spine and wanted nothing more than to disappear at that moment. He swallowed, trying to find his voice. "I didn't. I started to cry."

He steeled himself for derision but the answer seemed to satisfy them. Tall nodded, as if pleased, then placed his palms on the table.

"Well then, welcome. Let us introduce ourselves." From right to left, Tall was Dalle; Woman was Vet, and Growler was Lucien.

"And you all are . . ."

"Yes," Dalle nodded. "We are Storytellers."

Tomas felt his stomach flutter. They were different from the Nahan around them; it was obvious to all present. He took a deep breath to steady himself.

Vet seemed to read his mind. "You're not in the program yet, dear. Didn't Albion tell you anything?"

Tomas shook his head and Lucien muttered, "Typical."

Vet gestured to the photos before her. "Let's throw you into the deep end, then, shall we? Before us are photos of common who need to be put on, shall we say, a different path. For whatever reason, their activities are not pleasing our companies or organizations and we are being petitioned for alternate possibilities. Do you understand?"

Tomas nodded uncertainly. "I'm sure I'll learn as I go along."

"I'm sure you will," Dalle said, pulling out a photo, "or you won't last long."

Lucien pointed a finger at him. "You do know this is just an audition? You make it through this and if you are very, very good, you'll get to train and if you are even better than good and exceptionally lucky, you get the title."

"And then," Vet said, "your luck goes right in the toilet and you rue the day you ever applied." The three laughed and turned back to Tomas as one.

Vet held her hands over the photographs like a hostess offering a buffet. "So what do you say, kid? Want to give it a try?"

"Try what?" His mouth was so dry, Tomas could hardly speak.

"Try your hand at Storytelling. Look at the pictures before you and tell us what you see. What you know. You don't have to give us the solution; just tell us the problem." They sat back expectantly to watch.

Tomas could feel his hands tremble as he tried to focus on the photographs before him. They were upside down, but when he reached to turn one around, Dalle stopped him.

"It shouldn't make any difference, kid. Just look at them."

Tomas nodded, panic closing his throat. He saw nothing, thought of nothing but his own embarrassment as he skimmed over the unknown faces before him. Nothing was coming to mind but failure and the knowing smirks on the three faces before him.

Even Lucien's whisper was gravelly. "Getting anything, kid?"

Tomas shook his head. He couldn't meet their eyes until all three erupted in laughter. The sound silenced the room around them as everybody looked to see what could make the odd group in the back laugh so hard.

Dalle was the first to recover from the outburst. "Sorry, kid, we're just having a little fun at your expense. You're not going to see anything here. How long have you been in training? Forty-five minutes?"

Vet laughed, scooping up a stack of photos before her. "Yeah, it took Dalle ten years to be able to spin a decent story and Lucien nearly got an entire municipal board sent to prison." The Storytellers laughed among themselves, swapping insults and boasts, ignoring Tomas, who continued to peer at the photos.

"I know him."

They didn't seem to hear him, so Tomas put his finger on a photograph in front of Dalle. "I know him."

They quieted down, immediately serious, and stared, not at the photo, but at Tomas.

"And?" Dalle asked.

"Who is he?" Vet asked.

"His name is Kevin. I met him in Arizona."

Dalle looked at the photo, then shook his head. "Wrong guy, kid. He's from Pittsburgh."

Tomas wouldn't remove his hand from the picture. "But I met him in Arizona. He was on business. It was in a bar."

Dalle read the file on the back. "What do you know about him?"

Tomas closed his eyes, struggling to remember. "He was in trouble at work. Some kind of money thing. And no one knows he's gay."

"How do you know he's gay?"

"It was a gay bar."

"Are you gay?"

"No."

"But he thinks you are."

"Yes."

Dalle passed a look to Vet, who continued to question him.

"Did you have him?"

"Yes."

"Does he love you?"

"Excuse me?"

"Does he love you?" She leaned on her elbows. "Did he love you? Did he want you and feel for you?"

"I guess. I . . . I don't know. He talked a lot."

"So he trusted you."

"Well, he didn't think I spoke English."

"Why didn't you speak English?"

"A gay bar?"

"And you're not gay?"

He didn't know whom to answer or how, so he shoved his hands into his pockets. "It's a long story."

Dalle leaned forward. "We're Storytellers, kid. They're all long stories."

Lucien flipped through the file and shrugged. "Nothing in here about being gay. Apparently our people missed that. Could help." He looked to his colleagues, who seemed to join him in his silent conclusion.

"Okay, let's send these to Resources." Lucien opened another file and began reading, then looked up as if surprised Tomas was still standing there. "That's it, kid. We're done here. Go enjoy a few days in Chicago on us. We'll send a car for you when we're ready for you. Now get the hell out of here, Desara *Acte*. We've got work to do."

Tomas stepped away from the table, into the busy crowd surrounding them. His ears were ringing as he tried to make sense of what just happened. Nobody paid him any attention as he pushed open the doors and stepped into the quiet hallway. The heavy hotel carpeting muffled the sound of his voice as he repeated aloud what he had heard.

"Desara *Acte.*" He smiled, tasting the new word. "*Acte.*"

Apprentice.

Chapter Five:

ACTE

....

Acte: apprentice

"Shit, Stell. There's a garbage can under the desk. Why don't you use it?"

"I'm saving it all up so I have something exciting to do tomorrow."

"Ah sarcasm—that's refreshing." Tomas pulled two licorice whips out from under him and tossed them off the bed. His head was pounding, having spent his third day in deep meditation training. "You know, you don't have to spend all day in the hotel. Chicago's a big city. There's a lot to do here."

"Oh, I know. I'm allowed to go to movies. I'm allowed to go to museums. I'm allowed to be surrounded by common all day as long as I stay with my escort. I had more freedom on Calstow Mountain."

"It's for your own protection. You ran away from the True Family."

Tomas threw his arm over his aching eyes. He didn't want to have the argument that they had been having for nearly two weeks. He knew Stell was unhappy; she was bored and she missed him. He missed her too, but he didn't have the luxury of empty hours to think about it. After the riotous info confab, his life had become a grueling parade of interviews, physical disciplines, and meditation. It seemed someone was forever boring holes into him with their eyes or peppering him with questions. He was the punching bag of the Storytellers.

It wasn't just the Storytellers who picked over him, either. Accountants, doctors, and record keepers had pummeled him with questions, pumped him for facts, measured him, recorded him, taken blood and hair samples, along with fingerprints. This morning, which seemed like a lifetime ago, he'd had to practice his stillness meditation while some kid took a plaster cast of his face, hands, and feet.

Every evening as the car drove him from the industrial complex where the training was taking place back to the hotel, his skin and nerves, even his hair screamed with overstimulation. He would fumble into the always dark hotel room to find Stell bored, prickly, and ready to fight.

Tonight she wore just his boxers and a tank top. She looked small. And sad.

"I'm sorry it's like this, Stell."

"I'm sorry to be so bitchy."

Tomas laughed and rolled onto his elbow. "Bitchy? Where did you learn that word?"

Stell nodded to the television. "Tyra."

"Tyra?"

"Tyra Banks. She's a very famous woman that people go to for advice. Experts from all over the world come on to speak with her and the people cry and dance. She had a doctor on today helping a woman who called herself a Big Bad Bitch. She has a problem with something called PSM. I'm not sure what that is but maybe that's why I'm so bitchy."

Tomas stroked her thigh. "It's PMS and I'm pretty sure you don't have it. It's a common's problem. Besides," he rolled into her and kissed her ankle, "you're not being bitchy. I mean, not unnecessarily so. I know you're bored and I'm never around."

"You're busy. I know. This is important to you."

"You're important to me too." Tomas pushed himself forward until he lay across her crossed legs, his head resting on her inner thigh. "I promise it won't go on like this forever. Even if I have to leave the program, I won't live like this forever."

"I miss you so much." Stell stroked his hair and his face. Her hands moved down onto his chest. "I know how tired you are, so if you want me to stop I will."

Tomas kissed the tender skin of her inner thigh, his hands reaching up to encircle her waist. She fell back onto the bed as he kissed his way up her body. He could feel her hesitation; he knew he'd hurt her by pulling away the last few nights.

Tomas breathed in her hunger, could smell her blood and hear her heart pounding as his earlier exhaustion faded. Tasting the sweet saltiness of her skin, he climbed on top of her, pinning her arms over her head and kissing her deeply. She moved beneath him, wrapping her legs around his and he felt the heat from her body through his clothes.

She tested his grip on her wrists. "If you let me go, I'll tear you to pieces."

He ran his tongue along the hammering pulse of her throat. "Maybe I'll just bite right through your skin."

Stell groaned and arched against him, her legs pulling him tightly to her. She raised her head and tried to bite Tomas, but he pulled back, teasing her.

"You can't resist me forever, Tomas. And when I get my mouth on you, I'm going to swallow you whole."

Tomas bit her chin, then followed with small bites along her jawline. "Swallow me whole, huh? Do I get to pick the part you swallow first?"

Tomas sighed and dropped his head when a knock sounded at the door.

"Tell me you don't have to answer that."

He released Stell's hands with a whispered warning. "Stay right there. Keep thinking those thoughts." She giggled as Tomas walked to the door, adjusting himself in his pants. "If it's Housekeeping, we're killing them and eating them."

"Good. I hope it's Housekeeping."

The knock sounded again. "I'm coming." He looked back at Stell and waggled his eyebrows. "Eventually." He opened the door to a common man and woman.

"Good evening. I'm Nancy, this is Kanai." She gestured to the tall, dark haired man behind her. He was well-built, with smooth brown skin and almond-shaped eyes. "The Council sent us over. They said you haven't been able to go out."

Tomas came back into the room and dropped onto the edge of the bed, rubbing his face with his hands. Nancy and Kanai followed, waiting patiently for some reply.

"Who are they, Tomas?" Stell asked, sounding worried. To Kanai, she asked "You are common, aren't you?"

"Yes." Kanai said. "Mr. Vartan said you find my body type appealing."

"Your body type?" Stell whipped around to Tomas. "Who's Mr. Vartan? Tomas?"

"Mr. Vartan is the Coordinator of the Council."

"And so he sends two commons to our room? For what?"

"To feed you." Nancy stepped forward in front of Tomas and slipped out of her jacket. In the crook of her left elbow was a small tattoo. Beneath the ink, a faint scar. Kanai pushed up his sleeve to reveal an identical mark. "Where would you like us to sit?"

"What is this, Tomas?" Stell asked. "Who are these people? Get off my bed!" She pushed at Kanai, who moved to sit beside her.

Exhaustion flooded back into Tomas. There were so many things Stell didn't understand. It took him two days to explain television to her; this could take forever and he felt his patience wearing thin. "They're Kott, the common who work for us. We have to feed and we can't go out so they've sent someone over to us."

"Like the pizza we ordered?" Stell stared in disbelief at the two strangers. Kanai's face was passive, but Nancy met her glare with a cold stare.

"Not exactly," said Nancy. "If you don't find us pleasing, we'll send someone else."

"No." Tomas took Nancy's hand. "This is fine. It's just been a long day."

"This is not fine!" Stell jumped from the bed when Nancy sat down next to Tomas. She stood before Kanai, looking up into his calm face. "What did you say about body type?"

Kanai looked at the wall behind her as he answered. "Mr. Vartan said you preferred my body type to feed. I didn't ask any specifics. If you'd like me to leave, I will."

Stell turned to look at Tomas, who sat with Nancy on the bed they had just vacated. "So we're not allowed to go out and hunt. We have to sit here and eat what the Council decides we'll like? How do they know what body type I prefer?"

"They've asked me about you. I told them you like large men. Smooth skin. Soft voices."

Stell grabbed Kanai's hair, pulling his face before her. "Do you also have a big dick?"

Nancy's voice was low but sharp. "We don't have sex with you. We don't get put under. You feed from us and we leave. Simple as that."

"Simple as that, huh?" Stell moved past Kanai and stepped into a crumpled pair of jeans. She pulled a sweater over her head, slipped on boots, and hissed at Tomas in Nahan. "First we have to obey your parents. Then the Council. Now we take orders from our food?"

Tomas said nothing as she stomped out the door. Nancy shifted uncomfortably.

"It seems we've upset you. I apologize. We'll go."

"No." Tomas held her arm. "Sit down, Nancy. You too, Kanai. I'm hungry."

....

Stell pounded her fists on the walls of the elevator. Rage and hunger and frustration threatened to burst out of her and she felt as if she would scorch anything that crossed her path. In the hushed lobby of the elegant hotel, Stell stomped across the marble floor, glaring at the Nahan woman pretending to read a newspaper in the lounge. The woman moved to rise but Stell waved her down. Past the reception desk, Stell was stopped by a muscular Nahan man.

"Ma'am, did you hire a car?"

Stell stared at him. She had never seen a Nahan with tattoos before. Not much taller than she, his muscular arms and broad chest conveyed a power that made her pause.

"I'm going out for a walk." She tried to move past him but he blocked her way.

"I'll go with you."

She spoke in clipped Nahan. "I don't want company."

He glanced over his shoulder to be sure they weren't drawing the attention of the common working at the reception desk. "We don't speak in Nahan in public."

"Let me work on my English then. Fuck off. How's that?"

She heard him laugh when she pushed past him and stepped through the revolving door into the night. He followed close behind as she strode down the sidewalk. Stell didn't know where she was going. She only wanted fresh air and freedom, not another shadow. She spun around to confront him.

"Why don't you leave me alone?"

"I was told to stay with you if you left the hotel." He stood before her, relaxed. "There somewhere you wanna go, I'll take you."

"Don't you have to check with your Council first?"

"Yeah, I don't check with the Council too much."

His smirk irritated her. "And yet they tell you to watch me and here you are."

He shrugged. "I got a few errands to run so I volunteered. You wanna come?"

"And run errands for the Council?" She clutched her chest. "My big day!"

He laughed again. "I thought you True Family types were supposed to be little sheep."

Stell stepped back. "How did you know I was True Family?"

"The Almighty Council told me." He gestured over his shoulder to the front of the hotel. "Ever ridden a motorcycle? No? Let's go." It didn't sound like a request. Stell followed him to the bike more out of curiosity than from fear of defying him.

"By the way, my name's Adlai. Anton Adlai."

"I'm Stell," she said, climbing on.

"I know." Before she could ask him another question the bike roared to life and pulled out into the nighttime traffic.

Stell watched the city pass by, the cold air bringing tears to her eyes and a flush to her cheeks. He pulled onto the expressway, uncongested in the late hour, and opened the bike up. Stell felt her heart race as the world sped by. She could feel the power of the machine beneath her and let her head fall back to watch the halogen lights blur above her.

The neighborhoods deteriorated as they drove. Office buildings gave way to warehouses, run-down apartment buildings, and shabby homes. Graffiti covered every surface and even over the rush of the wind Stell could hear the bumping of car stereos. Adlai pulled up in front of a dilapidated house with a large porch and every interior light lit. On the porch, a half dozen young, heavily tattooed men lounged, while several slim, hard-eyed girls moved among them. Inside the house, salsa music made the glass rattle. All eyes turned to the motorcycle and one tall man with a scarred face stepped off the porch to greet them.

Adlai spoke under his breath. "You hungry? You can get something here." He added, without a touch of sarcasm, "Don't kill anyone."

Adlai and the scarred man engaged in a complicated handshake that was part greeting, part frisking. When both were satisfied, they began speaking in a rapid language Stell couldn't understand. Adlai looked at her, let loose another torrent of sound and both men laughed.

"You don't speak Spanish?" The scarred man asked with a heavy accent. Stell shook her head as Adlai headed her toward the house. The group on the porch rose and cleared out, except for one man who looked Stell over with relish.

"Hey, babe, we got some business to discuss." Adlai slapped her on the butt and settled into a rusty lounge chair next to the scarred man. "Go inside with Esai. He's got a little something that'll keep you busy."

Esai pulled a twisted baggie from his pants pocket, showed her a small white rock and leered at her. With a quick look to Adlai, who offered her no help, Stell nodded and followed Esai into the house. She was glad she didn't speak the language because she had no idea what she was supposed to say about the bag with the rock or how Esai thought that would keep her busy. She had plans of her own, however, that involved Esai in ways he would never foresee.

He led her through the living room, where the crowd from the porch was packed in around a large screen TV, then down the hall. Esai said something to her in Spanish and she followed him into a tiny laundry room packed with piles of rumpled clothes. He pulled the curtain closed behind them, pulled out the baggie and a small glass pipe. More unintelligible words and more leering revealed the black roots of Esai's teeth.

Stell pushed down her revulsion and leaned in close to him. A warm breath on his face and soft fingers on his eyes and Esai swooned. She caught him and the pipe easily with one arm. With her free hand, she pulled her knife from her pocket and made a small cut under his chin.

She couldn't stand the smell of him for more than a few deep swallows. Closing the wound, she pocketed the white rock and put the pipe back in his hand. A sharp whistle brought Esai back to his senses.

He shook his head and mumbled something guttural at her. It was a sound that would be an insult in any language, but Stell feigned ignorance. When he realized the pipe he was about to offer was empty, his insolence turned to surprise that bordered on panic. Esai patted down his pockets, checked the floor around him, and glared at Stell. She went on the offensive, gesturing toward Esai for the pipe. She almost laughed at his helpless bewilderment and was a little sorry to hear Adlai calling to her from the porch. With a disgusted scoff, Stell pushed past the confused man and headed back outside.

"There's my girl. You get what you needed?" Stell smiled and slipped under his protective arm. "Then we're done here." He slapped palms with the scarred man and led Stell off the porch. "See you next week, Tito."

"Yo, man, see you in a week. Feel free to bring your *puta* by anytime."

Stell could feel Adlai stiffen. Motioning for her to stay put, he turned back to the house.

"What did you say?"

Tito grinned and stepped closer with a swagger. "I said feel free to bring your *puta* by anytime. The boys like her."

Adlai nodded, as if listening to voices only he could hear. Then, faster than a whip, he pulled the taller man down in a headlock. From the waistband of his jeans, he pulled a pistol that he shoved into Tito's eye. The trapped man struggled for only a moment then began whimpering rapidly in Spanish.

"Don't apologize to me, you fuckwad. Apologize to her."

Red-faced and gasping for air, Tito held out a desperate hand to Stell. "I'm sorry, lady. I don't mean nothing by it."

"Now tell her you're a pig." Adlai shoved the gun harder into his eye socket.

"I'm a pig! I'm a pig, man. Let me go!"

"Now, tell me one more thing." Adlai's voice was low and soft. "Who's the *puta* now?"

His answer was a squeak. "I am."

"Who?"

"I am! I'm the *puta*. All right?"

Adlai whipped Tito out of his grip, nearly breaking his neck. "Don't forget that."

He started the bike and as she climbed on, Stell could hear a volley of Spanish hurled at their backs. She wrapped her arms around Adlai as the bike sped up and felt his even heartbeat and easy breathing.

"How'd you like your first Spanish lesson?"

"Don't call me *puta*, that's for sure."

He laughed and opened the bike up even more. "You get something to eat?"

Stell licked her lips and grimaced. "Yes. It tasted funny. And it's making me feel dizzy."

"Yeah, Esai's a tweaker. Just don't have any caffeine tomorrow, you'll be fine."

"I took that rock he had in his pocket."

Adlai pulled the bike off to the side of the road and turned around. "You did what?"

She pulled the small, white crystal from her pocket. "I took it. I don't know why. Just thought it would be funny. He was so confused."

"Damn, Stell." He took the rock from her and started to laugh in earnest. "You took Esai's crack? He's going to have some serious 'splaining to do to Tito. Damn . . ." He laughed again then pitched the rock into the gravel beside the road. "You are one crazy girl, Stell. *C-R-A-Z-Y.*"

As he pulled back onto the highway, Stell smiled and leaned back to watch the streetlights fly by.

. . . .

Tomas showered and dressed without waking Stell. He hadn't heard her come in last night. He smelled blood on her skin and from her deep breathing he gathered her feeding had been more satisfactory than his. Tomas stood at the foot of the bed watching her sleep. One smooth leg poked out from under the sheet, her toes pointing lazily off the bed. He resisted the urge to stroke her foot, to feel her warmth before he left for another long day.

His driver, a fair-haired Kott named Carlson, let Tomas out at the far end of the parking lot of the sprawling industrial complex. It had taken Tomas three days and a sharp tone to finally convince Carlson that he didn't want to be dropped off directly at the door. Carlson had his orders, which he took very seriously, but Tomas won out. For Tomas the act of opening the door was a gesture of intent, a physical way of saying "I'm doing this." The walk across the parking lot was a brief moment of fresh air before disappearing into his training.

The complex was enormous, made up of dozens of rectangular metal buildings, some with shipping bay doors, some with banks of windows, some sealed off from any outside view. The units were connected by a series of carpeted hallways that only some of the occupants knew were color-coded. Red carpet signified a public zone. To the west end of the complex, yellow carpets led to businesses run only by the common. If the carpets were green, the businesses were Nahan-owned and common-run. On the far east end of the complex, where Tomas was headed, the carpets were blue, the buildings windowless, and security thorough.

Security guards, a registration desk, fingerprint identification panels—Tomas passed through them on autopilot, knowing every step was being videotaped. Reinforced steel doors bearing the sign PITTINGER RESEARCH INDUSTRIES: RESTRICTED AREA opened onto a sterile white hallway lined with metal racks of boxes and odd-looking instruments. They were only for show, on the off chance that anyone uninvited should happen to peek through the open door. The hallway ended in a T, and turning left or right, the building took on a decidedly different feel.

From this point on rich cobalt wool carpeting replaced tile; fluorescent lighting disappeared. Soft, incandescent lamps made golden Venetian plaster glow. The plaster, he'd learned, hid layers of lead and soundproofing material. It was all designed to relax those working within its confines, to keep out the electronic whine of the outside world that so often gave the Storytellers a ringing headache, particularly when meditating. Rooms with electronic systems, like televisions and computers, were kept closed, their doors heavily lined with insulation. Tomas stepped past these rooms and into the reading room marked VEHN, the Nahan word for *listen*.

The furniture was ornate but tasteful; the stained glass windows (that he learned were false windows, opening to nothing) colored the room with rich shades of red and purple and blue. Oak shelves lined two walls of the room, filled with thick, leather volumes and carved boxes. At first he had been impressed, shocked by the transition from urban Chicago to regal drawing room in the space of only a few yards, but he'd grown accustomed to the texture of the place. This morning, with a dull headache behind his eyes, he began to question if the books on the shelves were as fake and empty as the artificial light behind the windows. He settled into a leather chair and awaited his instructor.

Even with his frustration and fatigue, this was one part of his day that he did enjoy. It was true Storytelling. For the past two weeks, he had spent at least two hours a day listening to the legends of the Nahan, the stories told in their entirety in the ancient oral tradition by the Storytellers themselves. Some of the stories he knew; some he thought he knew but learned had been altered for his childhood; some were wondrously unknown. He was expected to learn all of these tales, all of this history, by heart, verbatim, so that he too could carry along the story of the Nahan, the tales and truths that could never be written down.

Tomas was glad to see Dalle, one of the three Storytellers he had met at the confab, come through the door. Dalle had stepped forward as his mentor and Tomas enjoyed the melodic sound of his voice.

"Good morning, Desara. As you see you are stuck with me again."

Tomas rose and gave a small bow as the tall, slender man settled into the matching leather chair across from him. "Please, Mentor Dalle, you can call me Tomas."

Dalle stared at Tomas, a shadow over his gray-blue eyes. "First off, don't call me Mentor. Just Dalle. You're not a kid anymore. This isn't Heritage School."

"I'm sorry." Tomas felt his face redden at Dalle's suddenly harsh tone. Everything about this place made him feel eleven years old.

Dalle scratched his forehead, a habitual gesture. "And don't tell anyone to call you Tomas. In here, you are simply Desara."

"Why?"

"Why?" He leaned forward in his chair. "Because if you complete your training, you will belong to everybody. You will have the world laid open in ways you could never imagine. You will know tragedies and furies and atrocities. You will carry burdens that should never be yours and know secrets about others you would never even reveal to yourself.

"Listen to me, Desara." The command was unnecessary. Tomas was enrapt by the low, urgent tone. "Your mother will die. Your father will die. The people closest to you will fear you because they will see in your face their darkest nights and everyone who has ever called you by your name will turn away from you. From this point forward, never tell another soul your given name so that decades from now, when your story is no longer your story but the story of Ourselves, if you find someone who can call you by your name, you will remember what it is to be held in another's heart. And if it is never uttered again, you will at least go to the fire knowing there is still one thing, one small piece, that is yours and yours alone."

Tomas couldn't swallow. His hands had turned to ice and he had been nailed to the seat beneath him. Dalle didn't smile or try to comfort him. He met his gaze openly and patiently. The moment stretched before them, from Storyteller to apprentice as it had for centuries. Finally closing his eyes and breaking the connection, Dalle shifted in his seat and began to speak in a melodic tone.

"So, why don't I tell you the story of Icus, the woman who gave birth to fire."

. . . .

Stell awoke with a headache and a bitter taste in her mouth. Tweaker. That's what Adlai had called Esai. She had to find out what that meant and avoid it in the future.

She could smell Adlai on her hands. Had Tomas smelled him as well? A hook of guilt nicked at her stomach as her mind roamed over the memory of Adlai's body. He was so different from Tomas. Where Tomas was tall and angular, Adlai was solid, his muscles thick and well-defined. His movements were controlled and contained, like a dangerous animal in a cage. He held an air of disdain that Stell found compelling, especially as he had brought Tito to submission without so much as raising his pulse rate. She wondered what his business had been in that shabby neighborhood with those disreputable common.

Maybe she would get to find out.

Maybe he would be her bodyguard again this evening.

. . . .

"Feel the warmth of the coin in your palm."

Tomas breathed in deeply, trying to feel the penny that lay in his right hand. It was an isolation meditation, something he had excelled at, but today he could no more distinguish the warmth of the penny against his skin than he could tell one hair on his head apart from another. Mentor Sylva tapped him on the shoulder.

"Where are you, Desara?" Her voice was gentle.

"I'm back in the Mountains of Ur watching Icus grit her teeth."

Sylva smiled and nodded. "It's quite a story. 'And Baush was so fierce a child, his labor pains tore into Icus's heart and she gnashed her teeth such that sparks flew and set fire to the gore of his birth.' Pretty image. I hate the part about the hyenas."

"Maybe you should tell the stories and I'll lead the meditations. Not that I'm any good at that either."

Sylva settled down on the carpeted floor beside Tomas. "Discouragement already? You've only been here a month." There were flecks of gray in her black hair and the slightest touch of a wrinkle in her forehead. Tomas wondered how old she was.

"Somewhere around two-fifty." She laughed at the startled look on his face. "What? You didn't think I saw you checking out my face? You don't think I know about these wrinkles?"

"You look so young."

She winked at him, a youthful gesture that matched the twinkle in her blue-green eyes. "It's my life. I'm a meditation teacher. I get to relax for a living and help others do the same. It keeps me young. And you, my young apprentice, need to relax. You have decades to learn and centuries to forget."

Tomas threw his arm over his eyes. "I wish people would stop saying things like that."

Sylva laughed again and lay down beside him. "Let's look at the ceiling, Desara. See that plasterwork up there?" Tomas examined the honey-colored swirls. "That looks exactly like the ceiling of the villa my father owned in Umbria many years ago. Sometimes when I lie on this floor, I look up at that ceiling and I'm a six-year-old girl. I have no idea about the woman I'll become. And in that plaster, I see oceans and stars and faraway lands. I see all the things I dreamed I would see when I became a woman. Now I am a woman, an old woman, and do you know what I see?"

"No, what?"

"I see fake plaster."

Tomas waited but nothing more came. "Is that supposed to mean something?"

"No. Just killing time until you're ready to get back to work." She laughed and nudged him with her elbow. "Look, kid, you've got a lot of years ahead of you, a lot of misery but a lot of joy too. I've been working with Storytellers for almost two hundred years. I'm always surprised at the things they don't tell you. Maybe they want to make sure you take it all seriously. Maybe they figure if they paint a bleak enough picture the good times will be a nice surprise, but there will be good times. Trust me, Desara. If you truly endeavor to feel the people around you, you will know pain. You'll know betrayal and anger and loneliness but you'll also know joy. Ecstasy. Hope. All those things that keep our hearts beating, keep us telling our stories and moving our people and raising our children."

Beneath his arm, a warm tear slid onto the carpet. "I know I have a lot to do, Mentor Sylva, but could we just lie here for a little longer?"

"Kid"—she entwined her fingers in his—"that's exactly what we're gonna do."

. . . .

"Is there a reason we're pushing him so hard?" Sylva propped her feet up on her desk. As usual, the Storytellers were using her office as a lounge. She'd left Desara asleep in the meditation room to find Lucien and Dalle sprawled on her couch, their feet on her coffee table.

Dalle scratched his forehead. "This isn't summer camp. It's supposed to be hard."

"Oh please," Sylva said, "let's not get all military about this. You sound like Vartan." Dalle rolled his eyes at the mention of the Coordinator. "He's just a kid. Whatever happened to apprenticing?

Letting him work for the Storytellers for a few years before becoming one?"

"Apprenticing is overrated." Lucien's gravelly voice was emphatic. "What else does he have to do?"

"Maybe have a life? You've seen him. He's exhausted. I mean, how old is he? Twenty-five? Not even? He's only just left his parents' house." Sylva threw a wrapped peppermint at Dalle. "I worked with you when you apprenticed. You were nearly fifty before you reached his meditation level. And you already have him doing memory drills? Pattern recognition? While he's just learning the stories? What next? Are you going to shoot him out of a cannon?"

"He can handle it," Lucien said. "He is handling it."

"He is not handling it. You're going to burn him out."

Dalle had scratched a red spot on his forehead. "It's a tough call. He's so hungry to learn and he did apply young."

"You applied young, and it was years before you were doing what he's doing."

Dalle gave his forehead a rest and folded his hands before him. "He's just so good. I mean, he's really good but there's something—"

"Something holding him back." Lucien finished his sentence.

Dalle nodded. "Something draining him."

Sylva snorted. "Gee, I wonder what it could be. Maybe his fifteen-hour training days?" She sat back in her chair, shaking her head. She had an affinity for Storytellers and held a special affection for Dalle but his attitude toward the young apprentice was puzzling.

Lucien growled. "The girlfriend can't be helping. At least Vartan's keeping her busy working with Anton Adlai. He says they make a good team."

Now it was Dalle's turn to snort. "You'll forgive me if I don't put a great deal of faith in Vartan's judgment."

Sylva stretched her arms over her head and groaned. "Let's not talk about Vartan. That officious bureaucrat talks about himself enough. We're here to talk about Desara, who's crashed out in Meditation Room Two, by the way. Are you sure you're not driving him too hard?"

"I'm not his mentor," Lucien said. "But if he's going to fall apart, make him fall apart now before anyone is counting on him. There are no shortcuts on this path."

Sylva heard the tightness in his voice and didn't bother to argue. She was only a meditation coach, not a Storyteller. She didn't know what it was like to mentor an apprentice but she knew that even now, after four years, Lucien still couldn't utter the name Hess.

....

Tomas heard the shower running when he returned to the room. As he fell back onto the bed, he realized the room had been picked up. There were no clothes on the floor or junk food wrappers in the bed. The sun was still up. It had been days since he had been home before dark. He could hear Stell whistling in the bathroom and smiled when he recognized the tune. It was the theme song to *Bonanza*.

"C'mon out, Little Joe."

Stell ran out of the bathroom, naked, toweling her hair.

"Well howdy, pardner." He sat up and admired her. "I'm pretty sure they never had anything like that on the Ponderosa." Stell moved to join him on the bed but stepped past him when the phone rang. Before it could ring twice, she snatched the receiver from the cradle.

"Yes?" Stell turned her back to Tomas and kept her voice low. "Where are we going? Give me five minutes."

"Who was that?"

"It was the bodyguard." She didn't meet Tomas's eyes. "I wanted to go out and he won't let me go by myself."

"Where are you going? Where you fed last night?"

"Adlai picked out this neighborhood. He said it'd be okay."

"Adlai? Is that your bodyguard?"

"Yeah." She reached under the bed for her clothes. "He has tat-toos. Isn't that weird?"

Tomas didn't answer, only watched the back of her head, remembering Dalle's words from earlier today. Was it already difficult to look into his face?

"Stell? I'm sorry I didn't tell you about the Kott last night. I didn't know they'd send anyone over to us. If I'd known I would have told them not to. I knew you wouldn't like it."

Stell finally looked at him. "I didn't like it. I'll never like it. Do you?"

Tomas shrugged. He wanted to touch her face but didn't. "I haven't really had a chance to think about it. There's so much other stuff."

"Yeah. You have a lot of stuff to do." She pulled her boots on and rose. Wrapping a scarf around her neck, she hesitated at the door. "I don't know how late I'll be."

"I could go out with you."

Stell looked down at the ground. "It's a motorcycle. He's already down there."

"Yeah, yeah, all right. I'm just gonna crash."

"I'll try not to wake you when I get back."

Before he could answer, she was out the door.

. . . .

The silence in the room hammered at his ears. All day he had longed for silence and now, surrounded by it, he thought it might make him scream. He crawled back onto the bed and saw the red message light blinking on the phone. Tomas dialed into the message service. Just the sound of Louis's voice made his heart leap.

"Dude, we are heading to a place called McGympsies Irish Pub. Find it. Be there or I swear we're going to storm the hotel." Tomas was out the door before the phone hit the cradle.

. . . .

They pulled into a coffee shop on the side of the highway. Adlai led her to a booth in the far corner. "What are we doing here?"

"Waiting for that motel room door to open." He pointed to the Sunset Motel across the road. "Number two-seventeen." She wanted to ask him why they were waiting but didn't want to seem intrusive. After the waitress left, Adlai leaned in. "How do you like Chicago so far?"

"I haven't seen much. I've always got somebody attached to me. The Council seems to think that movies are going to change my life."

"You don't like movies?"

She shook her head. "They're not bad or anything, I just don't care about them. It's nothing but commons in them. Why do we pay so much attention to them?" Adlai began to answer but she held up her hand. "I know, I know, Tomas has told me a thousand times. We have to live among them to feed among them. We can't protect ourselves if we don't understand them, blah-blah-blah. Are they really that complicated? It's not like we marry them."

"Some do." He shrugged at Stell's surprise. "We do what we gotta do. Besides, the movies can be kind of entertaining. And the art and the music. It's not like we can put out any of our own. The Council would make short work of that."

"The fucking Council." The words began to roll out before she could stop them. "Ever since I ran away everybody has acted like I've been freed from some prison. People keep saying how lucky I am and how nice it must be. But you know something? I was freer on Calstow Mountain than I am here. There, I had church and school, but I was free to run onto the mountain. I was invisible. All I had to do was stay out of sight and I could be as free as I wanted. Here? Everybody is always watching. So many rules and jobs and work to do."

"Busy, busy, busy. That's the Council's way. Takes a lot of work to keep the great Nahan machine running."

"Doesn't anybody not do what the Council tells them?"

Adlai leaned back and let the waitress set down their drinks. "My folks did. I grew up in the Reaches." He saw she didn't understand. "The Reaches? Outside of Council reach? You know, they got their own identities, their own cash. They moved around on their own to stay anonymous. I grew up in New Mexico mostly. My mom was a photographer. She grew up in Boston but the Council got nervous about her success. She wouldn't stop taking pictures so she took off for the desert."

"And your father?"

"He's in Detroit, last I heard."

"But I thought . . . the *Eihl* . . . they were paired."

Adlai stirred his iced tea with his straw. "Dad always told me 'don't confuse biology with psychology.' Most of the time they couldn't stand each other, fought all the time. They always said they loved each other in their way and that way was the highway."

Stell put her chin in her hands. This went against everything she had learned about pairing and the *Eihl*. For a Nahan woman to conceive there had to be consistent exchange of blood over a long period of time and, if the pairing was correct, both the man and the woman would become fertile and, even then, only with each other. That the bond could be broken by simple personal likes and dislikes seemed impossible. Was that what had happened with her own father? Had it been no more complicated than a common's divorce?

"There's so much I don't understand."

"Then ask."

"Yes, and when I ask you roll your eyes and talk to me like I'm stupid."

Adlai tipped his head at her.

"I mean, not you but—"

"Your boyfriend."

"Tomas. He gets really impatient with me. Like it's my fault I've never seen television before or seen the Superman or worked a microstove."

"Microwave."

"Microwave. See? I just don't see why any of it is so important. And if it is so important, tell me before I come across it. Two weeks ago, he shows me the television. He tells me there is news and show games and sit-down comedies and I have no idea what he's talking about. But I listen and I try to keep it straight because I'm so bored in that hotel room and I hate the woman they sent as my *chagar*, my escort." She slapped the table, her frustration making English harder to form.

"So I am watching the television and there are men stealing horses. That is very serious. Tomas comes in and I tell him and he laughs and says it's something called *Bonanza*, that the men aren't real and the horses aren't being stolen and he looks at me like I'm an idiot." She began to shred the paper napkin under her drink. "I mean, now I understand that it's just a program, but I thought it was where the true show was, the news thing. How was I supposed to know?"

"I gotta admit, I would've loved to hear that 9-1-1 call." He flicked his crumpled straw wrapper at her with a wink. "Don't worry about it. I don't think you're stupid and I doubt he does either. It's weird to think of all the stuff you don't know about. Ask me anything."

Stell considered him for a moment. "Why do you have tattoos?"

"That's your question?"

"You said anything."

"So I did. Well, I just like them." He pushed up the sleeves of his shirt to show her a series of black intertwined lines.

"Aren't they permanent?"

"For them. Not us. They fade every two or three years. So I keep changing them. I like them. They're like art for your body." Without thinking Stell traced a thick black line with her finger. She stopped where the curve of his bicep disappeared under his sleeve. He watched her hand, then pulled his sleeve down. "So now you know where I'm from and what kind of tattoos I have. You know more about me than most of the people I work for."

The waitress set down two heaping plates of onion rings. Adlai poured out a puddle of ketchup. "What do you say we talk about something besides me? You got to be curious about more than that."

Stell swirled an onion ring in his ketchup. There was something she was curious about but was hesitant to bring up. The embarrassment of the horse rustlers episode was burned into her mind. She didn't want to be made a fool of again by the television but this particular show was about more than horse thieves and Adlai had already shown more patience than Tomas.

"Have you ever heard of vampires?" Adlai didn't laugh, which gave her courage to continue. "I saw this show on the television and it was all about vampires."

"What about them?"

"They're like us!" Stell caught herself and lowered her voice, leaning in to whisper across the table. "I mean, not exactly because they can fly and stuff and are supposed to sleep in coffins. But still, the whole blood thing, does the Council know about this?"

He cocked his head to the side and squinted at her. "I gotta tell you, sweetheart, it is outrageous that you have been turned out into the world with so little information."

He explained to her what was second nature to any Nahan. Yes, the Nahan were the basis of the original vampire myth, that every culture in the world had some version of it and each could trace it back almost entirely to the Nahan. Of course, these cultures didn't know the origin themselves and the Nahan had always carefully cultivated the misperceptions, the superstitions. Give them a monster to chase, he told her, and they'd never come looking for you.

"But in this movie," Stell said, "they're monsters but they act so common. The commons loved them and hated them at the same time."

"Does that ring any bells with you?" Anton laughed. "Get head, get fed? It's kind of crude but, you know, the easiest way to eat is to get them into the sack."

"But this was different. These vampires *wanted* to be common. They had these powers, cool powers that I would love to have, like being able to fly. And they can grow these fangs whenever they want. That would really come in handy but all they wanted to talk about was becoming common."

"That's because according to the myth they were common to begin with. They were turned into vampires by drinking vampire blood."

"But that's stupid." Stell said. "Commons eat steak and they don't become cows. Why would they think drinking blood would make them like us?"

"You're missing the most important point." He leaned forward on his elbows. "You know what our biggest advantage is over the common? Not that we can mesmerize them or that we age more slowly. Our real advantage is that the common are unable to consider the possibility that they may not be the pinnacle of life on Earth." He grabbed an onion ring. "They're so certain that they're the crown of creation that they have to create monsters to put a face on the abyss."

"So who is the crown of creation?"

He shrugged. "Who says there is one? I don't think it's us. I know it's not them. My vote is for honeybees."

"Honeybees?" Stell laughed, thinking he was kidding her.

"Yeah, honeybees. They work together. Nobody really knows how they communicate. The very essence of their work is the life of this planet. Everything benefits from them being alive, being vital. And the by-product of all their pollinating is honey, the only food that never spoils. Doesn't that say something for them?"

Stell put her chin back in her hands. Adlai tossed a bill onto the table.

"Room two-seventeen. Here we go."

. . . .

McGympsies was packed. It was Friday night and Tomas had to fight his way past a collection of burly rugby players at the corner of the bar to have any room to search. "Tomas! Over here!" Aricelli waved to him and when he was close enough, she pulled him past a dancing couple and threw her arms around him. "You made it! It's so fabulous to see you again!" Louis jumped to his feet to greet him.

"Dude," he shouted over the music, "you look like shit."

Tomas knew he had lost weight; his clothes were loose. His hair had grown out to the point where it had to be pushed behind his ears to keep it out of his eyes. It had been days since he'd looked in a mirror but the last time he'd looked, his cheekbones were sharp, his lips pale and chapped, and the dark circles under his eyes set off the angry red rims beneath his lashes.

Tomas mustered the last of his exhausted resources to maintain his composure but Louis would have none of it. He grabbed his cousin and pulled him into a tight embrace, putting his hand on the back of Tomas's head and pushing it into the warm privacy of his neck. They held each other, and Tomas knew Louis felt his ribs and shoulder blades sharp under the woolen sweater. When Tomas began to relax Louis held him at arm's length and arched a wry brow.

"So, how's things?"

Tomas laughed and Louis handed him a beer. Aricelli brushed his hair behind his ear.

"Is it that bad?"

He shook his head. "It's not bad. It's just intense, you know? Really long days and all this . . . this . . . stuff I'm supposed to learn in, like, five minutes. And there's all this, you know . . ." He sighed. Louis and Aricelli watched him, waiting as they always did for Tomas to fish around for his words. He didn't realize how much he missed that patience. He took a long drink from his beer. "Man, I'm so glad to see you guys."

"Where's Stell?"

"She's out. She's not really, you know, into it. I shouldn't be surprised. Everybody told me it would be like this but . . ." He held his arms open in surrender. "Feel free to be the first to say 'I told you so.'"

"Never, man. It's only been a month. Maybe she'll get the hang of it." Louis clinked their bottles and Aricelli jumped in to change the subject.

"So what sort of things are you learning? Can you tell us?"

He began to explain the different disciplines. There were isolation meditations where he was to make himself as still as possible and fully focus on one point, either a part of his body or an object nearby. The idea was to fully invest his energy into one single point. "They haven't explained exactly what the point of it is, but I'm really good at it."

"As you've always been at really pointless things."

"True." The boys toasted each other. "There are also these memory drills that are cool. There's all this chanting and stuff you do." He waved his hand, dismissing what was in reality a grueling physical undertaking, "But at the end of it, you can pull up any point in your life. I don't mean big things like the first time you fed but the smallest minutes of time in total recall."

Louis tried in vain to wave down the harried waitress for another round. "So that's the kind of shit you do all day? Go down memory lane?"

"No, there's a lot of other stuff. Location exercises and pattern recognition. They're obsessed with patterns; I'm supposed to see them everywhere. They're always watching me, waiting to see if I'm going to catch them. They're just always watching me. It's like they're trying to take my brain apart and put it back together differently." He didn't want his friends to hear the strain in his voice. "It is cool hearing the legends though. Do you remember the story of Roizo and Llan?"

"Ooh, I love that story." Aricelli clutched her heart. "There was war and Roizo was afraid that Llan's beauty put her in danger so he bricked her into the castle wall to keep her safe. But Llan could feel her *Eihl* was in danger and punched through the bricks with her bare hands to save him. So romantic."

"And so not true."

"Bullshit. Says who?"

"Says Vet, the Storyteller. The real story is that Roizo was a merchant and was on the brink of making a fortune when Llan threatened to kill the local warlord, which would have totally tanked his deal. He drugged her and bricked her up and when she came to she tore through the wall and killed the warlord anyway. By then Roizo had made his deal but it wasn't until after that that war broke out."

Aricelli considered the story for a moment and then nodded. "He did make the deal, right? So that's okay." Louis and Tomas laughed. "Hey, I'm my father's daughter. She had her *Eihl* and she had her money. It's a win-win."

Tomas realized his bottle was empty. "Are we drinking or what?"

"I can't get her attention." Louis waved again for the waitress, but in the press of the crowd he was invisible. "This place is a madhouse."

"I like it, though. I like the energy." Tomas let his eyes drift over the crowd. "But I want a beer." He closed his eyes, breathed in deeply, and whispered, "I want a beer."

A waitress delivering beers to a nearby table appeared at his elbow and put a bottle before him. Behind her, the waiting table cried out in protest, demanding she bring them their drinks, but she ignored them and waited at Tomas's shoulder. He told her he wanted two more, which she promptly placed on the table. He thanked her, his eyes and voice soft, and she smiled. Stepping back into the crowd, she turned to the enraged table behind her and yelled something about shutting their cake holes. Tomas passed the bottles to his wide-eyed friends.

"What? Don't you want another beer?"

"Dude, how did you do that?"

"Do what?" Tomas asked. "I ordered us beer. She's a waitress. It's her job."

Aricelli stared at him. "You didn't order a beer from her. You just said 'I want a beer' and she brought it to you."

"I asked her for it." He looked at his friends as if they had lost their minds. "She came by, I ordered three beers and she brought them." Aricelli and Louis shook their heads. "You guys, she even told us her name. It's Tammi, remember? Tammi with an *i*?" His friends continued to stare at him, shaking their heads. "Are you all playing with me?"

Louis took a drink and grinned at Tomas. "Dude, I think you might have picked up a few new skills here."

. . . .

They followed a sky-blue Nova down the highway. Adlai stayed several car lengths behind and lost sight of the car more than once.

"Aren't you worried we're going to lose him?"

He shook his head. "Nah. I know where he's going."

Since meeting Adlai, Stell felt like a thirsty plant suddenly hammered by a thunderstorm. She knew she would have to address what was happening with Tomas, but for now she was content to be carried along. He had his "stuff" to keep him busy; now she had her own.

They arrived in another run-down neighborhood, this one lined with dilapidated row houses. Porches hung askew and windows were boarded up on many of the facades. The Nova pulled into a narrow driveway next to a shabby, yellow, brick house. As they drove past, Stell saw the driver enter the house with a brown paper bag crumpled under his arm. They circled the block, pulling into the alley behind the house, and Adlai shut off the bike.

"I guess we should have talked about this at the diner. I'm a pretty good judge of character but I want to hear it from you first."

"What do you want to hear?"

"That you understand what we're going in here to do. That you're ready to do it."

A tremor of fear ran through her. Was this another thing everyone but she understood? Was there some sign she was unable to read? She didn't want Adlai to look at her with the same disdain she had come to fear from Tomas. "Tell me what you want me to do. I'll do it."

His eyes were cold but not impatient. "There are four people in that house. Maybe more. There are guns and a lot of drugs. Nobody is going to be calm. You understand?"

"Tweakers. Like Esai." She could still taste the bitter nervousness of his blood.

He nodded. "That's right. Just like Esai although even more wound up. We're going in there and we're gonna kill them all."

Stell blinked at him, not trusting her dawning revelation. "Feeding?"

"No. Not feeding. Not *r 'acul*. We're going to kill them all. Then we're going to blow up the house. Then we're going to ride away. If you don't want to go in, stay on the bike and wait for me, but I could use your help."

Breath caught in Stell's throat. Power glowed from Adlai's skin, the smell of strength and fearlessness. That he could want her help, that he could look at her and think she had the skills to help him in his dangerous work sent a thrill through her. She nodded, unable to speak, fearing not for her own safety, only that she might disappoint him.

They climbed off the bike and slipped into the backyard. Adlai's voice was low and steady. "We'll go in quiet. Be as still as you can. Wait until we're all the way into the kitchen for my sign. When you go, go like hell. Don't wait to see what they're going to do. Just turn it on and go. And Stell?" She stared at him, riveted. "Don't get shot."

"How do I avoid that?"

"If you see a gun, move."

"What?" She grabbed his arm, but he held his hands up before her face. Looking into his eyes, she felt a calm settle over her. His palms touched in a prayer position and he lowered them between them. As his hands dropped, so did her tension until her breath was as calm as a sleeping child. He nodded and then headed up the back steps.

The crowd at McGympsies had gotten thinner but drunker, and Tomas and his friends were feeling no pain. The conversation had turned silly and all three were laughing. Tammi-with-an-*i* became a faithful source of beer for the three, much to the displeasure of many of the surrounding tables. Especially enraged were the four people who had lost the first round Tomas had ordered up. The two large, muscular young men accompanying a buxom pair of girls had spent the evening glaring at Tomas and, as alcohol gave them volume, getting more creative in their insults. The three took little notice of them, jokingly labeling them Thing One and Thing Two and Miss Thing One and Miss Thing Two.

After a funny story, Tomas slipped off his barstool and embraced his much-missed cousin. Over backslapping and 'I love you, man,' Tomas overheard Thing One shout out.

"Get a room, faggots."

Louis laughed, climbing back onto his chair, but Tomas mouthed 'Watch this' and turned to the table behind him to stand behind the two Miss Things.

"How ya doing?" He spoke to the men, his hands resting on their dates' shoulders.

Thing Two spoke first. "We'd be doing a lot better if we didn't have to sit so close to a faggot like you."

Tomas peered down at Miss Thing One, or more specifically, into her impressive cleavage. "Do you think I'm a faggot?" She didn't answer, only laughed behind her hand. "Because I'm not." He began to caress her neck. Thing One rose, knocking back his chair.

"You want to start something, faggot?"

Tomas glanced over at his friends. Aricelli seemed a little worried but Louis was laughing. "Um, yeah, I do. Let me tell you what we're gonna do. All of us." Tomas blew out a deep breath and saw

Thing One and Thing Two relax. Both men followed his hands as he slipped them into the necklines of their dates. His left hand cupped the heavy breast of Miss Thing One. His fingers pinched the nipple of Miss Thing Two. Both girls had their eyes closed, relaxed as he groped them. Tomas's voice was low but clear.

"I'm going to take your women home with me and I'm going to fuck them. And you're fine with that." The men nodded, unconcerned. "But that's not all. You, Thing One, you're going to go with my friend, Aricelli, there."

Thing One nodded and Aricelli laughed and mouthed the word *thanks*.

"And you, Thing Two, you are especially lucky. You're going to go with my friend Louis and you're going to enjoy yourself big time."

Louis looked over the muscular man before him and laughed. "Double thanks, dude." Thing Two smiled, glad to be the lucky one.

"And so, throw down some money for our tabs, and let's get out of here."

The seven new friends stepped out of the bar into the cold night, four of them relaxed, two of them surprised and one of them moving as if in a dream. Making their way down the sidewalk, Thing Two wrapped his arms around Louis, who tried hard not to laugh as he caught the sleepy eye of his cousin.

"Are you kidding me? You can do this? This is what they train you for?"

Tomas said nothing. Louis's words had become distorted and he was having trouble remembering exactly what was going on. It was as if he were flickering in and out of numerous dreams, a sensation he had felt before in the training rooms of the Council. Miss Thing Two raised her mouth to his ear and began to suck on his earlobe. He turned and kissed her, feeling her tongue move hungrily within his mouth. Her name was Theresa. He could hear it in her heartbeat. She tilted her head back and opened her eyes, looking directly into his.

A bolt of pain shot down his legs. When her eyes met his, a floodgate of sensation burst and all she was came pouring into him. Like a wave, he knew her, her name, her family, the scar on her knee, the cysts on her ovary, the humiliations of ninth grade, the money she stole from her father, the desire she felt for her friend's boyfriend. All this and more came shrieking out of her glassy eyes into his brain like a pack of howler monkeys, throwing him back from her.

He staggered out of her grip, pushing the other girl away as well. Then, as if a film were being wiped away, the night came back into sharp focus. He could feel the cold wind on his face, the sour beer in his stomach, and before he had time to react, the sharp pain of Thing Two's fist connecting on his cheekbone.

Blood burst from his skin as he collapsed onto the sidewalk, Thing Two's rage-distorted face hovering over him, flailing fists pummeling his ribs and face. He covered his body as best he could as pandemonium broke out around him.

Aricelli reeled in shock after Thing One slapped her hard across the face, pushing her out of the way to get to Louis, who fought Thing Two. The Miss Things only added to the chaos, screaming and kicking at anything before them, even their own boyfriends who tussled on the ground. Aricelli recovered, her eyes filled with tears at the still-stinging sensation on her face, but she found Thing One easily, swinging a backhand that lifted him off his feet, off of Louis and Tomas, and into the gutter.

Louis finally got purchase on Thing Two, whose rage had given him super strength. A crushing punch to the nose and a kick to the side of the head toppled the larger man, giving Louis the chance to pull Tomas up by the armpits. The Miss Things screamed and kicked at him until Aricelli grabbed them both by the hair and slammed their heads together.

Stunned, injured but engorged with fury, the Thing party struggled to their collective feet. Louis and Aricelli grabbed Tomas and began to run as fast as they could down the sidewalk, blood from Tomas's face cut running freely. Aricelli had the presence of mind to hail a cab. Pulling Tomas in between her and Louis, she screamed at the startled cabbie to drive. They pulled into traffic, passing Thing One, who stood howling on the corner.

"Someone want to tell me where we're going?" The cabbie looked at his bloody party.

"Away from here. Just keep driving." Louis could hear the hysteria in his voice and struggled to calm down. Aricelli panted, her heart hammering, and between them Tomas made a choking sound. Louis pulled his head back, afraid he was injured, but saw Tomas was laughing. Not just laughing but guffawing. Blood covered the lower half of his face and an ugly welt rose on his cheekbone but his mouth split into a wide, crazy smile.

"Fuck you, Tomas. You almost got us killed."

Aricelli echoed the sentiment, watching the night fly by out the cab window. "He slapped me so hard my teeth almost came out. Do I look like a sidewalk brawler?"

Tomas looked around, laughter still rolling out in great, wracking waves. He'd never felt pain like he felt in his body at that moment but he'd never felt so alive. He caught Louis's eye and, helpless against the flood of adrenaline, Louis began to laugh too. They collapsed against each other, holding their bruised bodies, until they heard Aricelli snicker as well.

"Fuck you both." Then she too let loose a snort of laughter that caused all three to huddle together, helpless in their glee. The cabbie drove on, certain he'd eventually learn his destination.

"Give me two shots of Jack with two shots back. And two shots to wash them down." Adlai leaned on the bar. Stell hovered beside him, gripping the bar and bouncing on the balls of her feet. Her teeth chattered and when she didn't have her eyes squeezed shut tight, her pupils shone black and huge. The bartender lined up six shots between them. They downed the first pair in unison, Stell's trembling fingers dropping the glass on the bar. She winced at the heat in her throat. The bartender placed a wet towel before her.

"Look at me." Adlai took the towel and dabbed at her face. She felt his fingers tremble.

"What's on me?"

"What do you think?" After Adlai wiped his own face as well, the towel was streaked with black and red and the bartender discreetly dropped it behind the bar. Despite his casual stance, Stell could feel the energy crackling off of Adlai. He looked into her eyes and Stell couldn't read what she saw there. Was he angry with her? Had she done all right?

"I didn't know you could shimmer. You didn't even know you could do it, did you?" She shook her head. Adlai settled onto the barstool and pushed another shot in front of her. "Tell me what you saw, what you think happened."

Stell perched on the stool beside him, her spine so tense she felt she was levitating above it. She began to speak, her sentences merely fragments as the memory coalesced in her mind. She spoke of their entrance into the stinking house, the bitter smell of chemicals in the air. She had seen two men in the kitchen, where they entered and could see two more in the adjoining dining room. She could feel more but couldn't tell where they were. Adlai nodded at her recollection. There had been a total of seven people in the house, five men and two women.

She'd slipped into the room as silently as he had, so silently even the keyed-up addicts hadn't sensed their presence. When she'd moved to surround the men, she'd been so utterly still, even he, an experienced shimmerer, had had to blink to keep sight of her. If the common had noticed her she would have seemed to them to be disappearing and reappearing in spots across the room. It was clear in her retelling she had no knowledge of her ability.

She talked of the moment the killing broke out. A third man had walked into the room on Stell's side, had spotted her and called out, sparking action. She'd twisted the first man's head quickly, snapping his neck, and shoved the body into the other man, blocking his weapon. She recalled tearing at the other man but not how she'd reached him. She'd been aware of gunfire and a third and perhaps a fourth man in her killing hands. She'd heard nothing but from the rawness of her throat she suspected she'd been screaming. The whole episode, which seemed both instantaneous and eternal, had lasted less than seven minutes.

She remembered Adlai pulling her up by her waistband and tossing her toward the door. There was blood and water and wreckage everywhere. She recalled Adlai pulling something out of his pocket and placing it on the burner of the gas stove and turning the knob, then they were on the bike. When the explosion occurred, it was no more than a distant pop in Stell's blood-hammered ears.

Adlai pushed the third and final shot before her and she drank it as she had the first two. The bartender didn't wait for instructions. He refilled the six shot glasses. Stell opened her eyes wide, noticing the bartender for the first time.

"Did you see that guy?" Her voice was a wondrous whisper. "He's Nahan."

This time Adlai did laugh at her. "Look around you, sweetheart."

She was surrounded by Nahan. She hadn't even noticed she was in a bar, much less surrounded by Nahan men and women of varying ages. There were common among them as well but they were the minority. There was a pool table being used by two Nahan women and a heated darts tournament going on in the corner. In a booth by the restrooms, a heavily made-up common woman flirted with two Nahan men. As she watched, three common skinheads entered the bar, thought better of it, and headed back onto the street.

"Never been in a bar before?"

"Not like this. Not with so many Nahan."

Adlai pushed the next set of shots before her. "Couldn't take you anywhere else. We were pretty conspicuous on the street." He gestured to the dark stains on his dark shirt. "If I had taken you to a common bar, you would have started a riot."

"What do you mean?" She was no longer afraid to ask Adlai anything.

"I mean you're humming like a top. We both are. Have you ever been around the common like this?" Stell shook her head. "Well, try to avoid it. Let's just say it awakens their herding instinct."

"You mean their stampeding instinct." The bartender set two beers before them. "From Frances and the girls. They said you look like you could use them." Adlai tipped his beer in the direction of the pool table, where three Nahan women tipped their own bottles back at them. Stell peered over Adlai's shoulder at the group.

"Who are they? Friends of yours?"

"I guess you could call them coworkers. Let's just say they are people devoid of a herding instinct of their own." The bartender laughed and went back to wiping up the bar.

. . . .

"Looks like we're bunking together tonight, gorgeous."

Aricelli stepped from the bathroom, brushing her teeth, and rolled her eyes. She had scrubbed the night's filth from her face and even in the dim light, Louis could see the traces of a welt on her cheek, where she'd been struck. They had carried Tomas up to the room they were sharing and he now lay diagonally across one of the beds, his arm thrown over his eyes, his mouth open in sleep. Louis began removing his cousin's shoes.

"I don't think you need to be so gentle. He's not going to wake up."

Louis put Tomas's leg down softly onto the bed and began working on the second set of laces. Aricelli was right, of course; a marching band wouldn't have awakened him now. Maybe it was the angry bruise on his jaw or the dark circles under his eyes or the hollows of his cheeks, but there was a brittleness about Tomas now. Louis felt compelled to show him even a small tenderness.

"I want the side closest to the bathroom." Aricelli went back into the bathroom and closed the door, cutting out the only light in the room. In the dim glow of the city below them, Louis sat on the edge of the bed watching Tomas sleep, wondering what he dreamt about.

· ·

"Tell me your last name." Adlai pushed a beer before her.

"I don't have one."

"What?" His beer hung forgotten from his fingertips. "What's your mom's?"

"She won't tell me."

"She won't tell you?"

"She never told me a lot of things. Nobody would. Like who my father is. I never met him. I don't know his name either." She worried her lip. "Nobody ever spoke of him. I wasn't even allowed to ask about him, but it was always like . . ."

"Like?" He touched her softly shoulder to shoulder.

Stell shook her head, unwilling to discuss that painful memory. "You're the only other person I've ever heard of who didn't grow up with two parents together. I thought I was the only person in the world like that."

"Well we're a pair then, aren't we? A couple of lonely *acul 'ads.*"

"Killers?" Stell asked. She'd only heard the word used in Uncle Rom's sermons and then only as a terrible sin. "That's your title, *acul 'ad?*"

"My title?" He snorted. "More like a category, I'd say."

"Do you think I'm *acul 'ad?*"

Adlai cocked his head. "Well, let's look at this. Why haven't you asked why we killed those people? Or who they were? Or why they had to die? Aren't you curious?" Stell thought for a moment then shook her head. Adlai laughed. "See? I'm feeling pretty good about you not needing a career counselor."

"I didn't think about it. Maybe I'm tired of thinking, of trying to figure out everything that everybody else seems to know." She couldn't tell if he was laughing at her. "I trusted you. You said to do it so I did it. Is that wrong?"

His placed a warm hand on her thigh. "No, that wasn't wrong. And to tell you the truth, I don't care who they were either. It was just business and not everyone can do it."

"You can."

He nodded. "So can you, apparently."

"Does it bother you?"

He examined her face. "Why? Does it bother you?"

"No." She leaned in close, feeling like this should be a secret. "My mother said it would but it doesn't. It hasn't yet."

Whatever he was looking for in her expression, he nodded as if he'd found it. "Yeah, we don't always feel things the same way everyone else does, you know what I mean? That's why the Council finds us so useful—we can do what the others can't, what the others won't. They get to keep their hands clean; we get to get high. And, as *acul 'ads*, we smooth over a lot of life's little bumps."

"I thought the Storytellers smoothed over life's bumps."

He eyed her over his beer. "Who do you think we work for?"

Chapter Six:
DA SUTE

....

Da Sute: literally *the ache*; growing pains; the reality of the
path of adulthood

Sylva blew into her tea, watching through the steam as Coordinator
Vartan grilled Desara's driver, Carlson. The Kott man flushed and
stammered, explaining his attempts to find the young apprentice.
He'd phoned the hotel repeatedly, then pounded on the door, and
then finally bribed a housekeeper to let him into the empty room.

As a Storyteller-in-training, Tomas was discouraged from carrying any sort of electronic device, including a cell phone, to avoid
the exhaustion their interference could cause while meditating.
This meant that the newest investment of the Council was out in
the wind with his ex-True Family girlfriend. To say that Mr. Vartan
was displeased was an understatement.

Vartan spoke in a low, even tone that told everyone he was out of patience. "How is it we have set out every security protocol in existence on this complex and nobody thought to watch the little bastard at his hotel?" He glared around the table, resting his gaze on a young assistant who reddened under his stare.

"Well, sir, we had heard that Adlai was on it. He was with the girl and the emphasis seemed to be on keeping her out of trouble so we just thought—"

"Maybe he just needed a break." Sylva said, not impressed with Vartan's bullying. "We discussed the possibility we were working him too hard. It's too early to panic. He's young."

Dalle nodded. "I agree. It's too soon to start thinking our boy has run off. Maybe he was with the girl and they spotted the True Family and decided to hide."

"You think they can hide themselves better than we can?" Vartan's face was a deep red.

"I didn't say they could; they might just think they can."

Vartan rocked on his heels, grasping the table in a white-knuckle grip. "Where the hell is Adlai? Does anyone know how to reach him?"

"I had him out on a job," Lucien said. "The Fuentes situation. I haven't seen anything on the news yet but Adlai tends to get his work done early. If he succeeded in his errand, he'll check in. And if he's been entrusted with the girl, I don't think any of us need doubt he'll know where she is. Adlai is nothing if not thorough."

Heads nodded and Vartan began to relax until Dalle spoke up. "There is always the possibility that Desara was not with his girl last night." All eyes fell upon him and he held up his hands in surrender. "While he's not everyone's cup of tea, Adlai has his charms and all of us working with Desara have felt the strain between him and the girl since his training began."

Vartan fell back into his chair and stared up at the ceiling for several minutes. With a deep breath, he motioned to the assistant.

"Go out to Communication; tell them to start monitoring police bands and newswires for the Fuentes situation. Also feel out the True Family. Tell everyone to watch for Anton Adlai. If anyone sees him, tell him to get his ass in here pronto and bring Desara and the girl in with him. Go." The assistants fled the room. "Worst case scenario. What do we do?"

Dalle spoke first. "It's too early to worry about that yet."

"It's not your call to worry about timing!" Vartan slammed his hands down on the table. Sylva could see the effort it took to cool his temper. The ice in Dalle's stare must have helped because he lowered his tone. "With respect, I'm the one coordinating this complex and it's my ass if something happens to another apprentice. Maybe I'm overreacting but we don't need another Hess on our hands. Do we have a plan?"

The Storytellers passed hooded glances. Finally, Vet spoke up, her voice crackling with lack of use. She had been pulled out of a two-day deep meditation for this meeting.

"If something has gone wrong, we'll have to perform a full assessment on his mental state. We all remember how violent that can be. Depending on his level of mental dissonance, we can either work to reverse any damage or, worse case scenario, we remove him from the complex into full-time care."

Vartan rubbed his eyes. "What a shit storm. Not placing any blame but do we have any idea why our last two viable candidates for Storyteller have gone nuts?"

Sylva placed a hand on Lucien's arm, holding the Storyteller back. "Please mind your choice of words, Mr. Vartan." She sweetened her rebuke with the respectful address. As meditation teacher and adviser to the Storytellers, she didn't need to address anyone by their title but Sylva felt the anger in the room. "It hasn't been twenty-four hours. Let's give him a chance to resurface on his own before we assume the worst."

"Forgive me if I don't share your optimism. As Coordinator of this complex, assuming the worst is my job. May I remind you"— A tap at the door interrupted Vartan and he snapped at the young woman peering through the doorway. "What is it, Fiona?"

"It's Desara. He's calling from the Drake Hotel. He says he needs a ride."

Mentor Sylva cupped her hands over her face to hold back a laugh as the Storytellers collapsed back in their chairs. Vartan turned to Fiona, his voice wry. "Put him on speakerphone."

. . . .

Tomas paled as he listened. Several times he pulled the phone away from his ear and Louis could hear the angry tones coming through the handset. The conversation was mostly one-sided, with only an occasional "Yes, sir" or "No, sir" from Tomas. After a lengthy period in which Louis could make out several voices talking at once on the other end, Tomas wrapped up the call with a promise to meet the car in front of the hotel.

"How much trouble are you in?"

"I would guess a truckload, judging from the fact that it felt like every member of the Council within five hundred miles was screaming at me. I think even the janitor yelled at me."

"For staying out all night? Seems a little extreme. What did Stell say?"

Tomas busied himself tying his shoes. "She didn't say anything because apparently she never came back to the hotel last night." Louis started to speak but Tomas held up his hand. They heard the shower shut off in the bathroom. "Don't tell Aricelli any of this, especially about Stell. I just, you know, I can only deal with one thing at a time. Right now I have to put on my stainless steel underwear and prepare to get my ass torn by my mentor."

"For what it's worth, man, it was really good seeing you again."

Stell rested her head on Adlai's shoulder as the bike tore down the highway. The sun was rising, burning off the remnants of fog that had shrouded the city. Fatigue dragged at her body, making her eyes burn and her mind slow. All she wanted right now was to climb into bed and sleep. Tomas would probably be gone by the time she returned and the thought made her cling more tightly to Adlai. She missed feeling a body in her arms; she missed Tomas, even when he lay beside her. She was too tired for such thoughts and closed her eyes to let the rhythm of the bike lull her into a light sleep.

She came awake when Adlai pulled off the highway into an unfamiliar part of the city. They pulled onto a side street and came to a security gate where a striped barrier bar blocked their way and an armed security guard stepped out of the booth to question them. Adlai took off his glasses and the guard waved them on. They were in the parking lot of an enormous industrial complex, rectangular buildings abutting one another like oversized children's blocks. Adlai steered the bike around speed bumps and cargo platforms, stopping outside a loading bay marked PITTINGER RESEARCH FACILITY: STOCK LOADING. AUTHORIZED PERSONNEL ONLY.

"Let's go."

Stell climbed off and followed him up the metal stairs into the open bay. Two armed Nahan security guards stepped forward but Adlai never slowed down. He simply nodded at the two men and the guards let them pass.

"Where are we? Is this another errand?"

"You haven't been here yet? I thought you would have polished your boyfriend's apple at least once before you dropped him off."

"This is the Council?" She was running to keep up with him.

"This is one of their complexes. They have dozens of these all over the world, but this is one of the biggest; built special for the

Storytellers." At a set of heavy steel doors, Adlai pressed his thumb onto a scanner. After four metallic clicks, he pushed open the doors and led Stell into the complex.

The thick carpet muffled their footsteps and Stell marveled at the silence of the place. There was none of that annoying hum that seemed to emanate off of every surface in the common world. No TVs, no radios, no appliances or trucks to whine and grind. Her eyes scanned every door, every sign as she ran along behind Adlai.

As they passed one open door, a young woman called out. "Anton! Mr. Adlai, wait!" Adlai stopped so quickly Stell nearly barreled into him. "Mr. Vartan has been looking for you. Emergency."

"It's always an emergency with Vartan. I'll meet him in the conference room."

They were at the door before she could stop them. Adlai and Stell stepped into the large conference room, interrupting what was clearly a very unpleasant meeting for Tomas.

A man standing at the table spun on the newcomers. "Adlai. You've got the girl. Good. Get your ass in here and tell her to sit down and keep her mouth shut. Her turn is next."

Adlai leaned against the doorframe. "Tell her yourself, Vartan. She's right here."

Vartan smiled a saccharine smile. "Let me rephrase that. Please, have a seat."

A man at the table spoke softly to Tomas. "I believe the point has been driven home. Desara, do you understand how important it is to us that you remain in touch at all times, especially now that your training has made you volatile and perhaps vulnerable?"

"Yes, Dalle." Tomas nodded. "I understand."

Stell ached at the exhaustion in his face. His skin was so dry and his lips were cracked. It even looked as if he had some sort of bruise on his cheek. Anger welled up inside of her as she considered the treatment he had been receiving in this place. She wanted to reach across the corner of the large table that separated them, but Tomas wouldn't look in her direction. He also didn't look up as Vartan began to wrap things up.

"Okay, crisis averted. This time. So if we're all on the same page now, let's get back to business. Desara, I believe you're scheduled to work with Mr. Dalle this morning. We'll let you get back to that while Mr. Lucien, Adlai, and I discuss—"

"I want a day off." Tomas said.

"I beg your pardon? You just had your vacation and it—"

Tomas spoke in an eerie impersonation of Vartan. "Let me rephrase that. I am taking a day off. I'm taking a day off with Stell. If she still wants to go."

Vartan visibly struggled to spit out the words. "Adlai may have plans for your friend."

Adlai shook his head. "Nothing that can't wait a day or two."

"Very well then, Resources mentioned something about your apartment being ready this week. Why don't you talk to Fiona about hurrying it along?" He bared his teeth in a bad impression of a smile. "We'll see if we can accommodate your refined tastes."

"All it needs is a door," Tomas said. Stell felt proud of the way he held Vartan's gaze. "And a lock."

Vartan looked away first, closing his notebook and the meeting. Adlai held the door for him. The two women filed out behind him; one of them winked at Tomas. The two other men at the table followed. The one who had spoken earlier, Dalle, paused before Tomas. He stared for a moment and then brought his thumb up to stroke softly across the bruise on Tomas's cheek. It looked oddly intimate to Stell but Tomas allowed it. The man started to say something but instead just chuckled and left the room.

When the conference room door closed, Stell threw her arms around Tomas's neck, pushing him up against the table. He struggled to keep his balance as he buried his face in the warmth of her neck. They spoke over each other.

"I'm so sorry, Stell."

"I'm so happy, Tomas."

"I've been such a dick to you since we've been here. I've just pushed you away and I never even asked them to make any kind of concessions for you." Stell tried to shush him but he continued. "All I could think about was the training, becoming one of these people that the Council fawns over and fears so much. I wanted to be like them but after this morning when I heard no one could find you I started thinking about the Family and if they had come for you and what I would do if they took you." He pulled her tight against him.

"Nobody's going to take me, Tomas. I would kill them if they tried."

Tomas leaned back to look at her. "You'd be in the right company to do it. I hear Anton Adlai is a real badass."

"He's taught me a lot." Stell shifted under his gaze.

"I guess you're supposed to stick with him now?"

Stell pulled his face back down into her neck and squeezed him tightly. "I don't care what I'm supposed to do. Have I ever?" Tomas laughed and his breath tickled her skin. "Do we really have our own apartment?" Stell pressed her body against his, her intentions clear. He bit down on the tender skin of her throat.

"Let's go."

. . . .

After two hours and a few persuasive phone calls from Fiona, Tomas and Stell had an apartment with a door that locked, utilities, and best of all, a freshly made bed. Vartan's assistant had promised them their belongings would be moved, furnishings and groceries delivered, and she assured them with a smile that nothing would arrive for several hours.

Those hours were spent in a succession of lovemaking, feeding, and sleeping; neither speaking any more than heated suggestions or cries of delight.

The howling of the wind woke Tomas from a light sleep and he pulled Stell tight into his chest. She murmured, wrapping her legs around his and sliding her hand up his chest. He breathed in the smell of her.

"Hey, you."

"Hey, you, too." She kissed him, then traced the planes of his face with her fingers. He closed his eyes and tasted the tips of her fingers as they passed over his lips.

"I've missed you so much, Stell. I didn't even realize how much until I saw you this morning. This place, these Storytellers, it's like they're trying to tear everything about me apart to rebuild me in their image."

"Is it working?"

He sighed, letting her fingers trace his eyebrows. "I don't know. I feel different."

"You do feel different." Tomas opened his eyes at the odd tone in her voice. "I mean, your body feels different. It smells different." She pulled the covers back and let her eyes roam over his chest and stomach. "It's like there's this electricity that burns just on the surface of your skin, like the way the forest smells after lightning hits a tree." Tomas waited to hear more as Stell dipped her head to run her tongue along his collarbone. "I like it."

He closed his eyes, relieved. He did feel different. The training, the meditations, while exhausting, had strengthened his body, although his discipline still needed some work. "I really screwed up last night when I was out with Louis and Aricelli." He told her about his encounter with the Things. "They didn't deserve to be treated like that. And that poor waitress, Tammi-with-an-*i*, she could have lost her job catering to me like that."

"I think you worry too much about it." Stell dragged her fingernails down his stomach, making goose bumps rise. "It's not like you killed them, right? That's the big worry."

"It's just that now they're going to wonder how they wound up out there with us, if we drugged them or something. They could get nosy, start some kind of investigation. You never know with the common. They can be weirdly persistent about things."

"They don't even know we exist. They think we're vampires."

Tomas laughed and pinched her chin between his thumb and forefinger. "Vampires, huh? You mean you've never heard of the Brady Bunch but you know about vampires?"

"I saw it in a movie. Adlai told me about it."

"Anton Adlai." Tomas pushed Stell's hair back and looked into her eyes. "It looks like the Council is going to have you two working together a lot."

Stell rolled her eyes. "How would I know? I just get 'tell the girl this, tell the girl that.'"

"Adlai doesn't talk to you like that though, does he?" Stell turned her head from the question. "Tell me about him."

Stell sighed. "Why?"

He didn't know why. The last thing he wanted to think of was the burly Anton Adlai putting his hands on Stell and yet the thought wouldn't leave him. Plus, and this had been weighing heavily on his mind of late, it seemed all the Storytellers were unpaired. They lived in their own worlds, in the midst of the Nahan and yet apart. Tomas hadn't yet worked up the courage to ask about their personal lives. Somehow casual sex chat seemed out of place in the demanding hallways of the Council but he needed to know if his path as a Storyteller was one he would always have to walk alone.

Stell pulled him from his reverie in his favorite way, by sliding her hands along his body. "I don't want to think about anyone but you. I have all the days in the world to think about everybody else, but I have this night with you and you are the only one in the bed with me." She narrowed her eyes with playful menace. "Understand?"

"Yes, ma'am." Tomas let his mind and his body wander to far more pleasant lands.

. . . .

Later that evening, furniture arrived along with their luggage from the hotel and a small selection of groceries. Tomas hurried the assistants out of the apartment as quickly as possible, prompted by Stell's giggles and sighs where she sprawled in the off-limits bedroom. At midnight he declared the apartment closed to all workers and spent the night wrapped in Stell's arms. In less than twenty-four hours since leaving the complex he felt rejuvenated, as if he had been gone a month. Back at the complex the next morning, it took five words from Vartan to erase any trace of his well-being.

"You're on a funeral chain."

. . . .

"Nervous, Desara?"

"A little, sir."

"You'll be fine." Vartan wrote out a series of directions and handed them across the desk. Tomas didn't move to take them. "Something wrong?"

"It's just that, sir, if you were called to the funeral chain, why aren't you going? Why am I? And why are you telling me where to go?"

Vartan cleared his throat. "You don't need to worry about that, son."

"Actually, sir, I do." Tomas looked at the paper as if it might bite him. "If there is anything inappropriate about this chain, if there is some sort of disrespect and I take part in it . . ." Vartan could hear the fear in the boy's voice. He stepped around the desk and stood before Tomas, who stepped back sharply, making no attempt to hide his discomfort.

"You're right. You deserve an explanation. We are not in the habit of disrespecting the dead here. Believe it or not, we are well aware of what the abominations are. What we all have to understand is that times have changed."

"But the funeral chain, sir, that can't change. It can't . . ." Tomas clasped his hands behind him. "The dead have to be alone. Among strangers. Seven times, sir. They have to move seven times before the fire. And move with strangers—"

Vartan held out his hand to stop him. "Our population centers are too dense to ask just anyone to perform the final rites of release. I mean, it just isn't feasible to expect people to be able to safely and legally burn a fire hot enough, especially those of us who live in the cities. So we sent out word among all the communities within a few hundred miles that, at the fifth exchange, when the fifth knot is tied, we are to be called and we will send someone out to pick up the chain. You'll tie the sixth knot and take the box to the final location for the fire."

Tomas thought this over then shook his head. "But that means you know where the final fire is. You know where everyone goes. You're not a stranger to the dead. The dead have to be with strangers. You made their plans and if I'm driving—"

"No, Desara. Only you'll know. It's just as if the chain found you naturally. On this sheet of paper are four locations within one hundred miles that are capable of the fire we need. You pick one, either by location or randomly, it doesn't matter. I'll never know which one you picked and the chain will be intact. Nobody on the other end is expecting you."

"But my errand." According to Nahan Tradition, the dead had to be seven times removed from their family. Those transporting the dead had to have an errand. It was considered vulgar, to say nothing of bad luck, to transport the dead in an idle vehicle.

"I have four packages to be delivered, one for each town on the list. Drop one package off in person; that's your errand. Drop the others in the mail. Nobody will know anything about their journey. Does this satisfy you?"

Tomas wiped his damp palms on his jeans, then nodded and took the paper. Vartan clapped him on the shoulder and settled back into his desk chair. Once the door closed, he sank back into the soft leather. His hands trembled as he drummed his fingers on the desk, trying to calm his own heartbeat.

He knew the trepidation Desara felt. No matter how many times they did this, the fear didn't pass. He and his people had worked and reworked a plan that would keep the strict tradition of the funeral chain without alerting the common municipalities to what were blatant health and safety violations. Nobody on the Council gave half a rat's ass about the health code, but the thought of a funeral chain being broken by some nosy county employee was too disastrous to even consider. Were the concessions enough to completely avoid any disrespect or abomination? Vartan sure as hell hoped so.

From the farmers to the Storytellers to the coordinators of the Council, even the *acul 'ad*, all of them had one thing in common. Few of them feared their own death, but all Nahan feared their dead.

. . . .

Tomas heard the TV as he unlocked the apartment door and called out for Stell. He found her propped up against the headboard, dozing upright, the bed littered with candy wrappers and soda cans. Her eyes flew open as he kneeled on the corner of the bed, leaning across to kiss her. He picked up a handful of cellophane wrappers.

"I see my old Stell is back."

She scooped them up, scrambling across the bed to reach them all. "Oh, Tomas, I'm sorry. I didn't know when you were coming home and I couldn't sleep. I'll throw them away."

He grabbed her arm and brought it to his lips, kissing skin and plastic and chocolate by turns. "Leave them. They're the closest thing we have to leaves and pine needles. Let 'em crackle underneath us." He pulled Stell onto his lap and she wrapped herself around him.

"How was it?" Her eyes were serious. "I know you can't talk about it, but how was it?"

Tomas smiled. "Well, since I can't talk about it, I can't tell you that it was fine. It wasn't nearly as scary as I thought it would be. As a matter of fact, I kind of feel like a grown-up. Now that it's over, that is. I was freaking myself out on the drive but then once I met the fire man, it was okay."

"So you're not hearing anything like a loud wind?"

Even the True Family had their horror stories about the dead and funeral chains. "No wind at all. See?" He tugged on his ear. "Still attached, no howling, no bloody eyes." Stell smiled and rested her head in the crook of his neck. "Your eyes are kind of red though. Why can't you sleep?"

"I thought of my mother," she whispered as Tomas stroked her hair. He kissed her eyes and her cheeks. Over her shoulder, on the nightstand by the bed, he saw the battered copy of *Wuthering Heights* underneath a box of caramel corn. It was the only tangible reminder Stell had of her mother. She kept it hidden in her duffel; he'd never seen her pull it out.

"Can you forgive me for being such a selfish dick?"

Stell shook her head, wrapping her arms more tightly around Tomas's neck. "You're not selfish. I didn't want to say anything because I was afraid if I started thinking about it I wouldn't be able to stop. So I got all this stuff"—she gestured to the empty wrappers—"and kept myself awake all night waiting for you."

Tomas pulled a wrapper out from under his leg and examined it. "Cow Tales?"

"Sounds gross, doesn't it? I had to know what they were." She reached behind them and pulled out an unopened package. She tore at the paper and pulled out the long, skinny caramel column. "They're really good." Tomas bit into it, made a noise of approval, and shoved the whole length of candy into his mouth.

"Hey!" Stell pushed him down onto the bed laughing as he tried to chew the huge wad of caramel and candy cream. Trying not to choke on the sugar, he let her pin him to the bed.

"*Botcha kella oobatchee?*"

"What?"

Tomas swallowed a mouthful of candy. "What the hell are you watching?"

"Oh, the marathon!" Stell spun off Tomas and perched on the edge of the bed. "It's a twenty-four-hour bloodsuckers marathon for Halloween. I've been watching it all night."

"Bloodsuckers marathon?"

Stell nodded, drawn back to the TV. "All night they are showing this program about a vampire who fights crime. He's a detective although he can only work at night because vampires can't go out in the sun. And see her?" She pointed to the screen. "She's common, of course, but I mean she's common on the program too. They say *human* which is insulting. Aren't we all human? Anyway he's in love with her and she's in love with him but for some reason they pretend they're not, but she's a cop and he helps her solve all the crimes."

Tomas smiled, watching Stell's profile glow by the TV light. She pointed at the screen. "She knows he's a vampire and in the last three episodes, the murders were all done by other vampires. And he killed them! The other vampires, I mean. He killed his own kind. Like it was okay. It doesn't make any sense. And there's another thing I don't get." She was talking very quickly, her hands fluttering before her. "She knows he's a vampire. He knows he's a vampire. All these other vampires keep popping up all over this city. The whole show is about vampires but nobody on the show says they believe in them. They treat her like she's crazy and keep saying there's no such thing as vampires but they're on every show. It's nothing but vampires, but everybody is like 'I don't believe in vampires.' And then they get eaten." Stell turned to him, exasperated. "What does it take to convince these people?"

Tomas climbed back against the headboard and patted the bed, inviting Stell to join him. She did, pulling the covers over them both as she crawled. "When Louis and I were little, his mom used to let us watch all the vampire movies. We'd laugh all night, asking those same questions. They have this weird fantasy about vampires and I doubt they could even explain it to themselves. All I know is that some of them take it really seriously. Not just movies and stuff, but buy the whole enchilada. One of these nights, I promise you, we're going to find a group of them and we're going to have some fun."

Stell grinned at the lascivious tone in his voice and kissed him on the neck.

"Now let's watch us some bloodsuckers, huh? Got anymore Cow Tales?"

. . . .

Adlai pulled away from the curb. Desara was back. Stell wouldn't be going anywhere for a while. He could get some sleep and be back before they had pulled themselves from the bed. He had spent the night propped up on a bench across from the apartment building, watching the lights of the television flicker through the window he knew was Stell's. It was still his job to watch her and Adlai never let the job slip.

It was a better gig than most. He liked the girl. She was a real killer, better than she even knew. He had thought more than once how it would feel to take her as a lover. He imagined she'd be fierce and wondered how a kid like Desara could handle it. Then he shook his head. Desara was a Storyteller, or at least an apprentice. They were supposed to withstand an awful lot, *supposed to* being the operative phrase.

Adlai opened the throttle on the bike, cutting through evening traffic. There was a reason he was still in Chicago. There was work in San Francisco and Seattle, but he'd passed on it. He had to stay in Chicago. His best friend needed him. He had let him down before but it wouldn't happen again. The lake air was cold as it whipped over his bare face but Anton Adlai's mind was in the hot, dry nights of his New Mexico youth.

. . . .

He had just hit his twenties and was miserable in the Reaches, outside of Santa Fe. It was 1975, the recession; they were broke and had no other Nahan to turn to for help. The closest Nahan girls were forty miles to the north and Anton had no way of getting there. It would have been a disastrous autumn if Shelan and his parents hadn't stepped off that Greyhound bus. Anton had seen them arrive and was so shocked to see others of his kind he'd walked up to them in front of the drugstore and said *"Nahan da li?"* The woman had smacked him across the face.

"What's the matter with you?" she'd hissed to a shocked Anton. "In public?" He'd only stood there as the parents stomped past him, dragging their son, who looked over his shoulder and laughed. That look, that laugh, had told Anton everything he needed to know about Shelan.

The parents learned quickly just how far out in the Reaches they were. They had come from rural Pennsylvania looking for work, the father having had a falling out with the Council. They expected Shelan to find work of his own but once the boy discovered he had a kindred soul in Anton, work was the last thing on his mind.

The boys were night and day. Where Anton was muscular and brooding, Shelan was wiry and plugged in, his body constantly in motion, his mouth running. He buried Anton in filthy jokes, horror stories, and outrageous lies and Anton ate it up. They spent the winter hitchhiking and jumping freight trains trying to find any town with Nahan girls. They beat up common boys, fed off common girls, stole from common stores, and ran from common cops.

Shelan's parents fought constantly with each other and with anyone who crossed their path. For once, Anton felt lucky to have his parents separated. They only fought on the rare occasion his father ventured out to the desert from Boston. Shelan said repeatedly he wished the Adlais would adopt him since he hated his own family.

"We could tell people we're twins. We're a miracle!" Anton laughed at that and Shelan began weaving the story that would sell the improbable truth.

"Nobody is gonna believe us, brother, trust me on that."

"You have no imagination, Anton."

It was true. He didn't possess a tenth of the Shelan's ability to create stories and read people. Maybe it was from years of tuning out his parents' fights or maybe he just didn't have it in him. He knew his strength was fearlessness. He was strong and he was fast and he was just young enough to think nobody could beat him.

Shelan counted on that confidence, his mouth forever getting them into scrapes they would narrowly escape. Anton didn't care. He felt more alive with Shelan than he had his entire Reaches-imprisoned life. That was why when Shelan suggested they leave New Mexico and head west to the party scene of Hollywood, Anton couldn't pack his bags fast enough. They stole a car and were gone before the sun came up.

For five years, the two tore through the country like a wildfire, stealing anything they wanted, letting women run through their fingers like water. Shelan tried to teach his friend what he called *the fine art of seduction* but it was clear neither young man was interested in pairing up with a Nahan girl anytime soon. The world was theirs for the taking, they thought, and no woman, common or Nahan, was better than the rush of pushing each other to the limit. They skirted the edges of society, running drugs for cash, jacking cars, one time even robbing a bank outside of Cheyenne, Wyoming. Anton had taken a bullet in that caper and, although there was no scar, some nights he could still feel the twinge in his side.

"I know you said you'd take a bullet for me, man, but you didn't have to prove it," Shelan had said. There was nothing in the world they wouldn't do for each other.

Everything changed one summer night on Fremont Street in Las Vegas. The heat was crippling even after the sun had set but Shelan had it in his mind that they needed the kind of trouble only Las Vegas could bring. They went into a dingy casino, Shelan rattling off possibilities ranging from rolling the blackjack dealer to seducing the weary cocktail waitress. Anton let him talk, his eyes scanning the room, ready to follow whatever scheme his buddy came up with, ready to knuckle down any problems that arose. He felt like a fight and knew that with Shelan the odds were good he'd get one.

"Good evening, gentlemen." A well-dressed Nahan man stood before them, looking cool in a natty sport coat despite the heat wafting in from the street. "Nice of you to join us."

Shelan grinned. This wasn't the first time they had run into a mainstream Nahan big shot. From Buffalo to Miami to Seattle they'd been lectured and warned about cleaning up their act, getting a job, "doing their part" for the community of Nahan. No one had gotten through to them yet. Judging from the look on Shelan's face, Anton doubted this greased-up joker would have any better luck.

The man's diamond pinkie ring glinted under the flashing casino lights. "You boys gonna behave yourself in my casino tonight?"

"Oh yes, sir." Shelan purred.

"Sorry to hear that. I was hoping for someone with a little hell in their eyes."

Anton looked to Shelan who nodded. "Go on."

"My name is Mr. Delson. This is my place and there are some people who are not following the fair rules of my establishment. They have abused my generous nature. I am hesitant about involving the law due to the private nature of my ownership. I'm sure you understand. If I had someone I could trust, someone discreet to handle the more difficult aspects of my job, someone of my own kind . . ." The boys grinned. Mr. Delson shook their hands and just like that, they worked for the Council.

Their work took them beyond Las Vegas. They moved money and vehicles up and down the West Coast, learning their way around the hierarchy of the Council. Shelan was amazed at the intricacy and scope of its reach. Nahan business intertwined with mobs—Italian, eastern European, Asian. There were legitimate businesses and enterprises that fell in the gray area in between. There were enormous amounts of money changing hands but that wasn't what kept the two friends working. It was the world the Council opened up. There was no place in the country they couldn't go and be welcomed; no hotel that would turn them away; no car they couldn't get their hands on if they so wished. The Council played to their strengths, relying on Shelan's quick mind and Anton's fast fists.

They were in Reno for Shelan's first *r 'acul*. Despite all the scrapes, all the violence, Anton had taken the heat through the rough stuff. He had killed numerous times, sometimes *r 'acul*, sometimes for work, sometimes just for the hell of it, but Shelan still had never taken a life until a cocktail waitress named Dixi had gotten too coked up. Her heart was beating a little too hard for Shelan to resist as he fed on her and before he realized what he was doing, he felt the explosion of death rock through him. He collapsed on the carpeted floor of the motel room, his head erupting with light. Anton finished off the girl he was working on in the bed beside him, although he had had no intention of killing her before, and joined his friend in the post-kill high.

"We've gotta get down to the casino! I've got to see this!" He dragged Anton to his feet and the two ran across the street to the Big Hat Casino and Gaming Hall. Anton laughed, loving the smell of the night and the exploding stars and was happy to finally see that same ecstasy in his best friend's face. Once they passed through the swinging western doors of Big Hat, however, Shelan's eyes grew enormous. His mouth dropped open and his hands grasped helplessly at the air before him. Anton laughed at what he thought was a joke. Then he saw the tears dripping off his friend's cheeks.

"Shelan, brother, what is it? You okay?"

Shelan's head rolled on his neck as if it were broken, his gaze spinning across the room. His voice was thin and panicked. "What are they?" Anton looked around him, seeing only the usual collection of commons in polyester they had seen at every casino.

"What, man? The slot machines? Is it the lights? Are they too bright?"

Shelan's knees buckled and Anton caught him and took him out onto the street. Once the swinging doors had closed behind them, Shelan began to relax.

"Do you see that every time you kill?" Shelan asked.

"I don't know. What did you see?"

"It was snakes, man. They were covered in snakes."

"Who? The people in the casino?"

Shelan nodded, wiping his eyes. "They weren't real snakes, they were, like, made of smoke or something. And they were everywhere, just reaching for me, reaching for each other. There was all this . . . this desperation and rage and jealousy. Holy shit, I thought my heart was going to explode."

Anton wrapped his arms around his friend, holding him while he shook. "We'll figure this out, brother. We'll talk to somebody. Somebody'll know what to do." Anton continued to rock Shelan, ignoring the cars and noise that surrounded them. They were part of the Council now. As soon as Shelan could walk, they would find a phone and call the office. Someone would clean up the mess in the motel room. They had cleaned up more than their share of other Nahan messes; it wasn't too much to ask. Then they would find somebody on the Council, a doctor or somebody, who could take care of Shelan. Anton rocked his friend, feeling him beginning to relax. They always took care of each other.

Three hours later a Cadillac picked them up and took them to a house out in the desert where the Council conducted its more delicate business. Surrounded by Nahan, Shelan was feeling better but for once Anton did the talking. He explained to their handler what had happened, trying to describe what his friend had experienced. After hearing them out, the handler made a phone call, repeating the story to someone on the other end. He listened, nodding, occasionally looking over at them. He hung up and turned to Shelan.

"You'll stay here tonight. Someone is coming to see you tomorrow. Adlai, the car will take you back to town."

"No way, man." Shelan said. "If I stay, he stays or no deal. I don't give a shit what's wrong with me. If I gotta ditch my brother to fix this, it'll have to kill me first."

The someone coming to see Shelan turned out to be a Storyteller and the one night they were supposed to stay became more than a week. Both young men were interrogated, Shelan more intensely, for hours on end. On the eighth day, which Anton had spent playing pool alone in the billiards room, Shelan strolled in and collapsed on the leather sofa.

"You're not gonna believe this one. They say I'm Storyteller material."

"No shit."

"No shit, brother. They want me to go into training." He smirked but Anton knew his friend well enough to recognize the anxiety.

"And what does that mean?"

"Well I'm hoping it means free booze and lots of pussy but I'm doubting it. They want me to go to Chicago. There's some big complex out there where all kinds of training happens. Feel like taking a drive?"

"Am I invited?"

"Are you kidding me? I told them you're my twin brother. We're the miracle twins."

"Did they buy it?"

Shelan shook his head. "No dice. And do you know what the real bitch of it is? They told me to stop telling people my first name. They want me to go only by my last name. I asked if I could change it to Adlai but he wasn't biting."

Anton flopped on the couch. "My dad should have signed those adoption papers."

"No shit, man. I've spent my whole life trying to forget my parents and now I'm saddled with their fucking name for the rest of my career." He waved a finger in Anton's face. "Let me tell you something, you little bastard, no matter what they say, the first time you call me Hess, I'm kicking your ass."

....

The icy Chicago wind numbed Adlai's face as he sped along. It wouldn't have mattered had it been a soft tropical breeze. He had long ago learned to keep his face a mask. There was a quirk among the *acul 'ad*. While most of them were not gifted in reading people, they were also difficult to read even by Storytellers. He believed it was one of the reasons the two groups were drawn to each other. For the *acul 'ad*, the Storytellers were a link to a world that was essentially closed to them, a translator of the emotional language spoken all around them, which they themselves could rarely speak.

For the Storytellers, the opaque nature of the *acul 'ad* was a blessed oasis of silence from the constant and often painful barrage of emotion that besieged them. Both groups were admired by the Nahan but within that admiration lay traces of fear and mistrust. The Nahan survived by working as a unit, a hive mentality. Anyone within that unit who resided on the fringes could be perceived as a danger, even if it was understood they were a necessity.

Adlai could still see Shelan's face the night they took him down. The Storytellers, the Coordinator, and the Council had pushed him and pushed him even while he begged to be released from his training. Shelan had grown increasingly paranoid the deeper his meditations went and his handlers had decided to keep him in isolation for his own safety. That's what they told Adlai, who'd been forbidden access to his only friend. Adlai hadn't argued. His years in the business had taught him that when you were outnumbered and outgunned, a frontal assault was a mistake. Instead he worked and waited, lurking about the complex in the hope of just laying eyes on Shelan.

That moment had come four years ago at daybreak when Shelan's screams could be heard roaring through the corridors. Adlai raced toward the sound and arrived in time to see Shelan, wrapped in a sheet, strapped head-to-toe on a gurney being rushed toward the loading bay doors. His pitifully thin body bucked and thrashed, straining at the straps; his voice was harsh and raw as he screamed again and again.

"They'll kill us all! They'll kill us all!"

There was one brief moment of silence when Shelan's eyes met Adlai's as the attendants raced the gurney to the waiting van. Adlai stood frozen, helpless to stop the Council from removing his best friend. Once eye contact was broken, Shelan resumed his rant, the attendants continued their race, and the Council went back to the business at hand.

"Mental dissonance." That was the term they had used. "A danger to himself and the Nahan." Adlai had listened to their explanations, had put on a little show of outrage and despair and finally resignation as the Storytellers and the Coordinator explained Shelan's removal into private care. He could feel it—all the while their sad and sympathetic voices rubbed up against him, they were feeling him out, trying to read if he truly bought their bullshit.

Shelan was still alive. He was sure of it. Anton had been biding his time, doing his job. He didn't have Shelan's gift of prescience, but he knew with every fiber in his being that the new *acul 'ad* and her Storyteller boyfriend were the keys to freeing Shelan. He would find him, free him. He couldn't kill the people who had done this—Nahan didn't kill Nahan—but he could bring a world of hurt down upon them.

Sylva sat on the edge of the carpet, watching. Someone unfamiliar with Storytellers might have been bored watching two men sit cross-legged, facing each other, eyes closed for two hours. That someone might also wonder why the temperature in the room had risen several degrees for no apparent reason.

She couldn't explain the physics of it but Sylva knew the amount of energy being spent before her. This was a private guidance meditation, meant only for Storyteller and apprentice. Dalle and Desara had joined in a way she could never understand, Dalle leading the young man with gifts she knew a person had to be born with. Across the carpet, still as a stone, sat Lucien. He didn't join the meditation, only sat by in case something went wrong, something only a Storyteller could see. Sylva's job was to monitor Desara physically, to watch for outward manifestations of distress.

She saw no distress, nothing acute, but she saw plenty going on.

Although their positions never changed, Sylva could almost see the exchange of energy between them. Dalle would twitch and then Desara would flinch. Dalle shifted his shoulders and Desara groaned.

Lucien saw it too. Sylva saw his attention on Desara's finger-tips, which fluttered and twitched where they rested on his knees, and more than once the apprentice's skin broke out in goose bumps despite the rising temperature. She began to worry when she heard the boy's teeth grinding, saw the tendons in his neck pull taut. Dalle reacted as well, leaning forward, still deep in meditation, his breathing speeding up to match the almost-pant of Desara. Lucien got to his knees when she did, both of them prepared to break the meditative bond if necessary but Dalle broke it first.

His hand shot out, gripping Desara's jaw, his thumb pressing hard enough to stop the gruesome grinding sound. The boy's breath was part sob as he bent forward, slipping from Dalle's hand, his head resting on his mentor's crossed legs.

Dalle breathed a long sigh. Sylva saw the fatigue on his face. He nodded to her and, without a word, rose from the floor, letting Desara's head hit the carpet. Lucien rose as well and the two men left the room.

Sylva slid her hand beneath Desara's forehead. Gently she helped him sit up and then cradled his skull as she laid him out on his back. He never opened his eyes but smiled when she brushed the hair from his sweaty forehead.

"Enough for tonight, Desara."

He sighed and turned his cheek toward her palm.

In her office, Dalle and Lucien were muttering to each other, refilling their water glasses from her cooler. "So? What's the verdict?"

"His concentration is not great." Dalle said. "He kept popping in and out."

"That's to be expected in any meditation." Sylva kicked back in her chair, her feet on the desk. "He's still way ahead of the training arc."

"If he'd get his head out of his crotch he might be even further," Dalle said and Lucien snorted. "Good god, for a girl who doesn't talk much, Stell seems to have some extraordinary oral skills." Both men laughed as Sylva looked on confused. "It's just that when Desara gets frustrated, he tries to take his mind to a calm space, but it often goes on without him to a happy place."

Sylva laughed. "At least we know he has some balance in his life."

Dalle looked from one to the other. "He's different now, but . . ."

Lucien nodded. "It's still there? The block?"

Sylva had heard them mention something blocking Desara several times before.

Dalle scratched his forehead. "It's not . . . I don't know what it . . . where it's coming from. The cold. There's something very,

very cold that blows through him. So cold. Tooth-shattering cold. But no matter where I look, I can't see it in him." He folded his hands together. "I want to take him deep. I want him to call out the *Vint.*"

"Already?" Sylva's feet hit the floor. "You can't be serious."

"I can't see any further into him."

"But that doesn't mean you need to break him open. He needs time. He's not strong enough. Not yet."

"Time won't make any difference," Lucien said. "If something is broken in him, if whatever this coldness is comes from something wrong, some fault—"

Sylva kept her voice soft. "This isn't Hess we're talking about."

Lucien lunged toward her, jabbing his finger in her face. "You don't get to talk about Hess. Not now. Not ever. You have no idea what it means to see the *Vint*, to feel it. End of story."

Sylva held her hands up in surrender. She waited until Lucien had stormed out, slamming the door behind him. "I know I'll never see what you see."

"Sylva . . ."

"But I know pain when I see it. And I know a boy when I see one. Why you want to rush into this and drag him through—"

"Because it's already alive within him. Lucien's right. You don't know what it is to feel the *Vint*. And to know it's waiting within someone you've come to care about. We could wait a hundred years. When it comes, it'll still tear him to pieces."

Sylva stared at Lucien's empty chair. "We should send the girl away."

. . . .

Vartan paged Adlai and Stell to the complex early the next morning.

"So where's the job?"

"Indianapolis."

181

"Isn't Daskolias there?"

Vartan shook his head, not looking up from the envelope he was stuffing. "Had to go to Maine or some such place. Someone had a baby, having the naming ceremony. I didn't ask for details. You know Daskolias, she didn't offer any." Adlai said nothing. Behind him, Stell kept sticking her head out into the hallway trying to spot Desara. "Besides, the girl ought to meet some people. You say she's good, I'm prepared to take your word on that."

"And what is the job?"

"The usual, move some money, send a few messages. The Venezuelans are trying to muscle into our man's territory with some high-grade heroin. You might want to bring a few more of those exploding things you use when the house has to go." While drugs themselves were not Nahan business, the people who fought over them fought on Nahan property. Several decades earlier, the Council had seen fit to take a closer hand in who made money where and Adlai had a reputation for dealing with the heated and heavily armed participants.

This job was bogus, Adlai knew it. There was no problem with the Venezuelans in Indianapolis; he'd have heard about it by now. This was just a clumsy way to get Stell away from the complex so they could tweak her boyfriend. Did they think he would have forgotten being sent on a snipe hunt like this just four years ago? Did they think he would forget what was waiting for him when he returned?

None of this showed on his face. He followed Stell out the door and into the hallway. He would help her find her Tomas, give her plenty of time to say goodbye. He held back as they met outside the kitchenette. Adlai noticed the boy had not yet adopted that strange half-walk, half-shuffle of the Storytellers around him, always watching where they were going without looking anyone directly in the face. They must have told the kid he'd be going through some heavy work while she was gone. He was probably relieved Stell would be busy while he was out of contact. Such a lucky coincidence. Well, Adlai figured, if they were being banished, he would put the time to good use and feel the girl out on her willingness to help him.

. . . .

Tomas had been told to expect an especially long and physical session. After yesterday's one-on-one with Dalle, he was glad for the more physical workout with Sylva. He tried to pace himself as he moved into his fourth position in the eighteen-position motion meditation Mentor Sylva had taught him. Similar to *tai chi*, the positions moved from one to another with exquisite slowness. A moderately paced session would last just under three hours; Sylva had told him she expected them to be in motion for over four. He followed her lead, his muscles trembling under the strain, his blood pumping smoothly in time with his calm breath.

A month ago, four positions would have been more than he could handle. It was not only the physical strain—moving in such slow motion required an astonishing amount of strength—the mental focus required to mind the delicate shifting of balance was exhausting. Tomas had stuck with it, his body and mind responding to the gentle discipline of Sylva and now he found that after eighteen positions his mind and body felt clear and clean.

A bead of sweat slid down the inside corner of his eye, down along the curve of his nose to rest, suspended, off the tip of his left nostril. He didn't focus on it nor did he fight to ignore it. The sweat, like the twinge in his right thigh and the tic in his shoulder, spoke to him. They were expressions of the machine of his body.

"When your body needs to be heard, you must let it speak." Sylva had told him early in his training. "These small sounds, these physical glimmers, are no more than the sighs of the flesh, your body dreaming of its freedom."

Tomas began the slow pivot on the ball of his right foot. His right arm made a graceful descent toward his waist, while his left hand turned palm up and, led by his middle finger, rose slowly toward the ceiling. On the edges of his vision, he could see his motions mirrored in Sylva. Like him, she wore a pale-blue cotton tank top and loose cotton shorts. Like him, she was bathed in sweat, the clothes clinging to her slim body. Early in his training, Tomas would find himself distracted by her presence, transfixed by the loveliness of her movements and the distance in her eyes. Now, moving in time with her, he felt a stronger bond, a fluid connection as the air moved about their bodies.

Four hours and twenty-eight minutes into the discipline, Tomas's mind was transformed. His muscles had moved beyond fatigue into that state of strength that drew from a source the conscious mind could not tap. He had no thoughts, no words in his mind, only the shift and flow of the meditation. Position eighteen brought him back to a simple standing pose, his hands before him in prayer position. He closed his eyes, mindful but not alarmed at the weakness in his shoulders and calf muscles. Before him, Sylva mirrored his position. He let his breath restore his strength as he listened for his teacher.

Sylva broke position and crossed the room. They were in the swimming room in the basement of the complex, the long narrow pool of water reflecting the candlelight in erratic patterns on the low ceiling. They often practiced here, the acoustics making the second part of the meditation more challenging. She moved to a table near the door and picked up a bag of marbles. Tomas could hear the stones clink against one another. Carefully, she emptied the bag into the top of a tall, bamboo box.

Inside the box were a series of narrow chutes that pivoted on tiny fulcrums. At different levels within the box were small brass bells. The marbles of differing sizes and weights moved across different chutes at different speeds. Some dropped quickly, some rolled slowly, finding balance until another marble knocked them loose. Sylva tiptoed silently away from the box, preparing for the second meditation.

Sweat evaporated from his skin and he listened for the bell. He didn't squeeze his eyes shut; his lashes barely touched his cheeks as his energy went inward to the part of his mind that was always aware of his surroundings. This was a location meditation. Each time he heard a bell, he was to point his hands in the direction of Sylva.

His eyes were closed and the echoes of the water hall made his hearing unreliable. He had to turn to his mind's eye, the eye that saw when his physical eyes were blind. Tomas relaxed and allowed his mind to see the shadows of the room around him. Part of it was memory. He knew the contours of the room as well as he knew the contours of Stell's face. Part of it was sensory—an awareness of air displacement and the whispers of sound as his teacher moved as silently as possible. The biggest part of the ability was internal.

A bell sounded and Tomas tipped his hands to the left, directly at Sylva. He was not allowed to open his eyes to check if his answer had been correct. The teacher moved silently again as another bell rang. Again, Tomas located her instantly, pointing his fingers over his right shoulder. Bell after bell sounded and each time Tomas located his instructor. In his mind, the room glowed a watery shade of blue as he felt, more than saw, Sylva move around him. Finally she stood before him, very close.

Tomas smiled. He loved Sylva, loved the feel of heat her body radiated. He wouldn't open his eyes until instructed to do so but he felt a yearning for the soft hands of his meditation teacher, for the way she would gently stroke his hair or rub his back. He remained still, his breathing calm, waiting for her cue to move.

His eyes remained closed when he felt the sudden draft of air between them. They remained closed at her sharp intake of breath.

But his eyes flew open when Sylva's fist crashed solidly and painfully into his solar plexus, doubling him over and dropping him to the floor.

He rolled to his side, gasping for air that would not come. Sylva fell on him, pulling a thick cord out of nowhere and tying his hands behind his back. She was impossibly strong and lightning fast. In his struggle to breathe and make sense of what was happening, he was only partially aware of the door to the swimming room opening, footsteps rushing across the floor and rough hands pulling at him. He had just a moment to see Lucien and Vet over his shoulder before he broke the surface of the water, his desperate attempts to breathe succeeding only in sucking down warm water as he sunk to the bottom of the pool.

Chapter Seven:

VINT

....

Vint: the physical manifestation of human desire and
emotion, visible only to Storytellers

"Nothing here strike your fancy?" Stell shook her head. There was
a couple at the table near the dartboard who had been eyeing them
for most of the evening. Adlai recognized the type, married couple, probably both on their second or third marriage, cruising bars
looking to spice things up. Chicago, Indianapolis—it didn't matter
what city it was. Some things never changed. "Aren't you hungry?"

She was. Her appetite had been growing, her hunger making
itself known every couple of days rather than every other week. She
missed Tomas. She had never hunted with anyone else before. She
didn't realize how heavily she relied on his ability to read a room
and weave a story. Out here with Adlai, who was as reticent as she,
the fun of luring people lost its luster. It seemed too much trouble

to introduce themselves to the couple across the room, listen to their chatter, burning time until they could get them alone and vulnerable. She would rather drag them out back and bash their heads against the wall to get what she wanted.

Adlai slid his hand over hers.

"There's nothing for us here. Let's go."

"Where are we going to go?"

He chucked her under the chin with his finger. "We'll just follow our noses."

Outside Stell headed for the bike but Adlai pulled her along the sidewalk. The neighborhood they walked through changed from suburban chain restaurants and bars to progressively seedier nightclubs with smoked-glass windows and steel grates on the doors. Stell clutched Adlai's hand tighter, feeling a familiar rush of heat move through her. She snuck a glance at his face and caught his hard stare as he scanned the streets before them.

At this moment she didn't miss Tomas. Where Tomas would always look for the story, the bond to form with his prey, Adlai seemed to understand her need for the rush of fear. A shiver passed up her spine as she knew tonight she would have *r 'acul.*

Shouts came from the alley they were approaching. Glass shattered and Stell heard male voices laughing loudly. Adlai surprised her and pulled her tight against his body. His lips crushed hers as together they staggered, locked in an embrace, and crashed against the brick wall in the mouth of the alley. He forced his legs between hers, one hand pulling her thigh up onto his, the other pulling at her clothes. Stell climbed onto his body, slipping her hands under his jacket and clawing at the t-shirt beneath, not thinking, only wanting. Her heart hammered in her ears as the heat from his body burned against her, the rough brick cold at her back. She clung to him, a moan escaping her throat as she heard footsteps approaching from the blackness of the alley.

"Aw, isn't that romantic?" The voice was male, high-pitched with a nasal Midwestern accent. Stell opened her eyes and saw the voice perfectly matched the source—a scrawny white boy with bad skin and a worse mustache. Adlai looked at the kid and scoffed.

"Fuck off, man." He went back to his hot-breathed lovemaking on Stell's neck.

"Did you hear that?" Mustache asked. "Brady, you hear that?"

"I did. That fucker just told you to fuck off."

Adlai sighed, resting his forehead against Stell's, meeting her eyes with contained glee. There were three of them behind him. She could tell by the look in his eyes, he was thinking the same thing: Can it be this easy?

Adlai turned around and looked from one thug to the other, as if he just realized he was outnumbered. "Hey man, I don't want any trouble."

"Hey, he doesn't want any trouble." Brady, a tall, doughy manboy, said with a laugh.

"Oh well," Mustache's high-pitched voice got even higher. He got up in Adlai's face, his breath stinking of beer and cigarettes. "In that case, why did you tell me to fuck off?"

Stell watched the three men close in on Adlai. She could smell their adrenaline and it made her mouth water. She slipped up behind Adlai, cowering behind him, and whispered in a small voice, "C'mon honey, let's just get out of here." She opened her eyes wide, broadcasting a fear she did not feel. The third man, in a stained Colts jersey, took the bait.

Adlai began backing out of the alley. Colts Jersey stepped behind him, blocking his way. Brady laughed again as Mustache feinted left then right, trying to spook Adlai.

"What do you want?" Stell almost laughed at the affected tremor in Adlai's voice.

Mustache sidled up alongside them and with surprising speed, pushed Adlai toward the other two men while pulling Stell into a choke hold. All three men had knives ready, one at Adlai's throat, one waving in front of his face, Mustache pressed the third against Stell's cheek. It was clear they had done this before. Mustache backed away, dragging Stell with him as his cronies laughed. Adlai began to bargain, then to beg, offering them all the money he had if they would just leave them alone. Brady elbowed him hard in the stomach to shut him up.

Mustache waited until Adlai had straightened up to pull Stell close to his chest. Holding the knife under her chin, he unzipped her jacket and pulled it open. Stell whimpered in his grip, begging him not to hurt her, even mustering up a desperate tear. She could feel his body pulsing behind her, could feel the start of a pitiful erection pressing into her back. She couldn't meet Adlai's eye for fear she would begin laughing. Adlai barked angry obscenities to his captors as Mustache lowered the knife to the hem of her thin t-shirt.

"You got a nice-looking woman here, dude. Maybe you ought to take her to nicer places." He purred in her ear, running his tongue along her throat. He pulled the t-shirt hem taut with the tip of the knife as his two buddies giggled stupidly on either side of Adlai. Colts Jersey held Adlai by the back of his jacket, the knife falling away from the target's neck as he watched the show unfold in front of him. On his left, Brady was paying more attention, his hand locked on Adlai's arm in a powerful grip, his knife positioned for a messy gut wound.

Confident his buddies had the muscular man contained, Mustache let the knife cut through the fabric of Stell's shirt. She followed the blade's progress up her stomach, between her breasts and up to the neckline of her shirt. Mustache's cold hand slid across her stomach as he popped the final inch of fabric, letting her shirt fall back, exposing her bare torso to the night. Adlai closed his eyes at the sight, biting his lip. The attackers thought it was from anger or shame or modesty, but Stell knew differently.

Mustache pinched one of her nipples between his fingers and heard her gasp. "I think she likes me, boys. What do you think?" His two comrades were reduced to wheezy giggles as he whispered loudly in Stell's ear. "You like that, don't you? You been looking for a real man, haven't you?" Her eyes half closed, Stell tried to maintain the pretense of fear but seeing Adlai's tongue dart across his lips and the flash of his teeth as he waited for what was coming, her body reacted on its own. Her back arched, bucking her body into Mustache's open hand. His hands moved over her bare skin, hot in the cold night air.

"We're gonna have us a party. You and me and my buddies here." His breath was ragged as he pulled Stell deeper into the alley. "You tell Mr. Muscles over there that you want a real man." Stell said nothing, trying to prolong the anticipation. "Go on, say it."

Stell closed her eyes and whispered. "I want a real man." Brady and Colts Jersey clutched Adlai tighter as they laughed.

"You tell him you want us all, all three of us tonight, right here, right now."

She met Adlai's eye. "I want all three of them. Right now."

Adlai winked at her. "Greedy, greedy, greedy."

Mustache tried to kiss Stell's averted lips as he eyed Adlai. "She's gonna like it, you stupid fuck, three real men, one after the other."

Stell let her head roll back on her captor's shoulder. "It sounds wonderful but I think I may have to share." Mustache looked at her, confused at the laughing tone in her voice.

Before he could recover, she threw her head back, smashing his nose. Adlai wrenched his arm free from Brady's grip and threw a sharp jab to the larger man's nose, followed by a quick backward elbow to the jaw that rattled Brady's brains and dropped him in a heap on the alley floor. Colts Jersey stood by stupefied as Adlai turned to face him. With a snapping grip on his neck, Adlai lifted Colts Jersey off his feet and slammed him onto the alley floor. He pulled the knife from the stunned man and used it to open his throat. A dozen feet away, he could feel and smell and hear Stell tearing at the skin of Mustache.

. . . .

Tomas's lungs burned as they filled with water. With his hands tied behind his back, he flailed helplessly, disoriented, his head bumping against the concrete. He forced his feet below him and pushed off, the muscles in his stomach screaming from Sylva's punch. Just as he broke the surface and sucked in air, the water erupted. Lucien and Vet leapt into the pool. One Storyteller grabbed a handful of hair and yanked Tomas back under the water; the other lunged onto his shoulders, pushing him deeper.

Panic flooded Tomas; he screamed, taking in more water as he struggled to break free. He was yanked to the surface long enough to spit out a mouthful of pool water and suck in a blessed breath then the two Storytellers thrust him deep under the water again and again. Tomas could feel knees and fists and feet pushing at him as his fear set off a keening sound in his brain.

After an eternity under water, Lucien and Vet dragged him from the pool, throwing him over the edge to land roughly, his hands still bound, on the concrete edging. Tomas vomited water as he hacked, the skin on his cheek and forehead torn against the rough floor. His muscles screamed from exhaustion and oxygen deprivation, and his left shoulder felt dislocated from the painful binding of his wrists. He lay curled on the floor, his only thought getting air into his body and water out of his lungs, when he saw a new pair of feet. He looked up, still coughing, and Dalle looked down at him.

He tried to speak, to beg for help, but could only hack and gasp. When Dalle bent down, Tomas wanted to cry in thanks, but Dalle jerked him up by his right elbow, dragging him across the concrete, tearing more skin off his face and shoulders and knees. Tomas screamed as his shoulders jerked violently. He tried to get his feet under him once again but Dalle was moving too quickly.

He dragged Tomas across the concrete patio to an unmarked door. Slamming Tomas face-first against the wall, he slid the bolt that held the door closed. Tomas tried to push off the wall, to turn around and defend himself, but Dalle pinned him against the brick with an iron grip to the back of his neck. Blood ran into his eyes and filled his mouth as he struggled to breathe in the crushing grip. The door swung open and Dalle, grabbing a handful of hair, threw Tomas onto the floor of the small room and shut the door.

Tomas slid across the concrete floor into the brick wall on the far side. His hands still tied behind his back, he couldn't stop himself and the rough brick cut a deep gash in his scalp. His shoulders were on fire, his hands numb, his body convulsed as blood pooled beneath him. He could hear his panicked whimpers and rattling breath. He lay on the floor, waiting for the next barrage, his mind desperately trying to catch up to the assault.

There was no sense, no pattern; in one heartbeat the universe had gone insane. If he couldn't get himself together, he would be killed. The pain in his shoulders and back was beyond excruciating, lightning bolts of heat firing one after another from his skull to his wrists. Blood blurred his vision and his diaphragm cramped so badly he couldn't straighten up.

Breathe, he told himself. If he could breathe he could think, if he could think he could survive. Drawing from deep within himself, he struggled to draw in precious air and silence the pitiful mewling that threatened to bury him in panic. His heart raced when he couldn't silence the sound; it seemed to come from outside himself and Tomas felt a new wave of terror breaking over him.

He wrenched his arms, the pain in his shoulders giving him something concrete to focus on. He cried out from the torturous sensation but the mewling didn't stop. Blinking blood from his eyes, his vision cleared and there, just four feet away, hanging by her hands from a hook in the ceiling was a common girl bound and gagged.

She screamed behind the bandanna tied around her mouth, writhing helplessly from the rough ropes that bound her to the industrial hook in the ceiling. Her eyes were wild with panic, her terror keen as she kicked and twisted, trying to keep this new intruder at bay. Tomas stared at her, his own pain forgotten. His sense of unreality deepened as her eyes locked onto his, her terror and confusion mirroring his own. She stopped her struggles when Tomas began to scream.

The room erupted in a swarm of black snaking figures. Tomas scrambled to the far wall, crushing his incapacitated hands beneath him as he pressed his burning body into the brick. All around the girl writhing appendages whipped through the air, black with the texture of armadillo skin. They burst from her chest and flew about the room, each tendril ending in a gaping maw that snapped and whistled as it tore through the air.

The creatures slammed against the wall, scrabbled across the ceiling, snaked across the floor, screaming for escape, for connection, for life. Tomas heard only his own shrieks as several of the larger figures locked onto him, their hollow gaping mouths chomping air as they lunged for his chest. There was nowhere for Tomas to escape and the blunt heads of the creatures punched against his chest, bumping and probing. He couldn't close his eyes and his screams turned to whimpers as he felt burning spots erupt on his chest where contact had been made.

Then there was stillness.

The creatures hung suspended, their motion slowed to the point of silence. The only sound in the room was his jagged breath. As the nearest black figure withdrew slightly, Tomas found the girl's eyes. Her terror was gone. She began to make muffled cooing sounds behind her gag. She was trying to comfort him.

"No. Oh no." Tomas slumped against the wall, his voice a ragged whisper. If the snapping, voracious creatures had been terrifying, what came next was even harder. Some small part of his brain knew this was the same phenomenon he had experienced in the diner after his *r 'acul* with Stell, that these visions were a manifestation of the girl. As her terror turned to compassion, the tendrils became graceful, rushing at him with all the venom of a butterfly, brushing against him with soft fingers. The tenderness was more than he could bear as he felt their warm tips pushing softly through him, piercing him, running through him like sunlight through glass.

He wished he could close his eyes to escape the terrible sweetness of it. That this girl, this common surrounded by predators she couldn't understand, fearing for her life, could step past her own terror to comfort him without knowing him, having no connection to him but an inborn compassion, was more than he could bear. He wanted to scream at her to stop, but couldn't as the truth of her flooded his mind. Her name was Rebecca. She had a daughter and a drug problem and money worries and fear and, above it all, she had a hunger for life. She had joy and hope and tenderness despite all that surrounded her. She believed in life.

. . . .

Through a narrow mesh screen on the door, Sylva watched the room with Dalle. Like the girl on the hook, she couldn't see what Tomas saw. She saw only two people bound and frightened, one bewildered by the other's panic. Next to her, she heard Dalle's uneven breath. His forehead was pressed against the mesh, tears flowing down his cheeks.

She knew he and Tomas shared a vision invisible to outsiders. Tomas had drawn the *Vint*. Sylva handed Dalle a bath sheet and a knife.

The sliding of the bolt broke the silence in the room. Tomas was finally able to close his eyes, breaking his connection to the girl, and he crumpled against the wall in misery. Anything was better than this. Dalle stepped into the room and the girl faced him bravely. She kicked at him but he easily avoided her feet and stepped behind her. Her eyes widened in fear as his thumbs pressed against the sides of her neck. He didn't squeeze hard, but he pressed until she slumped unconscious. He lifted her free from the hook and laid her on the floor. Lucien and Vet slipped into the room, picked her up, and carried her out.

Tomas let his body slide to the side until his face was pressed against the concrete. He was beyond caring what happened now.

Dalle laid the bath sheet out on the floor. He rolled Tomas onto his side, straddled him, cut his bindings. Quickly, before Tomas could react, Dalle cut away the shoulder straps of his blood-soaked tank top then slipped the blade along the front of the shirt, opening its length. Tomas closed his eyes and felt the cold blade slide up each leg of his shorts, pulling the wet fabric from his skin as the shorts were cut away from his body. Dalle peeled the fabric away, leaving Tomas naked on the floor beneath him.

Tomas cried out as the agony in his shoulders was reawakened. Dalle moved quickly, lifting Tomas from his wet clothes and placing him on the bath sheet. The fabric was soft and warm beneath him and Dalle wrapped the sheet around his shivering body. His muscles screamed at the manipulation, but there was comfort in the swaddling. Tomas wished his mentor would wrap the sheet over his face as well, to put a warm, soft end to this nightmare.

Dalle lifted Tomas and slipped under him, resting the boy's head in his lap. Tightly bound and exhausted, Tomas could not resist as the Storyteller lifted his head and held a stone mug to his lips. The water was warm with a flowery smell that wasn't unpleasant. His throat burned as he swallowed, tasting an evergreen essence in the water. He could see white flower petals clinging to the inside of the vessel. He recognized those flowers, had seen them growing on Calstow Mountain, but before he could register the knowledge, new pain began.

A fist of heat punched into his stomach, drawing him into himself. His lungs seized up, shutting off all but the thinnest ribbon of air. His skin caught on fire beneath the sheet, alternating with blankets of ice that froze him. It was pain like nothing he had ever known before. His teeth gnashed together and his body twisted in a tortuous spasm.

. . . .

All that could be seen of his eyes were bloodshot whites but Dalle looked into his face, watching the muscles in his cheeks twitch and jerk, his nostrils flare as his body struggled for air. He held the boy, the swaddling containing the worst of the spasms. There was nothing to do now but wait as the deadly tea cast its evil spell over the young man.

. . . .

A freezing rain pounded against his back when Adlai pulled himself off of Colts Jersey. He could see the drops bouncing off of Stell's white back as she dragged Mustache closer to the curb. She had shed her torn shirt and woolen jacket despite the icy rain, the blood and the kill turning her body into a furnace. Adlai caught her eye and for a moment they stared at each other, blood and rain puddling beneath them. She slid her tongue along her lower lip and Adlai began to laugh. She looked like a firecracker, her enlarged pupils turning her eyes glossy black, the rain sparkling off her in the exaggerated night like diamonds. He tossed away Colts Jersey and stood, waiting for her next move.

She stood on unsteady legs, the blood high making her stagger. The rain picked up power and she turned her face to it. The blood streaked down her pale body, darkening the waistband of her jeans. She giggled as Brady, the only surviving member of his gang, struggled toward consciousness in an icy puddle.

"You want him?"

Stell thought for a moment then shook her head. "I'm full."

"Me too." In two steps, he crossed behind Brady and snapped his neck with an easy twist.

"What are we going to do with them?" The alleyway was turning into a sludgy river of mud and blood. Adlai put his hands on his hips and tried to think. It was a messy scene, sloppy and careless. There could be witnesses. There could be evidence. He looked back at Stell.

"Fuck it. Let's just leave them here." Stell laughed out loud, clapping her hands together as he continued with a giggle of his own. "Let's give the Indianapolis Police Department a mystery to solve."

Stell leapt with both feet into a deep puddle, splashing water everywhere as she laughed and danced her way out of the alley. Adlai scooped up her jacket and shirt and ran out after her.

"You forgetting something, Lady Godiva?"

"Who?"

He wrapped the jacket around her shoulders and pulled her close to him as they headed back toward the bike. Along the way they passed busy restaurants and nightclubs and diners full of common. Stell was relieved to learn that Adlai had no more interest in the common during his blood high than she did. The night was so much more interesting. They let the rain wash the evidence of their crime from their faces, climbed onto Adlai's bike, and sped out of the city, looking for a quiet place to watch the stars burn through the heavy autumn clouds.

· ·

The pain stopped, or rather, Tomas left the pain.

He was freezing. And filthy. His skin felt gritty and greasy, sticky with the darkness that hung in the air like a cloud. He'd never seen darkness like this. It moved around him like a living shadow, stalking him, confronting him. The cold drilled through him, throbbing in his bones and in his teeth.

There was Stell. The darkness parted around her and he wanted her to wrap him in her arms, to ward off the creeping cold but she held something to her chest. A black stone. Stell hugged a black stone to her body and smiled at him. Tomas longed for her, for her touch. Longing twisted through him and then she was gone, swallowed by the darkness.

Cold. So cold. That strange darkness pressed against him, his ears and his jaws and his teeth aching with the darkness, with the cold.

He wanted to leave this place. More than Tomas had ever wanted anything, he wanted to leave this place. *Out, out, out,* he thought. Then he felt foolish.

He was at the door.

Not just a door. A thousand doors. A sea of doorknobs spread in every direction, each with a small window above it. He knew those windows. They were the colored windows of the Storytelling room, although the darkness now covered each window like soot. Funny, he thought, that he had never noticed the doorknobs.

Which door would let him out? Which knob to turn? He had to pick the right one, he knew. If he opened the wrong door, he knew he would never leave the darkness. He swiped his hand over one of the windows, wiping the darkness away long enough to see a room crowded with common. A party. They laughed and drank and waved to him through the glass. He tried the knob but it wouldn't turn and the darkness clouded the window.

Knob after knob he turned, desperate to escape until one knob froze his hand. His knuckles ached with the cold but before he could pull away, the knob turned, the door opened, and the darkness held its breath.

There was a man, thin and bent, seated on the floor, his back to Tomas, rocking back and forth. He clutched at his black hair and hid his face behind bony hands.

"Who are you?" Tomas didn't feel his lips move, but heard his voice ask the question.

"S-s-s-s-s-s." The man answered.

"I don't understand. Who are you?"

"Hesssssss."

Tomas moved to stand in front of him. "What do you need?"

The man pulled at the skin on his throat. He pulled at the tendons and muscles that strained taut until the skin gave way. Rather than blood, however, something black poured out of the wound, something black and moving. Bees, hundreds of black, buzzing bees. They tumbled out around his fingers, some clambering and climbing, some flying up to his chin onto his face, others falling to the floor and skittering away.

"Can I help you?" Tomas felt calm despite the horrible show before him.

"Help me get them out."

The floor grew black with the teeming bodies.

"I don't know how."

The man pulled his head up and Tomas could make out dark blue Nahan eyes beneath the undulating mask of bees. "You take them. Take them with you. I don't want them." Tomas didn't want them either. The man bent his face into his hands, the bees fleeing his grip. He fell forward, clutching his face, and the black insects swarmed his head and body. Tomas stepped back as the pulsating cloud of bees converged on the bent man, climbing over his thin back and over each other until he was nothing but a humming mass of black bees.

Another step back and Tomas could feel a pressure building within him. His stomach cramped and he could feel a clutching sensation in his lungs. He looked down at his torso, terrified he would see a bulging mass of the stinging insects erupting from his abdomen.

Instead he saw a blue light glowing beneath his shirt. The light burned intensely, a pinprick of brilliant blue, that grew, spreading out over his stomach, blinding him as it burst through his clothing. It blew through him like an explosion until all he could see, all he knew was the brilliant vibration of the blue light. He fell backward, tumbling with no sensation of up or down until he felt an icy knife cut through him.

· ·

Dalle held on tight as Tomas sucked in a deep gasp of air, color flooding his pale face and his lips losing their frightening shade of blue. The sheet that swaddled him was soaked in sweat and Tomas struggled in its grip. Dalle smoothed his hair, stroking his face and murmuring soft words as Tomas thrashed his way back to life. Vet pulled the wet fabric away from his body, stepping back quickly as Tomas shot his arms out above him, reaching for nothing. He kicked his legs, blood flooding his abused muscles, and the Storytellers kneeled beside him, waiting for his return to consciousness.

Tomas opened his eyes and saw Dalle at his head, Vet at his right, Lucien on his left. His breathing was harsh as his lungs sucked greedily at the air. He twitched helplessly as his teachers lifted him once again and moved him onto a thick, blue blanket. They pulled the edges around him loosely, keeping him warm rather than restraining him. Above his head, Dalle leaned over him. His mouth never moved but Tomas clearly heard the gentle voice of his mentor.

"Welcome back, Storyteller."

Tomas closed his eyes and dropped into a dark, dreamless hole.

. . . .

The rain showed no signs of slowing, so they decided to head back to the motel. Even with her blood high, Stell was shivering. She dumped her dripping clothes on the floor and headed for the shower. Adlai moved behind her, picking up the muddy jeans and ruined t-shirt and tossing them onto the counter of the sink outside the bathroom. He peeled off his own shirt and washed himself in the basin. Over the roar of the shower, he could hear Stell singing to herself. He had to laugh when he saw the amount of blood on the waistband of her jeans. She ate like a slob. He dumped the clothes into a plastic bag, tossed them into his suitcase, and lay back on the bed to wait for Stell.

Adlai had had dozens of lovers over the years. He still felt as he had a decade ago that he had no desire to pair. The women he slept with were entertaining, some were passionate, some were even fellow *acul 'ad*. In the past few years, he had chosen women within the Council who could help him get information he needed. Vartan's assistant, Fiona, had been his most recent encounter and they'd certainly found plenty to amuse each other. The physical aspect of it filled a simple need for him, an itch easily scratched. Never did any of the encounters eclipse the always burning, always hidden desire to find Shelan.

The shower shut off and Adlai smiled at Stell's coos of delight at the swirling patterns of steam that flitted before her enhanced eyes. Stell was different. She was fierce but not hard, dangerous but not vicious. No doubt it was a moot point to the common she killed but there was a kind of joy in her slaughter. When she stared at him with those pale eyes he could feel a part of himself unwind in the smallest way and when he couldn't sleep, he sometimes let his mind wander down the path of an impossibility.

The bathroom door swung open and Stell stepped out naked, toweling her long hair dry. There were no lights on in the room, both of them able to see in the darkness after their kills, and the wisps of steam dressed Stell in a phantom robe of glitter. Adlai sat up on the bed and watched as her every move made the air around her dance. She dropped the towel on the floor and climbed onto the bed on top of him.

Passing headlights on the highway illuminated her body for a heartbeat, leaving a brilliant burn of her image on his sensitive eyes. Stell straddled Adlai, her bare skin hot against his, and pressed her mouth against the pulse in his throat. Adlai breathed her in, every fiber of his being wanting to take her. He grabbed her under the arms and flipped her beneath him, pinning her wrists above her head. She moved beneath him like a python, the free parts of her body rising and seething against him.

"We can't do this."

She giggled, thinking he was teasing her. She wrapped her legs around his waist, preventing him from pulling away. He pressed down harder on her hands.

"I'm serious, Stell. I have to tell you something. About my best friend."

"Now?"

He nodded. "Right now, before I ruin my last chance."

By the time he finished telling Stell the story of Shelan and his breakdown, Stell was pacing the room in a fury. She threw her boots, the remote control, the duffel bag; anything she could get her hands on was hurled in a rage. She turned on Adlai, her black pupils enormous.

"You knew they were doing this to Tomas and you didn't tell me?"

"There's nothing you can do."

"Like hell. I'll kill every one of those bastards with my—"

"With your what?" Adlai grabbed her arms and pinned them to her side. "With your bare hands? What are you going to do, Stell? March in there and start busting heads?"

"I'll do something!"

"And you'll get killed and then you'll both be fucked. Use your head." He loosened his grip. "Listen to me. The Council is like the common. Never underestimate them especially when they're threatened. Right now the only thing tighter than security in that complex is Vartan's ass. You go in screaming and you and your boyfriend will be 'disappeared' just like that."

Stell pulled away from him. "Why are you telling me all this?"

"Because you may be able to help me find Shelan."

"How?"

Adlai rubbed his hands over his face. "I hope nothing happens to your Tomas. I really do. I wouldn't wish that on anybody. But if it does, if they take him away, they'll probably take him where they took Shelan." Stell moaned and turned away but he pulled her back to him. "Listen to me, Stell. It's the only way I know to find him. You told me you and Tomas have a bond, that you can call to each other. You said you used to do it on your mountain, that you would know when he was coming for you. That bond has to have gotten stronger, right? After all the blood you've shared? If they took him somewhere, you would be able to find him, right? And if you could, we could free them both."

Stell dropped onto the edge of the bed and put her head between her knees. She was having trouble breathing. The thought of Tomas being injured or destroyed by the Storytellers was too horrible for her to absorb. Adlai settled down beside her, his arm around her shoulder.

"That's why we can't be together. I can't take a chance that anything could cloud the bond you two have."

Stell looked up at him in misery. "We're going back. Right now."

. . . .

He smelled sandalwood. Peeling open one eye, Tomas tried to focus. Shimmering jewel-toned shapes hovered before him at a distance he couldn't judge. He peeled open his other eye and tried to make sense of them but the shapes remained indistinct. He turned his head and a razor blade of pain sliced through his muscles. He was lying on the floor, candlelight flickering off copper medallions on the walls. He was in a meditation room. Dalle's meditation room. Dalle loved copper.

He experimented moving his body, his muscles and joints arguing with every motion. His fingers dug into the plush Oriental rug as he struggled to pull his mind into the moment. There was a flat, gray stone between him and his thoughts, and all he could do was peek around the edges trying to remember how he had gotten here. The effort was enormous and the softness of the rug enticed him to drift away.

"Why don't you try to sit up?"

Tomas closed his eyes.

"You might want to eat something."

Large hands slipped behind his head and neck and lifted him into a sitting position. Tomas didn't resist, nor did he help. He allowed himself to be placed upright and breathed deeply into the pain that cascaded along his spine. Dalle settled cross-legged in front of him, holding out a bowl of a creamy liquid. Tomas looked at the offering in disbelief.

"It's just soup, really." Dalle took a drink from one side of the bowl and held it out again. "See? Just potato soup. It will help with your throat. And your stomach."

When Tomas didn't move, Dalle leaned forward, holding the bowl to his lips.

"Drink."

The flat, gray stone that had blocked his thoughts slipped.

"Get your hands off me."

Rage rose from the base of his spine, erupting throughout his body, a refreshing change from the fear and bewilderment that had suffocated him.

"Eat. Then you can fight me."

A buzz of blood and anger rang in Tomas's ears.

"Trust me. You're in no condition to fight me or anyone. Eat your soup." He held the bowl out again. "You'll have your chance. You'll have your say."

"Is the soup drugged too? Like you would tell me."

"I would tell you."

Tomas took the bowl. His hands shook so badly the ceramic clinked against his front teeth. He managed to swallow, grimacing at the shredded feeling of his throat.

"Tell me what you saw."

Tomas shook his head.

"Tell me. We need to talk about it. Where did you go?"

"Nowhere."

Dalle took the bowl and set it aside. He pressed Tomas's palms together, wrapping his hands around them and squeezing. "I know you're angry. You hurt and you're confused but this is not an insignificant thing that has happened, Desara. I didn't send you to that place lightly. That place where you went, that is your place in the world of Ourselves."

The warmth of Dalle's hands flooded Tomas. He stared down at the rough knuckles and blunt, chewed fingernails, wondering how something so warm and comforting could be so dangerous. He wondered why this had never occurred to him before. He raised his eyes to Dalle's face and his breath caught.

"Why are you blue?"

"What?" His mentor's eyes widened.

"Shit." Tomas pulled his hands away to cover his face. "Did you drug me again?"

Dalle pulled Tomas's hands down and held his chin, forcing the younger man to look at him. Dalle was smiling. "Am I blue?"

Tomas looked around the room, trying to find the source of the blue light hovering over Dalle's face. His mentor laughed.

"It's not a trick, Desara. It's a gift. It's a result of the poison. Sometimes we can see thoughts and emotions as colors, as auras. Does it frighten you?"

Tomas shook his head, watching the color shimmer over Dalle's face. "It's kind of beautiful. Will I see it all the time? On everyone?"

"Maybe. Maybe not. Gifts like this come and go. You're only just now unlocking your gifts. There's so much we need to do. Where were you? Where did you go?"

The soup soured in his stomach. "Nowhere. I was nowhere. It was so cold. And the darkness was thick and sticky like—What?" He stopped when he looked at Dalle. The blue was gone, replaced by blotchy orange and yellow. "You're worried." The colors vanished. "And now you're hiding it. You're hiding your colors. Why?"

"I'm shielding them for now," Dalle said. "I'll teach you how to do that too. I just think that right now they'll distract you while you're trying to sort this all out."

"But you are worried about me." Tomas studied Dalle's face. "Something is wrong, isn't it? Something is wrong with me."

"No." Dalle put his hands on either side of Tomas's face, leaning in close. "There is nothing wrong with you. You called out the *Vint* and you are here in one piece. Everything else we can work to make right."

"The *Vint*, that's what I saw, right? The snakes?" His throat closed at the memory. "Will I see that all the time?"

"No, no, no." Dalle rushed to reassure him, wiping a tear from his cheek. "I promise you. You'll learn; I'll teach you. You'll have a choice. You'll learn to control what you see, how it affects you."

"What happened to her?" Tomas asked. "Rebecca?" When Dalle said nothing, Tomas raised his voice. "Remember her? The common girl you kidnapped and hung from a hook? She has a daughter, you know? She was afraid and hurt and you just hung her there like a toy to be thrown away when you're done with it."

"She has not been thrown away. She will be given the opportunity at a new life, to become a member of the Kott in exchange for the service she provided us."

"And what if she says no? You kill her?"

"She will be strongly encouraged to never mention the incident and certain safeguards will be put in place to ensure her silence."

Tomas shook his head. "What a bunch of bullshit."

Dalle gripped Tomas's wrists tight. "And what would you recommend? How do you think this works, Desara? You think your pretty face and good table manners are enough? We have hard decisions to make every day."

Tomas tried to pull away but Dalle wouldn't let go. "She has a right to live."

"So do we. Listen to me very carefully." He jerked Tomas closer. "This is what we do—me, Lucien, Vet, Albion. There are fewer than a hundred Storytellers alive at any given time and we have to make the decisions that our people can't or won't make. We carry the burden. That's why we have to train so hard. That's why we have to be strong. To carry the burden."

Tomas closed his eyes, the memory of his vision seeping in. "Like Hess. Hess didn't want to carry the—ow!"

Dalle had thrown his hands down. Tomas's wrists ached where

they'd been gripped but that wasn't what Tomas felt. He felt space, absence.

He hadn't realized how accustomed he'd become to the feel of Dalle around him. Through his training and meditation, his mentor had turned him inside out, had prodded and rebuilt every inch of him in a way he could never explain.

Now Dalle pulled away. The sensation frightened Tomas.

"Who is Hess?"

"Where did you hear that name?"

"I met him in my dream. He pulled bees from his throat and told me to take them. Who is he? Is he real?" Dalle said nothing. Tomas reached for his hands, needing the contact. "Tell me. Stop masking your colors so I know you're telling me the truth. Dalle, you owe me that."

Dalle met his angry stare with a look Tomas couldn't read. "Take your hands off of me. I owe you nothing."

"Dalle?"

"He was an apprentice. Before you. He couldn't handle it."

"What happened to him?"

Dalle scowled at Tomas. "I need to think."

Before Tomas could react, Dalle pressed two fingers between Tomas's eyebrows, pushing him back onto the carpet, dropping him back into a dreamless sleep.

. . . .

Tomas came to with a start. He felt better than he had the last time he'd woken up but somehow he felt even more tired. Dalle was gone and Tomas couldn't find the strength to think about that or anything else. He wanted to drift.

Tomas watched candlelight play across the textured ceiling until one dark spot caught his eye. At first he thought it was a shadow from the swirled stucco but its darkness didn't follow the lines of the moving light. The darkness moved on its own in small, pulsing waves, like the shadow of wings flapping. Tomas squinted trying to make out what he was seeing and realized the spot was growing, the shadow lengthening. Everything in the room disappeared for him except that growing darkness.

The shadow constricted, then pulsed, then blossomed across the ceiling like a cloud.

Bees. A cloud of bees, a silent swarm floated just below the ceiling, bumping and gathering along the ridges of stucco. Tiny black bodies, silent despite their number, floated above him, the cloud of their swarm opening and closing like a hand reaching for his hair. Tomas, transfixed, was rising up on his elbows to greet the interloper when angry voices could be heard in the hallway.

"You can't go in there!"

He heard a scuffle and a growl of obscenities and then Stell burst through the door. She threw herself on the ground beside him, holding his face in her hands.

"Tomas, are you okay? Can you hear me?" Tomas nodded, bewildered at the sudden rush of cold air and exhaust fumes that clung to her heavy woolen clothes. She pulled him close to her body, burying his face in her neck. "I thought they had killed you or taken you away from me." Tomas pushed himself more deeply against her skin, murmuring reassurances into her hair.

"You cannot be in here!" Sylva screamed from the doorway. "You can't storm in here and disrupt our meditation. This is a room of peace, of calm, not violence and blood. This room is for silence and—"

"Then why don't you be quiet?" Stell hissed, clutching Tomas close. This struck Tomas as funny and he laughed out loud. He saw Dalle and Lucien crowd the doorway with Sylva. Everyone looked tense.

"Desara, I know your girl is worried about you."

Tomas tilted his head. "She has a name."

Dalle nodded and began again. "I apologize for that. Stell, I know you have been worried about Desara and you have every right to be. This is a difficult path he has chosen and there are many profound challenges before him, before us all."

"Oh, shut up." Stell stroked Tomas's hair and kissed the top of his head. "All this talking. Let's get out of here."

Lucien joined Dalle and Sylva in protest, shouting over each other why Tomas couldn't leave the complex.

"Give us five minutes, please."

Sylva held firm. "I'm not closing this door."

Tomas laughed again, the tension and posturing around him striking him as absurd and surreal. "I promise we won't rush the door." He leaned back on his elbows and looked up at the luminous face above him, the crowd at the door forgotten.

Stell examined his face in dismay. She picked carefully at his hair, pulling it back from the bloody gash on his hairline. He smiled up at her.

"What did they do to you?" She whispered.

"It's not important now." The smell of her breath relaxed him more than any incense he had breathed in this room. He reached up to touch her cheek. "I'm okay, Stell. It's poison. It's got to work its way out of my system."

Stell's expression told him all he needed to know about her opinion of the poison. She pulled Tomas to her chest and slipped in behind him, like they were boarding a bobsled. She pushed up the sleeve of her sweater and put the crook of her elbow before his face. With her other hand, she pulled out a knife.

"Open it. You need to feed."

"You can't do that!" Dalle gripped the doorframe. "Desara, stop! Put the knife down."

"He's hurt. He's not healing," Stell said. "He needs blood to heal."

"He's not hurt. He'll heal." Dalle entered the room, his hands out, palms up in surrender. "Listen to me, Desara. You do not want to feed right now, not while the poison is in your system. There is so much we need to do still."

Tomas looked from him to Lucien and Sylva, whose faces were shining with oranges and yellows, the colors of anxiety. Dalle's face remained clear.

"Remember what you told me the first time we fed on Calstow Mountain?" Stell whispered into his hair, her lips brushing the sticky wound on his forehead. "You told me 'this is Nahan. This is natural.' I believed you then. Believe me now. Drink."

Dalle was blocking the colors. He was hiding something.

Tomas stared at Dalle. "Show me your colors."

"If you drink right now you will negate all the poison," Dalle said. "You will never have another chance to see within yourself like this again."

Tomas opened Stell's knife. "You mean *you'll* never have another chance."

Dalle slapped his hands to his face as Tomas cut into the tender skin of Stell's arm and began to feed. He settled back into her warm body, his eyes half closed. His vision drifted toward the ceiling and for just a moment he wondered where the bees had gone.

. . . .

Dalle had never felt such utter exhaustion. Even his own induction had not left him as battered and hollowed as the last two days. He lay back on Sylva's office couch as she and the other Storytellers settled in around the room.

Sylva cracked her knuckles. "So, Desara's left the complex to go see his family. After feeding on his girlfriend, we can assume the effects of the vision poison will be wearing off very quickly. We don't know much about what he saw or if he is aware of any new gifts he's uncovered or if he really understands what happened at all."

Vet touched Dalle's arm. "Was there anything unusual in his vision that you could tell?"

Dalle laughed an unfunny laugh. "You could say that. How about this? He saw Hess."

Lucien could barely whisper the words. "That's impossible."

"It has to be a coincidence," Sylva said. "He heard us talking about him."

"Do you ever talk about Hess?" Dalle asked. "Any of you? Because I don't. I can't."

Vet shook her head. "You must have planted the idea during a thought-circle. After the fact, I mean. Maybe he saw a young man in his vision, but how did he know it was Hess?"

"Well," Dalle said, "maybe because the man told him 'I'm Hess.' And pulled bees out of his throat. Would anyone like to take a wager on what that might mean?"

"Bees?" Sylva drummed her fingers on the desk. Like all human dreams, images and objects had their own meaning for the dreamer but certain objects reappeared in Nahan dreams and visions with consistency, like the black stones whenever one dreamed of an *acul 'ad*. There was no meaning she could think of for bees. "Do you know if Desara is especially afraid of bees? Maybe they're a phobia for him?"

"There's been no sign of it during meditation. I'd have seen it."

Lucien ripped open another candy pack. "What did you say to him about it?"

"Well, I wanted to start with 'Help! I'm having a heart attack!' but I was afraid that would draw too much attention." Even Lucien laughed at that. "I told him what I could, that Hess couldn't handle the training."

"And that was it?" Lucien asked. "He didn't ask anything more?"

"The poison was still shaking him up, rattling him. I couldn't get him to open up."

Vet reached for a candy. "Could that be one of his gifts? Could he be able to read people from objects they've touched? To read residual energy?" While all of them were gifted in general, some were endowed with extra gifts, like Vet's ability to always see colors in the Nahan. Lucien often had prescient dreams, although their hectic and violent nature kept him from calling them an actual gift. Part of the induction and the poisoning was to not only draw out the *Vint* and judge the candidate's ability to handle its presence, but to also shock the mind into opening doors that would otherwise remain closed.

"I suppose it's possible. Hess did train in the same facility, get locked in the same room. Maybe the trauma of it left some sort of resonant energy that Desara was able to tap into. Maybe he can reach out to Hess."

Lucien's voice cracked as he spoke. "But will Hess reach back?"

. . . .

"It's time for your dinner." The young woman pushed open the door and carried in a wooden tray. "It's spaghetti with tomato basil sauce and garlic bread."

"Don't you know we're not supposed to like garlic?"

"You seemed to like it plenty last week in your Caesar salad. I also have a nice super Tuscan wine for you. It's not Barolo, but it's good, especially with it being so cold out tonight."

Hess lay back on the bed and stared at the ceiling. He wished she would stop talking and get out. He had no appetite, although lately he had taken to eating everything on his plate, his body suddenly hungry to build its strength. The girl, a common named Missy or Cassie or Lassie or some such, continued to fuss around the room, laying out his table setting as if he were in a five-star hotel, rather than an isolated house on an isolated island in the middle of an icy lake somewhere in Canada. At least he thought it was Canada. It was cold enough.

He sat up in bed abruptly. "You know, it's bad enough I have to listen to the drone all day. Do I really have to listen to your idiotic chatter, too?"

She adjusted the rose in the vase on the table and smiled placidly. "You might want to eat this right away. Spaghetti is no good cold."

"Get the fuck out." She did and Hess fell back once more onto the bed. At least she no longer offered to join him for meals. He had made his opinion on that topic painfully clear. He pulled the covers back over his legs and searched the ceiling. There, in the shadows of the window, he could hear something small banging against the glass, an insect buzzing, fighting insensibly to break through the glass. Before he could wonder why anything would want out in this cold, the drone kicked on. Then all Hess knew was pain.

Chapter Eight:

DI CRUN FETA

···

Di Crun Feta – literally, *rocks in a puddle*; figuratively, a mess
below the surface; hidden danger

"You talked a lot in your sleep, like you were having nightmares."

Tomas nodded, watching the highway roll past from the back-seat of the town car heading for Deerfield. Stell perched beside him, watchful as she'd been since leaving the complex.

Nightmares didn't begin to describe what went on behind his eyes.

Cold, fear, confusion, exhaustion both physical and mental. Visions of Hess flashed over and over, the pain and horror of the bees worse now that he had returned to the physical plane.

And worse than that? The doubt. Doubting Dalle hurt almost as much as his mentor's rough tone, his abrupt withdrawal.

Almost. Nothing hurt as much as Dalle's withdrawal. Tomas knew he had become addicted to the attention of his mentor, to his presence.

He didn't know who had mentored Hess but he could understand the strange man's anguish if his mentor had pushed him away.

"I was dreaming of someone." These were the first words he had spoken in hours and his throat felt raw. "About an apprentice who was there before me."

"Shelan Hess."

He stared at her. "How could you know that?"

"I'm supposed to talk to you about him."

As the highway fell away behind them, Stell related Adlai's tale of his youth in New Mexico and his friendship with Hess. She ended with Hess's removal from the complex and Adlai's warning to Stell about Tomas's possible fate.

"Can you help him?"

Tomas shut his eyes and saw bees pouring from the ruined throat. He opened his eyes again quickly, needing to see Stell's clear, open face.

"He's not right, Stell. There's all this, this . . . blackness inside him."

"It's been four years since he's seen his best friend. If you went four years without me, what would be inside of you?"

A strangling panic made it hard to speak.

"I don't know what I'm supposed to do. I don't even know where he is."

She ran her fingers over his face, smoothing the furrows between his eyes. "You'll do the right thing." She kissed his eyelids, then settled in beside him on the leather seat.

....

"We're pulling up to the house, Mr. Desara."

"Thank you, Carlson."

The house was dark in the early November dusk. "Do they know we're coming?"

"I told them not to make a big deal about it. Maybe they're watching TV in the back of the house." He hoped so. He wanted the quiet, the calm predictability of his childhood home. He pushed open the door and the room lit up. A chorus sounded.

"Surprise!"

A sign hung over the living room: "Welcome Home, Storyteller!" Beneath it, two dozen Nahan neighbors, friends, and family smiled, holding up champagne glasses.

Tomas squeezed Stell's hand.

His parents stood front and center, Beth's arms out wide waiting for an embrace. To Tomas, the area around her eyes and cheeks glowed an emerald green streaked with glimmering flecks of gold. She looked like a brilliant jewel-toned beacon and he allowed himself to be squeezed tight in her embrace.

"You shouldn't have done this, Mom."

"Oh, pooh!" She held his face between her hands. "I'm so proud of you I could fly!" She kept one hand on his cheek and turned to address the crowd. "Our son, the Storyteller!" Everyone cheered once more and Tomas laughed graciously. Richard slapped his son on the shoulder and Beth made the goodwill gesture of handing Stell a glass of champagne. The crowd moved forward, hugging and hand-shaking, congratulating Tomas.

. . . .

His grandparents hung back from the door, neither wanting to be part of the crush. Tatiana had voiced her opinion that a party at this time would be a bad idea, that it would not be something Tomas would want, but Beth and Richard had disagreed. Seeing Tomas now, Tatiana wished she'd fought harder.

"Things have changed, no?" Charles whispered. "Look at his face."

"He looks tired."

218

"He looks more than that. Watch his eyes." In the course of his life, Charles had had the occasion to work with two Storytellers and, beyond their expected eccentricities, the one thing he remembered about both of them was their strange pattern of eye contact. It wasn't quite shifty, just a hair away from bashful. Tomas was acting the same way. His eyes would flit over a person's face, then down to one side. The longer the person held his hand or demanded his attention, the shorter the sweeps of vision would be. And always, after each encounter, Tomas would raise his eyes to Stell and not look away. It was as if he were breathing through his eyes and all the people in the room were deep bowls of water. He held his breath to see them then turned to Stell to refresh.

Tatiana watched Stell as well. The change in her was remarkable. Gone was the hesitant, awkward country girl. The woman Tatiana saw stood tall and relaxed. Clad entirely in black, she seemed feline in the way she scanned the room. She remained always at Tomas's left shoulder, her fingers grazing his arm as he was pulled through the crowd. She spoke very little but not out of the shyness she had shown over the summer. Rather she seemed removed from the noise and a little bored by it. When Tomas would turn from another well-wisher, she would lean close to him, glad to offer him whatever comfort it was he found in her face.

"It's like she's protecting him."

"It certainly seems that way."

. . . .

The champagne was still flowing two hours later and Tomas had taken to gripping Stell's hand tightly for support. So many faces had moved before him. For the most part they'd been happy for him and proud for his parents but among the crowd he had seen flashes of jealousy and resentment and the hunger of people who were looking for ways to exploit their relationship with a Storyteller. Tomas made no sign that he had seen any of these things glimmering across their faces. Sometimes the colors had been vivid, other times like a faint mirage, but after every encounter he had turned to Stell, whose face remained as clear and pale as the day he had met her. She moved through the room with him, ignoring the partygoers as they ignored her.

At the door to the den in the back of the house, Stell grabbed Tomas by the wrist and pulled the door shut behind them.

"Let them wonder what happened to their precious Storyteller for ten minutes." Her hands worked his shirt from his waistband and moved along his skin.

"Yeah," a voice called out from the corner, "Nobody will find you here." They turned to see Louis and Aricelli bent over a computer reading something online.

Tomas rushed to his cousin. "Louis. Oh, Louis. You're here. How did I miss you?"

"Of course I'm here. Where else would I be?" Louis hugged Tomas, then stepped back to examine him once more. "You look like shit, man. What are they doing to you?"

"You wouldn't believe me in a thousand years."

Aricelli moved in to hug Tomas.

"You look like shit, man. What are they doing to you?"

"You did it!" Tomas ignored him, laughing as Aricelli moved in for a hug. He ran his hands over her face, then turned to Louis to stroke his cousin's cheek as well. He felt light-headed with his relief at seeing them, at being back with them.

"What?" Louis asked. "I shaved? I've been shaving for a while now."

"No." Tomas laughed. "You had your *r 'acul*. I can see it in your faces. Am I right? Did you do it together? Oh my god, did you guys hook up?"

Aricelli leaned in laughing. "It just happened. We were in Boston at this concert and all hell broke loose. The whole city was high that night and we took these two back to our hotel room and the next thing you know, boom, they're gone, we're high, and I'm like 'Oh my god, Louis, you're totally hot!' It was the craziest thing. We just—"

Louis put his hand on her arm to stop her. "That's enough. You don't have to tell him anymore, right? You can see it, can't you?"

Tomas hesitated, bewildered by the shadow on his cousin's face that was punctuated by angry stripes of deep red. "I didn't . . . I didn't, you know, look for it. It's just there."

"Right there on our faces. Right there for you to read anytime you want, like an email we don't have to send."

"Louis," Aricelli said, "I don't think he meant anything by it."

"No, of course he didn't. He's a Storyteller, right?"

"What is this, Louis?" Tomas asked. "Are you pissed at me?"

Louis leaned in close to his face and started to speak but instead made a sound of disgust and turned away. Tomas pulled him back. "No Louis, please, don't just walk away."

"Why not? You did."

"That's it?" Tomas let go of his arm. "That's what you're pissed about? That I'm not around? To do what? Be your wingman? Do you have any idea what I've been going through in this training? How hard it's been?"

"No, I don't, Tomas. I don't have any idea. You know why? Because somewhere along the line, I became some guy you used to know."

"You're my best friend!"

"Bullshit. The Council's your best friend. The Storytellers." Louis pushed Tomas away and Stell stepped forward quickly. "And put a leash on your fucking guard dog."

Tomas went after Louis, who crossed the room to get his drink. He could hardly breathe. First Dalle, now Louis. "Tell me what I can do to make this right. Please." They turned their backs to the room, leaning against the desk, and stared at their reflections in the night-blackened window. Tomas spoke so that only his cousin could hear him.

"They don't call me Tomas at the complex. I'm only allowed to use my last name. When I asked my mentor why, he told me it's so that when all the people who have used me have gone, I'll be able to tell the ones who really knew me. He said that people I've been close with won't be able to look me in the eye and that I may go to the fire without anyone knowing my name."

Louis shook his head. "Sounds like a fun place to work."

"You have no idea." He stared at his cousin in the glass. "I don't mean to see those things, Louis. I haven't learned how to not see them yet. I wish I could. It's exhausting."

Louis sighed. "Dude, I don't give a shit what you see in me. Don't you understand? I'd never hide anything from you. But you're hiding everything from me. I didn't even know you were coming home tonight until Aricelli's mom told me. People keep asking me how you're doing and I just make stuff up so they think we still talk."

"I'm sorry."

"I never heard what happened to you after we stayed out all night. I don't see you for forever when you go into your training and then we hang out one night and you look like shit—and you still look like shit by the way—and you disappear again. You tell me you're in all this trouble and I don't hear a word from you all week. Don't you think I'd be worried about you? I've spent my whole life looking after you, standing in front of you and making sure you don't walk into walls. I can't just turn that off."

"I know." Tomas wondered if his cousin could hear his silent begging that Louis never, ever turn that concern off.

"Dude, I know the word's gone out and you've gotten your Storyteller secret decoder ring or whatever, but are you sure this is what you want? What you want to be?"

Tomas tried to laugh. "It's a little late for that. Those cows are so far from the barn, I can't even tell you."

"Screw that." Louis leaned hard against him, his face serious in the dark reflection. "I don't give a shit what they say. They can give you any title they want—Storyteller or Junior High Prom Queen—you're my cousin first. Underneath it all, you're always going to be Louis Besson's goofy little cousin, got it?"

Tomas nodded, relieved that this roller coaster of emotion finally seemed to be taking an upswing. "I think the word Aricelli used was *daffy*."

"Dude, are you kidding me?" Louis shook his head in mock disapproval. "You saw her naked and you can even think of another woman? That was almost enough to make me change teams." Slipping into classic Louis-regaling mode, he filled Tomas in on the more sordid details, making him laugh out loud, until Aricelli stomped across the room.

"Are you guys talking about me? You are!" She slapped them both and began adding her own details to the story.

The three friends laughed, finally at ease, leaving Stell alone at the front of the room. She curled up in a leather chair, happy to be away from the chatter, happy to see Tomas relax, and happy to be free of the need to join in.

. . . .

Aricelli was loading the dishwasher and Richard was closing the door on the final guest by the time Tomas found his grandparents. Charles and Tatiana sat on the stairs, smiling as Tomas came into the living room carrying a handful of dirty glasses.

"Remember us?"

Tomas dropped the glasses on the coffee table and ran into his grandfather's outstretched arms. "I didn't think you could make it."

Charles kissed the side of his grandson's head as they rocked in their embrace. "Miss this day? Who do you think you're dealing with, kid?"

Tomas pulled away and kissed his grandmother. "It's not a big day. I don't know where Mom got the impression that I had graduated or something. It's really not like that."

Tatiana placed her hand on his cheek. "You look perfectly dreadful."

Tomas settled on the stair next to her, his grandfather on the step below him. "I know. Louis has told me. Stell told me. Would it help if I told you that I look a lot better than I feel?"

Charles reached up to push the hair off of Tomas's face. The tenderness of the gesture brought tears to both their eyes and Tatiana laughed.

"You'll never be able to deny each other, you two. Tomas, you inherited your grandfather's tender heart and copious tears."

"I've given up fighting it, Grandma. It's a losing battle."

"Good." She patted his knee. "It's a good quality. It's one of the many reasons I fell in love with Charles all those years ago. The ability to be moved in a hard world is a sign of strength. Don't ever forget that."

"You forgot to mention that he also inherited my good looks."

"That goes without saying, Charles."

"Speaking of good looks," Charles tilted his head toward Stell, who relaxed on the living room couch, ignoring the glares from Aricelli, Louis, and Beth, who were busy cleaning up from the party. "Stell looks good."

"She's kind of come into her own, you know?"

"She's *acul 'ad*, no?" Tatiana smiled at Tomas's surprise. "What? You think we've spent our whole life on Calstow Mountain? Tell me, Charles, who does she remind you of?"

"I was thinking the same thing. Nadia. When your grand-mother was at court, when we had only known each other a short while, she had a maid who was *acul 'ad*. And let me tell you some-thing, Tomas, in those days a poor Russian *acul 'ad* was a black stone indeed." His grandparents laughed, sharing the memory.

"You never told me this, Grandma."

"There are many things I've never told you." She slapped his knee. "And I'm not going to tell you tonight. Why are you chang-ing the subject? We are here to talk about you."

"I'm sick of talking about me." Tomas buried his head in his hands. "I'm sick of being me."

Tatiana rubbed his back. "You have chosen a very difficult path, a Storyteller advising the Council. But always remember, Tomas, the Council serves the Nahan, not the other way around. Never let the institution become more important than"—

Tomas raised his head. "Please, Grandma, don't start quoting Benjamin Franklin."

She patted his cheek. "Tomas, you are a good man. You are a man like your grandfather with a true heart and generous nature. Despite what you may believe, I'm not an anarchist. While I do believe your father, our son, has been too easily misled by his bureaucracy-loving wife,"—Tomas sighed but Tat forged ahead— "I understand the Council has done a great deal of good. This is not the aristocratic court of France; I know the world has changed a great deal. But we are still Nahan. We are still Ourselves, apart. And if we do not work as one for one another we will not survive."

Tomas wanted to close his eyes. He wanted Stell to get him away from this place. He loved his grandparents with all his heart but he knew that once his grandmother got on this topic, she could hold forth for some time. The words felt physically heavy against his ears. Still, this was his grandmother.

"Yes, Grandma Tat, I know. I assume you're going somewhere with this?"

"I am. You remember Elmer Braddus, who grows those delicious Braeburn apples that you love so much." Tomas nodded. There were miles of apple and pear farms around Calstow Mountain held and managed by a handful of Nahan families. "He came to us over the winter. He knows our Richard and Beth have connections to the Central Council. It seems someone has decided that the Council will be better served if ownership of the land is handed over to them and handled from their headquarters; that the profits of the orchards could be increased if the farming techniques were updated."

"Maybe they're right," Tomas said. "There are cooperative Nahan farms all over the country that turn a profit. There are scientists who know how to make crops disease-resistant."

"Tomas, these people have grown heirloom, heritage quality fruit for two centuries. They do not do it for money. They do it to sustain their lives and their land. They ask for very little help. Even if there were a way to do it 'more efficiently,' is efficiency the only goal of life? Or more money?"

"But if they've asked for help—"

"Then we should give it to them because we are Nahan and we take care of each other. Does this mean we force each other to live like Louis's family? Or Aricelli's? Or even our own? I have no interest in being an apple farmer but I have a great deal of interest in allowing an apple farmer to be. Do you understand what I'm saying, Tomas?"

Tomas put his head down on his knees. "I do, Grandma. But I'll ask you the same question I asked Stell. What do you want me to do about it?" Tatiana answered as Stell had.

"The right thing."

· ·

Louis thumbed through a comic book. They were crowded into Tomas's old bedroom, Louis and Aricelli on one twin bed; Tomas facing them on another. Stell lay on her stomach at the foot of Tomas's bed pushing a yellow Matchbox car around in circles. Downstairs, they could hear Charles and Tatiana laughing with Beth and Richard.

He hadn't asked his friends to join him but after the party cleanup had finished, he and Louis had wandered up the stairs together. Aricelli followed, Stell behind her. Nobody spoke. Nobody needed to.

Tomas was the Storyteller but Louis and Aricelli could read him like the comic book Louis flipped through. They knew he needed to be here, that he needed the silence.

How many lifetimes had he spent in quiet suburban rooms like this, his cousin waiting, never losing his patience, for Tomas to ask him his questions? Tomas turned to Louis to explain everything—blood, girls, wet dreams, cars, how to pass algebra—every new discovery eased by his cousin's experience and easy charm. And now? Now an ocean, a planet, a universe of knowledge had been crammed into his skull and where did he go? Back to his room, back to Louis and Aricelli and the memory of safety there.

"They think there's something wrong with me."

Tomas saw Louis struggle not to react. Aricelli looked up from reading over Louis's shoulder. "What did they say?"

Their attention felt like heat. "They didn't say anything. They hid their . . . they didn't say anything." He stared at the illustrated panel Louis had stopped on, gunfire drawn as starbursts, the same yellows and reds of anxiety Dalle had masked.

Louis kept his voice soft. "Then how do you know there's something wrong?"

"Dalle, my mentor, was hiding something from me." Stell drew closer, rising to her knees beside him. "There was someone before me, an apprentice who didn't . . . He was in the same program I am, doing the same training, and they said he couldn't take it."

"And?" Louis asked. "You could take it, right? I mean, you graduated or whatever."

"It's not like that. I'm not done. I don't know if I'll ever be done." He finally met Louis's eye. "And I think I screwed up by leaving the complex before I was supposed to. There was this other stuff they wanted me to do but I left."

"Why?"

Tomas didn't want to say the words aloud. "Because they were lying to me."

Stell leaned forward. "They lied to Adlai."

"You don't know that, Stell. You only know what Adlai told you." He saw Louis and Aricelli waiting for an explanation. "Adlai is Stell's escort, her bodyguard, and his friend Hess is the one, the apprentice . . ."

"The one who didn't make it," Louis said.

"They hurt him." Stell grabbed his leg. "Adlai said they hurt him and sent him away. The Council did, the Storytellers. They're holding him prisoner."

"Stell—"

"Tomas! You said he was hurt. You said—"

"I said there was something wrong with him."

"So you think Adlai is lying?"

"I don't understand," Aricelli said. "I thought once you were a Storyteller you could tell who was telling the truth."

"It's not that simple," Tomas said. "Truth is what we believe it to be. People can hide things if their reasons are strong enough to them. Plus Adlai's *acul 'ad* so he's really hard to read."

"Holy shit." Louis leaned in. "He's *acul 'ad*?"

It hadn't occurred to Tomas until that moment how much their lives had parted paths. Storytellers and *acul 'ads* and security systems were an everyday part of his life now. This wasn't the case for his friends. He didn't dare think how they would react when they learned that truth about Stell. "That's not the point. Even if I could read him, the truth is fluid. He may really believe his friend is in danger, even if it's not technically true. I know Stell believes it."

He saw the look his friends shared. Deciding between the reliability of Stell versus the Council whose boundaries they had lived within their entire lives wasn't a difficult choice. Stell didn't seem to care about their verdict; she looked only to Tomas.

"What would you want someone to say to me, Tomas? If you were missing, if you were hurt after all they put you through? If I saw you carried out screaming and I never saw you again?" She squeezed his knee. "What would you want someone to say to me then? Or to Louis or Aricelli? Or to your parents, your grandparents?"

He saw the answer in her face. "I'd want them to say they'd do anything to save me. But Stell, you didn't see this guy. You didn't feel him. He pulled bees from his throat."

Louis and Aricelli drew back as one. This wasn't some little kid crisis. This wasn't a bully on the playground or a dreaded invitation to a dance. Tomas lived in a different world now, behind the scenes of the authority that had shaped their lives. How could he ask them for help?

"All right, you guys, bees aside, let's stay on point. Are you absolutely certain this guy is still alive?" Tomas nodded, relieved at Aricelli's take-charge attitude. Louis too seemed to relax with the conversation headed toward practical matters. "What are we looking for? First, we need information. We need to find out if this guy is actually being detained. If he is, we need to find out details about the facility. Can we visit him? Is he there against his will? If he is being imprisoned, what can be done to get him out? And is that a good idea?"

Tomas drummed his fingers on his knees. "What kind of place could hold him? It couldn't just be a regular kind of facility. Remember what happened at the Irish pub? And that was after just a few weeks of training. This guy could be way better at manipulation than I was. The only people who could hold him would be Storytellers."

"Would they?" Aricelli asked. "Would they hold him?"

"Not against his will," Tomas said, hoping they felt more convinced than he did. "Not unless, you know, there was no choice. If he was a danger to himself."

Louis spoke up. "Okay, let's look at it this way. Regardless of where this dude is, there is one surefire way of never finding him and that's to call anyone on the Council and say, 'Oh, by the way, where's that Storyteller prison place?' If the Storytellers want it to be a secret, the Council will make sure you never find it."

"He's right," Aricelli said. "I don't know what kind of hoodoo-voodoo the Storytellers use, Tomas, but this is the Council we're talking about. It's power plays and maneuvering. Information is like money. You gotta have it to make it and if you don't have it, you gotta fake it until you do."

Tomas felt the familiar sensation of being in over his head. "Are you guys going to tell me what this means?"

Louis slapped his knee. "It means, bro, you're going to go back into that complex and act like you already know all you need to know about this Hess guy and his incarceration. You're going to need all your best bullshitting skills."

He let his head hang. "I don't even have the words to explain to you the impossibility of bullshitting my mentor, Dalle. When I tell you he's inside my head . . ." He squeezed his eyes shut. "Let's just say these aren't drunken sorority girls we're dealing with."

"You just head back to the complex and do your thing." Louis used the same big-brother tone he'd used to guide Tomas all their lives. "My family is in security; Aricelli's is money; yours is real estate. We have channels in the Council. Let us work that side. For now, find out what you can about this Hess guy without looking like you're pumping them for information."

Aricelli reached across and took his hand. "We're your friends, Tomas. We've always been. If this is important to you, it's important to us."

. . . .

Tomas excused himself to make his goodbyes to his parents and grandparents. Once he and Stell had left the room, Louis lay back on the bed. "You're being very helpful in all this."

"Of course I am. Why wouldn't I be?"

"Questioning the Council to help Stell's friend? I didn't know you girls were so close."

"Grow up, Louis. If there is something unethical going on inside the Council, I think we have an obligation to do what we can to uncover it."

"Hmm, when you put it that way, I can see you're right." He leaned in close and tapped a finger on her forehead. "Thank you, Alien Pod Person. Now, may I speak with Aricelli?"

She brushed his hand away with a laugh. "What?"

"Unethical? Your father is the king of unethical and he doesn't give a rat's ass what the Council does. He's in it for power and money and he's good at it. And you are a chip off the old block. You want me to believe you're rushing in to right a wrong? Save it for Heritage School."

"Hey, what kind of person do you think I am?"

"Everyone else may have you pegged for a beauty queen but I know you are a born *tu Bith*, the original moneymaker. And if I thought for a second you were drinking the Council's Kool-Aid I'd have you committed. Look, I've had to hop-step to that 'Council Knows Best' crap with my parents my whole life. I don't care what the Council does and neither do you, except for how it can work to your advantage. So why this urge to start crusading all of a sudden?"

"Do I have to say it out loud?" Aricelli rose with a huff and flopped down on the other bed. "Come on, Louis. You heard Tomas. He saw this guy pulling bees out of his throat?"

"What are you saying?"

"I'm saying that Tomas is sweet. You've protected him his entire life. You know I love him too but he's not the toughest person you'll ever meet. Maybe the reason there are so few Storytellers is because a lot of them crack up."

"Aricelli, don't."

"I don't give a shit about some kooky friend of Stell's. If this place exists, we need to find it before Tomas winds up there."

. . . .

They rode back to Chicago in silence. All the talking, all the noise fell away behind them with the miles. As hard as he tried, however, Tomas couldn't shake the metallic twist of anxiety that ran down his neck. Stell sighed and kissed his hand.

"Thank you for trying to find Adlai's friend."

"I'm glad I can make Adlai happy."

"And me."

He leaned his head back against the leather. "And you. Especially you."

. . . .

As Carlson pulled up before their apartment building, Tomas felt that twinge of anxiety again. He searched his mind for what could be triggering this metallic twisting in his neck but before he could come up with anything, someone tapped on the driver's window.

The window beside Stell lowered. It was Adlai.

She brightened and reached for the door handle but Tomas stopped her hand.

"We just got home. It's the middle of the night."

"Nature of the beast." Adlai rested his muscular forearms on the window. "I'm afraid most of our work is done in the dark."

For one terrible moment, Tomas saw himself driving his fist into the smirking face of the *acul 'ad* at the window. He could feel the electricity coming off of Stell as she thought of heading into the night with Adlai. Tomas wanted to demand that she stay but knew such a move was not only futile, it would make him look pathetic to both Stell and Adlai.

"Yeah, if you've got to work, by all means, work."

Stell kissed the side of his face then climbed out of the car. "I won't be that late, I promise. Oh, but you'll probably already be at the complex, won't you? So, I'll see you tomorrow, yes?" She didn't wait for his answer, but climbed on the back of Adlai's bike. Tomas pulled the door shut behind her but not before the motorcycle's exhaust fumes tainted the air within the car.

Carlson cleared his throat. "Would you like me to get your bags, sir?"

"No." He looked up at the darkened windows of their empty apartment. "Let's just go on over to the complex. No point in going home now."

Tomas sighed as Carlson pulled out into traffic. It was such a stupid situation. What did he expect? Of course Stell would want to ride off with Adlai. He was dangerous and muscular and unpredictable and so fucking muscular. He certainly was not constantly exhausted and pulled in a thousand different directions and counted on to always do the exact right thing at the exact right moment for the whole world at the drop of a hat.

"Excuse me, sir? Mr. Desara?" Carlson broke Tomas' torturous train of thought. "Um, I was wondering if I could talk to you about something. It's, well, it's not exactly within my job description."

Carlson struggled to find the words and Tomas watched the muscles in the man's jaw work. Maybe it was a trick of the light in the dark car but there emerged around the driver a tangle of lines, like the cloud of dust that always followed Pigpen in the Peanuts cartoons. The driver was oblivious to their appearance and Tomas realized that Carlson was the source of the anxiety he had been feeling the entire drive.

"I don't want you to think that I eavesdrop because I don't. I take my job very seriously, Mr. Desara, and I understand how sensitive the work at the complex is. I'm sixth-generation Kott and, believe me, I'm well aware of the importance of secrecy."

Tomas put his hand on the driver's shoulder to reassure him. "I understand."

Carlson pulled off the road into the parking lot of a shopping center and turned to face him. "It's about what you were talking about on the way out to Deerfield, about Mr. Hess. I drove for him like I do for you. For over a year. He was a great guy. I mean, he was really a pleasure to work for." The tangle of lines around Carlson's face twitched and darkened.

"Why are you telling me this?"

The web wrapped tightly around Carlson's throat and Tomas had to look away. It was clear this was hard for the Kott to talk about but the image of his strangulation was disturbing. "It's the way he was just gone. I know it's none of my business but it was just so sudden and, well, Mr. Hess was a really nice man to work for. Funny, you know? Please don't tell anybody, but we used to stop at bars on the way back from his training. He'd buy drinks and we'd laugh and talk. Even Mr. Adlai would laugh."

Tomas rubbed his eyes, the strain of trying not to see the pulsing web of anxiety over the driver's face exhausting him. "What is it exactly that you're trying to tell me?"

Carlson sighed. "I think I know where he is. I mean, I don't know exactly, like an address or anything, but I wasn't the only one who liked Mr. Hess. He had this really nice way about him, not nice like waitress-nice, but sort of funny and crazy that got on some people's nerves but a lot of us really liked. Especially, you know, us." He tapped his chest.

"Kott."

"Yeah. Us. Sometimes, and I don't mean you, and I don't mean any disrespect, really I don't, but sometimes we're kind of invisible around here. You all will talk around us and say things like we can't hear you."

"And you heard where Hess is?"

"Not exactly."

"What exactly?" Tomas was beginning to regret not getting out at his apartment.

"Just a name. Westin. I think it's the name of a facility. A private one."

"Do you know where it is?"

Carlson shook his head. "But I do know that it's run by Kott. See, when I was driving for Mr. Hess, we went to a confab in Detroit and I met this Kott girl and we started talking. We're not allowed inside the confabs, so there's all this time to kill. Anyway, she was going to college and was having trouble because"—

Tomas dropped his head back against the leather seat. Like his grandmother, Carlson could talk endlessly. Unlike his grandmother, however, the driver needed no particular topic. Tomas dug his nails into his palms, struggling to keep from drowning in the ocean of words pouring from the Kott's mouth. Something about a girl with epilepsy and a PhD. A solitary assignment. Needing to find a replacement. Tomas didn't want to offend any member of the Kott but he thought his ears might be bleeding from the assault.

"Carlson, please. It's very late. Can we get to the point?"

"Yeah, sure, I'm sorry. I'm nervous, you know?" He smiled and wiped a line of sweat off his upper lip. "Okay, so here's what happened. I'm assigned to pick up a new Kott assistant at O'Hare, Katie something or other. She's real young, college girl, and as soon as she gets in the car, she's on her cell. And, like I said, I don't want to eavesdrop but I've got ears and I hear things and she asks, 'How long a drive is it to Westin?' Well I've never heard of Westin but I file it away in my mind, you know? I'm very verbal. Words just stick to me. They always have." Tomas believed him completely.

"So after she gets off the phone, we start talking. She tells me she's here for some *sensitive*—that's the word she used, *sensitive*—project and that she's real excited about it. Then this beep goes off on her cell phone and I think she's taking another call but no, it's an alarm and she pulls out a bottle of pills. Well, I don't want to pry but she sees me looking and tells me she has epilepsy. And I say, 'No kidding! I've got a friend with epilepsy.'"

Tomas fought the urge to throw himself out of the car.

"I tell her about Deb and she says, 'Deb McKinley? You're kidding! That's who I'm replacing!' Then, I guess she figures since I knew Deb, I knew about this Westin place, and she tells me how nervous she is about being alone with just this one guy. I act like I know what she's talking about because, you know, I don't want to seem stupid or anything, and she starts talking about isolation studies and how even the Nahan are nervous about this guy and all the security protocols she's got to learn. You see what I'm saying?"

Tomas had gone so long without blinking his eyes were dry. He squeezed them shut and tried to speak slowly. "It's very late, Carlson. I'm sorry, I don't seem to be following you. What do two girls with epilepsy have to do with Hess?"

"They didn't just have epilepsy. They both studied the psychology of prisons and prisoners. Deb got her gig the week Mr. Hess was taken away. She's done and this girl is brought in. Same major, same illness, same hush-hush status. Now I don't claim to understand how you all operate in there but Mr. Hess told me things about what he did for a living. Most of it didn't make sense, you know, and he liked to pull my leg a lot but you could tell that he was treated differently inside that complex just like you are."

"How do you know how I'm treated inside the complex?"

Carlson held his palms up. "People talk. And they don't see us when they do."

"Apparently not." Tomas chewed the inside of his lip. The lines that had entangled Carlson's head were thinning and fading now that he had unburdened his soul. "So why didn't you tell any of this to Adlai? He's been looking everywhere for his friend."

"He hasn't been looking here. I know him and Mr. Hess were good friends but they weren't much alike. Mr. Adlai is one of those guys who doesn't look at us, any of us. He's, um, kind of cold, you know?"

Tomas laughed without humor. "I know. Trust me. Can you find out where this Westin place is? Do you still stay in touch with this Deb lady?"

"Yeah, but she won't tell me."

"Even if you tell her it's important?"

"Look, Mr. Desara. I really want to help Mr. Hess. I'm worried about him. It's not like him to just disappear like that but I've got to be careful. Deb's not going to say anything because they made it really clear that it was top secret. I know I told you sometimes we Kott are invisible but we've got to assume we're not, you get what I'm saying? I mean, this is not the kind of job you get fired from, if you get my meaning."

Chapter Nine:

PETILN

....

Petiln: literally *to desire another*; the requests for life
guidance from Storytellers

The industrial park was nearly empty. Tomas covered the hallways,
passing darkened offices of common and Nahan alike. Carlson's
words haunted him. He walked past these doors every day. How
many people did he just blow by without noticing? The two common
security guards waved him on into the secure blue-carpeted area and
the Nahan receptionist smiled up at him as if showing up at night
were the most natural thing in the world. He pressed his thumbprint
to the scanner and entered the halls of the Council complex.

Most of the offices were dark; Vartan's light was off. A few people whispered among themselves in the Communication Room but
for the most part the business of the day was over. From the very

last conference room on the right side of the hall, light spilled out from under the door. Tomas poked his head in and found Dalle kicked back surrounded by files. The Storyteller scribbled a note, tossed the folder onto the floor, and reached for another one. When he saw Tomas in the doorway, he paused mid-reach.

"Good lord, tell me I haven't worked all night."

"No," Tomas said. "It's still night. I couldn't sleep."

Dalle gestured to an empty chair. "You feel okay?" Tomas slipped into the seat quietly. "It's not a trick question, Desara."

"I feel okay." He wished Dalle would look at him. "I'm sorry. About leaving the way I did. Have I really fucked things up?"

Dalle made a sound that could almost be a laugh. "Oh, on the list of fuck-ups that have come from this building, yours isn't even in the top one hundred." He smiled at Tomas.

And there it was, the flood of Dalle's attention, like a warm front pounding across the room. Tomas couldn't have explained it to anyone, he didn't have the words, but he felt it pour over him, easing the pain in his chest.

"You'll find, Desara, that the line between good decisions and bad is very, very blurry. But that's what we do as Storytellers. We keep making decisions." He tapped a pile of folders in front of him.

"What are those?"

"*Petiln*." Dalle said.

Tomas cocked his head. "Infidelity?"

Dalle looked up. "That's kind of literal. *Petiln* are our day job. You didn't think we just sat around poisoning each other, did you? These are the itsy-bitsy pieces that make up our big world. Complaints, requests, job recommendations, identity swaps, you name it. Most of the time people make their own decisions, for better or worse, but sometimes they feel stuck or unsure or just bored with their own decisions and they request advice from us. Here's one."

He slid a folder before Tomas. Inside was a photograph of a young Nahan woman at a desk in a cubicle.

"This is Elena. Just outside of Indianapolis. She's working in an insurance firm and has been very helpful putting paperwork through for us on a number of medical claims. She's reaching her first century mark, needs to flip, doesn't know what to do with her life. The Council wants her to stay in the industry, albeit under another name, doing what she's doing now because she's good at it but she wants a change."

"So what do we do?"

"We look at her," Dalle said, "dream about her and come up with something for her."

Tomas looked up to see if he was kidding. "How am I supposed to do that?"

"I already told you." Dalle held up the photo of Elena. "Look at her, Desara. Dream about her. This isn't rocket science."

"But won't I just be making it all up?"

Dalle spoke in a singsong. "Maybe that's why they say 'Life Could Be a Dream.' Just try it. No harm in it. She doesn't have to take your suggestions if she doesn't want to."

Feeling silly, Tomas leaned back in the chair and studied the photo of Elena the Insurance Agent. He focused on nothing really, just letting her eyes look into his through the camera lens. As he stared, the planes of her face began to lighten, the shadows under her eyes darkened. He saw her bitten fingernails and the paper cut on her right index finger. Behind her, her in-box overflowed and a cup of paperclips had spilled on the blotter. The tail end of a croissant stuck out of a crumpled wrapper next to a short cup of espresso. On the bulletin board behind her, he could just make out a picture of a full moon. He heard a faint whispering in his head and sighed.

"Can she go to Paris? Fashion? She's got an excellent head for business. Do we have any boutiques she could run? Or be a personal assistant? She'd like Paris."

"We'd all like Paris." Dalle grinned.

"Yeah, but I think she needs it."

He slid Tomas a pen. "Write it on there."

"What? Where?"

"Right there on the bottom of the situation request. Say 'recommend Paris, business training or personal assistance.' We'll forward it to Resources and they'll find her a match. There's always someone who needs an assistant somewhere."

"Just like that?"

"Just like that. If she takes it, you just cost the Council several tens of thousands of dollars and a reliable insurance agent."

Tomas hesitated in his writing. "Is that a problem?"

"Does it feel like a problem?"

"No."

Dalle laughed and opened another folder.

. . . .

The offices around them were coming to life by the time they'd cleared half the files. Despite the hours of work, Tomas felt energized.

Dalle was also bright eyed. "This part of the gig doesn't suck, does it?"

"No, it doesn't. It would be nice if this is all there was."

Dalle straightened a stack of folders from the floor. "I hope you're not waiting for me to tell you that's how it is because it isn't, but there are some bright spots. And for your first crack at *petiln*, you did a pretty nice job. Expensive but nice." He stood up and stretched his back. "Come on, let's go see what Sylva has in her snack drawer."

In the darkened office, Dalle moved easily, finding Sylva's stash of snacks. Tomas flicked on a small silk-covered lamp, bathing the room in a soft golden tone. He and Dalle flopped on the couch.

"It's a good thing you came back, kid," Dalle said, holding up a bag of Reese's Pieces. "Sylva got these just for you."

"Those are my favorite."

"I know."

Tomas rolled his eyes. "Of course you know. Want some?" His mentor picked out a few pieces and popped them into his mouth. "Dalle, how long have you been here in Chicago?"

"I moved here when they built the complex. We used to be in St. Louis until we got this land and built this center. It was quite a feather in the Council's cap." He glanced at Tomas and shook his head. "It's strange to think how this must look to you. You've never known anything but the Council, have you? They've been established your whole life. In this form, I mean."

"Was there another form?"

Dalle waggled his hand. "It hasn't always been so formal, so established. In many ways it has made things easier for us, even for, you know, *us*. Less minutiae,, less squabbling. Or at least, we don't have to squabble." He laughed to himself. "Now we have professional squabblers, little people who just love fighting over minutiae. It's practically Vartan's reason to breathe."

When Tomas said nothing, Dalle nudged him. "Does that make you uncomfortable?"

Tomas knew there was no point in hiding it. "Yeah, kind of. I mean Mr. Vartan is the Coordinator of the Central Council. My mom works for the Council. The group I grew up in, everyone works for the Council. The Coordinator is the boss; he's responsible for everything."

Dalle patted his knee. "Oh Desara, you have a lot to learn. I don't envy your transition, coming up in the middle of a Council family. I have to make a note to address this in Heritage School. Vartan is a bureaucrat. A good one, if such a thing exists. He knows protocol; he likes meetings; he's good at surrounding himself with smart people. But he operates within strict guidelines. He has profits to make; he has to protect the Kott; he has to stay on top of the paperwork." Dalle grabbed some more candy. "I wonder what you must look like to him."

"What do you mean?"

"I mean that for the first time in his life, he may think there's a Storyteller that will call him boss. Someone that grew up in Heritage School. Make no mistake, Desara"—Dalle pointed his finger at Tomas—"you don't call him Mr. Vartan anymore. You don't answer to him. He answers to you. We try not to flaunt this obvious dominance of authority but it seems we may need to refresh the point. I need to keep reminding myself how new this must seem to you, questioning the Council."

"Believe me, Stell is on board with teaching me that lesson."

Dalle laughed out loud. "I like her. I'm glad you have her. I even like that she told me to shut up." He nudged Tomas. "But tell her not to do that again. It's good that you've had her with you through all this. She's quite a girl. A black stone, indeed."

"It hasn't been easy." Tomas knew Dalle could hear the strain in his words.

"I know, kid. It never is. It's such a strange pairing, Storytellers and *acul 'ads*. Irresistible but strange. We're both able to do things that the rest of our people cannot. But for all we can see, it's hard to understand what drives them. But there must be a reason behind it because there are two things every young Storyteller has—a grumpy mentor and an *acul 'ad* friend."

Tomas took the risk. "Like Hess and Anton Adlai?"

"Exactly," Dalle said. "If you think I'm grumpy, you should have seen Lucien. He suffers from vivid dreams, prescient, sometimes even apocalyptic. That's one of the reasons Lucien can be such a prick."

Tomas laughed. "That's not how I imagined Storytellers talking about each other."

"We're still Nahan, kid. We still screw up and want things and fear things and forget things." He sighed. "We're still human. Lucien wakes up a nervous wreck half the time. When he realized Hess had those same types of dreams, long before his induction, Lucien felt a sort of kinship toward him, kind of an empathy. Me? I never could get a handle on Hess. We were always apart, at corners to each other."

"You didn't like him?"

"It's not like that. We just didn't connect. He was nervous and prickly and tough, always being funny and looking for the angle. I found him exhausting. And she never said it but I think he irritated the shit out of Sylva. And as for Anton Adlai," Dalle chuckled at Tomas's groan. "*Acul 'ads* are a story unto themselves."

. . . .

The crowd was thin at Petey's, the Nahan bar that had so surprised Stell her first night working with Adlai. The bartender set two beers before them as Adlai pulled out a cell phone.

"I thought you didn't carry a phone."

He finished reading the message. "No. I said I don't carry a Council phone. This is private. Just like the job."

"What is the job?"

"It may not be anything. Or it may be something you're really going to like."

The bartender slid a small cloth-wrapped bundle across the bar. Adlai pulled back a corner of the rag, revealing what looked to Stell like a wad of electrical tape and gum. He nodded his approval and slipped the package into his jacket pocket.

"Hopefully I won't have to use this."

The bartender laughed. "Yeah, I know how you hate violence. You got the address?"

Adlai nodded and tipped back the last of his beer.

. . . .

He pulled the bike up to the freight elevator of a factory building not far from Petey's. Stell watched as he pulled out key after key on his key ring, unlocking a labyrinthine lock system, before lifting the gate and rolling the bike into the grimy car. She hopped in behind him and Adlai pulled out even more keys to make the elevator carry them to the top floor.

"Where are we?" She peered into the darkened room as Adlai rolled the bike out.

"My place. Dropping the bike off. We don't need it tonight."

Stell tried to make out details of the apartment in the darkness but could only sense its size. Their footsteps echoed and the dim lights of the city below barely pierced the enormous grated windows that covered one wall. She assumed they would go back down in the elevator; instead, Adlai pushed open one of the glass panes and climbed out into the darkness.

"You coming?"

He was halfway to the roof as she scrambled out the window, a rusty fire escape groaning under his heavy boots. She climbed quickly to join him and they headed off across the tar paper expanse of the roof. At this end of town, the buildings were close, sometimes touching, and the two *acul 'ads* moved from building to building easily.

At the end of a long block of warehouses, he darted right and headed to the raised edge of the roofline. Not waiting to see if she had followed, he gripped a cluster of drainpipes and swung down into the darkness below. Stell knelt on the edge of the roof and watched as he shimmied down the pipes, slipped onto the narrow ledge, and pounded the window frame. She couldn't see how he held on, his grip on the brick maintained with the tips of his fingers, but at last the window gave way. The upper half of the pane vanished within the building, the lower half swung out, and Adlai shifted his balance and leapt inside. A moment later, he stuck his head out and looked up at Stell.

"What are you? The lookout? Let's go, Slick."

Without a thought, Stell slipped off the edge of the roof, trusting Adlai, trusting her own strength, and shimmied down the pipes, along the ledge, and in through the open window. She followed Adlai through a maze of broken pallets and crates, industrial shelving, and massive columns of faded cardboard boxes. She followed him up into the metal catwalk that crisscrossed the ceiling of the loading area. He circled the large room, checking for lines of sight, and settled down on a rusted metal plate overlooking the largest of the loading bay doors.

"What are we doing?" Stell asked, sitting down beside him.

"Waiting to find out if some friends of mine are getting ripped off. I've got a buddy who moves precious stones for people. It's about eighty percent legit, if you know what I mean." Stell nodded, not knowing what he meant. "So there's been some talk that one of his employees has been ripping him off a little bit here and there and has now decided to make one final haul. The word is that if this cat's grabbed a bundle, he's going to be moving them here tonight for a large sum of cash."

"What if it's not true?"

Adlai shrugged. "If it's not true, we spend a night chilling in a dirty warehouse. If it is true and that piece of shit shows up with Boxi's diamonds, it's going to end really badly."

"For him."

"For all of them."

"How many do you think it will be?" Stell bit her lip and Adlai chuckled.

"Enough. For both of us."

She swung her feet, her body gearing up at the thought of the excitement to come. Her eyes scanned the doors, willing someone to enter.

"Relax. We've got some time to kill, so to speak. The drop's not until three a.m., although if there's going to be a double cross, somebody will be here early to get into position."

"What do you mean, double cross?"

"These are bad guys, Stell. They cheat and steal and rip each other off. Don't get me wrong. I don't mind cheating and stealing but when it comes to the common, they'll cheat the eyes right out of your head. Supposedly the deal is with some Russians and they're usually good for some ugly gunplay so we're going to sit here and see who shows up. If a sharpshooter shows up first and gets into position, we'll know the deal is on and we know he'll probably do most of the killing for us."

"Not all of it, right?"

Adlai laughed out loud. "No, sweetheart, not all of it, I promise."

. . . .

In less than an hour, a door groaned somewhere beneath and to the left of them. They leaned over the railing and watched as a slim man in a black jacket and watch cap darted through the loading area. Putting his finger to his lips for silence, Adlai slipped to his feet and pulled Stell up with him. Below them, the sharpshooter scanned the warehouse, looking for a hiding place, and spotted the ladder up into the catwalk. The sounds of his feet banging on the metal steps hid the sounds of Adlai and Stell as they climbed up into the girders in the ceiling. The sniper ran quickly and silently across the catwalk, choosing to set up his shot less than three feet from where they had been seated just moments before. Adlai looked bored as he watched the man screw a silencer onto a large gun he had pulled from his jacket pocket.

"They'll be here within a half hour." His breath was hot on Stell's ear as he whispered to her and a shiver of anticipation rippled through her. Another metallic clanging sounded below and the sniper hunkered down, frozen in place.

"I'll be damned." Adlai shook his head.

"What is it?"

He pointed to a dark figure climbing a tall stack of cartons to the right of the loading door. The figure made it to the top of the stack and lay down on his stomach, propped up on his elbows. In his hands was a long gun much like that of the sniper above him.

"That is proof that there's nobody like the common for screwing a deal." He pulled Stell close to him so he could whisper in her ear. Her body was already heating up as the adrenaline began to pump. "The good news is there are going to be a lot more people than we expected. The bad news is they're all going to be killing each other. Son of a bitch, it's a wonder we ever get to kill them."

The catwalk sniper checked his aim, ready to kill the gunman below him. Stell looked from one to the other. "So who works for who? Which one is the bad guy?"

"They both are and they're both going to die. This guy," he pointed to the sniper on the catwalk, "is just going to live a little longer, since he's going to start the killing for us."

As if on cue, the sniper on the catwalk leveled his gun and with a whistling *ssst,* the gunman on the crates below collapsed off his elbows, his head turned at an uncomfortable angle. Adlai glanced at Stell. "Nice shot. We're going to have to take him out quickly. Why don't you hang here behind him while I get in position by the ladder. Once the shooting starts, you drop this guy quick. We'll wait for the gunplay to die down and anyone left standing is ours. Sound good?"

Stell nodded, shifting on the girder to let Adlai crabwalk past her. He moved quickly over the girders, crossing the space over the loading area silently. Stell watched him, enjoying the sight of the muscles of his back and arms as he balanced himself and jumped from beam to beam. Restlessness pricked at her own muscles and she swore she could taste the blood that would soon be spilled below.

Stell could smell the adrenaline pumping in the common below her. He wiped his hands on his pants then reestablished his grip on the gun. It was time.

A small man with long arms stepped into the loading bay holding a briefcase. He was joined by an even smaller man whose hands were stuffed deep in the pockets of his varsity jacket. The two whispered to each other, scanning the room. The steel door beside the darkened office swung open, a sliver of streetlight casting the new arrivals in dramatic shadow.

Even Stell paused at the impressive entrance. Four men, the Russians, she presumed, clogged the doorway, their long coats filling out their already impressive bulk. One man stepped forward, the other three falling into step behind him as all six met in the middle of the warehouse floor. Stell couldn't make out their words but saw the long-armed man open his briefcase and pull out a cloth pouch. From among the Russian giants, one man pulled out a matching case, opening it to reveal neat stacks of money. The conversation was brief, the packages exchanged hands, and both parties began to retreat.

The two skinny men almost made it into the shadows of the door. The sniper caught the long-armed one, who collapsed in a heap. His partner's skinniness turned out to be an asset as he twisted and leapt, avoiding a spray of bullets and diving behind a pallet of wooden crates. The sniper rose to find him, never hearing Stell as she dropped onto the catwalk behind him. One quick snap of his neck and he folded gracefully upon himself. She hurried to catch up to Adlai, who hung from the top rung of the ladder while guns popped and bullets whistled below.

"Looks like Boxi's guy brought more backup." Adlai pointed to a hunched figure behind a forklift, firing from a protected spot. "They knew what was going down tonight. Ouch, that's gonna hurt." Adlai chuckled as one of the Russians spun from a ricocheted shot.

They watched the drama unfold beneath them, men chasing each other, firing wildly, screaming and swearing, each side taking turns losing its advantage.

Stell made a sound of impatience. "They'll all be dead before we get down there."

"Give it a minute." Adlai scanned the scene. He could see two Russians out of commission, soaking in their own blood. The third, with an exploded knee, howled in pain and Stell could see the jagged hole in his shoulder as well. He wouldn't last long. That left one giant Russian lurking in the aisles unhurt. The surprise second shooter hid in the shadows.

"Two men left standing. How's that suit you?" Stell nodded and they slid down the ladder. They moved behind the Russian hunter, whose gun pointed up toward the ceiling.

"C'mon," the Russian yelled. "Let's finish this. I promise I'll kill ya quick."

Adlai peeled off to the left, knowing where the skinny man was hiding with senses unavailable to the big gangster. Stell stayed in step with her prey, relishing the sight of his thick neck peeking out above his woolen collar.

"There's no way you're getting out of this building alive. You're in way over your head. I'm gonna find ya and I'm gonna put a bullet right between your eyes. Now if you're a good boy and stop wasting my time, maybe I won't spend the next six months tracking down every member of your family and popping a cap in their asses too. What do ya say?"

"Fuck you!" Stell recognized Adlai's voice but the gangster had only one man in mind.

"You stupid *S-O-B.*" He took off running toward the voice, stepping out into the open floor of the warehouse only to stop short. "What the . . . ?"

Stell slipped out beside him and saw what made him stop in his tracks. Adlai stood behind the other gunman, holding him up under his armpits, his mouth locked in a bloody bite on the limp man's neck. The Russian stared, trying to absorb what he was seeing, muttering incoherent questions as he watched a thick ribbon of blood spill onto the floor in front of him. Stell clamped her hands over her mouth to stifle a giggle as Adlai pulled his mouth from his meal and held the body out on his arm like a salesman showing a suit.

"Did you want some?" He smiled at the gangster, his mouth coated in gore.

"What the . . . ? Get the . . ." He lifted the gun with a shaky hand and Stell vaulted onto his back, wrapping her legs around his waist and burying her teeth in the fleshy softness of his throat. She tore at his skin, her bite like iron as blood erupted.

The large man screamed at the pain, swatting at this unseen assailant as he spun, trying to shake her off, trying to keep his balance as blood loss and panic overwhelmed him. The screams echoed through the warehouse, ringing like bells in her ear, and she swallowed again and again. She could feel the pulse of death coming. She tightened her grip on the large man, who managed somehow to

stay on his feet. They cut back and forth across the floor like danc-
ers, Stell swaying to his erratic rhythm.

Adlai watched, enthralled, his own blood high making his eyes
glitter. Neither saw the gun nor heard the scream of the man on the
floor behind them, he of the exploded knee and destroyed shoulder,
who summoned up the strength for one last act of courage.

Squinting one sweat-filled eye and rolling onto his ravaged
shoulder, the fallen Russian raised his gun one last time and fired,
hoping if not to kill the fiends, then to at least put his fellow coun-
tryman out of his misery.

The bullet pierced Stell's side, making her cry out, breaking her
seal on the man's throat. She dropped to her feet, her victim falling
like a tree in front of her, as she twisted her body to see the wound
on her back. A cloud of blood darkened the back of her shirt and
Stell spun in circles trying to see the back of her waist.

"Shit, shit, shit! Ow, this hurts! Ow!"

Adlai dropped on the gunman, driving his knee into the bloody
pulp of the man's damaged leg. The man screamed, helpless to stop
Adlai from ripping the gun from his hands and tossing it into the
darkness.

"Let me see, Stell."

Stell turned her back and lifted her shirt, hopping from one
foot to another like a child who had to pee. "Did he shoot me? Is
that a bullet? Goddam it!" Her voice was shrill, full of blood but
not high from a kill. "Am I bleeding? It hurts!"

"Yeah, the blood's stopping but you gotta get high or that's
gonna take longer to heal."

Stell saw the obviously dead body of her target. "He's dead!
He's dead and I didn't get it. Damn it!" She spun on her attacker,
who continued to scream with what voice he had left. "I'm gonna
tear your fucking head off!"

Adlai caught her with one arm. "You don't want to tear his head off, Stell."

"Yes I do and then I'm gonna shove it up his ass. He shot me!" She hung from Adlai's outstretched arm, screaming into the dying man's face, spraying him with blood and spit.

"Finish him, Stell. Let him die in your mouth. You've gotta get high. Hurry, there's not much left in him."

Stell swore again as Adlai dropped her onto the man beneath her. She tore into his throat with even more savagery than usual. As the blood drained from his body, the last thing he heard was his own skin tearing and a sickening sucking sound. The room slipped into darkness quickly and for the last three seconds of his life the Russian was grateful for death.

. . . .

When the room exploded in light, Stell heard the musical sound of bells. Falling back on her heels, she stared up into the expanse of the warehouse, marveling at its transition to soaring cathedral, its grimy windows now brilliant stained-glass masterpieces. The sound washed over her as the dust motes glittered like floating diamonds. Her head lolled on her shoulders, her eyes rolling to find the source of that magical sound. It was Adlai, still kneeling, with his head thrown back laughing. The sound banged around the empty space, doubling and tripling in size.

"'I'm gonna tear your fucking head off and shove it up your ass.'" Adlai howled, clutching his stomach in laughter. "Where did you learn that?"

"On TV."

He collapsed on the floor, trying to catch his breath, then rolled onto his back and stared into the glittering darkness.

"I can't remember the last time I laughed this much."

Stell crawled toward him, tracking gore on her knees. "Are you laughing at me?"

He looked up at her, his black pupils obliterating the blue of his eyes. "Yes."

"Oh, okay." She laughed too, straddling Adlai where he lay. "As long as I know."

He grabbed her by the back of her head and held her face close to his. "Come here." He ran his tongue along her jawline and tasted what he found there. "You're a mess."

"Says you." She licked him back, running along his chin to the corner of his mouth, leaving a clean streak through the drying blood. The sensation tore through her body and Stell ground her hips against the growing bulge in his jeans.

"We've got to move the bodies," he said.

"Oh fuck the bodies. Why can't they move themselves?"

Adlai turned his head toward the destroyed Russian beside him. "Hey you, Pavel, get in the truck." He looked back at Stell. "I don't think he's going to listen." He began to giggle, an infectious sound that soon had Stell laughing as well. The adrenaline, the blood high, the nearness of their bodies had them ratcheted up and both were helpless when the laughing fit hit them. Twice Stell tried to get up to start on the cleanup and twice Adlai barked an order at the dead Russian, reducing her once again to stitches.

"Are we going to spend all night here?" she said climbing off Adlai, trying to keep from laughing. Adlai turned his head and Stell covered his mouth with her hands. "No! No more! Get up. Let's get out of here. Why do we have to move them anyway?"

Adlai sighed and sat up to survey the room. "Because if we take out these three," he waved toward their kills, "the police will come in, see Russian mobsters and guns and say, 'It was the mob.' End of story. If we leave these three, the police will come in and say 'It was the mob. And a pack of wolverines.'"

"So what do we do with them?"

"We put them in whatever car is outside. Then"—he pulled out the package the bartender had given him earlier—"we blow up the car. Goodbye suspicious throat-trauma victims. Hello suitcase full of money."

. . . .

They were back on the roof of the warehouse before the SUV in the parking lot exploded. The sight was magnificent. Adlai held the waistband of Stell's jeans so she could lean out into space and feel the heat from the fire below. The wind blew her hair out like a fan around her, the light from the fire coloring her pale skin in glowing flashes of yellow and red. The heat made the sky shimmer and Stell watched the night move. Adlai watched Stell.

When the sirens sounded in the distance, he pulled her back and they ran across the rooftops, racing each other. Stell's long legs, fueled by the kill, covered the distance easily. Together they leapt over roof edges and ventilation pipes, around chimneys and generators. Adlai fell behind to watch her cutting through the night like a knife. She was laughing when he pulled her arm and spun her around.

"You gonna run all night?"

"Yes, I am. It's so beautiful up here." She let her head fall back and spun in a lazy circle. Adlai caught her and pulled her tight against him.

"It's beautiful downstairs too. First window on the right."

"Are we here already?" She focused on Adlai, seeing his shiny, black eyes. Blood stained his face like a haggard beard and made his breath irresistibly sweet. She pressed her body against him, letting her face skim his, breathing in the scent of him, hearing his heart hammering beneath his clothes. She twined one leg around his, grinding against him, and clutched the back of his neck, whispering into his ear.

"Don't say no to me."

"Get inside."

She jumped through the window first, the darkened room now brilliant with her blood-high eyes. It was as empty as it had felt but Stell spied a rumpled bed at the near end of the room. As Adlai landed on the floor behind her, she dropped her jacket and headed for the bed. Before she could peel her t-shirt off, he came up behind her and grabbed her around the waist.

She could feel his hands everywhere as she spun to face him, kissing him roughly as they staggered several feet into the room. His coat disappeared and her hands tore at his shirt, trying to get to the burning skin she could smell beneath. He tipped his head back as her mouth explored his chest and shoulders. She loved his arms. Biting into his shoulder, she watched the light ripple like mercury over the contours of his muscles and the sounds he made as she worked her way over his skin thrilled her.

She climbed him, wrapping her legs around his waist, wanting to be as close as possible to his body, but he pushed her down. He had to push hard but held her at arm's length. For one horrible moment, she feared he would refuse her again.

"Take off your shirt."

She ripped the shirt over her head as his grip tightened on her hips. His eyes moved slowly, obviously, over her body and his vision felt like fingers on her hypersensitive skin. She squirmed in his grip, wanting to be in contact with his skin once more, but he held her away.

When she was sure she would scream from anticipation, he jerked open the button fly of her jeans, pushing them down to just above her knees. Stell gasped at the cold air on her skin. Free of his restraint, she pulled at his jeans as well, pushing them down and plunging her hands in. She freed his cock, white-hot in her hands, and tried once more to climb his body but her jeans at her knees restricted her. Not wanting to release her grip on him, she kicked and squirmed, swearing at the restraints as Adlai watched her dilemma.

"Shit." She used both hands now to try to push the jeans down off her legs but he stopped her. She huffed in frustration. "I'm stuck."

"I know."

He leaned in and bit her lower lip. She opened her mouth for more but he whipped her around by her hip, slamming her forward into the rough brick of his apartment wall. Her fingers dug into the brick as he kicked her legs apart, one arm wrapping around her body, his hand sliding between her legs, holding her in place as he entered her from behind.

Still trapped by her jeans, her movement was restricted and Adlai took full advantage of his control. The fingers of his left hand massaged the tender cleft of her body in time with his vigorous thrusts while his right hand slid up her body, over her shoulder and grabbed fiercely at a handful of hair.

The sounds coming from Stell weren't human as she arched and writhed, growling at the restraints, crying out at the intensity of the pleasure. The rough brick scraped at her aching nipples as she bent backward, trying to push him even more deeply within her. Her hands scratched at the wall then clawed backward, trying to find purchase on his pale bare skin.

He bit down hard on her neck, not yet breaking the skin. "*Oascaru li da.* You are so fierce, Stell, so fucking deadly."

She groaned as he bit more deeply into her skin and she reached back to wrap her hands around the back of his head. She pulled his ear to her mouth and bit down sharply on his earlobe. "Wait until I get my hands on you, you'll know *oascaru.*"

"I'm counting on it." A sharp bite and Stell smelled her own blood and felt the ecstatic sensation of his lips and tongue feeding from her.

....

Tomas left Dalle asleep on Sylva's couch. His mentor had told him he planned to spend most of the day in deep meditation. "Recuperating," he'd said. Tomas watched Dalle's eyes flutter shut and heard his breathing even out. It hadn't occurred to him to wonder about the toll training an apprentice would take. Despite Dalle's reassurances, Tomas worried he'd acted too rashly, feeding so soon after his induction, missing the chance to fully explore his vision.

He slipped out of Sylva's office and headed for a meditation room. The hours of flip requests he'd done with Dalle, dreaming decisions for Nahan he had never met, had lit him up. He felt giddy and warm, better than he had in days. Before he could open the door of Dalle's favorite meditation room, the door to the right opened and Tomas heard an unmistakably gravelly growl.

"Desara."

"Lucien, hello." The Storyteller looked terrible, like he'd just run down a hot highway. His hair stuck up in clumps and his eyes were painfully red. He smelled sour and Tomas tried not to flinch when Lucien crowded him against the door.

"Don't you look fresh, young Storyteller." Tomas didn't know what to say to that so he tried to lean away from Lucien's bitter breath. "Back in the trenches so soon? All recovered from your induction? Even with blowing it by feeding from your little girl?"

"Dalle said it was all right, that I'd be okay."

"Well, Dalle is a good mentor, isn't he?" Lucien looked him over from head to toe. "You really lucked out with him. It could be a lot worse, but you know that, don't you?"

Tomas looked for someone, anyone, to come down the hall and rescue him from this odd confrontation. Lucien saw him search. "Nobody here but us, kid. Storytellers make the rest of them nervous. They give us a wide berth." He put his hand on the wall beside Tomas's head.

"Is there something I can do for you, Lucien?"

The Storyteller's breath was hot on his face. "Tell me what he said. Hess. Did he ask for me?" Lucien grabbed Tomas's arm. "Can you talk to him?"

"I don't know." Tomas winced from the grip. "I haven't meditated since—"

"You talk to him," Lucien hissed. "You tell him—"

"Lucien!" Sylva ran down the hall. She pulled Lucien off Tomas, pushing him back against the other wall. Lucien let the tiny woman manhandle him. "This is not appropriate. You want to have this discussion, you go through Dalle. Am I understood?"

He nodded, his head falling back against the wall. Tomas could see tears streaking his cheeks. Sylva turned him, pushing him down the hall away from Tomas. He let her move him several feet before he called over his shoulder.

"Desara. You tell him I'm sorry."

· ·

"That couldn't have been easy for you." Sylva followed Tomas into the meditation room and waited for him to settle cross-legged on the carpet with her. "You should really talk about this with Dalle. He's your mentor."

"He's meditating." He touched her hand. "You're my teacher too. Why won't anyone tell me about Hess? What happened?"

Sylva stared into the carpet, her voice low. "Hess had dreams, awful visions, they were killing him. They were worse than Lucien's ever were and Hess hadn't even been inducted yet. The meditations only made the dreams worse. The more he meditated, the more focused his dreams became until he begged Lucien to release him."

"Why couldn't he just leave?"

"And do what?" Sylva asked. "You can't unring that bell, Desara. You can't unlearn how to meditate. He was petrified of the common; he was petrified of himself. The last thing any of us need is another branch of the True Family popping up. If we had let him loose, they would have gobbled him up and then there would be even more people in rags living in the woods bleeding themselves."

She smoothed the nap of the carpet. "We were desperate. We even used the drone to calm him down."

"The what?"

"Just a stupid idea Lucien had." She waved it away. "A noise machine, an electronic droning. It made it impossible for any of the Storytellers to meditate. It made them all miserable but it did help Hess for while. It held his dreams off. He began to relax. Not being able to meditate kept him from being so afraid. When Lucien thought he was rested enough, we turned off the drone. We took him to the pool for the Eighteen-Step Meditation and, well, you remember what follows that." Tomas nodded, still haunted by the confusion of the attack and the horror of the *Vint*.

"He called out the *Vint*. It was terrible to watch just like it was with you. Like it always is. But before Lucien could give him the oleander, Hess just . . ." Sylva's voice disappeared. She took a deep breath. "His screams were so horrible. It was all horrible. His fear was like a bitter smoke, you could smell it everywhere. I looked into his eyes and there was no doubt he was gone. He was completely gone."

Tomas didn't know what to say. They sat in silence until Sylva smiled up at him. "I'm sorry we never told you this. I should have known there would be some energy left over from all of it that only a young Storyteller would have picked up on. It was just so horrible for all of us. Everyone in the complex suffered. Dozens of people left and never came back. Forgive me. Forgive us all."

Tomas took her hands and held them between both of his. He still loved her hands after all they had put him through. He trusted these hands and trusted this woman and so he asked her the question that started it all. "Where is Hess now?"

"With his family. I don't know where. He never wanted to see us again. He wanted his family to take care of him."

"And the drone? Do you use that anymore?"

"God, no. That's long gone."

"What happened to it?"

Sylva shrugged. "Vartan took care of it. Like I said, the whole incident rattled everyone, seeing a young Storyteller shatter like that. Vartan removed the drone, took care of moving Hess, everything. It seems even a bureaucrat will cooperate if you frighten him badly enough."

Chapter Ten:

TU BITH

....

tu Bith: class of Nahan responsible for
moneymaking; bankers

Thirst woke Stell. The apartment was sweltering, the steam radiator
beside the bed popping and singing. Sweat pooled on her stomach,
where Adlai's arm lay across her. She slid out from beneath his arm
and rolled onto her side to study him with her still-sensitive eyes.
He looked like he had been in a fight or maybe thrown through a
window, the pale skin of his chest and shoulders torn and bruised.

She traced a long streak of four cuts, her fingernail tracks, along
the curve of his rib cage ending at a fading bite mark on the cut of
muscle just above his pelvis. The wounds excited her and she would
have run her tongue along the cuts on his collarbone but she was
too thirsty to swallow. Sliding off the mattress, Stell padded silently
across the dark loft.

The bike sat in the center of the space surrounded by tool chests and racks and greasy rags. It was clearly Adlai's favorite, if not his only, real possession. Under the window, an industrial-sized washer and dryer sat silent, their clothes from last night peeking through the round window, dry and wrinkling. It was too hot to dress so Stell didn't bother to fetch her clothes. She walked naked the length of the loft to the open kitchenette, really just a small refrigerator and gas stove with a set of shelves between them. Stell opened the refrigerator and poked through the contents. There were several take-out containers with Chinese and Mexican foods, which Stell pushed aside to pull out a can of grape soda. She popped it and drank half of it in one pull. With a quiet belch, she continued her tour of the hidden world of Anton Adlai.

She could smell him everywhere. There were no bookshelves, no magazines, no mail or catalogs strewn about. On the other side of the refrigerator sat an industrial sink, battered and scarred with grease and paint. The concrete floor dipped slightly under her feet toward a drain in the floor. She puzzled over its location, several feet from the wall until she noticed copper pipes trailing along the wall. Above her head hung a shower nozzle. Apparently Adlai preferred to shower in the open. That wasn't all. In a dark alcove, a toilet crouched, open to the room.

The space felt good and Stell could feel her body relax as the blood high waned. She made her way back the length of the loft, stepping over a set of free weights in the floor. As she lifted her leg over a weight bench, she saw an ugly purple half-moon on her thigh the exact size of Adlai's bite. She rubbed the mark, knowing it would fade, and felt a sharp twinge in her side. The bullet hole had closed but the bullet remained inside. Adlai had told her the kill would help the wound heal faster but the damage wasn't gone.

She twisted her back, bracing herself on the wall to stretch. The wall was bare, a long expanse of exposed red brick, broken up occasionally by pipe ends or bolts but two thirds of the way down the wall, Stell spied a small, white square. Stepping closer, she saw it was a photo balanced on the edge of a jagged piece of brick. She held the photo up to catch the light from the street and could make out two figures.

Two young men leaned against a big car. The one on the left stood with muscular arms folded, long, stringy hair covering a good part of his scowling face. It was Adlai. Beside him, a taller and skinnier young man with wild, curly hair had his arm around his friend and his head thrown back in a widemouthed laugh. Stell smiled, tracing her finger over the image of Adlai in younger, happier days.

"That's Shelan."

Adlai had slipped up behind her, resting his chin on her shoulder.

"You're young."

"Uh-huh. That was our first car. Legal car, that is. A Nova. Had a V-8, an eight-track tape player, and kicking speakers. We were bad motherfuckers." He wrapped his arms around Stell's waist and pulled her closer to him. She leaned back, enjoying the solidity of his body.

"I wish I could see his face. He's laughing. All I see is teeth."

"You'd have to be quick to catch Shelan not laughing about something. We used to laugh so much. We had more fun and made more money and got more pussy than . . ." The words disappeared in a heavy sigh and Stell could feel his grip on her tighten.

"Just so you know, I'm glad your Tomas survived that place. I'm glad he didn't have to go through what Shelan did. And even if your friends can't find out where he is, I'm going to. I'm getting him out of wherever they put him and then we're gone."

"I know."

"If it goes wrong, if something goes wrong," he dropped his voice to a whisper, "you can come with us."

"What's going to go wrong?" She didn't want to ask but couldn't stop.

"Tomas might be different."

"He's not different."

He nodded against her cheek. "But if he is. That's what they do, Stell. The Storytellers, those bastards in that complex, they change people. It's what they do, what they tried to do to Shelan."

"Don't."

"If you need to get out, if you need to get away from the Council, you can come with me. Come with us. You never have to look back." Stell squeezed her eyes shut, his words swimming before her. He kissed her neck and pulled away.

"How's your back? The hole is closed."

Stell nodded, not trusting herself to speak.

"It shouldn't hurt too much until the bullet starts working its way out. I'm not going to lie to you. That'll hurt because it's got to break the skin to get out. It'll feel like you swallowed a mouse with really sharp claws." He stepped away from her to the laundry machines where the Russian's briefcase sat and tossed her a bundle of wrapped bills. "This'll make you feel better."

Stell examined the money like it was an alien artifact. "I thought this belonged to your friend, Boxi."

"No, the diamonds belong to Boxi. The money is windfall. I'll take what I need and give the rest to him. Boxi will take the money and the word will go out that there's cash around and if any of our people need it, they'll get it. Simple as that. Don't need the Council to tell us how to do it. It's a lot easier than begging that fucker Vartan for pocket money, isn't it?"

"I don't know. I don't have any money."

"Where do you get your food? Your clothes and stuff?"

Stell shrugged. "Commons bring in groceries. They do our laundry too. And clean the apartment. They even bought my clothes."

Adlai sat back on his heels and watched her as the morning sun filtered through the grated windows. "Then consider that your first payment toward independence, Stell."

. . . .

Stell let herself into the apartment, listening for Adlai's motorcycle long after it had passed out of earshot. Still in her coat, she examined the apartment she shared with Tomas with new eyes. She and Tomas were no more evident in the well-appointed apartment than Adlai was in his bare loft. They had picked out none of the furniture. There were pictures on the wall of places Stell couldn't identify. Paintings of wine bottles and blurry renditions of French cafés, hung in their small dining alcove, a woven bowl with an African design that had never seen an African waited on the entrance table for mail that never arrived.

She stepped into the kitchen, opening a stocked cabinet. The crackers and dips and pastas and sweets within were all satisfying enough but for the first time Stell wondered what she would have bought for herself. The Kott were attentive. If the stone-ground crackers didn't get eaten, they never appeared again. When the M&M's were gone in a day, three packages took their place. The sight of an open package of the peanut butter cookies Tomas loved so much made Stell's breath catch in her throat, loneliness soaring in from nowhere and punching her in the stomach. She let the cabinet door slam shut.

"Stell? Is that you?"

She turned, gripping the countertop behind her, and called out to the bedroom. "Tomas? I thought you'd be at the complex. Why are you home?"

"Oh, I went over last night after you left and worked all night." She could hear dresser drawers being pulled. Tomas would make sure all his clothes stayed neatly folded in their drawers, not just paw through them looking for something to wear like she would. "Hey, I called Louis about some information I found out on Adlai's friend. He and Aricelli are on their way over right now. He thinks he might have a way to—"

Tomas stood in the doorway, his mouth open in mid-sentence as he stared at her. Stell didn't move, feeling as if a movie screen had appeared behind her and the activities of the previous night were playing in vivid color for Tomas. Neither spoke until Tomas dropped his chin to his chest and let out a ragged breath. He headed back toward the bedroom.

"You might want to shower before they get here."

. . . .

Stell came back into the living room after her shower, her skin rosy from the steam and scrubbing. Tomas didn't look up as she came in even when she dropped the towel she was using to dry her hair on the floor. He hated when she did that and would usually insist she pick it up. Today, however, he paid no mind to the damp heap on the carpet or to the woman who dropped it. Stell knelt beside where he sat on the couch.

Tomas arched an eyebrow. "Kneeling? Really?"

"I don't want to sit in a chair. My back hurts. I got shot."

"Shit, Stell. Let me see." She turned and lifted her shirt. The marks from Adlai's lovemaking were gone but a small purple welt remained from the bullet. Tomas touched it gingerly, feeling her wince. "You know you can die from these things, right? You can be shot to death. If it punctures an organ or there are too many of them, you can bleed out. Did he tell you that, Stell? Or did he just throw you into gunfire and wish you luck?"

Stell pulled her shirt down and settled back on her heels. "I've been around guns before. I'm okay. These were Russians. With the knob."

"The knob?" Tomas looked into her earnest face. "I think you mean the mob."

Stell dropped her gaze and Tomas hated himself for embarrassing her. He hated her for embarrassing him. "What are we doing, Stell? Are you happy?"

It took her a long time to answer. "I miss you." Her voice was small. "I miss . . ."

"I know. I miss it too. But everything's different now, isn't it?"

"No, Tomas. I just—"

"It's not that. It's not that you slept with him." He saw her blush. "You don't need to be a Storyteller to see that. And it's okay. I mean, obviously I would rather, you know, but we've got to face facts. You and I are on different paths now. Neither one of us is going to be a banker or an insurance salesman. We have very different callings."

"Adlai says that *acul 'ads* work for the Storytellers. I could work for you."

"Dalle said something about that too. But Stell, if Adlai's right—and I'm not saying he is—but if Hess is being held against his will, something is very, very wrong. Something that could be dangerous." Tomas closed his eyes. "I think when we find out what's going on, maybe you should leave. You should go with Adlai."

"What? No." She grabbed his hands. "You said you'd never send me away. You said that. And if something is dangerous, I can help."

"This isn't gangsters with guns, Stell. These are Storytellers." He stared into her pale eyes. "Believe me, this is some serious shit. And if they're imprisoning Hess, if anyone is imprisoning him, then everything I know is wrong. Everything I've trusted all my life falls apart."

"You can trust me."

He brought her fingers to his lips and whispered. "Maybe you can't trust me. Maybe I have this all backward. Maybe it wasn't

Hess they broke. Maybe Hess was removed because he wouldn't break. Maybe I'm the one they broke."

A knock at the door cut off Stell's protest. Tomas pulled away when Aricelli and Louis arrived in a flurry of coats and scarves, coffee cups and pastry bags.

Tomas counted eight tall cups of coffee. "Are we having a party?"

Louis threw his coat on the floor. "If you're going to drag us out at this unspeakable hour, it requires strong fuel."

"It's almost noon."

Aricelli dropped into an easy chair and grabbed a cup. "Fortunately we're staying in town. At the Drake. Well, I'm staying at the Drake; Louis is using my bathroom as a changing room while he cultivates some new urban relationships."

Louis lowered himself gingerly onto his coat on the floor. "And those relationships require solid hours of nocturnal attention. This morning conversation thing is bullshit."

Tomas pulled Stell down to sit with him on the couch. He knew she was still upset. He was too but this wasn't the time to discuss it. He had other business at hand. Tomas didn't know which was worse—how badly the pieces of his life fit together now or how used to it he was becoming. He fumbled with his coffee, just wanting to get started. As usual, Louis led the way.

"So, Westin. It doesn't officially exist."

"But my driver said—"

"And I said it doesn't *officially* exist."

Aricelli went on. "It's not easy keeping something like that a secret. Real estate brings taxes and utilities and all sorts of paperwork. I checked as many places as I could. It would take some doing to keep that off the record."

"Who could do that? Who could pull off a place like that?" Tomas asked.

Aricelli glanced at Louis before speaking. "Well, if the money people don't know about it and the security people don't know about it and real estate people don't either, that narrows it down pretty well."

Tomas felt his stomach sour. "The Storytellers."

Louis gave a sympathetic nod. "He was their mess to clean up. He was their mistake."

"It's not a mistake," Tomas said. "It's not like that. He couldn't handle it. Not everybody can."

"Okay, so what do we do?" Aricelli asked. "Is that it? Do we drop it? Assume the Storytellers are exercising their authority to handle this their own way?"

Louis shrugged. "I don't see that we have any choice, do we? It's not like we can question them. On the other hand . . ."

That was when Tomas saw it—Louis and Aricelli had practiced this argument. They were dancing around him. For once in his life, Tomas didn't feel like being handled by his friends.

"What is it, you guys? Just say it."

Aricelli cleared her throat. "If the Storytellers are out of line, if they're doing something dangerous, maybe people ought to know."

"They poisoned him," Stell blurted.

"Who?" Louis turned to her as if just noticing she sat with them. "Who poisoned who?"

Tomas tried to talk her down but she spoke over him. "The Storytellers. They poisoned Tomas. I bet they poisoned Hess too."

"They didn't, Stell." Tomas shook his head. "He didn't make it that far."

"How far?" Aricelli asked. "You were poisoned?"

He kept shaking his head. "It's not like that. That's not what happened to Hess. The poison is . . . is . . . it's part of our training. It's what makes—"

"Does Mr. Vartan know about this?"

"Vartan doesn't have any say over it. It's a Storyteller issue. It doesn't concern him." Tomas stopped short, catching the surprised looks of Louis and Aricelli. "I didn't mean it to sound like that. He's the Coordinator but the Storytellers are their own authority."

"The authority to poison and imprison people," Louis said.

"No, no." Tomas felt a dull ache building behind his eyes. "It's not like that. Hess's mentor Lucien was really upset about Hess breaking down."

Aricelli cocked her head. "From the poison he'd been given by said mentor."

"Shut up about the poison!" Tomas flew to his feet. "You don't understand."

Aricelli looked into her coffee. "Obviously we don't but you seem okay with it. You're the one in training with the Storytellers." Tomas could feel how carefully she chose her words, could almost see her verbal tiptoeing. "All I'm suggesting is that if we're looking for someone else who was poisoned, regardless of how necessary it might have been, perhaps we ought to utilize the Council resources at our disposal." She looked up at him. "It's not like you'd have a difficult time convincing Mr. Vartan to launch an investigation."

"What do you mean?" Tomas asked.

Louis kept his voice in the same careful tone as Aricelli. "It just means that we have avenues of recourse. The Council has certain checks and balances in place that—"

"Would you guys stop talking like Council leaders?"

Louis stared up at him. "If you'll stop holding forth like a Storyteller. We still call you Tomas, remember? You haven't totally crossed over."

Tomas took a deep breath and settled back down on the couch. "I'm sorry. I am." He looked to each of them. "This is really hard for me. I feel pulled in all these different directions and I don't know who to trust. Besides you guys." He made sure to include Stell in his glance.

"It's all right, dude." Louis punched his knuckles against Tomas's knee. "That's what we're here for."

"Strange days indeed," Aricelli said with a wink, defusing the tension. "Who'd have thought that of the three of us, Tomas would be the first one to get a real job at the complex? The only person alive who ever came close to flunking out of Heritage School."

Louis laughed. "All we're saying is that Mr. Vartan would certainly be interested in any shady goings-on regarding the Storytellers. His ego took quite a hit after the famously failed Vartan Plan."

"The what?"

Louis laughed again and Aricelli shook her head. "You really do live in the clouds, don't you? Do you never listen to Council gossip? My father loves to tell that story." She sipped her coffee and settled in to tell the tale.

"They were building the complex and Vartan had all kinds of plans to make it even more of a command center than it was already supposed to be. We're talking about the business communities paying taxes to it and reporting all their income to them; Heritage Schools having to send kids there for free internships: all kinds of crazy stuff."

"It sounds like he was dreaming of a feudal castle with him as the Lord Mayor."

"I guess," Louis said. "But in some ways he was just trying to modernize the Council, bring it more in line with business, less in the hands of the magical, mystical Storytellers."

"Daddy said his mistake was that he overstepped the bounds of the money people. The *tu Bith* went to the Storytellers to complain. From what I heard, a Storyteller slapped the taste out of Vartan's mouth. He didn't just veto the new plans but even cut back on the authority already established for Coordinator. So you tell me, you're Paul Vartan. You've just been bitch-slapped and humiliated in front of the entire community. How do you feel about Storytellers?"

"I can't imagine he'd complain about a complaint," Louis said. "That kind of dressing-down must have stung like a sonofabitch."

. . . .

Stung. Stung like a bee.

Tomas closed his eyes, the words floating before him.

Like bees.

Bees.

Patterns everywhere. That's what Dalle had told him. Always look for patterns.

. . . .

Stell leaned forward, her hand on his arm. "Tomas?"

"Bees." Tomas said, the word tingling on his tongue. He felt phantom drifts of the poison under his skin and the room seemed to fade away from him. "Bees."

"Bees?" Louis asked. "Dude, are you okay?"

Tomas opened his eyes. "I'm a Storyteller."

Louis stared at him. "Well you look like a crazy person."

"I know. I need to meditate. About the bees."

Tomas stepped away from the couch, his back to his friends, muttering under his breath. "Where? Where? Where?"

"You're going to meditate," Aricelli said in disbelief. "Right now. About bees."

Tomas held up his hand to silence her. "Here. I have to do it here. If I go there, they'll know. Dalle will know."

"Dude," Louis said, "if you're going to do some yoga shit, I'm going back to bed."

"Not yoga. Meditating. It's what—" Tomas caught himself and smiled. "It's what we do. Can you give me a few minutes? And I'll need you to be really quiet."

Stell folded her legs beneath her on the couch. Aricelli huffed out a disgusted breath and Louis sprawled out on the floor.

"Dude, all you're going to hear from me is snoring."

....

Tomas settled on the floor behind the couch. In front of him sat a narrow hallway table with spindly legs that framed a square of beige wall. A blank screen. Behind him, through the sofa, he could feel the solid silence of Stell.

He moved into lotus position, breathing deeply, and turned his focus to the small black lump that rested at his core. He'd felt that lump within him for so long. It was cold and dark.

It was fear.

Sylva was wrong. He wasn't feeling the residual echoes of someone else's fear. He couldn't have explained how he knew but he knew that he had to fully understand his fear before he could begin to address it.

Remaining still, he let breath run through his body until he sensed the small black lump begin to move. He didn't react. It was his mind working to reveal to him what needed to be done. The black lump shifted, replicated, copying itself, spreading open from the center like a flower.

No, like a honeycomb.

Bees.

A cloud of bees had poured from Hess's throat in his induction vision. Bees—industrious and necessary, lives of honey and hierarchy. Queen bees and drones.

He groaned. Drones.

The black honeycomb spread, filling him from within, pushing open his lips.

From his mouth flew a black bee, then another and another. Tomas watched as a dozen or more black bees flew from his mouth, landing on the blank wall before him. They landed in a random pattern and froze, waiting.

"Show me," he said.

And they did. Flying together, their slender black bodies created lines and shadows, moving and shifting until Tomas could see the pictures being drawn on the wall before him. It was a storyboard, a living graphic novel drawn before his eyes by the black bees of fear that had taken up residence in his being after he had placed his life in the hands of the Storytellers.

He stared at the story laid out before him. "Look and dream." That's what Dalle had told him to do. He looked at the story his fear was telling him and he dreamed.

Could he do it?

. . . .

Back at the complex, Tomas checked the door to Dalle's meditation room. It was still closed, a blue ribbon hanging from the knob. Dalle had settled in for deep meditation. Tomas slipped into the Storytelling room.

As he had been experiencing the vision, he had been so sure of his plan of action. Aricelli obviously bought it and was preparing to follow it. Adlai and Stell and Louis would also be at the complex waiting to see if it worked. As the immediate effects of the meditation wore off, however, Tomas could feel a different sort of fear settle into his stomach.

To call what he had planned inappropriate was laughable. His plan was insane.

He paced the room, trying to calm himself. Like the meditation rooms, this room had been the scene of change for Tomas. He traced his fingers along the seams of the chairs in which he had learned the stories of the Nahan. He had passed their tests. His mentor had found him worthy to be called Storyteller. Now it was time to put that faith in himself. He took a deep breath and felt the insecurity ebb. Another deep breath and confidence began to seep in.

Without giving himself another chance to delay, Tomas headed down the hall into the north end of the Nahan complex where the Kott were allowed to work.

He had been in this part of the complex before many times and for the same reason he was here now—to visit the *Kott'del*. These were the Kott who had agreed to avail themselves to be fed from for the convenience of the Nahan who didn't wish to hunt. There were strict guidelines in place for their safety and they were regularly rotated on shifts for their health but there was still a level of nervousness among them anytime they were asked to provide blood.

The more veteran *Kott'del*, like Nancy and Kanai, who had come to his hotel room to feed him last week, were allowed to be fed from off-site and without supervision. The newer recruits operated under the watchful eye of Mrs. Studdard, a sixty-something, ninth-generation Kott who was rumored to be utterly fearless.

She might be fearless but Tomas was counting on her appreciation of hierarchy. And her patience. And her outrage. In that order.

Bracing himself for the worst, Tomas pushed open the door and smiled.

Her name was Rene. She was twenty-two and from the neck up looked no older than sixteen. Tight brown ringlets were pulled back from her face with a red hair band that matched her red-and-white striped cardigan. She rose when Tomas entered the room and he could see the girlishness ended at her face. Rene was blessed with a body that would best be described as luscious, with full breasts and a round bottom. He would have gone through with this regardless of what *Kott'del* was on duty, male or female. This just made it easier.

If he was going to flip off the strict protocol protecting the Kott, he might as well enjoy it.

He held open the door and addressed Mrs. Studdard. "Leave us. Now."

"I'm very sorry, sir, but the policy is that—"

"I know what the policy is. I wish to feed in private. Leave us now."

Mrs. Studdard bristled. "Your wishes are not my concern. My job is—"

"I know what your job is. Do you know mine?"

She did. Mrs. Studdard had been raised among the highest levels of the Nahan and was well aware of the special regard held for Storytellers. She was also all too aware of her limited clout. Picking up her pocketbook, she marched to the door.

"I shall be right outside. I would appreciate your respect for our rules."

Tomas nodded to her as she marched out. He pushed the door closed softly and turned the lock. Ten feet away he could sense Rene's heartbeat begin to gallop. He knew the feeling. His own pounded but for much different reasons. Mistreating the Kott was its own world of trouble.

He joined her on the overstuffed couch, smiling at the furious blush on her cheeks.

"I'm Rene. I'm happy to serve you today." She was breathing so shallowly she could hardly spit out the rehearsed lines. "Where would you like me to sit?"

Tomas took her left hand between both of his. It was tiny and the pulse in her wrist beat hard enough to be visible. He traced his fingers along her forearm to the crook of her elbow. The *Kott'del* tattoo there was dark and vivid against her freckled skin. He flicked his fingertip over the blue ink and could feel the skin was smooth.

"Is this your first time, Rene?"

"Yes," she nodded, several long strands of ringlets breaking free from her hair band and tumbling around her young face. "But I'm ready. I mean I'm prepared. I know what to do. If you'll just tell me how you want me to sit. Or lie. Or stand. I mean, however you want to do it."

He placed a finger on her lips. "May I let down your hair?"

He slid his hand along her neck and gently tugged on the elastic, coaxing her hair loose. He never broke eye contact with Rene and could see the effect his nearness was having on her. Her lips grew rosy and full, her eyelids began to lower and a mottled flush rose along her throat.

He leaned in closer to her, his breath a whisper over her open mouth. Where his wrist brushed the side of her throat, he could feel her blood pounding beneath her skin. He had almost forgotten the delightful ease of seducing a common woman.

Cradling her head, he leaned her back against the arm of the couch. With his other hand, he unbuttoned her cardigan, letting his fingers flick against her skin. He pushed the fabric back and traced the edges of her pink bra. When his fingertips slipped underneath the lace edges, Rene moaned softly, his thoughts of desire transporting her to a realm of sensual delight.

He slid her pants off and smiled when he saw that what she wore underneath was the same pink as her bra. It had been a long time since he'd seen lingerie. Stell refused to wear underwear of any kind. Rene sighed, arching her back, her mind taking her some place wonderful.

He ran his fingers along the side of her face and he could feel the power he wielded over her. It wasn't the same seduction he had used on the road with Louis. His mind was stronger now, his intentions clear. He realized he could take Rene far away in her mind and bring her back to the present with ease. He brought her attention fully to him, fully into the moment.

Even when fully consensual and not feeding-related, intimacy between Nahan and Kott was frowned upon. Sexual intimacy while feeding from the Kott'del was forbidden. A Storyteller coercing a Kott'del without her permission? Outrageous.

That's what Tomas needed, that's what the bees had made clear. Tomas needed to create outrage to achieve his goal. And he pursued a noble goal—helping Nahan, seeking out a possible injustice, sacrificing his own reputation regardless of the repercussions to discover a truth.

Noble. Admirable. Maybe even brave.

So why did it feel so shitty?

Rene didn't feel shitty. She felt luscious and delicious and the baser side of Tomas argued that he was overdue for some sexual satisfaction. He could ensure her pleasure as well. Her body already responded willingly.

But not really though. Not truly willingly.

Rene loved a boy named Trent—a boy with a scraggly beard, a lot of sweaters, and a ukulele. She loved Trent and she really loved that ukulele. Tomas could feel it all over her. But because of Tomas, because of his coercion, she wasn't thinking of Trent. She wanted only Tomas. She wanted only to please him.

She didn't deserve this. He needed the outrage; he needed the truth, but Rene didn't deserve to be treated like this.

Tomas didn't want to be the person who would do this.

Protocol aside. Hess, Storytellers, outrage aside.

Tomas would not be that man.

With a sigh of regret he pulled his hand from Rene's full breast, his fingertip slipping over the pink lace longingly. They would see that he hadn't completely stepped over the line, that he neither bedded her nor fed from her. He had gone too far, no doubt about it, and he hoped it provoked enough outrage for his plan. But he wouldn't go any further.

The bees would just have to understand.

....

"Thank you." He kissed her on the cheek. "That was wonderful." Rene made no move to dress so he piled her clothes on the couch next to her and winked.

"You might need these. Before Mrs. Studdard comes back." The mention of her supervisor snapped Rene out of her trance and she scrambled to straighten out her clothes. Not waiting to see if she was decent, Tomas strolled out of the room, leaving the door ajar.

It had to be enough.

....

He counted his steps as he headed back to the meditation room. On the nineteenth step he heard Mrs. Studdard's voice; at twenty-six he heard a door slam and heavy footsteps following him. He turned the corner and slipped into Meditation Room Two. Folding his legs underneath him, Tomas relaxed and waited. He resisted the urge to go over his plan again lest he begin to second-guess himself. It would either work or it wouldn't. When he heard Mrs. Studdard's raised voice down the hallway, he smiled. So far, so good. He knew the door would swing open seconds before it did and didn't bother to open his eyes at Vartan's angry tone.

"What the hell is going on Desara? Answer me."

"What are you doing?" Sylva charged in to block the Coordinator from the door. "You can't barge into a meditation room when a Storyteller is meditating."

"The hell I can't! I can when he rapes one of our *Kott'del*. I am personally responsible for their safety. Desara, you know very well what the rules are and purposely betrayed the trust placed in us by the—"

"Are you speaking to me?" Tomas opened his eyes and turned his head to the enraged crowd waiting for him. Sylva used her small body to fill the doorway as Vartan and a red-faced Mrs. Studdard leaned in. "It's okay, Mentor Sylva. I'll get up now."

"You're damn right you'll get up. You'll get your ass out here and explain to me who the hell you think you are taking advantage of the girls in the *Kott'del* that are entrusted to my care."

Tomas stretched and yawned, pushing through the trio at the door. He padded down the hallway, turning only when Mrs. Studdard complained.

"He's not even listening to you, Mr. Vartan. Tell him to stop."

Tomas remembered that he had once found the old woman intimidating. She held a very high rank among her kind. Oh well, too late now. He pointed at Mrs. Studdard.

"You are Kott. You do not belong in this end of the complex. Please leave."

Mrs. Studdard paled under his gaze even as Vartan defended her.

"She's here with me. She's lodged a complaint about you taking advantage of one of her people."

"She has a complaint about me?" Tomas stepped very close to Vartan's face, feeling as if he were stepping to the edge of a cliff. "And she came to you? How cute." Tomas turned to go but Vartan grabbed his arm.

"Don't turn your back on me."

"Why not?"

"You work for me."

It was exactly what Tomas was waiting for. Time to step off that cliff.

He spoke loudly enough to be heard by the small crowd that had gathered in nearby doorways to eavesdrop. "I believe you have that backward. I am the Storyteller. You are a bureaucrat. If memory serves me correctly, you work for me. At least, that's what the Council says." He turned his back on Vartan and headed for the Storytelling room, half expecting to feel the blast as the Coordinator exploded in rage.

The silence in the hall created a vacuum that sucked every nerve in the building into it. Out of sight, Tomas collapsed against the closed door and let out a nervous breath. Vartan had turned purple at Tomas's rebuke and that had not been an intuitive vision. The veins in his forehead had nearly ruptured as Tomas had brought up the sorest of Vartan's sore spots, a public reminder that the Council had backed a Storyteller over him. Given time, he would find a way to counter Tomas, to put him in his place but right now Tomas was counting on the element of surprise. He was also counting on Aricelli showing up on time. A voice spoke outside the door.

"Mr. Vartan? I'm sorry to bother you but there's a Miss Capp to see you?"

They were getting closer.

. . . .

Aricelli acted as if she didn't notice the blistering tension in the group before her. Paul Vartan's eyes were red-rimmed as he strained to control his temper and the people around him looked one loud noise away from fainting. Sticking to her script, Aricelli flashed her best smile.

"Mr. Vartan? You probably don't even remember me."

Vartan shifted gears with difficulty. Marcus Capp carried a lot of weight in the Council. As his daughter, Aricelli knew she would not be dismissed. Instead, Vartan turned away from Mrs. Studdard with muttered promises to look into the incident.

"Of course I remember you. How could I forget?" He took Aricelli by the elbow and led her past the Storytelling room. She caught the look of heat he threw at the closed door. "Let's not talk here in the hall, Miss Capp. Let's go to my office."

"Please, call me Aricelli."

. . . .

Tomas heard her name and forced himself to count three slow beats. Certain they had had enough time to make it down the hall but not enough to get into Vartan's office, Tomas threw open the door and tumbled into the hallway.

"Aricelli? Is that you?" He made a show of trying to smooth his hair and straighten out his wrinkled clothes. Vartan spun on him with a look that could have stopped a cat's heart but Aricelli smiled vacantly.

"Oh, Tomas. Tomas Desara. Hi." She looked to Vartan for help.

Tomas leaned against the doorframe. "I work here now. I'm a Storyteller."

The look of shock on Aricelli's face was so perfect, Tomas almost believed he'd surprised her. "Really? You? I mean, you made it? Wow, that's really something."

"Yeah, you know"—Tomas smirked at Vartan—"it's a lot of work but it's cool."

"I bet." She eyed him up and down, the shock not entirely wiped from her face. "Well I'd better get on with my meeting. It was really great seeing you again."

"Call me sometime."

With an apologetic laugh, Aricelli allowed Vartan to lead her into his office.

When the door had closed, she whispered to herself, "You've got to be kidding me."

"You seem surprised."

Aricelli let conflict show on her face for a moment and then replaced it with an insincere smile and a honeyed voice. "It's exciting to meet a Storyteller."

"Excitement isn't exactly the word I would have used to describe your reaction."

"Well, you know." She fumbled for the right words. "I didn't really know Tomas very well. He was . . . I just . . . that he would make it as a Storyteller is, well . . ."

"Exciting?" She laughed, letting Vartan know she knew she had been found out. "Miss Capp, you'll find here in the day-to-day life of the Council that the glamour of the Storytellers wears a little thin."

"I can see why. Just between you and me, he was a total nerd. And if what I heard was true, I think he was even a bed wetter until he was about twenty." She blushed as she laughed. "Oh my god, I can't believe I'm sitting with the Coordinator of the Council making fun of a Storyteller. You won't report me, will you? What am I saying? People report to you."

Tomas had explained his plan. If the Storytellers had a secret operation, only someone with Vartan's clout could begin to unearth it. But even the Coordinator of the Central Council wouldn't launch an investigation like that lightly. Especially Vartan. Especially after the smackdown he had received.

Unless they used that humiliation to set him on the path.

Tomas had told her he would prime Vartan, rip open that old wound. A young Storyteller putting him in his place would outrage Vartan. Then they would need someone else to come in and let him know about Westin, let him know the Storytellers had even more going on behind his back. They could find out what, if anything, the Coordinator knew about the facility and somehow convince him to share that information.

Aricelli assured Tomas she would handle that. She knew what she looked like to the Coordinator—beautiful, pampered, silly.

Just another Council darling counting on Daddy to keep her world perfect. Marcus Capp was an incredibly powerful man among the money people. Even though the Coordinator technically outranked him, Aricelli knew Vartan was ambitious. She bet he'd do just about anything to please the *tu Bith's* darling daughter.

She slid her jacket off her shoulders. The sweater she wore beneath the blazer was sleeveless, high in the front with a low, scooping backline. Knowing he watched her, she swept her thick black hair up in a clip, revealing a long expanse of smooth white skin. There weren't many Nahan men who would look away from a sight like that.

Vartan was smiling. "So what is it, Miss Capp, that has brought you into the city?"

"Well for one thing, I would have made the trip just to get you to stop calling me Miss Capp. Or are you sending me back to Heritage School?"

"Forgive me, Aricelli. I'm happy to help you in any way I can, if you call me Paul."

"Okay, Paul." She reached into her purse for her notebook and pen. "I'm here to ask you to help. I'm trying to get in with Henri Besson." She unfolded a piece of cream stationery with the distinctive Besson letterhead. She knew Vartan would recognize the personal stationery of another of the most powerful families in the Council and, just in case, Louis had duplicated his father's writing across the page.

"Henri has given me a list of secure facilities he would like me to visit. I've been to several Kott vaults, the printing center, which was filthy by the way. If you can avoid it, I would." She tried to sound bored as she scanned the list. "There's an identity maintenance facility I'm supposed to see, among other things."

"It sounds like quite an adventure," he said. "I assume we're also on your list?"

"You are. This facility is considered state of the art, a fortress of silence and safety in a dangerous world. Those were Henri's words, not mine." She could see the effect saying Mr. Besson's first name was having on Vartan. No doubt, in this office, Henri Besson was referred to as Mr. Besson. "I must admit I'm impressed at the size and scope of the facility. It's not easy to get in here with the fingerprint scanners and guards."

"And yet you just seemed to stroll in."

Aricelli laughed and tucked a loose curl behind her ear. "It would be disingenuous of me to pretend that my name doesn't open doors. Or, I should say, my father's name."

"Which leads me to my next question. Why exactly is Marcus Capp's daughter having to jump through hoops for a job? Even with Henri Besson?"

She bit her lip, visibly weighing her words as she considered him. "It's not exactly a job I'm looking for."

His eyes moved over her body. *In your dreams, Vartan,* she thought. *I'm not that ambitious.* None of her thoughts showed on her face.

"There have been some situations. The *tu Bith* are not entirely thrilled right now."

"I haven't heard anything."

"My father told me about you and your difficulties with the Storyteller, about your plans for the Council."

Vartan's face reddened. "Ah yes, my own moment of infamy. No doubt your father enjoys regaling his guests with that little anecdote."

"Things have changed." They watched each other. "I'm not in the inner circle of the money people, but I hear things and there seems to be a groundswell of concern."

"About the Storytellers? I find that hard to believe. After all, what's good for the Storytellers is good for the Nahan, correct?"

"That's what I've always been told." She flipped her pen across her fingers, broadcasting her anxiety to Vartan. "Can I be honest with you? I mean, you're not going to report me to Bobby the Bed Wetter down the hall?"

"I promise you, anything you tell me will remain in the strictest of confidence." By the flicker of his smile, Aricelli had no doubt he would retain that nickname for future use.

"Certain people are questioning our dependence on the Storytellers. Our blind obedience to a class of people who appoint themselves and make the important decisions for our people with no accountability."

Vartan blew out a long breath. "Those are dangerous words, Miss Capp. You're talking about the principal decision-making body of our people."

Aricelli didn't need to fake her anxiety now. With her next sentence, she could bring a storm of trouble down on the Council. Or she could look like a fool.

"The *tu Bith* are very interested in Westin."

She had seen statues with more animated expressions than Vartan's at that moment.

"Westin? I'm not familiar with that name."

And then she saw it, the nervous ripple of his left eyelid. A tic. Aricelli didn't know how the Storytellers did what they did but she knew how to read men.

Vartan was lying.

She dropped her pen and notebook back into her purse. "Well then, I guess I've wasted your time. I apologize. I know you're a busy man." She could feel him study her.

"I'm sorry you wasted the trip."

"Oh, you know how it is." She pasted on an obviously forced smile, trying a different tactic. "Maybe Daddy just sent me on a snipe hunt, something to put me in my place. Maybe they're all having a good laugh at my expense, getting ahead of myself with my ambition."

Aricelli gathered her things to leave, wondering what Tomas would make of Vartan's lie. He knew about Westin, she was sure of it. Was he covering for the Storytellers? Would he tell them about her questions? Would it come back on Tomas? Regardless, Tomas had overestimated Vartan's vulnerability.

"What do they want to know about Westin?"

Or maybe not.

Aricelli hid her smile, settling back in her seat. "How it works. Where it is." She knew she had to be careful here. She didn't want to tip her hand but she had to learn what Vartan knew. "They want to know how they're pulling it off with such secrecy."

"To shut it down?"

How to answer that? She couldn't be sure which side of the issue the Coordinator took. Best to let Vartan wonder the same.

"To gauge its viability."

That must have been the right answer. Vartan leaned forward on his desk and studied her.

"You trusted me. Now I'm going to trust you. What I'm going to tell you is highly confidential. Less than a handful of people are aware of it and I am taking a great risk getting you involved."

Aricelli tried to remain cool. "Anything you tell me will go no further."

"For now I hope that's true. Once our project has gotten a little further along, once we have some concrete evidence of our success, I hope you will help me get the support we'll need in the Council. I'll tell you right now, it's going to be a tough sell."

He scribbled on his stationery and handed it across to her.

"What's this?"

"Directions. To a house on Lake Wenneset in Michigan. There's a machine there that I think the *tu Bith* will find very interesting."

He watched her fold the paper and slip it into her purse. "What we are working on, what we are attempting there, is delicate in nature. The community at large is not ready for this innovation. I cannot emphasize enough the need for discretion. You've given me your word that I can trust you. I will be deeply disappointed if you prove me wrong."

Chapter Eleven:

NAHAN

....

Nahan: Ourselves

Tomas heard the assistant knock on Vartan's door. Voices in the hallway moved past the Storytelling room where he hid. It was time to find out if Aricelli had succeeded. He eased the door open to slip out. His stealth was wasted.

On the other side of the door stood Dalle, waiting.

Words froze in Tomas's throat. He couldn't move, could barely breathe as the blue eyes of his mentor stared into his, unreadable. They stood face-to-face, close enough to touch noses. He could smell Dalle's skin and he felt the familiar sensation of being utterly transparent before the man. He finally managed to choke out the only word in his mind.

"Mentor."

Dalle huffed a soft breath that Tomas could feel against his face. "No."

Dalle took Tomas's hand and turned it palm up. In the center, he placed a black bee.

"Is this yours?"

Tomas couldn't speak; his thoughts raced. How did Dalle know about the bees? Where did he find a black one? In the middle of winter? In the complex? Were black bees even real?

Before he could ask anything, Dalle squeezed Tomas' fingers, closing his fist over the buzzing insect. Tomas couldn't stop him, even when he felt the small body fighting then breaking under the pressure. He didn't want to open his hand. He didn't want to see the death there.

Instead he looked at Dalle, at his mentor's hand held up before him. As Tomas clenched his own fist, the dead bee shifting within his grip, Dalle opened his hand, showing his palm to Tomas.

In the center, surrounded by an angry red welt, a long, black stinger protruded.

"Why didn't it sting me?"

Dalle smiled. "It did."

He brought two fingers of his injured hand and pressed on the center of Tomas's forehead, whispering one word:

"*Epatu.*" Open.

He felt the world fall away around him, held up entirely by the contact of skin on skin.

Then the contact was gone. Tomas opened his eyes, not knowing when he had closed them. Dalle was gone. His hands were empty.

. . . .

"Do we have any sort of plan?"

Tomas said nothing as Aricelli drove. Adlai, Stell, and Louis sat quietly in the backseat of the SUV. He knew they were watching him, worried about him. His hair stuck to his face and his neck was damp with the sweat that covered him after his odd encounter with Dalle. He kept clenching his fist, trying to remember the feel of the bee, trying to figure out what was real.

Louis leaned forward and stuck his head in between the front seats. "Mr. Vartan knew about Westin. Have we decided what this means? Is this good news or bad?"

Tomas continued to stare at his fist.

"Well," Aricelli said, catching Louis's eye in the rearview mirror, "if he knows about it, the Storytellers aren't keeping it a secret from him."

Tomas unfolded his fingers. His palm was smooth and unmarked.

"Then that's a good sign, right, dude? It means whatever the Storytellers are doing, it can't be that bad, right? Mr. Vartan would be obligated, as the Coordinator, to report—"

. . . .

Tomas let the words fly by. Buzz by. Like bees.

Dalle had placed a bee in his palm.

Dalle had opened his mind.

Epatu—when a mind had to open to let something in. Or let something out.

Sweat dripped down the back of his neck but he ignored it as he ignored Louis and Aricelli, the *acul 'ads*, and the road rolling past.

Bees. Drones. Fear. Pain.

The bee had stung him.

Dalle had felt the pain.

He saw Lucien's red eyes, his tear-stained cheeks.

"The Storytellers aren't doing this."

"What, Tomas?" Aricelli reached out to push a sweaty lock of hair out of his eyes. Tomas pulled away. "How do you know this?"

"It's killing them. It's killing Lucien not being able to reach him, to feel him."

Adlai growled. "That's pretty damn good since he's the one who broke him."

"No. Lucien didn't break him. Hess just broke."

Louis put a hand up to hold back the *acul 'ad*. "Well then, who's taking care of Hess? And do we really want to bother them?"

"I don't give a shit who's taking care of Shelan," Adlai said. "He's coming with me."

"What if he needs help?" Aricelli asked. "What if that machine Mr. Vartan mentioned is helping him heal?"

"The drone." Even the word made Tomas's head ache. "It might be why Lucien can't reach him, can't feel him."

Louis leaned in closer, speaking softly. "Dude, are you feeling him? Or whatever? I mean, how can you do it and the Storytellers can't?"

"I don't know. Maybe it's my gift? What I was supposed to learn from the poison?" He looked into the darkness flying by. "Maybe it's Hess's gift that he never got to learn. Whatever it is, something keeps telling me about the drone."

Aricelli shook her head. "But didn't you say the drone was removed? That it didn't work?"

"It worked."

"So then why would Mr. Vartan still want it?"

"Maybe because it works."

"It's just a house."

Aricelli shut off the ignition and all five of them peered up at Westin.

. . . .

It was just a house, two stories, weathered porch, surrounded by miles of woods. Dampness from the lake in the distance hung in the air.

293

Louis looked back through the rear window. "Nobody followed us. There doesn't seem to be any security."

"Carlson said it was just one girl up here guarding him. It's a solitary assignment."

"She's Kott," Aricelli said. "What if she won't let us in?"

Nobody said anything until Stell huffed. "What do you mean she won't let us? She's common. We'll make her."

"She's Kott," Adlai said. "We can't touch her."

Before Stell could protest further, Tomas opened his door. "Maybe we won't have to touch her. We'll just ask her if we can see Hess. She doesn't know Mr. Vartan didn't send us. She'll let us in. We'll talk to Hess and decide what to do."

They had almost made it to the porch when Tomas heard a sound like a motorboat engine being revved underground. He dropped to the dirt, clutching his head.

The sound was more than a sound. It punched through his skull like a bolt, making his teeth clamp together and his thoughts go white. Nausea ripped through his body and Tomas feared he might lose control of his bowels. The sound abated and he was able to gasp a breath.

Stell reached him first, wrapping him in her arms and pulling him to her chest. "Tomas? Tomas? Speak to me. We've got to get him out of here."

"No. I'm okay. That sound, it"— Another short burst of sound rang out and Tomas's teeth clacked together. Just as quickly, the sound vanished. Tomas was pale and struggled to sit up. "Change of plans." He waved his friends closer.

On the ground, wet with sweat, the taste of blood in his mouth, Tomas understood. It was the drone he had been feeling all along. The blackness. The cold. The pain.

"You've got to get her to turn it off. I can't go in there with it on."

"I'll go in there." Adlai said. "I'm going to rip that fucking thing out of the wall."

"No." Tomas grabbed his arm. "We've got to get her to turn it off. There might be a fail-safe or an alarm trigger." His mouth tasted like ash. "This might not be the worst it can do. Go carefully. If she can amp this thing up, if this is what the drone can do, we can't leave him here. Go, before it starts up again."

. . . .

Aricelli banged on the door and didn't wait for an answer. She marched into the foyer of the house, followed by Louis and Adlai. In less than a minute, a young blond woman ran into the hallway with a panicked look.

"Hello? Who are you?" She wore flannel pajama pants and a Purdue t-shirt. Her hair was dirty and had a pencil stuck within its tangled mess.

"Katie, isn't it? You need to turn off the drone now."

"Who are you? I'm not turning anything off until you tell me what you're doing here."

Aricelli looked to Louis, who gave her a small nod. He knew what she was going to do.

"Damn it." Aricelli fumbled in her purse. "Didn't Paul call you?" Katie only stared at her. "Paul Vartan? Your boss? You do know who you work for, yes?"

"I answer to Mr. Vartan."

Aricelli pulled out the directions Vartan had written on his own stationery. "And who do you think sent me?"

"Get Vartan on the phone!" Louis pointed a finger at Aricelli, ignoring Katie. "I told him to get his shit together or this was the last time we were taking care of this. Get the goddam drone turned off and let's get on with it."

"I'm working on it. Please, I'm sure it's just a misunderstand-ing." Aricelli almost smiled. Louis was such a natural. He had to know that nothing brought people together like a shared enemy. He would be the bad guy, Aricelli would be the ally.

"You people have no business being here. I don't care who—"

"Please, Katie. You have to listen to me. I don't know how our wires got crossed but Mr. Vartan sent us here. It's a maintenance thing. We do it every year and if I don't get that drone turned off, I'm going to be in so much trouble. I don't know why nobody told you about this. Deb was always ready for us when we showed up." They could hear the drone kick on once again and Aricelli tried not to think of what it was doing to Tomas.

Katie chewed her lip. "I was told never to turn it off. That it was for my own safety."

"Trust me." Aricelli tipped her head toward Adlai. "That's what this gorilla is for."

She held her breath and waited. Louis had ended his fake phone call and Adlai stood frozen, waiting to see what the girl would do.

Katie chewed her lip a little longer, looking at the note in Aricelli's hand. Then she nodded. Before relief fully flooded Aricelli, Katie spoke up.

"I'll turn it off. But I have to call Mr. Vartan first."

The drone kicked on again, the rumble seeming to go on for-ever. Aricelli thought she might be sick.

"Okay."

Katie kept nodding, her relief evident. "Okay, great. It's in my office right by the phone. We can just call—"

Aricelli didn't know which one of them would act first. One of them had to grab the girl. She could not be allowed to make that call.

The decision was made by the sound of the front door being kicked open.

· ·

They were just standing there. Louis, Aricelli, even Adlai, just standing there. Couldn't they hear the drone? Didn't they know what it was doing to Tomas?

Stell had Tomas, her arm around his waist holding him up. She dragged him into the house. Blood ran from his nose and his skin shone waxy with sweat.

"Turn off the fucking machine!"

Katie backed away. "Who are you people? I'm calling Mr. Vartan. I'm Kott and I demand"— She didn't get to finish her demand. Stell dropped Tomas and leapt for her, grabbing the blonde by the neck and hauling her onto her toes.

"Turn. It. Off."

Stell heard the others behind her. She didn't know if they would stop her or help her but the girl looked down at her stubbornly.

"Get your hands off me. I am fourth-generation Kott."

"And I don't give a shit." Stell squeezed a little harder.

"I'll report you," she hissed. "I'll tell Mr. Vartan."

Stell's nails dug into the soft skin of her neck. "With what voice?"

"Stell, stop." Tomas sat on the floor where she'd dropped him. His hair and his shirt clung to him, dark with sweat. Stell didn't loosen her grip. "Katie, I need you to listen to me. You need to turn off the drone. It's a dangerous machine."

Katie struggled to speak around Stell's grip. "Mr. Vartan said it's too dangerous to turn off. He said—" She gasped as Stell dug her nails in. Katie's voice came out in a reedy whine. "I'm protected by the Council."

Tomas laughed. "Does it look like she gives a shit about the Council?"

. . . .

Tomas left Katie in Stell's hands. Louis and Aricelli stayed downstairs as much to prevent Stell from killing the girl as to keep watch. The drone was off. He and Adlai headed upstairs to find Hess.

Tomas stepped aside and let Adlai move into the room. Under the window was a narrow bed and in the dim light they could see a figure lying still. Adlai hurried to the bed and caught his breath at the sight of Shelan, thin and haggard, staring at the ceiling unseeing.

"Shelan?" He whispered. "Shelan? Can you hear me?"

Hess brought his eyes into focus on Adlai's face. "Go away."

Tomas saw Adlai reel at the words.

"Shelan? It's me. Anton."

"Go away." He closed his eyes tight and a tear slid out the corner of his eye into his hair. "You're not real. You're not real. You're not real."

Adlai brushed his fingers over Hess's cheek and the Storyteller opened his eyes. "I'm here, brother. I'm getting you out of here."

Hess cried out and threw his arms around Adlai's neck, pulling himself up into his embrace. His thin fingers dug at Adlai's coat as he cried. "Be real. Oh god, please be real."

Tomas didn't want to interrupt but they had to hurry. He cleared his throat and Hess jumped at the sound.

"Who are you? I know you."

"There isn't time to explain it now. We've got to go. Please, trust us."

Adlai gave him his jacket to cover up. "We've got a car outside."

"They'll never let me leave. The drone will be coming on any minute. I can't go. They'll kill me. Please listen, Anton. I can't . . ."

Louis slipped through the door. "What the hell's taking so long? Let's go. We don't know if there's any kind of alarm or timer. Come on."

Adlai assured his bewildered friend that everything was taken care of and helped him down the stairs. Hess was light-headed and unsteady and had to lean on Adlai. Downstairs, Stell finished tying a red-faced Katie to a kitchen chair, a towel around her mouth as a rough gag.

Tomas saw the Kott girl's rage and heard the threat in her muffled words.

"Trust me, Katie. This is the right thing. And it could have gone a lot worse."

. . . .

Aricelli had the car running, Louis in the backseat, waiting for Adlai to help Hess down the stairs. Tomas, still leaning on Stell, walked along beside them. Adlai growled that he didn't need help, that Hess needed nobody but him now.

"We'll go to Detroit. My dad's there." He shifted his grip on his unsteady friend. "Dad can get us back to the Reaches."

They froze at the unmistakable *ch-chunk* of a pump-action shotgun.

"Going somewhere, sweetheart?"

Tomas heard Hess moan, taking the longest of the four of them to turn to face the two Nahan men pointing guns at them. One had the shotgun aimed directly at Adlai. The other stood smiling, his fingers on the trigger of a 9mm.

Adlai stepped in front of Hess, and the man with the handgun smiled. "You move, we fire. You may be fast but you're not faster than a bullet. You may be tough but you ought to see what a shotgun blast can do to a human skull, especially at this range."

Adlai grinned and Tomas felt Stell tensing, aggression moving through her. "That's a nice bluff." The *acul 'ads* inched forward, giving Tomas a clear view of Hess, eyes closed, swaying. Guns were raised, Stell and Adlai poised to attack.

"Stop," Hess said. "Put the gun down, Graves. I won't leave."

"Good boy," Graves said, lowering his weapon. The other man kept the shotgun trained on them as Hess pushed past Adlai's restraining arm.

"Let me go, Anton," Hess said. "They'll kill you."

"What? No, they're Nahan." Adlai shook his head. "I'm Nahan. They may shoot but I'm awfully hard to kill."

"They've done it before. They killed the men who brought me here."

Tomas felt a cold stone turn in his stomach at the sight of Grave's ugly grin. Sylva had told him that dozens had left the complex after Hess had been removed. They probably assumed the drivers had been among them.

Graves held out his free hand. "Let's go, Storyteller. You come back inside and let us clean up this mess. We'll call Mr. Vartan and he'll find someplace nice and safe to stick your buddies." Hess drifted forward. "Come on, that's right. You be good and I'll give you a nice treat. Be a good little Storyteller now."

Hess stepped away from Adlai, his hand outstretched toward Graves. Before their fingers made contact, he looked over his shoulder at Tomas. Tomas met his gaze, the icy fear in his stomach giving way to something colder, harder. Hess held his gaze.

The low ringing in his ears, an aftermath of the drone, grew louder as he looked into the dark Nahan eyes he had seen in his induction vision. The ringing became a buzzing, the sound of a thousand bees telling him a story.

Felson. That's who held the shotgun, Grave's partner. Tomas knew him in that instant, knew his pain, knew his madness.

Death—he'd lost someone, someone he loved. An accident. An explosion. The thousand invisible bees told Tomas about the pain.

Felson's wife had died during the construction of the Council complex.

He blamed the Storytellers.

Hatred and pain has twisted him, infecting him, drawing into his orbit a kindred spirit. Graves. Graves wasn't in pain; Graves was just mad. Together they had sunk to the bottom of the cesspool that was Vartan's ambition.

"Can you hear it?" Tomas asked. "The shrieking of the dead in your ears? You will." He sniffed the air, drawing deep breaths through his nose. "I can smell it too. Can you?"

"I can smell it," Hess said. "It smells like sour earth. Like rusted metal buried in rotting vegetables that somebody has set on fire then pissed on."

"You're never the same afterwards, after you taste the death of Nahan."

Back and forth Hess and Tomas spoke, telling the lessons they had learned at the hands of the Storytellers. Felson and Graves swung their guns, ordering them to be quiet but they kept speaking, kept drawing closer to the gunmen.

"It freezes inside your veins."

"You become paralyzed."

"Abomination."

"Abomination." Hess' voice grew soft.

"Get in the goddam house." Graves grabbed Hess's arm.

Hess glanced down at the hand that gripped his arm. "Do you feel how cold your hands are? You're going to be that cold forever."

Tomas continued. "You'll never be able to purge yourself of that cold, of that death. That's mud in your veins and the hottest fires on earth will never burn it out of you."

Graves yanked Hess toward the porch.

"This superstitious shit is the whole reason you Storytellers have to be put down."

"You think it's superstition?" Tomas asked. "You think the training we receive from the hands of our predecessors is just fairy tales and ghost stories?"

"Yeah, I do. That's the difference between you and me, between the future and the past. I don't have the luxury of sitting on my ass and dreaming dreams. I not afraid to do what has to be done to achieve my goals."

"Your goals?" Hess jerked his arm free and laughed out loud. "This is your plan, Graves? I don't think so. You're Vartan's trained monkey. You always have been."

"Don't listen to him, Graves. Don't let him get into your head." Felson pointed his gun at Tomas's forehead. "Shut your mouth, Hess. You talk too much, you know that? I never did meet a Storyteller who knew how to keep his mouth shut."

"You still haven't." Tomas stepped up to Felson, pressing his forehead against the muzzle of the gun. "I'm a Storyteller too. Are you going to kill me?"

"Yes I am." Felson smiled an ugly smile. Tomas tipped his head forward, Felson's gun pressing harder into his skin. He felt sluggish and heavy and he resisted a sudden urge to yawn. Around him the forest grew darker and quieter. He could smell the adrenaline in the air but it had none of its usual allure. Tonight it smelled sour and stale, like old smoke.

It wasn't like slipping into a trance. It felt like the opposite of meditation. The air, the light, the people around him, nothing had that vibrant allure of transcendental thought. Everything was suddenly dull. Everything was ugly. He turned his head, the gun grazing his temple, to look at Stell. Her normally luminous face was blotchy with anger and fear. Cool, tough Adlai looked small and skittish. He could see the white faces of Aricelli and Louis staring in horror from inside the car. So much fear hung in the air, so much anger wafted over him, yet none of it touched him.

Nahan didn't kill Nahan. It was one of those truths he had never questioned. Now that that pillar had been shattered, all he could think to do was yawn.

"Are we boring you, Storyteller?" Felson pressed the gun harder into his forehead.

"A little bit, yeah."

"Well, maybe a bullet tearing through your skull will liven things up, huh?"

Felson had every intention of killing him and Stell and everyone with them. In Felson's mind, it was already done and for just a moment Tomas wondered what it would be like to be dead, to not feel the warmth under his skin or the fluidity of his muscles as they moved him through the air. He rolled his shoulders back, releasing the tension that lay there, and tipped his head from side to side, loosening his neck.

Felson waved the gun before his face. "What the hell are you doing?"

Tomas ignored him and turned instead to Hess, who stood beside Graves like a prom date. "Do you think it's true? About the mud and cold?"

Graves had gone pale. Funny how Tomas hadn't noticed that. "That's what the Storytellers told me."

Tomas sighed and pressed Felson's gun once more against his forehead.

"It's time."

Felson hesitated for only a minute, scanning for signs of a trick. When nothing came, he tightened his grip on the gun.

"You're goddam right it's ti"—

Before the words were out of his mouth, Tomas slapped the gun away from his forehead, using it to jerk the man forward.

He lunged into Felson. His mouth clamped down on the guard's throat, tearing away skin and muscles, silencing the scream that shone in Felson's eyes. Grabbing him by the back of the head, Tomas ripped the man away from what remained of his throat and let the body drop to the ground in a spray of arterial blood. Felson pawed blindly at his ruined throat, shock and pain crippling him as his life puddled beneath him. The last thing Edmund Felson saw was the young Storyteller leaning over him, his face black with blood, spitting out the meat of his throat.

Nobody screamed. No one cried out. Graves moaned as he dropped to his knees before Hess and began to cry. Hess pried the weapon from his fingers. Graves rocked on his knees, his cries pitiful as Hess stroked his head. After several minutes, Graves lifted his tear-stained face up to see him, struggling through his tears and terror to utter one word.

"Mercy."

Hess gently wiped the wash of tears from Graves's face and cupped his cheek in his palm.

"No."

He leveled the gun at his captor's forehead and pulled the trigger.

. . . .

"I don't know what to do now."

Tomas swayed on his feet. He could feel bile rising in his throat and had to swallow hard several times. The blood on his lips was beyond foul but he couldn't bring himself to spit it on the ground. Before him, Stell and Adlai stood white-faced and slack-jawed, for once unnerved at the sight of carnage. They both staggered as Louis pushed his way between them and ran up to grab Tomas by the shoulders.

"Hold still." Louis wiped the gore from his cousin's chin with a soft cloth. "Whatever happens, bro, it happens to us both, okay? Just like the old days."

"I don't think this is going to be like getting grounded."

"Aricelli," Louis shouted toward the car. "Get out and help me with this. You two," he pointed to Stell and Adlai, "you get that one. We'll drag them into the bushes to hide the bodies. We don't know who else might come by here. Tomas, Hess, you two sit down. You both look like you're going to faint." When only Aricelli moved, Louis shouted louder. "What are you waiting for?"

"We can't touch them." Stell's eyes were enormous. "They're dead. They're Nahan. If we . . . they . . . we can't touch . . . that."

He marched up to Stell. "You listen to me very carefully. These men are dead. Two Nahan are dead because Tomas killed one of them." He stuck a finger into Adlai's face. "Your friend killed the other. They killed them and now we are going to take care of it because that is what Nahan do. That is what friends do. And I don't care if every ancestor that ever breathed howls in and tears the eyes from our heads; I don't care if we have to strap these bodies to our backs and walk them back to Chicago, we are taking care of this. Do you understand me?"

Stell nodded, shock draining from her face. She turned toward the mess that was Felson.

Aricelli joined Louis, who was waiting at the splayed feet of Graves. She wouldn't meet his eyes as she jerked the dead man from the ground by his wrists. It was so horrible, the pallor of death on a Nahan face. He understood now why the dead had their faces covered immediately by the closest family member. Aricelli's feet slipped on a spongy mass in the blood and she fought back a gag.

"On three . . ." They slung the body into the underbrush beside the house. Aricelli's hands were covered in blood and Louis could see them tremble. From his back pocket, he pulled the t-shirt he had used to wipe Tomas's face and rushed to wrap her hands in it, both to clean the blood and help her keep it together. "You're doing great." He whispered.

"I'm so scared, Louis."

"I know. Me too. We just have to do what needs to be done."

. . . .

From the porch, Tomas and Hess watched the silent endeavor. Tomas flexed his fingers, testing them to see if they felt any colder than they should. "Why did you kill that man?"

"Why did you?"

"He was going to kill us. He already had it in his mind. There was no other way. But Graves, he was down. He had surrendered."

"Are you telling me I should have shown him mercy?"

"No." Tomas watched a puddle of blood glowing in the light from the porch. "I'm telling you you should have let me kill him. I would have killed him for you, for all of us. You didn't have to put yourself in line for whatever is coming."

"Whatever's coming is already here," Hess said. "Those men killed my drivers almost four years ago. They never heard howling or felt the cold shrieks of the dead. They never went insane. They were already insane." He clasped his hands between his knees. "When I was training, the Storytellers told me about the mud and the cold but Lucien told me that the real abomination is not the killing; it's what you become afterwards."

"And what is that?"

Hess shrugged. "I guess it depends on who you were before."

"What are we going to become?"

"You are going to become a Storyteller who was willing to lose his own sanity for the lives of the people he loves. Think you can live with that?"

Tomas sighed. "You make it sound noble. It doesn't feel that way."

"Really heroic things never do. Or so I'm told."

"Is that why you killed Graves? To be a hero?"

He laughed. "Man, do I strike you as a hero? Would I be running with Anton if I was a noble beast? No, I'm going to become someone who gets as far away from Chicago as humanly possible for the rest of my life."

Tomas had nothing to say to that so they watched the end of the cleanup in silence. Aricelli and Louis covered the bodies with branches while Stell and Adlai threw mud and pine needles over the blood and tissue on the road.

"We need to figure out what to do now."

"Anything coming to you, kid?"

Tomas shook his head. "You?"

"Not a freaking thing. You know what we could really use right now?" He looked at Tomas. "A Storyteller."

. . . .

"We need everything—cash, ID, a car."

Adlai's father, Ivan, surveyed the bloody group gathered in his cramped Detroit apartment. "Got a Jeep that's clean." He studied Hess, who had collapsed in a battered recliner. "I don't know if it'll get you far enough away from whatever did that."

Adlai sighed. "Yeah, it's a bad scene. Gonna head to the Reaches. Maybe crash with Mom for a while."

"Good," Ivan said, rising and moving toward a pile of cardboard boxes in the corner. "You can take some of this crap back to her."

"What is all this?"

"Aw, we lost a storage unit. Gotta find a place for all this." He rummaged through a box and pulled out a photo album. "Remember these?"

Adlai grinned and took the book, settling on the floor next to

Stell in front of Shelan. On the couch beside them, Tomas, Louis, and Aricelli sat wide eyed and silent. Tomas hadn't spoken a word since Westin.

"Look at these, Stell. These are pictures my mom took from her days with the Reachers. She's got some great stories."

"Who are the Reachers?" Stell asked.

"I guess you could say they were our Beat Generation," Ivan said, as the others moved to look over Adlai's shoulder. "They got together right after the war, the first one. The Council was just getting their act together and started cracking down on the arts scene. Nothing like a little power to create a rebellion."

The photos were beautiful. In one, a petite Nahan woman straddled a steamer trunk wearing nothing but a wispy feathered boa. The photo captured the exact moment she bit into a ripe plum and the juice glowed on her chin. The image was incredibly erotic.

"These are amazing." Aricelli said as Adlai thumbed through photos of Nahan men and women, alone, in pairs, or in groups of three and more, engaging in many levels of sensual delight. Some were artistic, some were outright pornographic. "I notice the same models keep appearing. Were these all taken at the same time?"

"No." Ivan shook his head. "The Reachers tended to run together in waves. They were a tight-knit group but they were always moving. They'd descend on an area, grift the hell out of it and leave, usually with the law on their tail. These pictures span over ten, fifteen years."

Stell turned a page in the album. Adlai whistled.

"Look at her." In the photo, a voluptuous woman reclined on a tangled length of velvet, wearing nothing but a dazzling smile and an endearing dimple on her left cheek. Her long hair tumbled over her shoulders as she spread her legs for the camera and was caught mid-laugh. In the next photo, the woman still reclined, her head thrown back as a man in a tuxedo buried his face between her thighs. The photos progressed with the man, his back to the camera, moving his way up the laughing woman's body. Something in her face made the erotic encounter seem natural and friendly, not lurid or invasive. Ivan looked over and recognized the photo.

"Oh yeah," Ivan laughed. "I remember her; she was a hell of a dancer. Ran with your mom for a long time. She shows up in a lot of the pictures. That guy too. Keep turning the pages and you'll see why the Council kept trying to shut your mom down."

Tomas looked away from the book like it had burned his eyes. The woman in the photo, still naked, still sprawled on the velvet, now reclined against the man in the tuxedo. He had his face buried in the woman's neck, biting into her skin, blood running freely down the white expanse of her bare breast.

"It's something, ain't it?"

None of them had ever seen a photograph of that most intimate Nahan act. It was never photographed, never drawn, never described in anything but the most intimate settings. To see it photographed so boldly, so beautifully, was both exciting and disturbing.

Adlai turned the page of the album since Stell's hands had gone slack at her side. In the next photo, the man in the tuxedo finally showed his face. The woman still wore her brilliant smile, softened somewhat with satisfaction, but the man's face was hard, predatory, a strange contrast to the voluptuous softness of his partner. Adlai whistled again and moved to close the book but Stell stopped him.

"That woman." She ran her finger over the photo. "You knew her?"

Ivan grinned. "Oh yeah. She was a wild one."

"Was she?" Stell stared at her. "That's my mother."

Ivan was the only one who laughed. "That's *your* mom?" He eyed Stell's slim figure. "Wouldn't have seen that coming."

Stell traced her finger over the man in the tuxedo, the hard line of his eyebrows, the narrow lips, and the impossibly pale eyes.

Without asking permission, she peeled the photo from the album. "Are there more photos?"

"Yeah, sure, but they could be anywhere." Ivan said. "This isn't even all the boxes. You're welcome to go through all of them. Hell, you're welcome to pack them up and haul them out west to your mom's place. Save me the trouble of—"

Before he could finish, Adlai cut him off with a shout.

"Shelan?"

. . . .

Hess's back was arched, his eyes rolled far back in his head and his hands convulsed into tight fists. Tomas scrambled onto the chair and straddled him, pinning him down.

"Hold his arms. Hold him down!"

Adlai and Ivan each took an arm and Stell threw herself across his flailing feet. Tomas gripped the sides of Hess's skull, his palms pressing into his cheekbones, his thumbs meeting in the center of his forehead at the same spot on his own forehead that Dalle had touched hours earlier. The terror of the man beneath him shot through his body like a current and Tomas struggled to maintain his grip. Reacting on instinct, he pressed his lips to Hess's forehead and began to whisper one word over and over again. *Epatu.* Open.

The pain in his hands and arms was excruciating and Tomas's teeth clenched together so hard he feared they might crack but still he whispered again and again. Ivan and Anton struggled to hold Hess down until finally he sucked in a gasping breath and let out a pitiful cry. His body slumped beneath Tomas, who had gripped his face so hard he had to peel his hands away.

Hess opened his eyes.

"I still dream."

"I know. I felt you."

"For a long time I couldn't dream. I couldn't sleep. But then the dreams started seeping in when I was awake. I don't know what's real anymore. When I saw you, I thought you were death coming for me. I saw the world burning and I saw you taking me out of it."

"I'm not death. I'm just like you."

Hess closed his eyes. "You're not like me. I killed Graves hoping it would kill me."

"Do you trust me?"

Hess nodded.

"I need you to do something for me."

He grabbed Tomas's hand and pressed it to his forehead. "Anything."

. . . .

"Mr. Vartan?" Fiona peeked her head in the office. "Miss Capp called. She's on her way up. She says it's urgent."

"Thank you, Fiona." He waited until the door was closed before releasing the breath he felt like he'd been holding for twelve hours. He hadn't slept the entire night, hadn't left his office. All night he'd tortured himself with visions of destroying his career by acting so rashly.

He'd taken a huge risk. If something went wrong, if Aricelli Capp saw what was happening at Westin and grew squeamish or righteous, he would have brought a shit storm down on himself. If his partners knew what he had done, they would tear him apart.

But Vartan had a plan.

He always had a plan. That's why he always landed on his feet, because Paul Vartan tried to see two or three steps ahead. He had vision. More importantly, he had the guts to act.

The drone project was working. Graves kept him updated. The kid was falling apart, growing weaker and more desperate every day. They starved him of blood, kept him from sleeping, rewarded him when he was docile, and amped up the drone when he acted out. Graves predicted Hess would kill himself within two years. The plan was then to present the tragedy to select and sympathetic Council members, along with other documented evidence, with a suggestion that an investigation be launched regarding the stability and dependability of the Storytellers.

Then Aricelli Capp had strolled into his office and Vartan saw a new plan.

Lovely, luscious Aricelli Capp, so sweet and young, the delicate pampered daughter of the most powerful *tu Bith* in North America. He saw the whole plan roll out before his eyes. Send the girl to Westin unannounced. She'd surprise the Kott; she'd surprise Hess.

That beautiful girl, those delicious breasts. Hell, Vartan had hardly been able to keep his hands to himself. Hess would surely snap. And if an insane Storyteller were to assault the precious off-spring of Marcus Capp? It wouldn't take a Storyteller to imagine how the *tu Bith* would react.

Sure, he knew Capp would blame him for endangering his lit-tle girl but that would pale in comparison to the hell he'd bring down on the Storytellers. There would be a schism and the business of the Nahan would be taken out of the hands of those bleary-eyed wackos. It would be put into capable hands, responsible, practical hands.

His hands.

And if nothing happened to the girl, if Hess had been too broken to assault her, pathetic creature that he was, Vartan still had the girl in his pocket. She wanted what he wanted and knew he had a plan.

She would see him spearheading a revolution.

He wouldn't let her rush into anything. He would mentor her on their plan. For a moment, Vartan let his thoughts drift to the possible sensual repercussions of Aricelli joining their team at his side. Any minute now she would be coming down the hallways of the complex and he would know if he had made history or the worst mistake of his life. He couldn't wait at his desk to find out.

Vartan stepped out into the hallway just as Aricelli turned the corner. She smiled brightly and ran up to him, her cheeks flushed just as he had imagined. "Paul! Great news. I've brought Daddy!"

And like a child seeing Santa actually step out of the fireplace, Paul Vartan saw Marcus Capp striding down the hallway, surrounded by an entourage, yet entirely eclipsing them. Marcus Capp was neither overly tall nor especially handsome. Aricelli got her looks from her mother but she inherited her ability to make an entrance from her father. His presence was electric and Vartan struggled to maintain his poise.

"Paul, long time no see." Word of the powerful *tu Bith's* presence had spread and eyes peered out of every doorway. "Seems we have a lot to talk about."

If Paul Vartan had a machine that could capture and preserve one moment in his life forever, he would have used it at that moment. Surrounded by his employees, sharing the hallway with one of the most powerful men in the Council, and knowing he was about to change the world, Paul relished a sweet moment of perfection.

"It's certainly my pleasure to have you here, sir. Shall we go into my office?" He swung open the door and held his arm out in welcome.

"Perhaps we should." Marcus Capp didn't move. "Before we step inside, however, I'd like to introduce you to a very valuable assistant of mine." A member of his entourage stepped forward and removed his sunglasses. Vartan froze, staring into the face of Shelan Hess.

"I believe he has some rather particular issues he'd like to discuss with you."

Vartan staggered backward, bumping into the wall as the rest of Capp's entourage surrounded him. Adlai, Desara, and the pale-eyed girl formed a semicircle around him, leaving him no retreat but into the office. His eyes flew from face-to-face until they landed on Aricelli.

"You bitch."

She smiled.

Marcus Capp waved his hand toward the office and Vartan was helpless but to turn and enter. "You'll understand if I invite the Storytellers to join us, won't you?" The *tu Bith* bowed to Dalle and a very red-faced Lucien and stepped inside. Dalle went in behind him. Before he followed them, Lucien ran his fingers over the embossed plaque on the door. "Paul Vartan—Council Coordinator." With a vicious flick of his wrist he ripped the sign out of the wood. Wielding it like a knife, he closed the door behind him.

EPILOGUE

....

Three months later

Tomas sat on the bed and loosened his tie. Music and laughter fil-tered up the steps and he knew it would be hours before the party began to wind down. He lay back and closed his eyes. A moment later the door swung open and Aricelli breezed in.

"Hiding in my parents' bedroom? Kinky. I like it."

He sat up and rubbed his eyes. "I had to get away for a minute."

"I know. I just found Dalle outside on the patio with a neigh-bor's cat in his lap. Storytellers." She kissed his forehead and moved to her mother's vanity to smooth her hair. She wore a copper-colored velvet dress that fit her perfectly, like it had been made for her, which it had. Her hair was swept up in a loose chignon and a gold chain adorned her graceful neck.

"You look . . . celestial."

She smiled at him in the mirror. "Celestial?"

"Beautiful is not a big enough word for you."

She blew him a kiss and began to reapply her lipstick. "How I really look is irritated. Do you know that DeBoer just got here? He claimed he was too sick from the flight to make it earlier. I mean, if you can't handle twenty hours on a plane, why are you living in Australia?"

"I bet he has no clue that you're irritated at all, does he?"

"Of course not. After all, you never know when you're going to need Tasmania." Laughing, she stepped over to the bed and stood between Tomas's legs. He put his hands on her hips and leaned forward to kiss her velvet-covered body.

Aricelli had been invaluable in the aftermath of Vartan's removal. She had proven herself truly her father's daughter as well as a master negotiator. News of Vartan's betrayal of the Storytellers had rocked the Council around the world and the complex had become a war zone of meetings and arguments and reassignments. The work had exhausted Tomas and Dalle and the other Storytellers who had arrived to control the damage. Even Marcus Capp had aged in the ensuing chaos but Aricelli thrived under the pressure. Cunning and resourceful and adaptable, it seemed at times she was the only thing holding the Nahan enterprises together.

She ran her fingers through his hair, tracing her thumb along his brow the way she knew he loved. "I know these crowds exhaust you. I know how hard all of this has been but a lot of the Europeans are going home soon and it would mean so much if you could just make one more pass through the room. Everyone wants a little face time with Desara."

He nodded and kissed her hand. "It's you they should be looking for. I couldn't have done this without you, any of this. You deserve the attention."

"All I want is justice." She kissed him again. "And world domination."

He laughed. "And that's just right around the corner."

"Of course." She pulled away, trailing her fingers along his cheek. He thought she was never more beautiful than when she smiled at him like that. "Promise you won't be long?"

"I promise." The sounds of the party swelled in the room as she opened the door and vanished as quickly as she had come.

It was still cold in Chicago but the air had that wetness that promised the arrival of spring. Tonight snowflakes blew outside the window and Tomas watched their erratic flight. It had been snowing like this when Stell left. He stepped to the window, his face reflected in the dark glass. In his mind's eye he saw the parking lot of the complex, the battered red Jeep Cherokee idling there, Adlai and Hess inside, Stell standing beside it waiting for him.

It had struck him then that goodbye scenes were never like they were in the movies. No music swelled, there was no soft lighting. There was a bitter wind and blowing snow. He was freezing and exhausted. Inside the complex Aricelli was struggling to keep a fist fight from breaking out among three European Coordinators. He hadn't slept in two days. He knew Stell was leaving and knew there was nothing on earth he could do to stop it, even if he wanted to.

He had to say something but nothing seemed right. She looked up at him and he felt that silence, that peace that had always fallen over him when he looked into her pale eyes. He reached out and touched her cheek.

"I hope you find what you're looking for."

Her eyes drifted over his shoulder to the complex sprawling behind him. "You too."

She climbed into the Jeep and left. In the blowing snow, she was out of sight in seconds.

Tomas pressed his forehead against the cold window. He knew he wouldn't be getting any letters like he had sent her on his trip out west. There would be no postcards describing the sun on the red rocks of Texas or the sight of the mystical Joshua trees. It wasn't her way. But maybe someday she would be bored riding in the back of the Jeep or holed up in a motel somewhere lying low from the law and she would decide to pass the time reading the only book he knew she always carried. Maybe she would pull out that battered copy of *Wuthering Heights* her mother had given her, the only memento of the life he had taken her from, and maybe she would read as far as page 166 and there, tucked into the binding, maybe she would find the note he had left for her. It was just one line.

Come back to me.

Tomas straightened his tie and headed for the door. The Council was waiting for him.

GLOSSARY OF NAHAN WORDS AND PHRASES

Acte – apprentice

Acul 'ad – Nahan who are predisposed to killing; assassins

Avalentu – literally *flight*, a road trip that is a rite of passage for Nahan youth

Chagar – chaperone, escort

Da Sute – literally *the ache*; growing pains, the reality of adulthood

Di Crun Feta – literally *rocks in a puddle*; a mess below the surface, hidden danger

Eihl – The One; a Nahan's true love; partner with whom to have children

En Na 'u 'an – True Family, Nahan cult of repentance

Epatu – open

Kott – commons who have pledged to assist the Nahan

Kott'del – members of the Kott who voluntarily feed the Nahan

Nahan da li? – "*Are you Nahan?*" used more as an enthusiastic greeting than a question

Oascaru – deadly, fierce

Osviat –to disappear, to be liberated, usually when one's parents change identities

Petiln – literally *to desire another*; the requests for life guidance from a Storyteller

R 'acul – killing while feeding

Saht – flood, colloquially the feeling of being around young lovers

Set fealte, 'u di – formal welcome into a home

tu Bith – Nahan moneymakers, bankers

'u fealte, sed 'im sete – formal request for permission to enter a home

Vehn – listen

Vint – the physical manifestation of energy Storytellers can see in the common

ACKNOWLEDGMENTS

This book has gone through the trials. I have about a billion people to thank for reading this throughout its many incarnations and I should go ahead and apologize to all the innocent trees and ink cartridges who sacrificed everything for this. Let's hope your efforts are not in vain.

I strained the limits of common decency and friendship with the fearsome Hitches—Gina Milum, Debra Burge, Tenna Rusk, Angela Jackson, and Christy Smith. Thank you for reading, rereading, and rereading. And thanks for always showing up.

My sister Monica Rimer has sacrificed precious shelf, closet, and floor space keeping up with all the new pages. Love you.

My 47North editor Jason Kirk got thrown into the deep end with this one. I deeply appreciate your time, attention, tact, and enthusiasm, as well as your inability to be shocked or grossed out. This is the beginning of a beautiful friendship.

My copyeditor Hannah Buehler saved my bacon too many times to count with her amazing attention to detail and her ability to figure out what I was trying to say. This book is better for her skill and all mistakes are my own. Seriously, she tried. Hard.

Nobody gets anywhere alone and I could spend the rest of my life thanking people who have been generous with their time, attention, reading hours, enthusiasm, snack food, and all the other million things that keep a writer going. To my family, blood and otherwise, my friends, WV WIPs, Matera peeps, Patchwork Writers, my radio family . . . I am beholden to you.

And finally to Fang, who was with me every step of the way—I miss you, mouse.

ABOUT THE AUTHOR

Photo by Jessica St. James 2012

A fifteen-year veteran of morning radio, an avid traveler, and a so-so gardener, S.G. Redling currently lives in her beloved West Virginia.